SHAGDUK

SHAGDUK

SHAGDUK

DE RE DORDICA: BOOK ONE

JB Jackson

PILUM   Nantes   2022

THIS IS A FINE MISSILE BOOK,
PUBLISHED BY PILUM PRESS.

2022 Pilum Press Trade Paperback Edition
Copyright © 2022 by Pilum Press
All rights reserved.

The Library of Congress Cataloging-in-Publication Data
is available upon request.

ISBN 987-1-956453-04-01

Cover and setting by Luisa Editorial
Illustration by Eddie Black

First Edition
10 9 8 7 6 5 4 3 2 1

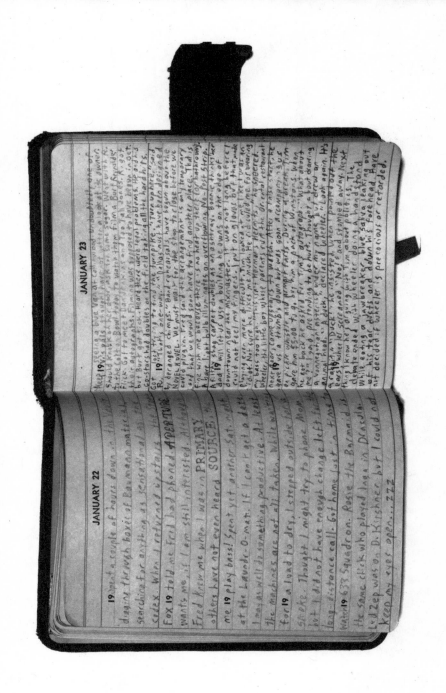

Basham & Winstead (San Francisco).
De re dordica: Items from the Seaberg Collection.
December 8, 1997. Sale no. 818.

1977

1977

Professor Sherwood gave me this five-year diary. The lock and key kind, salvaged from a donated carton of *National Geographics*. Not pretty to look at, but it is unused. Black leather, gilt edges. Had to wait until today to start writing in it. "*Nulla dies sine linea*," it says on the title page. An admonishment?

When I asked Sherwood what I should write in it, he lectured me about Socrates and the unexamined life.

"A diary is for recording one's quotidian adventures," he said. "One's most private thoughts, feelings, and reflections."

Of course I know what a diary is. My question was merely rhetorical. Rhetorical questions result in retired professors explaining to grown men what diaries are. Grown men who evidently live under rocks.

What shall I, a librarian at a rinky dink, Mickey Mouse liberal arts college, to whom nothing ever happens, possibly have to write about? As I recall some of the celebrated diaries I have read and enjoyed—those of Captain Scott, Sparwenfeld, or Pepys—it now seems like it might be fun to keep one after all. Someday, I suppose my grandchildren will find my diary tucked away in the attic and exclaim, "Grandpa was so boring!"

"I keep a journal," said Sherwood. This would have been in March. He opened a bulging leather satchel. The satchel was crammed with papers and notebooks, at which he gestured with a flourish, which I took to mean they were all his own journals. "Sometimes when I don't feel like writing, I doodle," he explained. To demonstrate, he traced circles in the air with his finger but then put his finger in his mouth, as if caught in a forbidden act. He laboriously extracted one of the notebooks from his satchel and opened it to a page on which he had sketched several robed figures with elongated heads and three-fingered hands. A doodler can save ten percent on labor if he draws them like Mickey's, I guess. Sherwood slammed the notebook shut before I could get a closer look. He seemed a little rattled.

"Down in the Vault," he continued, "we've a diary from the Nara Period. That of a mystic the Japanese call Mendo. Do you know Mendo?" To hear the professor say "the Vault" amuses me, because I dubbed it that after the episode where the Riddler and his cronies break into the library's "Vault for Rare Old Books" in search of a tome on the treasures of the Incas. I doubt Sherwood has ever seen *Batman*. He does know a thing or two about the treasures of the Incas.

"In his diary, Mendo chronicled the details of everything he did from the moment he woke in the morning until he retired at night. Meals, his bowel movements, whether it had rained or the sun had shone. He did this for the duration of his extraordinarily long life, which he lived in complete isolation on a fog shrouded island in the middle of Lake Mashin. A remarkable achievement for any diarist. The diary was bound in covers of yellow silk and is known in sinophilic circles as the *Yellow Book*. Not to be confused with that organ of decadent fame or the local *Yellow Pages*. Mendo even documented his—*ham!*—onanistic episodes. But I've said too much." Sherwood has a habit of frequently clearing his throat, which sounds like he is shouting the word "ham."

"They are written in the old *man'yōgana*, of course," he continued. "In the hermit's idiosyncratic hand. It's a dry and most difficult read. I can show it to you if you'd like to—*ham!*—accompany me down to the Vault." The professor sniffed sharply, then added, "You read the old *man'yōgana*." I do not, actually, but nodded noncommittally. Would rather read the *Yellow Pages*.

Sherwood has been at Porteous since the Punic Wars. He ostensibly retired years ago, but continues to handle book donations, assist researchers, and perform other duties known only to him and Dixie. He walks to and from the bus stop with the aid of a Japanese sword cane. I once witnessed him use the weapon to savage a piñata at Dixie's birthday party in the break room.

Sherwood's office on the mezzanine, which Dixie allows him to keep, is filled with antiques and curios. Vases bondoed together from shards, an old-timey diving helmet, and an ancient clepselaea. These were collected throughout his long tenure as Professor of Ancient History and Archaeology. Mounted above an Egyptian-inspired Art Nouveau divan is a stuffed rhinoceros head. He said it came from the Children's Museum where he was once one of the trustees. On his desk, an old Beam's Choice crystal bourbon decanter serves as a paperweight. Like Jeannie's bottle from the TV show. Not an antique, but fun. In the corner is a stationary exercise bike. Sometimes I pedal it while Sherwood explains long-winded theories about the Clovis people, his golf exploits, or some daft, loathed colleague called Bertie. Wires run from the bike to a hoary-looking terracotta pot in the corner.

"Found it near Yaxchilan in 1917," said Sherwood of the terracotta pot. "No one believes me when I tell them it's a galvanic cell. You're charging it right now."

"I believe you," I said, half-sincerely.

To usher in the new year, I hosted a party at Collinwood last night. It is the first party I have ever hosted. Invited an odd bunch who did not know each other well and did not mingle. Booze might have helped had it occurred to me to provide booze. Recognizing the party was a flop, I quietly latibulated until Fred found me. He offered me a drink from a flask. "Silver Dollar" tootled from the TV.

"Why are we watching this?" said Fred.

"Joan Crawford said the best parties are a wild mixture of people," I said, surveying the room. "Corporation presidents, a few lovely young actresses, a bearded painter, your visiting friends from Brussels, a politician, a hairdresser. Toss them all together and *voilà!*"

"Do you know any hairdressers from Brussels?" said Fred, rhetorically.

"The Bastard and I have beards. But we don't paint. Look around you. Bookish types and musicians. All guys except Debbie."

"She didn't want to come," said Fred. "I had to drag her here kicking and screaming." Debbie overheard this remark and shot Fred a dirty look. If someone attends a party against her will, is she even considered a guest?

"What's this?" said Fred.

"Bust of Liszt. Randy gave it to me for Christmas."

Fred ran his finger over its red flocked surface. "This is in poor taste. Do you rest your wig on it?"

Randy saw us with the bust and came over to introduce himself to Fred. "I thought Sherwood was coming," he said, addressing me.

"He was invited," I said. "Been a while since I've seen him"

Randy and Fred bonded over my card catalog. Whatever the Bastard told him, Fred bore an expression of incredulity. I am pleased to see those two getting to know each other. They have much in common. At least on paper.

No one touched the Rotel, which sat on the chrome and glass coffee table next to the black-eyed peas and some sweating cold cuts. Both were now covered in confetti after Spunt detonated a small device. So much for leftovers. When the countdown began and the ball dropped, I had no one to kiss. No one did.

The Royal Canadians launched into "Auld Lang Syne," a song that always makes me feel wistful. I turned off the TV and yawned conspicuously. It was time to hit the hay. Put on *The Sound of Music*, thinking that would induce people to go home, but then Monty started singing along. For the duration of Side A, the atmosphere of the room transformed from one of sober introspection to gaiety as others joined in song and dance. Should play *Metal Machine Music* next time. Only when I turned off the lava lamp and started stabbing all the balloons did people take the hint.

This morning I met my upstairs neighbor, Veronica. When I apologized for the noise from last night's party, she said, "A party? Are you sure?"

SUNDAY, JANUARY 2

Dear Diary, *lorem ipsum dolor sit amet*. Never mind. Can already tell that keeping a diary is going to be a chore. No point in doing it half-assed, though. Gotta do this full-assed. Maybe it will reveal some truths about myself. Or truth with a capital *T*. Or the meaning of life.

Why are we even here? Since we were nothing but mindless, feeble jelly, wriggling out of the primordial ooze, where life was simpler and the ooze cozy and rich in nutrients, we have been making it up as we go along. We were given no instruction manual. After millennia of trial and error, we at last stand upright, wear pants (surely an example of de-evolution), and eat food off conveyor belts. How was the world conceived? Is there really such a place as infinite space? Must I believe in the human race?

Woke up to sleet, which later turned to rain. After sweeping up confetti and other party detritus, I spent part of the afternoon listening to records. Really listening. Not while doing the dishes or anything else. I read the lyrics and the liner notes. Contemplated the album covers, which are often works of art. At some point I noticed movement out of the corner of my eye. My neighbor's black and white cat was busy shoving a piece of taffy under the door. His way of paying admission? I let him in, as I always do.

The cat jumped onto the coffee table and sighed deeply.

"What ails you, little buddy?" In a bid to amuse him, I offered him a wad of wrapping paper. He watched it slowly unwad for a moment before flopping over, disinterestedly. I then gave him a tour of the house in a bucket.

There is a green Bug in the driveway completely covered in cigarette ads. A traveling salesman? On a Sunday evening? It was still there when I turned out the lights.

MONDAY, JANUARY 3

Left the house to discover ice all over the windshield of the Rambler. Scraped it off with my Q-Card. Fishtailed my way down to Camp Bowie, which was not so bad on account of the salt. Arrived at the library to find the building cold and empty. Spent the morning sorting through boxes in the Vault. Found the door ajar again. Movement of air from a large vent keeps the door from clicking shut sometimes. You have to pull it closed behind you. Who was in there last?

While dusting off the top of a file cabinet, I discovered a list, teutonically-capitalized out of ontological respect, of Prohibition-era library rules which dictate that one must not:

>Enter the Library if unclean or suffering the Pox
>Consume Foodstuffs or imbibe Alcoholic Spirits
>Nap in the Reading Room or the Stacks
>Behave without Couth
>Partake of Pipes, Cigarettes, or Tobacco
>Destroy or deface Books, Newspapers, or other Library Property
>Bring Livestock or other Domesticated Animals into the Library

Figure I have broken all of these, except the livestock rule. Fort Worth has long been known as Cowtown, but when were students ever in the habit of leading cattle into the stacks? Did they really need a rule prohibiting that?

Regarding habits, I tend to jot down notes on the backs of old catalog cards. Notes like "Cash check" or "More Pibb." I do it in my sleep, too. Scraps of dreams and get-rich-quick schemes, none of which make any sense at sunup.

Covered for Jo Ann at the information desk in the afternoon. It was so quiet I just read the newspaper. The newspaper says the Fort Worth Public Library will offer language classes starting next week. Spanish, French, German, and Esperanto. I should volunteer to teach a class in Dordic.

Guy in a fringed leather jacket and no shirt strutted in and sold me some incense. Long hair. A real doom hippie. He was packing a pistol in the waistband of his filthy bell bottoms, so I was afraid to say no. He sold incense to Jenny, too. He loitered by the globe before I lost sight of him. Later caught him trying to steal *Steal This Book* by Abbie Hoffman.

"Stealing is illegal!" I said.

"Property is theft!" he countered, triumphantly, before fleeing.

Dixie emerged from her office to see what all the fuss was about. "That fringie's mother must cry herself to sleep at night," she lamented. Fringed jackets aside, anyone with long hair and a beard is a fringie in Dixie's book. Present company included.

"Why aren't you wearing a tie?" demanded Dixie.

"Told you we should keep Abbie Hoffman in the Vault," I said.

"You will wear a tie in this library. And why don't you shave that awful beard?"

"There's a tie in my desk," I lied. "I'll go put it on. By the way, have you heard from Sherwood?"

"Sherwood's AWOL," remarked Sarge as he rolled by. As is T-Bone, as usual. Where is T-Bone when you need him?

The phone rang at the information desk. All I heard through the receiver were shrieks and echoes. Was about to hang up when Fred spoke.

"It's *Songs of the Humpback Whale*. The neighbors probably think I'm strangling Debbie. Which I wouldn't mind doing, frankly. Come see the band Saturday night. We'll be at the Connexxion. You should audition."

"Pawned my Starfire months ago," I said. "Besides, Jeane Dixon predicts rock music is on its way out, to be replaced by melody. She also says the next dance craze is a modernized version of the waltz."

"Kemosabe! You hawked your axe?"

"Needed the dough."

"You have lost your goddamn mind. Do you still have your Vulcan?"

"Of course," I said. "I may have lost my mind but I'm not crazy."

"Let me know if you ever want to sell it. By the way, your sidekick Randy. He's a pretty weird guy."

"The Bastard is the weird one?"

"I'm a freak," said Fred. "Randy's just weird. Big diff." *Songs of the Humpback Whale* howled into my eardrum. I slammed the receiver down.

Checked out a duodecimo of Gnaeus Vibius's treatise on cosmetics and preserves on my way out.

"This says 'non-circulating,'" said Lloyd when I presented it to him.

"I know because I cataloged it," I said. "It's okay."

"If you say so, Steven."

The library cast its long shadow across Lot C. It is staying light later. Someone has spray painted a handprint on the hood of the Rambler. The Doom Hippie? But he likely would not have known which car was mine. Tried to wipe the hand off with some spit and an old date due slip but ended up just scratching the paint.

Watched *A Countess from Hong Kong* on Channel 11. Might have enjoyed it more if Sophia Loren had not spent half the movie hiding in the bathroom. To bed at midnight.

TUESDAY, JANUARY 4

Much warmer today. Spent a ridiculous amount of time writing an obscene and insulting memo to the Bastard in Dordic. Since Randy's idea of fun is translating Catullus into Dordic on his lunch break, he ought to get a kick out of it. Besides, he needs the practice if he intends to keep up with me. My Dordic is already much better than his.

Not a peep from Sherwood. Phoned him from my desk but there was no answer. When I went to his office I found the door unlocked. Before Christmas break, Sherwood had refreshed the contents of the display case in the vestibule. Piled on a book cart were the contents he replaced, including (according to their attached typed tags) a Mississippian-era carved stone disc, a Venus figurine with a frog-like face, a three-fingered gauntlet of unknown origin, and a plastic replica of the Gundestrup Cauldron. The latter I snatched for my office.

The Secret Societies of All Ages and Countries in two volumes caught my eye. It is an interlibrary loan item I requested for Sherwood before Thanksgiving, now overdue. Will read it on my day off tomorrow. We are pals, so I doubt he would mind.

Found myself perusing the classifieds but found not a single bass for sale. Think I might audition for Aperture.

WEDNESDAY, JANUARY 5

Up at five. How quiet and peaceful the world is at that hour. Or it would be, if Veronica were not pacing, or tossing horseshoes, or whatever the heck she does upstairs.

Studied Dordic all morning until the pawn shops opened. No luck in any of them, so I gave up and went to Bruce. At least there they don't have a motley bunch of shills telling you that mudbucker sparkles. Marquee out front said "Theremin for sale, never been touched." Ha ha. They had a secondhand Rickenbacker for two sixty-five. For two sixty-five I could get an a/c unit. Plugged the Rick into a Travler [sic] combo by Earth Sound Research. Peavey knock-off, but it rocks. Tuned up, then began thumping the theme from *Barney Miller*. The clerk made a throat cutting motion with his finger, then pointed at a handwritten sign that said, "No Barny [sic] Miller." Settled on a Fender copy because I can ill afford the real McCoy.

The brand is Pan, which I have never heard of. Pan, the god of rustic tunes and impromptus! Jap made. Has a rich sunburst finish with tortoise pickguard. Rosewood neck with trapezoidal pearloid inlays. Someone took real good care of it. Slim and fast-playing neck like my Starfire had. On a whim, I also bought a trombone. Marked down on account of a dented bell.

Sex Pistols received honorable mention in the morning paper for "vomitting [sic] and spitting" on Heathrow onlookers. If that is punk rock, then my interest is piqued. Will have to ask Fred if he has heard "*Anarchy in the U.K.*" But how does the punk rock ethos translate to grooves on a record?

There was also an article in which the author advocates an "American Diary Repository." A national clearinghouse for the preservation and use of the diaries written by Americans for what they record and reveal about life in America. From the historian's point of view, this is a fine idea. But I have to chuckle when I think of some grad student poring over these words a hundred years from now.

Windexed the hood of the Rambler, but the hand is still faintly visible. It only has three fingers. Chainsaw accident, no doubt. Could clearly see it in my peripheral vision when I pretended to be a passerby. But I think that is only because I knew it was there already.

Was ready to go inside and get warm when I decided to swing by Sherwood's place. Someone had dumped an aluminum Christmas tree in his front yard. It cannot be Sherwood's because he does not celebrate Christmas. Knocked loudly several times and peered through a couple of windows. Noted nothing amiss and reluctantly headed home.

Lit some incense and poured myself a stiff one. Watched the last rosy light of the winter day pour in through the drapes. Curled up on the divan with a blanket and a couple of dictionaries.

THURSDAY, JANUARY 6

Drizzly morning. The secret societies book was a long slog. Especially the chapters on Freemasonry. Not sure why Sherwood wanted it. Returned the volumes to his desk exactly where I found them.

Jo Ann called out sick, so I volunteered to give the library tour to new students. A small group had gathered in the vestibule, waiting for the carillon to ring ten. Meanwhile, I stared at the gold and white Penrose tiles beneath my feet. Looked up now and then to smile and make obligatory eye contact with the others. In retrospect, I should have waited in my office.

"The Porteous College Library occupies the first two floors of Blanston Hall," I began. "The business office and admissions are on the third floor. The dean's and president's offices are on the fourth floor.

"Blanston Hall is a Beaux Arts Revival affair dating to 1911, which makes it the second-oldest building on campus after Shawmut. It is said to have been designed by John Peter Howard on his death bed. In truth he merely described it to his nephew, who built it after Howard's death. Doesn't stop awestruck Howard fanatics from coming here with their sketchbooks and cameras. Don't get me wrong. It's a handsome edifice." At this last utterance, an elderly chap straight from the pages of Wodehouse grimaced.

"Well-endowed from its inception, the library is known for, among other things, the Reverend Ralph Henry Pogue Collection of material deemed somehow heretical or contrary to the morality of decent Christian folk just like you and me. Today, its catalogue reads like a Protestant version of the *Index Librorum Prohibitorum*. It includes apocryphal material and early editions

of Servetus, Linnaeus, and Descartes, as well as the more recent blasphe-
mies of Henry Miller, Anton LaVey, and Simone de Beauvoir. The Eustace P.
Hogg Collection features thirty-eight hundred exquisitely bound sermons. The
Willup Troutman Collection collects that prolific wordsmith's papers in one
convenient place. We also have a *Biblia sacra vulgatae editionis,* a.k.a. the
'Dalí Bible,' and a facsimile Gutenberg Bible, the latter which is displayed in
a climate-controlled Plexiglas case yonder. Every week I unlock the case and
turn the page. Gotta keep y'all coming back for more."

I winked at a couple of chicks who looked like Charles Manson flunkies.
They gave each other knowing looks. Why the hell did I do that?

"In the display case to my right, we have various *objets d'art* from the
Baumann Collection, which includes a replica of the Gundestrup Cauldron. It's
in my office if you ever want to gaze upon it. Beyond that, *The Yawning Guy.*
Rococo bust in bronze by Franz X. Messerschmidt. Also a copy."

"Where is the Baumann Collection kept?" asked the geezer.

"The Baumann Collection along with select theses, rare books, and other
special collections, is stored in the Vault. I mean, the basement."

As the small crowd dispersed, I overheard Dixie chewing out the Stone Fox
over her mismatched socks. Afterward, the Stone Fox seemed glum.

"Hey, I dig your socks, Jenny!"

She smiled and lifted her long skirt up a little to show them off. One was
orange and one was brown.

"Felt something in my shoe this morning," I said. "When I got to the library,
I took my shoe off. My sock had a goat head stuck to it. Couldn't pull it off.
Had to cut it off with scissors. Now there's a hole in my sock. It's getting bigger
and bigger."

Jenny regarded me with sympathy. Or was it pity?

"I'm Steven Miller," I said, speaking into the stapler. "And this has been
'Sock Update.'"

When Jenny first started working at the circulation desk, the Bastard had
asked, "Who's the stone fox?" unaware that her surname was Fox. The appel-
lation stuck.

Not only is Jenny a stone fox, but she is also the other kind of fox. Some
people are foxes and others are hedgehogs. With apologies to Isaiah Berlin, I
present my coworkers:

Mrs. Dixie Womack, Head Librarian (hedgehog)
Me, Chief Cataloger (fringie)
Randy "The Bastard" Kelso, Conservator (fringie)
Jo Ann Duhig, Reference Librarian (hedgehog)

Monty "Three Card" Harper, Circulation Assistant (fox)
Professor Sherwood (retired fox)
Edith Tibbets, Technical Services Assistant (hedgehog)
Hazel Lipske, Dixie's right hand (hedgehog)
Doris Trillin, Page (fox)
Nick Spunt, Serials Person (can't decide)
Lloyd Bemis, Circulation Assistant (fox)
Maxine Doakes, not sure what she does (hedgehog)
Kevin "Hey Now" Weems, Circulation Assistant (hedgehog)
Sarge, Page (fox)
Carlos, Facilities Guy (hedgehog)
Jennifer Fox, Circulation Assistant (stone fox)
T-Bone, Security Guard (hedgehog)

While Jenny was telling me incredulous stories about life at the Hacienda, I casually reached for a small cloisonné candy dish that was in one of the cubbyholes behind the circulation desk. Took the lid off and peered inside. There was a large toenail clipping and a used Band-Aid.

"Hey Now found the Band-Aid in a book and put it in the dish," explained Jenny. "Not to be outdone, Spunt added his toenail. They are so gross, both of them. They call it 'shenanigans.'"

Spotted a dead spider on the Gaylord. "This can be our contribution," I said, dropping it into the dish. Jenny grimaced.

"Wait, I might have something." She reached up under her shirt for a moment, then held up her pinched fingers. "Belly button lint." She flicked it into the dish.

Encountered the Bastard on a cigarette break. When I griped about the hand on the hood of the Rambler to him, how it damaged the paint job, he sheepishly took out his wallet and gave me twenty bucks. "Will accept this as a confession," I said.

"Thought you said you were going to Earl Scheib!" he said. "I'll paint any car any color!"

"Guess I have to, now," I said. "Do you have any New Year's resolutions?"

"Woody Guthrie's 'rulin's' from thirty years ago are still pretty sound, in my opinion. Wash teeth. Read lots of good books. Beat fascism, dot dot dot. What about you?"

"Don't usually have any, but I feel like I was in a rut all through '76," I said. "I need a change! Maybe travel. Be less aloof. Should probably try to get laid. By the way, what's with the three-fingered hand?"

Randy opened his mouth in mock surprise. "You don't recognize it? *Tsk tsk.*"

FRIDAY, JANUARY 7

Upon arrival at the information desk, I found Dixie's granddaughter Amber sitting behind it like she works there. The little black-haired girl's legs dangled above the floor. "You must be the fringie librarian," she said. "Mee Maw told me about you."

"That's my chair, kid."

"Mee Maw said I could sit here."

Did not have the energy to argue with her. I was also afraid to argue with her. Kid logic is unassailable in its outrageous cogency and utter disregard for truth. Amber regarded me with contempt while I lit the Doom Hippie's incense.

Wanted to put the lava lamp Randy gave me for Christmas at the information desk, but the lone electrical outlet had too many things plugged into it already. Think I have an adapter at home.

The telephone rang. "Good morning, it's a great day at the Porteous Library's information desk. This is Amber. How may I help you, please?"

What the hell? I sat there in awe as this kid answered someone's questions about Maximus the Confessor. Is Porteous paying her? I have so many questions.

A new security guard started this week. His name is Boggs. Today he introduced himself and asked where L.F.'s office was. When I told him it was on the fourth floor, he repeated me.

"Did you say 'fowuth flowuh'?" I said.

"Ha ha, you got me. I'm from Queens. My nephew says, 'Uncle Reggie, it's *dawg* not *dowug*.' By the way, I'm going to have to ask you to extinguish that incense."

Boggs seems more like a fox than a hedgehog. Time will tell.

People are whispering about Sherwood's absence, including L.F., who came looking for him today. L.F. said they were supposed to have met to discuss the Baumann Collection some time this week. He seemed more pissed than worried, but now I am starting to worry.

Swung by Roy Pope on the way home for a six-pack of Pibb. A big-titted slave girl caught my eye from a circular rack of yellow-spined paperbacks by the register. She knelt before a swashbuckler who twisted her arm cruelly. Opened to a random page but stopped reading after the eighth occurence of the word "master." What kind of culture produces such work?

All I went in there for was the Pibb, but ended up buying some Sta-Puf, a cat toy, and a couple of other sundries. And *Rogue of Siluria*.

"That will be $14.76," said the young cashier, eyeing my paperback in amusement. She blew three bubbles simultaneously, which popped in rapid succession. Resisted the urge to ask how she did that.

"A very good year," I said. "For, uh…William Caxton." So much for Randy's twenty.

The cashier stared at me blankly. "Whatever," she said. She handed me my change, bills first, then balanced the coins on top. Is there any hope for today's youth?

Professor Ziglar ambushed me in the parking lot. I watched in fascination as his hair did not move whatsoever in the gentle breeze as he asked me about an overdue notice he had received in the mail for *Worte Christi* by Albrecht Goes. "I returned that in December!" he insisted. Politely told him to give the circulation desk a call in the morning. It is like he is wearing a plastic Fisher Price wig. Seem to recall you could forcibly pry those off, if you wanted to.

Saturday, January 8

Slow day at the library. The Stone Fox showed me a note she found in the book return which said "So sorry. Dropped box of animal crackers instead of book by mistake. They are safe to eat." When I looked up, Jenny was holding up the aforementioned box. She was eating one of the crackers.

"Don't eat that, Jenny!"

She swallowed, then tried to force a cracker into my mouth. It seemed more serious than playful. Of course, I gave in. "If I die, it's your fault," I said, melodramatically.

Many students are still out of town. The Stone Fox and I played paper football at the circulation desk. Got tired of standing after a while, but did not want the amusement to end. Pulled up my socks and was mucho invigorated. After "Happy Trails," Jenny made the closing announcement in a ridiculous Cockney accent. A fairly bold thing to do in front of the librarian on duty, but she knows I am a fox. No patrons were in the library, anyway.

Stopped by the house to change and eat something before heading over to the Connexxion. Fred greeted me from the bar when I arrived. "Kemosabe!"

"I bought a bass," I said.

"Bravo. You should join us on stage."

"Too bad. Didn't bring it with me. Is Debbie coming tonight?"

"Naw, she took off with her Belgian hairdresser."

"You mean she dumped you?"

"He can use my acoustic," offered the guitarist in a Maple Leafs sweatshirt. "I'm Tim," he said.

"Gotta trombone in the trunk."

The trombone interested the others. They must have thought I was a real musician. Bonnie, a chick in a fringed suede vest and bolero corduroys, suggested there was room to play a solo during one of their longer songs. She said she would cue me when the time came, and quickly demonstrated a couple of the piece's themes on her Minimoog. Recalling something I had read about embouchure, I spent a few moments backstage trying to make sounds that did not suggest *Songs of the Humpback Whale*.

Bonnie gave me a copy of the set list, which was mostly cover tunes. I would play along on Tim's acoustic, providing a touch of Spectorian texture. Tim did not have an extra strap, however, which meant I would have to perform seated next to the drummer, Dave. They miked me and patched me into the mixer. After a quick sound check, it was determined no one could hear me. Nor could I hear myself, unless they turned me up. That only produced feedback. "Play anyway," whispered Bonnie.

Aperture went on after eight to a crowd which included more than a few fans. Because I did not know any of the arrangements I struggled to keep up, but the many mistakes I made seemingly went unnoticed. Spent half of "Tush" trying to shake the pick out of the guitar, to no avail. I fingerpicked the rest of the song.

The last number, which was the longest and also an original composition, was what I call "high prog." Packed with time changes, extensive instrumental passages, and plenty of room for solos for everyone at the end. Sat patiently next to Dave, waiting for my turn to blow. Tim, who also sings, is extraordinarily gifted. Even though his coiffure was short, he was musically hirsute. His own lyrical solo was surely the climax of the set. Paid close attention to the one-legged bassist. Plays at a level I could never hope to match. If that is what the others are used to, they are never going to want me.

Bonnie's Minimoog solo sounded a lot like something from *Das wohltem-periete Klavier* (most likely it was). Waited for my cue, then began my own demonstration, with which I intended to impress the others enough so they would want to keep me. To my dismay, I had badly underestimated how deafeningly loud trombones are. All I could do was pretend I had meant to play that loudly at first, then bring the volume down as much as possible. Afraid of hitting any bum notes, so I just riffed on a B-flat. A monotonous perpetration only the Five Satins could love, but being a showoff was never my style. For the sake of symmetry, I brought the volume back up at the end for a rousing glissando, piercing the veil between art and physics.

"Ladies, and gentlemen, the Pompatus of Love!" cried Tim, when I had finished. As if I had never heard that one before. Do not think my performance was a disaster, though I nearly slipped afterward in a puddle of my own saliva. Could have been a lot worse. No one commented on it either way, which I took to be a good sign.

Emerged from the club into a tempest of howling winds and ice pellets. The drive home was a bit tricky. The bricks on Camp Bowie were especially slick. Saw a couple of wrecks but managed to avoid one myself.

SUNDAY, JANUARY 9

While trying to fall asleep last night, I decided my trombone skills leave much to be desired. They probably all laughed at me after I went home. Oh, well, screw 'em. Was not looking forward to rehearsals and late nights again, anyway.

Got a light dusting of snow. It is so cold at Collinwood there is frost on the inside of my windows. All out of things to burn in the fireplace. Decided to leave early for Randy's so I could stop by Sherwood's again. Put an Otter Pop under the windshield wiper to see if it would freeze on the way there. (It did not.) Parked in the Polyflex parking lot, which was empty. The roof of the imposing gray building was crowned with a railing presumably to keep one from falling. But why would people be on its roof? The only sound was a cable slapping a flagpole. Good thing Sherwood is hard of hearing. That sound would drive me crazy.

Pulled bread bags over my shoes to keep them dry. Hurriedly crossed the lumpy asphalt street and approached Sherwood's front porch. A black-figured krater filled with frost-bitten cacti confirmed I was at the correct house. Have given Sherwood rides home but he never invites me in. Slipped on some ice and broke the tip off a Japanese stone lantern. Sorry, old man! Knocked until my knuckles hurt, then jiggled the doorknob. Looked through all the windows but most of them had drapes. I noted several newspapers in the yard.

Circling to the back, I snooped around a dilapidated garage, then peered down a dark well. Found the tornado shelter unlocked, so I hoisted open one of the bowed, termite-ridden doors and gazed down into the gloom. Save for a few cobwebs, the room appeared to be empty. Did not want a spider dropping down the back of my neck, so I turned to leave. As I did so, however, something caught my eye. At the bottom of the steps lay what appeared to be Sherwood's cane. It had been broken into several pieces. By now I was freezing my ass off, so I gathered the fragments and returned to the Rambler.

After a pit stop at Roy Pope for hot dogs, buns, a carton of Kents, and a couple of cat toys, I headed over to the Bastard's. When I arrived he was making homemade paper like any normal person. While he washed up, I told him about going over to Sherwood's. I showed him what I had discovered.

"This is his cane, all right," he said. "Or just the *tsue*. But where's the blade? And why do you have Wonder bread bags over your shoes? Those go over your socks, dipshit."

"I dunno. It was dark down there." I removed the tattered bags and tossed them into the trash.

Neither of us spoke for a moment, as we pondered what the broken cane could mean. Had Sherwood been in a fight?

"Come back over there with me," I said.

Randy cracked open a cold one and handed it to me. "After the Super Bowl," he said, persuasively.

For me, the game was more about just hanging out with the Bastard than who was winning or losing. Was pulling for the Vikings, though, because I like their colors more. When some guy kicked a field goal from a distance of forty yards, I said, "How hard is it to kick a field goal?"

Randy reached to adjust the rabbit ears. "It's a challenge to kick it far enough and have it go between the narrow uprights. First of all, you've got your holder. He receives the snap and has to set up the kick. He can't fuck around. Then you've got these huge dudes like Matt Blair flying at you, trying to tear your head off."

"Always thought it looked like fun."

"Dude, there's a football field right across the street from the library. Go kick one."

Shoved a fifth hotdog into my mouth, *sans* bun. "Why are there six weiners in a package but only four buns? That is some bullshit." Between bites, I added, "Getting dark soon. Barring some sort of miracle, it appears the Raiders are going to win. You ready to leave?"

"You're damn right they're going to win," said Randy. "Let me get a flashlight."

Arrived at Sherwood's at dusk. Once again, I parked under the jagged *P* of the Polyflex sign. I led Randy across the street and around back to the tornado shelter. The flashlight revealed a smooth, earthen floor. On the wall opposite the steps was what appeared to be a door drawn in chalk. Its frame contained an inscription.

"The runes are Dordic," I said. "But the language isn't. What beautiful calligraphy!"

"Dude, check this out." Randy pointed the flashlight at a shard of metal. I picked it up.

"Part of the blade," I said. "For what it's worth, I don't see any blood. Here are his glasses. Or what's left of them. What the hell happened here?"

"What does the inscription say?" said Randy. "Do you have a camera?"

"No, but I have pen and paper in the car." I stubbed my toe on something heavy. The ancient battery from Sherwood's office. But what was it doing here? Hurried back to the Rambler and when I returned, Randy was holding a leather doctor's bag. Inside was a toothbrush, a comb, and some pants rolled up like

Swiss rolls. There was also a canteen, a compass, and a thin blanket. The kinds of personalia you'd bring on a camping trip. Randy unrolled a plain shirt which looked more like a tunic.

"What's this? Halloween was months ago," said Randy. "This first aid kit still has the price tag on it. And here's a bottle of prescription medication."

After I transcribed the text from the chalk door, we tried the back door of the house and found it unlocked. We entered, and found ourselves in a darkened, musty kitchen.

"Professor Sherwood!" I shouted. "It's Steven and Randy from the library!"

I went through an archway into the living room while Randy disappeared down a hallway. Sherwood's house was as elaborately appointed as his office, filled with books, art, and antiques. "Whoa, I did not expect this!" I said.

Randy yelled "What?" from another room.

"An old pinball machine!" I said. "It's the Magic Circle. Man, I haven't seen one of these in ages." Removed a satchel from the top of it, and playfully tapped the flipper buttons for a moment. "Hey, I found Sherwood's satchel!"

Randy reappeared carrying a stack of books. "These were on his desk." He placed the books on the pinball machine and opened one.

"Ex Libris Adolf Hitler," I read aloud. Wide eyed, I turned to the title page, which read *Die Tür* in Fraktur.

"It also bears the embossed stamp 'Property of S.S.,' like some of the ones in the Baumann Collection."

"*The* S.S. or just S.S.?"

"You're seeing what I'm seeing," said Randy. "Besides, Nazis wouldn't say 'the' S.S., dumbass. Check out the verso."

I turned the page. "*Folium versum, folium rectum*," I sang. "Sounds like something the Romans wiped their asses with."

"That would be a *tersorium*," said Randy.

"Like wiping your ass with leaves," I continued. "I've done that before."

"A *tersorium*'s more like a sponge on a stick."

Another massive old tome was bound in what appeared to be some sort of well-worn animal skin. Its cover was embossed with a three-fingered hand. Like my diary, it also had a lock. Its key was attached to the lock with a new-looking piece of string.

"Sherwood must have brought these home," I said. "A big no-no. Unless Dixie gave him her blessing."

Randy inserted the key and opened the book to a random page. A color plate depicting a cloaked man standing before a door from which issued swirling mist. The door had indistinct writing around it. Traced my finger over it in wonder, as if that would osmotically impart further information.

"It's in Dordic," I observed. "What is this? A grimoire or something?" Randy stared at me with folded arms as I examined the text. Noticed several hairs that had ostensibly been used as bookmarks. These I yanked out and let float to the floor.

"Appears to be a codex," I continued. "Comprising different manuscripts. Most appear to be in the same hand."

"What's it say?" said Randy.

I read a passage aloud in a stentorian voice. Its meaning was roughly, "Oh, [word scratched out, ed.], awaken, he whose eyes are on the back of his head, whose tongue is in his anus, whose paw…"

"You're not supposed to say that out loud, dude!" Randy interrupted. He slapped my hand away from the page, closed the book, and locked it.

"You told me to!"

"Didn't know you were going to summon a major demon."

"So what if I did?" I said. "I mean, what did you think would happen?"

We both looked around the room, and Randy chuckled nervously.

"Don't see any demons," I said.

"We should take these with us. They're library property."

"Any of the Baumann Collection that we accessioned is stamped accordingly. So I haven't cataloged these yet. They might help us understand what happened to the professor."

"He could have kicked the bucket," said Randy. "He's ancient, after all."

"Of course, but where's his body, then? Wouldn't you say he was of sound mind?"

"He was never of sound mind. All joking aside, something sinister is going on, wouldn't you agree?"

We spent the next several minutes opening drawers and exploring closets. I checked the bathtub. Even looked under the bed, as if I expected to find Sherwood under there drinking tea.

A sagging bookcase caught my attention. Each title was more fascinating than the last. Removed a worn copy of *The Friar Untucked: Ribald Tales from Nottinghamshire* and showed it to Randy.

"Put that down and let's get out of here," he said.

"But these woodblock prints!"

Neither of us could figure out how to lock the back door behind us without a key. I removed the screen from the small window over the kitchen sink. Randy waited outside while I locked the back door, climbed out of the window, shut it behind me, and replaced the screen. At least it would prevent someone from wandering into the house from the street like we had just done. On the way back to the Rambler, we retrieved the mail from the mailbox and picked up all the newspapers. Along with the books and Sherwood's satchel, it was almost more than we could carry at once. He has been gone longer than I thought. As an afterthought, I went back down into the shelter and retrieved the ancient battery.

Night had fallen. A lone streetlight illuminated the Rambler, which looked conspicuous in the empty parking lot. I shut the trunk. Anxiously glanced over my shoulder and noticed a figure staring down at us from the Polyflex roof, its gloveless hands gripping the frozen aluminum railing. "What the fuck are you looking at?" I thought, as I stepped through ice into a puddle, soaking my shoes.

Back at Randy's, he sorted through Sherwood's satchel, while I attempted to make sense of the text I had copied in the tornado shelter. "It appears to be in Dordic but I don't recognize some of the words," I said. "Don't see how any of this is going to help us find Sherwood."

"We can stop trying," said Randy, irritably.

"That's not what I meant." I recalled the hairs I had found in the codex. What if they had been important? I now regretted pulling them out.

When Randy was in the bathroom, I rummaged through Sherwood's satchel. In an interior pocket, I found an amulet. It is bronze, with a remarkably beautiful gemstone in the shape of a triangular cupola. When I heard Randy flush, I quickly put the amulet in my pocket.

"What's burning?" said Randy. He sprinted across the room and grabbed my shoes, which were propped against the heater. "Are you trying to burn down my house?"

MONDAY, JANUARY 10

Did not get home until well after midnight. Yesterday's events have given me much food for thought. What does Sherwood's disappearance have to do with the scene in the tornado shelter? And the books?

The streets are still icy and I am surprised the library was even open. Freezing cold outside but a veritable sauna indoors. Brought an adapter from home so I could plug the lava lamp in at the circulation desk. As soon as I had done so, Dixie appeared and asked, "What's that light for?" When I returned later in the morning to see if it had started bubbling, it was gone. I asked her later, "What happened to the lava lamp?"

"There is already adequate lighting at the circulation desk," said Dixie.

"The library's too cheerless and institutional. Don't you think the lava lamp adds a touch of warmth?"

"It undermines the library's mission," she said, adding dubiously that a student had already "burned his hand on it" and that it "might explode" or "fall off the circulation desk."

"Fine," I said. "I'll put it in my office." The library has not had an official mission statement in over a year. I supposed Dixie has forgotten that.

"You can't have it in your office, either."

"We'll see what Carlos has to say," I snapped. Have no intention of asking him, of course.

In the afternoon, I checked my cubbyhole for mail. Sherwood's was stuffed, so I took it all. After sorting through it at my desk, I took out the interesting stuff and put the rest back. No word from him, still.

Sneaked down to the Vault for some peace and quiet until it was time to go home. It is the one place I can go that is cool in the summer and not intolerably hot in the winter. All the Vault needs is a more comfortable chair. And perhaps a hi-fi and an icebox. While browsing in the thesis cage, something triggered my memory of the amulet. I contemplated its origins for a moment before going back upstairs.

As soon as I got home, I placed the amulet in a cigar box for safekeeping with all my other tiny things. A couple of German-style TV dinners while watching *Man with the Golden Gun*. The prune-apricot compote was disappointing. The neighbor's cat hawkeyed me the whole time. Had to show him my hands like I'm a blackjack dealer.

"You don't want this, cat." I said it in Dordic, just for laughs. Maybe I can teach him commands.

TUESDAY, JANUARY 11

Sick of freezing my ass off. On my lunch break, I made a phone call and am having a cord of wood delivered to Collinwood tomorrow. Ah, modern living! Brought some of Sherwood's mail to work so I could examine it at my desk. His personal mail was pretty much just your usual bills (including an overdue notice from Columbia House, uh oh!) and junk mail, but among his work mail I found a response from the Seaberg Society in Van Nuys.

Dear Professor Sherwood:

We appreciate your interest in the Seaberg Society. Our mission statement is "To discover, procure, and preserve whatever may relate to the natural, literary, and anthropological history of the world, and to establish and maintain collections in art and archaeology; and to acquire by gift, purchase or otherwise, artifacts and other materials of historical significance; and to charge, collect, solicit and receive funds, donations and property, real or personal, to promote such purposes."

We are greatly interested in the Baumann Collection, and are looking forward to an exchange of information concerning its contents. If you would be willing to send us a complete catalog, we would be most indebted to you.

We look forward to hearing back from you. Thank you for your consideration.

Diane Nagy, Interim Director

Edith came up to the information desk and handed me a slip of paper upon which was written the words *quim* and *spintriae*.

"Steven, can you tell me what these words mean? I overheard two young gentlemen say them in the quad."

"The first one is, *ahem*, slang for female genitalia," I said. "I'll have to look up the second one."

"If it's going to be dirty then I don't want to hear it."

"Says here 'roman coins, or brothel tokens.'"

"I told you not to tell me!"

WEDNESDAY, JANUARY 12

Well, my cord of wood got delivered. Evidently, a cord of wood is a hell of a lot of wood. Should have done some research. This snafu cost me seventy-six simoleons. The delivery guy wanted ten more to stack it so I did it myself while he sat in the truck and watched like a pussy. Money will be tight for a while, but if I cannot pay my electric bill, at least I have a cord of wood I can burn to keep me warm.

Of course I built a fire right away. Spent most of the day studying the codex while listening to the *Ring* cycle as background music. By the time *Das Rheingold* was over two and a half hours later, I felt like Malcolm McDowell at the end of *A Clockwork Orange*. Please end the sickening pain!

Late in the afternoon, I needed a breather, so I drove down to Radio Shack for some speaker cable. Cold temperatures are causing water main breaks, the water from which is then freezing, creating slick spots. The Rambler's tires are bald, so I was lucky to get home in one piece. Common sense did not stop me from going back out to see *Logan's Run* and *Soylent Green* at the Bowie. Alone, alas.

THURSDAY, JANUARY 13

Dark, drizzly day. Today's meeting agenda:

Professor Sherwood

Microfilm reader

Steal This Book
New security guard
Dress code
Lighting at the circulation desk
Mr. Coffee
Rubber band usage.

Dixie wants Jo Ann and me to go to Turkey Knob College next week to see their new microfilm reader, a task I have little interest in.

Feel like such a phony sometimes. If I balk at reading professional literature, it is only because much of it concerns public service or collections. However, I am the one who eliminated a huge cataloging backlog last year. In addition to my usual duties, I have also taken on the monumental task of cataloging the Baumann Collection, which has been slow going. Due to the complex nature of the material, I cannot train a student assistant to do any of it. Not that my department could even afford one, on account of dwindling budgets. During Dixie's rubber band filibuster, I found myself thinking of food. My own fault for not packing a lunch, but I find room-temperature meals unappetizing. After the meeting was over, I ended up waiting in line for fifteen minutes at the Business School cafeteria for the "Meatloaf with Catsup." The scent of cologne is so overbearing in that place, I always close my nostrils and consequently can taste nothing.

While waiting for the elevator to take me down to the Vault, I absent-mindedly warbled the "Tuba mirum" from Mozart's *Requiem*. Monty heard me and spirited over. "Why, Steven, do you *sing*?"

"Not really," I responded, somewhat mortified.

"Oh, you do, too! I just heard you! You should join us on Thursday evenings."

"Us?"

"The Westworth Village Chorale. Our amateur choir. Last month we caroled our way through Ridgmar Mall and were mentioned on the Channel 8 news."

"Sounds like fun, but I don't read music." The elevator doors opened.

"Pshaw! Neither do I! Well, I do, actually, but you don't have to!"

Monty pronounced it like "pee-shaw." Is that how it is pronounced? Never heard anyone say that word aloud. Not sure I have ever even seen that word outside a Wodehouse novel. Sounds like a droll pseudonym from *Reader's Digest*: "Funnies by P. Shaw."

"You will mull it over, won't you?" Monty implored. "You have a lovely voice!"

"I will, Monty." Under the flourescent lights of the library, Monty's hair looks purple. Does he dye it?

FRIDAY, JANUARY 14

At some point each morning, I tend to walk by the dictionary stand by the information desk, flip to a random page, and choose a random word of the day. Typically, I read the definition aloud to Jo Ann. What I do not tell her is that I cheat by deliberately choosing the worst word on the page just to make her uncomfortable. Got lucky today with "hoarfrost."

Was just about to attack a stack of Baumann books when Dixie demanded I rush job some Ásatrú materials for a visiting professor. They looked a lot like *D&D* rule books (the same people probably wrote both). Alas, no accompanying miniatures or polyhedral dice. The publisher is in Waxahachie, of all places. It is nice to know heathenry is alive and well in North Texas. Hail Odin!

How to Recognize and Handle Abnormal People is conspicuously displayed on the corner of my desk. It amuses me to think that when Dixie is in my office, she sees it and wonders if I recognize her.

Am I the abnormal one? Are Dixie and the other hedgehogs normal? My aversion to hedgehogs aside, it is ostensibly the so-called abnormal people of the world, the fringies, with which I find common ground, and feel most comfortable being around.

Not all fringies are created equal. Sometimes, when I am in my office concentrating on something, I will hear a weird gooey sound. Spunt is standing directly behind me, his mouth filled with saliva, opening and closing it slowly in my ear. He will then ask, "What are you doing?" in a voice that sounds like he is gargling. I invariably shout "Get lost!" Spunt just laughs his wheezing Muttley laugh. Fringie? Or freak? Leave it to a librarian to classify everything.

Received a mysterious package, C.O.D. Brought it back to my desk and examined it. The return address was a P.O. box in Los Angeles. Opened it with great curiosity. Evidently, I had placed a mail order for five hundred custom matchbooks with "Steven Miller, Esq., Master Cataloger" embossed on them in Old Hamcherry. They do not have a phone number on them, so I cannot even use them as business cards. Not that I would ever need one, because whom would I give them to? Must have sent off for them after (or during?) the Christmas party in December. In the bottom of the box was an unpaid invoice.

Braunschweiger and grapes for dinner while watching a movie called *Fantasy Island* starring Bill Bixby. No matter what he is in, I will forever think of Bill Bixby as Eddie's father. Throughout the whole movie I kept wondering, "Where is Eddie?"

SATURDAY, JANUARY 15

Spent my shift at the information desk trying to write song lyrics. Amber asked me what I was doing. When I told her, she provided me with the title, "Subways of Your Mind." It is better than any of the titles I had been considering. But what does a little girl know about the subways of one's mind? If she had known them, she would not speak of them.

Found some sheets of Letraset in a desk drawer and used some to make a kick-ass "Vault for Rare Old Books" sign. Put the sign in a picture frame and nailed it above the door to the Vault.

Steak 'n Taters for dinner while watching *The Deadly Tower* about Charles Whitman. Kurt Russell played the sniper. The movie was ruined for me when I realized it was not filmed in Austin. Dinner was a disappointment, too. It didn't taste as good as it looked on the box. Nothing tastes as good as it looks on the box.

After searching high and low for it, I dug out my trusty Rhythm Master. Practiced playing bass all evening to a driving foxtrot beat. It is difficult to play when your fingers are cold. Especially when you are rusty. My calluses are starting to return, which means my fingertips are snagging on clothing.

Watched the Von Erichs in the ring for a while until I drifted off in front of the TV. Damn, I love it when Fritz does the Iron Claw.

SUNDAY, JANUARY 16

Damn cold. Set up my typewriter in front of the fireplace. Spent much of the morning typing up and filing subject cards for the latest additions to my personal library. One was for *Very Peculiar People: Portrait Studies in the Queer, the Abnormal and the Uncanny*, by Eric John Dingwall. It and a book on John Christie are the only books in my collection shelved under CT9990, the call number reserved for "Adventurers, eccentrics, misers, etc." Would Sherwood be queer, abnormal, or uncanny enough to warrant such a subject heading? I think so. He was certainly quite the adventurer back in the day. True eccentrics do not know they are eccentric. Sherwood would have scoffed at the label.

Was on my way out the door when I encountered Veronica. "You're crazy," she said. "Why are you wearing shorts in this cold?"

"I'm going to play hellball with a friend at the Y."

"What's hellball?"

"It's like racquetball, but instead of following the rules we just hit a bunch of balls around. Whatever's within reach in whatever direction we happen to be swinging at the time. It's chaos, reflex, luck, and bruises. The sadomasochism only stops when we're utterly exhausted or too injured to continue."

"Sadomasochism." said Veronica, raising an eyebrow.

"But it's fun."

"You're shivering."

"Yeah, I gotta get in the Rambler. Got to ramble on. Nice talking to you!"

MONDAY, JANUARY 17

There is a steep, wooded slope behind the Church of the Nazarene. I like to go that way from Lot C to the library. Grackles, raccoons, and other critters abound there. Beyond that, it is a brief jaunt across the FWTS campus. Then down a flight of steps to the street, across which is the entrance to Blanston Hall. Takes me longer to get to work, but it offers a few moments of peace and beauty before arriving to the disquietude of the library.

Had just started to ascend the muddy hillside when I saw Carlos up ahead. It was too dark to see what he was doing. Abort! Ended up stuck behind L.F. He was clothed in one of his trademark color suits. This morning it was yellow Stetson, yellow slacks, yellow shirt, bolo tie, yellow cowboy boots, and a yellow elephant belt buckle. Some call him flamboyant. A term I would concede for the attire if not the man. L.F. walks somewhat slower than I, so I ended up inelegantly reducing the length of my stride so I would remain behind him.

Later in the afternoon, I spotted L.F. again in the vestibule of the library. Instead of his yellow duds, he was now brownly attired. Why would he change clothes?

During a cigarette break, Randy told me that he heard it through the grapevine that L.F. hired a private investigator to look into Sherwood's disappearance. We also discussed Claudine Longet's murder trial. The police had seized her diary without a warrant. Wondered what kind of incriminating things one would find written in mine? Guess I could get in trouble for taking Sherwood's books. Was going to mention the amulet to Randy, but then chose not to. Would like to find out more about it first.

The sign I made for the Vault for Rare Old Books is gone. Who else even goes down there besides Sherwood and me?

TUESDAY, JANUARY 18

Today I inadvertently corrected Dixie's pronunciation of *Lustige Blätter*. Repeated it only to confirm what she had said, not because I was trying to correct or embarrass her. Could tell she was hacked off, though. You can always tell by her eyes.

Jo Ann was out sick, so I was stuck at the information desk most of the day. Today's questions included:

How do I find articles about MKULTRA
I need a book about Gary Gilmore
Can I use your stapler
Can I borrow a paper clip
Do you have back issues of *The Rassler*
How do you do the Heimlich manoeuver
How much does Tom Jones weigh
Is that Gutenberg Bible real (x2)

A young man came up and asked for books about "skeletons." Asked him for more information, and we ended up discussing bones, cartilage, tendons, and ligaments. On our way to 573.76, we paused in the reading room to look at a wall chart of the human anatomy, where I pointed out a few things to illustrate our conversation. Brought up chicken wings as an example of how most mammals have a separate radius and ulna. The kid looked like he has probably eaten a few chicken wings, so perchance he would grok what I was talking about. Instead, he looked at me, confused, and said, "You mean we have *chicken bones* in us?"

WEDNESDAY, JANUARY 19

After a night of tossing and turning, I returned to Sherwood's house before daybreak. Climbed through the kitchen window (it is easier to climb out than in) and wiped down every surface Randy and I were likely to have touched. Was quick about it. No more snooping. Would be in for it if the cops or L.F.'s P.I. caught me there.

As I was getting back into the Rambler, I heard a voice behind me. It was an old guy with a Polyflex patch on his shirt.

"We ask that you not park here unless you are doing business with us, Ace."

"Of course. Won't happen again." He waited for me to leave, as if I were going to trick him and stay. I rolled down the window. "Do you know the gentleman who lives in the house across the street over there?"

"Sorry, Ace."

"You haven't seen him lately, have you?"

Considered tossing him one of my matchbooks and asking him to contact me if he did, but decided to remain "Ace." Besides, I do not want to waste them. I only have five hundred.

Later in the morning, I headed over to Omaha Surplus. On a whim, bought a can of "Emergency Drinking Water." When you shake it, it sounds like there is something solid within. Also got one of those dog tag chains for my amulet.

Picked Randy up from work so we could discuss Sherwood's books over dinner at El Fenix. After taking Randy's order, the waitress looked at me.

"Two Cokes." I had already eaten and was not hungry.

"What kind?"

"Do you have Mr. Pibb?"

"No Pibb. Coke."

"What's up with the two Mr. Pibbs?" said Randy after the waitress left.

"I do that when I'm really thirsty and don't want to wait for a refill. You like Wagner, right?"

"*Oh! Welchen Wunders höchstes Glück! Der deine Wunde durfte schließen*," sang Randy. Several diners turned their heads in alarm.

"Tried listening to the *Ring* cycle last week. Wanted to dig it, I really did. Some of the music was pretty great, but it would be helpful if I understood German better. *Die Tür* has been slow going."

"No doubt. Which recording did you listen to?"

"Furtwängler."

"Ah, the anti-ideologue subjectivist *par excellence*. A philosopher in rehearsal and a poet in the evening. Have you heard Solti or Karajan? Two different *maestri*. Karajan's controlled suavity versus Solti's brassy, spontaneous theatricality." Randy fumbled for a cigarette.

"The *Ring* benefits from stereo," he continued. "What Furtwängler lacks in mono he more than makes up for in subtlety of tone color. His *fortissimo*! Then you've got the cast to consider. Solti's is arguably the best the sixties had to offer. Can't go wrong with Nilsson and Fischer-Dieskau. Anyway, I want to hear about *Die Tür*."

I pulled *Die Tür* out of my bag.

"What's that?" said Randy. "Macramé?"

"Do you like it?"

Randy shrugged. "If you feel it, carry it."

"Words to live by," I said. "Why is it so dark in here?"

"Anyway, I'd recommend Solti for *Das Rheingold* and *Die Walküre*, Leinsdorf for *Siegfried*—in glorious Living Stereo—and Karajan for *Götterdämmerung*."

"Don't think so, man," I said, shaking my head. "Not sitting through that whole shebang again." I did not tell him I only listened to *Das Rheingold*.

"Suit yourself, dude. Wagner's for non-pussies."

I carefully opened *Die Tür*. "Damn this Fraktur."

"If you let me take it home, I can check it out."

Was reluctant to do so, but Randy's German is better than mine. I slid it across the table, then took out the codex.

"This one's pretty crazy," I said. "Full of incantations and invocations, as well as evocations for dozens of demons, spirits, and their ilk, collectively referred to in Dordic as *kakoi*. There's a bunch of complicated geometry shit, too. Architectural drawings in nine-, ten-, eleven-point perspective. Besides being in Dordic, the calligraphy makes it even more of a pain in the ass to read because of all the ornamental ligatures. Beautiful to look at, though."

We looked at the demonurgical stuff. Randy studied several pages and furrowed his brow. "*Kakoi*, did you say?"

"Each is presented with its portrait and sigil," I said. "Here they tell you how to pronounce each one's name, followed by a description of their interests and expertise (geometry, astronomy, rhetoric), method of seduction (sloth, vanity), powers (noisome breath, psychic ability, flight)."

"Whoa," said Randy. "How'd you like to meet this scumbag in a dark alley?"

"Ugh. That's my worst nightmare. All my orifices involuntarily clenched at the sight of those slimy proboscides."

"No doubt," said Randy. He turned another page. "These *kakoi* are non-Solomonic. You'll find none of these in the *Pseudomonarchia daemonum*."

"What do you mean by 'non-Solomonic?'"

"The Testament of Solomon is associated with the Old Testament. The text describes how Solomon was enabled to build the Temple of Jerusalem by commanding demons by means of a magical ring that was given to him by the Archangel Michael."

"So if demons are real, then Jesus is, too?

"Not so fast. Demons aren't a Christian invention. They've been around for eternity. The ones in Solomon's encounters are of Greek, Egyptian, or Abrahamic traditions. The Buddhists have demons. And so do the Hindus, Zoroastrians, and Mesopotamians. The word *kakoi* does have an obvious Greek ring to it, though."

"I've noted superficial similarities between Dordic and Greek," I said. "But Greek is an Indo-European language while Dordic is certainly not." I was waving my hands around for emphasis when I knocked one of my Pibbs over next to the codex. Splashed all over one of the open pages and much of the fore edge. As quickly as I could grasp a wad of napkins, the Pibb beaded up and raced off the page, as if magnetically repelled. Ran my finger over the paper. "Doesn't feel waxy. What's the deal?"

Randy held the book up above the table while I cleaned up the sticky mess, then set it back down. "This isn't any kind of paper I've ever seen. The shagreen boards are badly worn, but the Mr. Pibb didn't seem to hurt it, either."

"What's shagreen?" I said.

"Could be stingray, or just untanned leather with a rough, granulated surface."

We took a moment to appreciate the cover. "Good thing the key was attached," I observed. "Lock like this looks easy to pick."

"One would expect a book like this to be sealed by magical means."

"Not this one, clearly."

"Unless the seal was broken," asserted Randy. Felt like he was arguing with me but about what?

When a couple sat down near us, I made a menu wall to give us some privacy.

"Look at these silky, tender chunks," said Randy, projecting his voice. He grinned at the nearby couple. "This is easily the best *mole* I've ever had," he announced.

THURSDAY, JANUARY 20

This morning I showed Dixie the "Rules for Students in Porteous Library." When I suggested we display them at the circulation desk, she resisted, arguing it would only "confuse people" and "make a mockery of rules in general." Foiled again!

Later, while searching for a book in the stacks, my eyes lingered upon the works of Hawthorne. Was repeating "Hawthorne" aloud in an exaggerated British accent when I heard two chicks snickering from the next aisle. Was tempted to explain to them that I knew Hawthorne was not British. Decided it was not a big deal and let it slide. Found myself thinking about the Stone Fox.

While filling in for Jo Ann at the information desk, Amber sat down and started asking me questions about my background and qualifications. What is this, an interview?

"When I chose to study Linguistics as an undergraduate, I had no intention of becoming a linguist," I said. "I just like languages."

"What languages do you speak?"

"None fluently. Nobody to speak them with. I do read the major European languages. Helps me a lot when I am cataloging. A little Japanese and Mandarin. Proto-Celtic but that doesn't really count. Wrote a paper on Cherokee once. What languages do you speak?"

"Spanish and Ubbi-Dubbi."

"*¿Qué es Ubbi-Dubbi?*" I said.

"*Wubouldn't yubou lubike tubo knubow.*"

"Impressive!"

"How did you end up being a librarian?"

"Let's see. I was born in '53. From an early age…"

"Fast forward," said Amber.

"While working in the library as an undergrad, Jo Ann told me about library school. Because of its vocational nature, I gathered a library degree was a prudent move. Now I get paid for sitting here talking to you. Jenny's studying for her M.L.S., you know."

"I want to be a marine biologist."

"Why a marine biologist?"

"Jesus won't save the whales."

Someone stole my sandwich out of the break room ice box. Zeke's for lunch with Randy. For some reason I was anxious to get *Die Tür* back. As soon as we sat down to eat, I broached the subject.

"*The Door*, in English," said Randy. "By one Durchdenmeer. Frankfurt am Mayn, 1844. A private reprinting of an evidently 17th-century work about the mythology of the island Vul Kar that existed ages ago. Somewhere in the Pacific according to the map within."

"Let me see the map," I said, eagerly.

Randy continued. "Theirs was an advanced civilization and as ancient as all get out. Its citizens dwelt in great content in cities of dazzling spires and stained glass, ruled by seven sorcerers. One of the seven, Zuberon, his mind ravaged by *qutum* leaves—whatever that is—and delusions of grandeur, became so powerful that he challenged the gods and incurred their wrath. As Vul Kar sank beneath the waves, Zuberon collected a vessel of soil, and by reciting an incantation, caused a new world to be. An act not of creation but of reproduction, imperfect and incomplete. Subject to the vagaries of demented imagination and whim. After hastily sweeping the contents of his workshop into his magical bag, Zuberon traced a door in the air with his finger and fled with his faithful into this new land Durchdenmeer refers to as Dord."

I raised my eyebrows. "Dord as in Dordic?"

Randy turned to a plate titled, *Vul Kars Agonie, 27. August, 8498, 13 Uhr*, which depicts a land beset by calamities. Waves crashing over rooftops, flames licking from chasms, bony fingers grasping sloughing flesh.

I held up my macramé bag. "My magical bag, ha ha. Did you say 8498, as in the year 8498?"

"Not the Gregorian year, obviously, although it does say August. Probably Durchdenmeer's doing."

"What happened to the other sorcerers?"

"They and their followers fled in ships born by the 'seven winds' to establish new colonies," said Randy. "That's as far as I've gotten." He turned to another plate, *Exodus der sieben Zauberer aus Vul Kar*. It depicts the sorcerers, with elongated heads, walking in formal procession, but one in the rear is rendered in pointillistic fashion, as if he were meant to be invisible.

"Don't recall this story at all," I said. "Unless Vul Kar is supposed to be Mu."

"Me, neither. And I read all twenty-four volumes of *The Children's Encyclopedia of Myths and Legends.*"

"Why are they carrying purses?"

"You see those at Göbekli Tepe as well as in the art of the Olmecs and Egyptians. The Annunaki carried them. Every explanation I have read seems unlikely if not implausible."

I returned to the map, which depicted more sea than land. Creatures peeked from the waves, while swirling lines suggested maelstroms and dangerous currents. "Here's Vul Kar. Are these supposed to be tunnels?"

"Those look like hachures, indicative of slopes," said Randy. "Hills or mountains."

"They look like worms," I said. "Why do you think Hitler had this?"

"Why Hitler had this should be obvious. We should probably be wondering what Sherwood was doing with it."

"Oh, miss," I said. "Can I get a doggy bag for this okra?"

On our way out to the Rambler, I said, "You know what? I don't recall wiping my fingerprints off Sherwood's pinball machine."

"Hang on, I want to say hello to the Colonel." Randy ducked into the Susu Lounge for a moment while I waited outside. Presently, he returned with two shots of whiskey. He handed me one and we drank to the Colonel's health. "Have you ever been arrested and fingerprinted?" he said, as we rolled onto Guilford.

"No. The F.B.I. says having fingerprints altered by plastic surgery doesn't work because they can make identifications from partial prints no larger than the end of a pencil."

"Wouldn't worry about it."

"Should we put his mail and newspapers back?"

"Do you want to get caught doing that?" said Randy. "What if someone notices the papers disappearing and reappearing? You're thinking too much."

Against my better judgment, I went to Sherwood's after work to wipe my fingerprints off the Magic Circle. As I approached his house, however, I spotted a brown Buick Centurion in the driveway. Kept going, turning onto Sam Calloway. Who could it be? Circled the block and drove by again, now headed south. Pulled into the Polyflex parking lot and began a stakeout.

Minutes passed, then an hour. At last, a man appeared from the side of the house. Did he emerge from the back door? Had he been in the tornado shelter? Tall, thin, baby blue leisure suit, white loafers, newsboy cap. No socks in this weather? Did not recognize him. He got into his car and headed toward White Settlement. For better or worse, I hesitated too long and missed my opportunity to tail him. Besides, I still wanted to wipe those fingerprints away, which I did. In and out, two minutes. No question of returning Sherwood's mail and newspapers, now.

I climbed out the kitchen window and dropped to the ground. Sure enough, I saw Roof Guy at the railing, illuminated by the weary pallor of the lone streetlight. He was watching me through binoculars. Had supposed the hedges in the front yard and the darkness would have afforded me some privacy, but apparently not from Roof Guy's vantage point.

When caught red-handed my m.o. is to act naturally, which I did. As I reached the Rambler, Roof Guy lowered his binoculars. He now produced a clipboard and was writing something down.

Leftover okra for dinner. Watched *Operation Crossbow* with Sophia Loren and some other people. Panavision sure looks rotten on my black and white. Felt like I was missing half of the movie because of the dimensions of my TV screen. Why don't they make TVs wider?

FRIDAY, JANUARY 21

To Turkey Knob with Jo Ann to look at their library's new microfilm reader to see if we wanted to purchase that model for the Porteous library. Jo Ann said she would let me drive if she got to be in charge of the radio. She chose KVIL, which was fine with me. I like my rock hard, soft, and in between. She was in an agreeable mood and chose not to pick a fight, even when I sang falsetto to the Bee Gees. Of course, she may later run to Dixie with some complaint or another. Spotted Veronica's Pacer in the parking lot.

In the afternoon, Randy showed me how to make phase boxes. Made one for *Die Tür* before returning it to my macramé handbag. Wanted to make a phase box for the codex but it was too big.

"Mind if I xerox that?" said Randy. "I'll give it back on Sunday. Are we still going to Dallas?"

I nodded, then reluctantly handed him the codex. Was irritated because I had planned on reading it at the information desk tomorrow.

Spaghetti and meatballs for dinner while watching a Bob Hope special. Veronica's cat joined me. Ann-Margret stole the show, but when does she ever not steal the show? After that, Humphrey Bogart in *Dead End*. Dead End Kids would make a killer name for one of those punker bands. It is uncanny how much Bogart and Ron look alike. Guess he and Mom are back in Aspen by now. To bed at ten.

SATURDAY, JANUARY 22

Spent a couple of hours down in the Vault digging through boxes of Baumann material, searching for anything as sensational as the codex. When I got back upstairs, the Stone Fox told me Fred had phoned. Aperture wants me, if I am still interested. Although Fred knew me when I was in Primary Source, the others have not even heard me play bass!

Spent yet another Saturday night at the Laundr-O-Mat. If I can't get a date, I may as well do something productive. At least the machines are not all taken. While waiting for a load to dry, I stepped outside for a smoke. Thought I might try to phone Mom but I did not have enough change left for the long-distance call.

Got home just in time to watch *633 Squadron*. Rosie the Barmaid is the same chick who played Inga in *Dracula*. Led Zeppelin was on *Don Kirshner* but I could not keep my eyes open.

SUNDAY, JANUARY 23

Keep seeing a blue van in the driveway at Collinwood. Undoubtedly one of Veronica's pals, though I have not gotten a look at its owner. Should knock on her door, ask for some sugar.

Went with Randy to the Cotton Bowl today to watch them film a Burt Reynolds flick. We got to meet Dan Jenkins and Too Tall Jones. Randy got their autographs. Filming was supposed to have begun in October, but Burt got sick. Heard there were legal problems. He and his co-stars had doubles on the field taking all the hard hits.

"Hey, look!" I said. "It's the Goodyear blimp. Do they think this is a game?"

Band rehearsals have begun above the Novel Hovel. We must wait for the shop to close. Fred said the arrangement is only temporary and that we would soon have to find another place. That is fine with me because there is no heat up there (or bathroom). A bare light bulb illuminates an overflowing no-pest strip. A filthy shag carpet doubles as an ashtray. Bonnie thinks her dad will let us use a building he owns on the edge of downtown near the Mixmaster.

It was not long before I could not feel my fingers. I put on gloves but that made playing even more difficult. Tim looked at me like I was an idiot. Not sure he likes me much. He ridiculed me for wearing my bass too high. "This isn't Herman's Hermits," he sneered.

Wheeler, the little boy whose parents run the Oriental restaurant next door, came upstairs to watch. After one false start, he gave us a thumb's down but was soon accompanying us on pickle whistle and armpit farts. During a break Tim gave him five dollars to go buy him a pack of Winstons from the machine in his parents' restaurant. When he got back he asked for Tim's autograph.

"What about me?" I said, pretending to be hurt. Thought about drawing a Vonnegutian asterisk under my name, but reconsidered and drew an animal head.

"A duck," declared Wheeler.

"Look again. It's a rabbit."

"Duck," he insisted. When I pointed out the ears, Wheeler screamed "No!" and stomped away. Next thing I knew, he was arguing with Tim about politics.

"Carter's a farter," proclaimed Tim.

"Ford's an automobile!" countered Wheeler, triumphantly.

"More accurately, Carter's leprosy and Ford's yaws," interjected Fred.

The debate ended with Wheeler doing a handstand while eating a jawbreaker, blue saliva leaking out of his tear ducts and down his forehead. Have not decided if Wheeler is precocious or retarded.

After running through all the covers, the rest of the evening was spent bringing me up to speed on the originals, which are complex and involve a lot of memorization. I do not read much music, but have my own musical notation. Just a mnemonic device, really. When I used it on the chalkboard to illustrate one of the arrangements, nobody raised objections.

Fred, a self-described non-musician, pretty much does his own thing. He provides embellishments, both musical and non-musical (fog, sound effects, liquid light projector, and whatnot). He invited me in after I gave him a ride home.

"Where'd you get this?" I said, referring to a life-sized cardboard cut-out of Todd Rundgren in the corner.

"Record Town. Doug said I could have it. It's a promotional gimmick from *A Wizard, A True Star*."

"Didn't think you were a fan."

"The boy wizard should have joined the Peace Corps. Do you want it?"

Fred lets me borrow whatever I want from his record collection. While pawing through his bins, I found "Anarchy in the U.K." and put it on the turntable.

"Hey, where'd you get these?" I asked. Fred had a pile of 8-tracks on his bamboo coffee table. I rattled *Wings at the Speed of Sound*.

Fred made a face and said, "Keep it."

"Why? Don't you want it?"

"Naw. Debbie left a bunch of junk here when she bolted. Keep 'em all."

"What have I done to deserve this generosity?" I said. "This is a decent album. Really dig the bass riff on 'Silly Love Songs.'"

"Just when we thought people had had enough of silly love songs, Paul looked around and saw that it wasn't so."

"What's wrong with that?"

"I'd like to know. I've rarely heard a guy say less over that many albums."

"Must an album say something?"

Fred jerked his thumb toward the turntable. "Ask Johnny Rotten."

On the way home, Todd Rundgren rode shotgun. Drizzle turned to sleet. Windshield wipers merely smeared the mess around. It made everything look blurry. Should probably buy new ones, but I do not know how to install them.

MONDAY, JANUARY 24

Brought Todd Rundgren to work. He now lives in the corner of my office. While covering for Jo Ann at the information desk, the geezer from the library tour approached and introduced himself. "My name is Bertram Harrington. I'm a visiting scholar from the Eswaran Institute. I am told the Baumann Collection is up my street." He had a British accent.

"Who told you that?" I know Jo Ann did not, and I doubt Dixie would have.

"Professor Sherwood, whom I understand is away."

"He's missing, yes, if that's what you mean."

"Of course. I was wondering to whom I would speak to obtain access. Not to the art pieces so much, but chiefly the printed matter. The manuscripts."

"I know the collection better than anyone else, I suppose, except for Professor Sherwood." Handed him one of my custom matchbooks.

He read it very seriously for a moment, then looked up and grinned wryly. "You're the one who cataloged the Ásatrú books for me." He handed the matchbook back to me. "I'll be in touch soon. Good day." He hesitated, then added, "I say, I'm thinking of staying on after the spring semester. I am in need of a flat." His tone was now warm.

"You're at the Men's Faculty Club?"

"For the time being. Do you know Fort Worth well?"

I perked up. "Sure do! I've lived here my whole life!"

"That's brilliant. Can you recommend a neighborhood?"

"Let me see. Arlington Heights is terrific. But there are many areas on the west side that are nice. Ridglea Hills. Ridgmar."

"Where do you live?"

"On Collinwood. Near the Showdown."

"Thank you for this information, Steven. Very kind of you."

"Professor? Before you go, may I ask the significance of the word, 'dogsbody'?"

"Dogsbody?" he repeated. "It means 'a person who is given boring, menial tasks to do.' Why do you ask?"

"Came across the phrase recently and was unfamiliar with it. Thank you!"

Lunch with the Stone Fox at the Student Union. Since her shift started at one, she wanted to meet at noon. This was a bummer because of crowds and because I usually eat at ten-thirty. Left my billfold in the Rambler. As I was returning across the quad, I overheard Jenny shouting to a friend, "I can't. I'm having lunch with Steven Miller!" It was weird to hear my name like that. Proof that I exist? Jenny's tone was one of smugness, like she was having lunch with Burt Reynolds. Her friend responded, "Steven who?" Did not let Jenny see me because I did not want to embarrass her, in case the tone in her voice betrayed feelings that she does not want me to know about. She did sound rather excited, however.

Suppose our meal could have been a date. Neither of us called it that, nor did it feel like one. We discussed work, her classes, and her Yes t-shirt, which had a colorful dragon on it. Have never met a chick who liked Yes.

"Did you see them last summer?" I said.

"At Moody? Yes, I was there."

"Me, too!" I mentioned that "Close to the Edge" was my favorite Yes song. "Its ecstatic organ interlude never fails to bring tears to my eyes," I explained. Jenny got a strange look on her face. Could not tell if she found my confession ridiculous or endearing.

When I brought up Chris Squire's stupendous bass solo on *Yessongs*, she suddenly asked me if I knew that Eskimos have over fifty words for snow. "Yes," I replied, after a long pause. "Franz Boas had claimed that. But there has been some debate over the number because of the polysynthetic way of forming words in Inuit. Don't Texans have fifty words for heat?" She smiled, but stopped when I began to list them all.

After lunch, I became self-conscious of my breath. Must they put garlic in everything? "I'm going to get a pack of gum. Back in a sec."

"I've got some." Jenny gave me a small square wrapped in paper. It looked like a neat little gift.

Unwrapped it, then popped the gum into my mouth. As I began chewing, some flavored goo squirted out of it, which caught me off guard. Reached for the pack and read the ingredients. "That must be the magnesium stearate."

Dixie dinged me again for not wearing a tie. "When I reach for the higher shelves, my shirt comes untucked," I complained.

"I understand, Steven, but the dress code comes down to us from L.F. I have nothing to do with it," she replied, curtly.

"Carlos doesn't have to wear a tie."

Dixie grimaced. "I don't know what to tell you, Steven. Rules are rules." What *yaje*.

TUESDAY, JANUARY 25

"Lloyd, would you please come here?" I overheard Dixie say in an orotund tone. Scooted my chair backwards so I could watch the show.

"Do you launder your shirts, Lloyd?".

"Yes, ma'am. I also do my father's laundry," replied Lloyd, who towered over his objurgator.

"Your shirt is stained."

"Yes, ma'am. You'll excuse me while I help this patron."

Dixie tailgated him. While Lloyd operated the Gaylord, she continued. "When you report for work, you will wear a clean shirt. You look like a refugee from a rummage sale."

Lloyd is such a gentle giant. He cares for his elderly father who is terminally ill. What little free time he has, he spends playing organ for his local church, music being the only thing that brings him joy. Lives out in Westland and takes the bus to work. So he has stains on his shirts. Is that a crime?

After pork and beans for dinner, I dusted off my book collection while listening to records with the TV turned down. When *City Beneath the Sea* came on, it looked interesting so I turned that up instead. It takes place in the year 2053, which means people had been eating Soylent Green for three decades by then. Imagine being alive in such a world. Evidently, in 2053 fire extinguishers look exactly like they do now, except they are kept loose on the floor instead of hung from the wall.

WEDNESDAY, JANUARY 26

The newspaper had another piece extolling the virtues of the dreaded metric system. Read with fascination about bumkyns of beer, puncheons of wine, and of cubits, swods, and tuffets. Those were the days! The imperial system is one of the last things that sets the U.S. apart from the rest of the world. If we go metric, it will be a sad day indeed.

Did not want to arouse suspicion by asking anyone at Porteous about my amulet. I took it to that rock shop out in the boondocks. The Rock Guy behind the counter took one look at it and said, "What do you have there?"

"Found this among my grandmother's jewelry," I lied. "Thought it might be alexandrite."

Rock Guy turned on a bright lamp. He contemplated the stone for what seemed to be a long time. "Can't even say what color this is. It's green and purple at the same time. Not alexandrite, though. More like dichroic glass."

"Like the Lycurgus Cup?"

Rock Guy stared at me but did not answer. He held the amulet up with tongs. Resting his hand against his cheek for stability, he positioned the gemstone close to his eye, then moved it slowly across his field of vision. "This is highly refractive. Beyond the range of our refractometer, even." He now squinted at the stone through a little magnifying glass.

"I'm seeing unexpected spectra," said Rock Guy. He reached for a small flashlight that was fitted with what looked like the end of a chair leg. When he turned it on, it produced a focused beam of light. When the beam shone upon the stone, the counter and floor were covered in colorful triangles. We both looked around in wonder.

After consulting various gemological tables, Rock Guy finally looked up with a sigh. "I'm in a little over my head here. Can't seem to arrive at a ballpark birefringence or refractive index. It's definitely anisotropic. Can check for some other things like hardness, if you'll allow me, but I can already tell I don't know what the heck this is. Say it was your grandmother's, eh?" he said, dubiously. He looked askance over his glasses. "Come back tomorrow when the boss is here. He'll know more than I do, but if you ask me, this stone is something strange."

The boob tube was nothing but doom and gloom. Charles Manson on Channel 4, radioactive waste on 5, threat of the "U-bomb" on *The Bionic Woman*, *The Execution of Private Slovik* on 11, a dreary Nova piece on coal mining on PBS, and *The 700 Club* on 39. No, thanks. Of course, my demonurgical reading matter of late is not any more cheerful. Opted to practice my bass playing. That always brings me joy. The strings on the Pan are old, so I boiled them. That ought to buy me some time.

THURSDAY, JANUARY 27
My cigarette break coincided with Randy's. We spoke in hushed tones of our readings outside the back door of the break room, which I propped open with *The Urantia Book* which exists for the purpose.

"Let's make this quick. It's colder than a penguin's perineum," said Randy. "*Die Tür* is turning out to be your typical screwball stuff. Durchdenmeer makes frequent allusions to a *Chronik von Vul Kar*, from which we learn of the fate of the seven sorcerers and their followers. Isn't that one of the titles we found at Sherwood's?"

I nodded.

"They took with them all of their magic, including amulets, rings, wands, staves, and weapons," continued Randy. "They also took their libraries. The author tells of how, since then, books, scrolls, and tablets changed hands and were stolen, destroyed, and lost. Over millennia they were copied, embellished, translated into languages of the day, and corrupted by the introduction of errors of thought and hand. Words began to lose their meaning. Scribes, once sorcerers themselves, now no longer understood what they were copying. Many ceased to care."

"Sounds like a philological nightmare," I said.

"Goes on to tell of the coming of man by sea and later over the ice road. The people of lost Vul Kar shunned him."

"Are the people of Vul Kar not men?"

"The text has *Mensch*," said Randy. "Battles were lost and won. Some fled to the mountains. Some went underground. Others took slaves, were enslaved themselves, or were interbred. Sorcerers grew weaker, while seers ceased to see and oracles to hear. Durchdenmeer writes of a *sub rosa* brotherhood of those who would regain the power and knowledge of Vul Kar by seeking out primary and secondary documents, magical items, and the like. Material that would be meaningless and perhaps even dangerous to ignorant slobs like us."

"Speak for yourself."

Randy stomped out his butt. "Gotta get back inside in a minute. Are you translating the Dordic parts?"

My teeth were chattering now. My voice did not sound like my own. "*Linguae dordica* is helpful, but there are many words and glyphs I can't decipher," I said. "There's also a bunch of geometry stuff that makes no sense to me, and I'm no slouch at geometry. I know a dodecahedron from a logarithmic spiral. But there are shapes in the codex that would disturb Escher."

When I got home from work, I discovered someone had been in my apartment. My card catalog drawers had been opened. Books lay scattered about. The Liszt bust was on the kitchen floor. His eyes had been gouged out. Veronica's cat did not do this, surely. Could be that damned DDT kid from across the street. I picked Liszt off the floor. Something gooey got on my fingers. Smelled sulfuric. I preserved some of the goo in an empty film canister and washed my hands for several minutes with shampoo.

Went upstairs to tell Veronica. She was surprised and concerned. "I've been gone most of the day. Didn't see or hear anything." Does she ever?

"As far as I can tell, they didn't take anything. Can't figure out how they got in, though. Front and back doors were locked. All the windows were closed and locked. Half of them are painted shut."

"I don't lock my doors because I know you," said Veronica, airily. "Which means whoever got into your apartment could just as easily barged into mine."

I followed her into the bedroom. She opened a box on her dresser. "My jewelry is still there." She held up her arms as if mystified. "Everything is in plain sight."

"Oh, goody," I replied, moronically.

Veronica stood there for a moment and then whistled for her cat. She turned about as if it were just behind her. "Yoo hoo! Figs!"

"I'll let you know if I see him," I said.

FRIDAY, JANUARY 28

Appointment with Dr. Grainger for a cleaning. His hygienist, Phyllis, has been calling me Steve from the time we met over two years ago. Since I did not object the first time, it is too late to do so now. Phyllis smears Vaseline all over my lips before each cleaning. Afterward, she wipes my mustache against the grain with a wet cloth. It is really unpleasant.

As soon as I sat down at my desk at work, I heard Randy's secret knock on my office door. A knock we have always done: *boom-tic, boom-boom-tic*. I hear it less and less these days. He spoke rapidly, in hushed tones. "Did you hear?" he said. "This morning L.F. announced that Sherwood's dead."

"What?"

"The P.I. he hired discovered Sherwood's body at his house. Natural causes. Guess they must have done an autopsy already. L.F. identified him personally."

"But when did they find him?" I said. "We know he wasn't there a week ago. Do you mean to tell me he disappeared for over a month, without telling a soul, then he came home and died?"

"I'm not saying that at all. It's all dubious."

"Makes no sense at all, but I doubt anyone knows enough to question what L.F. said. Including you and me, frankly."

"The memorial's next Friday," said Randy. "Hey, where'd you get that?"

"Todd? Fred gave him to me."

"Fred's a weird guy."

"Funny. That's what he said about you. By the way, someone was in Collinwood. No sign of forced entry, but they made a mess."

"They take anything?"

"Don't think so. But you know that bust of Liszt you gave me? They gouged his eyes out."

"Classical music lovers can be touchy."

"You're a classical music lover. Did you do it?"

Randy shrugged noncommittally, then pointed at a photo pinned to the wall above my desk. He read its caption aloud: "Where is John?"

"Found that tucked into a book I was cataloging." It was a photo of Le Corbusier and Yoko, both naked.

"Check out that dude's leg scar," said Randy.

"Boating accident. Pussy way to get a scar."

"Take a whiff of this." Opened the film canister with the goo sample and held it under Randy's nose.

"Oof," he gagged. "Why do you have that?"

"It was smeared on Liszt. How can we find out what this is?"

"Guess we could take it to Wicker."

"Who's Wicker?"

"You'll see. Let's run over there now. It'll only take a minute."

We walked across the quad to Comstock Hall, where we found Wicker in one of the labs. He was messing around with a Bunsen burner. "Wicker! We have a solid to ask."

Wicker removed his goggles and shook our hands. It was Rock Guy! Stifling a worried glance at Randy, I opened the film container. He studied it briefly then looked at me. "Is this your grandma's, too?"

"What? No!" I protested.

Wicker put his goggles back on. "What do you want?"

"Can you identify this?" said Randy. "Run some tests on it or something?"

"Looks like octopus jizz," said Wicker.

"That is unlikely," I said. We all stared at each other for a moment.

Wicker dipped a tool into some hydrochloric acid, then into the jizz. After holding the end of the tool over the Bunsen burner for a moment, he mixed it with a solution to see if a precipitate was formed. Next, he transferred some of the jizz into a test tube and held it over the flame. After a moment, a fulvous mist issued from the tube. "Let's see if it's soluble in water."

Randy and I watched Wicker with great interest. At last, Wicker turned off the Bunsen burner and removed his goggles.

"The jizz showed a precipitate with silver nitrate, which obviously wouldn't happen with a nitrate salt. However, the flame test indicated a clear positive for nitrate."

"Not bromine?" challenged Randy.

"Bromine gas is a much brighter orange red. Not the dirty red brown indicative of nitrogen dioxide. Besides, bromide salts don't spontaneously eject elemental bromine over a flame any more than, say, chlorides eject elemental chlorine gas when gently heated."

"The gas looked greenish-tan to me."

Wicker shrugged.

"So what is it?" I said.

"No idea. Octopus jizz. Can I get back to work?" Wicker now regarded me closely. He said nothing of my amulet, in which he had shown such interest at the Rock Shop.

"That was disappointing," I whispered to Randy in the stairwell. "How do you know so much about chemistry?"

"Dude, I keep telling you, I read a lot of kids' books. It's a quick and easy way to bone up on a subject." When we emerged into the quad, he mimicked Wicker: "Is this your grandma's?"

I shrugged innocently. "Why do you suppose he said that?"

SATURDAY, JANUARY 29

Left the house before dawn to head downtown for Led Zeppelin tickets. Wanted to get there before the lines got long. I underestimated Zeppelin fans. People had spent the entire night out in the brutal cold. By the time I showed up it was a mob scene. A scalper tapped on my window but I am not paying fifty bucks to see anyone. Nor do I wait in lines for anything, if I can help it.

Felt like I needed a break from serious matters. Considered going to the Stock Show but I did not want to go alone. Have never owned anything heavier than a light jacket, so I did not feel like freezing my ass off, either. Predictably, I ended up going to a few record stores—Record Town, LP Goodbuy, Peaches. Am always pleased when I leave a shop empty-handed because I know I've saved money. Today I did not save money. Brought home some E. Power Biggs, April Wine's *Electric Jewels*, Kayak's *See See the Sun*, Mike Oldfield's *Ommadawn*, *Sad Wings of Destiny* by Judas Priest, ZZ Top's latest offering, something funky by Automatic Man, Harmonium's *Si on avait besoin d'une cinquième saison*, some Hovhaness from the Poseidon Society, a Nonesuch LP of Balinese gamelan, and that Jean-Michel Jarre album they played on KERA the other night. Oh, and *Old Favorites by Jim Lowe*, for sentimental reasons. Spent a heavenly evening listening to it all.

SUNDAY, JANUARY 30

This morning when I walked into the kitchen I heard faint scratching and meowing. Took me a second to discover it was coming from the trash hole. When I opened it, Veronica's cat emerged. His whiskers were covered in cobwebs.

I threw on a robe and carried the feline upstairs. Veronica's door was open. Before I could knock, Veronica had taken the cat from my arms. "Figs!" she cooed. What an odd name for a cat. She cradled him and covered his face in kisses. "Are you okay? Where have you been?"

"He was in the trash hole."

"The what?"

"That chute thing in the kitchen."

"The dumbwaiter? The door to mine's painted shut. He must have entered through yours."

"Mine's really hard to open." Glad she did not ask me why I called it the trash hole.

"Surely he wasn't in there this whole time, though?"

"We would have heard him." Veronica looked at me like I knew more about this that I was admitting. Can see why she would think that, but I am as clueless as she is.

Hellball with the Bastard at the Calmont Y. He was late, so I ended up trying out all the weight machines until he arrived. Randy and I wore ourselves out on the court. Each time one of us got hit, we made up a curse in Latin. Then the other one would try to translate it. Randy is more creative at cursing than I am (and his Latin is far superior), so he won that game as well as the overall match.

At one point, Randy farted loudly and proudly. "*Unum saltum et siffletum et unum bumbulum!*" he declared.

I applauded. "Mesdames et messieurs, I present you the incomparable Monsieur Poo-Hole!"

"If you're referring to Joseph Pujol, I believe it's pronounced *Pujol*. Catalan name. But I was referring to Roulandus le Fartere, not Le Pétomane."

"I stand corrected," I said, irritably. Does Randy have to be right about everything?

MONDAY, JANUARY 31

The library was closed today because people were freaking out about the white stuff. Or just the threat of it. Went to work anyway because I wanted to examine the Baumann Collection undisturbed. My office was too quiet, so I tuned in to WBAP. It mystifies me when people say they find classical music relaxing. I find it too engaging for relaxation. Much of it is quite dramatic. Final movement of the "Moonlight" sonata, anyone?

Was flipping through an old U.S. road atlas when Guddu suddenly appeared, seemingly out of thin air.

"Where the fuck did you come from?" I said rather rudely. Still, that stealthy son of a bitch startled me. The hairs were standing up on my arms.

We looked each other up and down until the silence became unbearable. To break the silence, I blurted, "Do you want to learn how to find Kentucky on a map?"

"Prithee, what is *Ken-tuck-kee*?" he said, phonetically, like he had never heard of the place. Like he had never spoken English before.

"Here's his hat," I said, pointing at the map. "Iowa is his head, Missouri is his shirt, his pants are Arkansas, Louisiana is his shoes, Tennessee is his skillet. Here is the Kentucky Fried Chicken." I looked up at Guddu.

"Kentucky is a human?" said Guddu. The words lurched out of his mouth, which contorted to accommodate the phonology. What the hell accent is that?

With my fingertip I traced the man's shape. "These states here are shaped like a man holding a skillet of chicken. Kentucky is the chicken." I tapped Kentucky with my finger for emphasis. Was starting to doubt if I was doing this correctly.

"The chicken is where?"

"Kentucky is the chicken."

Guddu looked disappointed. "Would it please thee to see the earth from..." He searched for the word. "The welkin?"

"Sure, Longfellow."

On a piece of scrap paper, Guddu deftly sketched a rabbit, then two leaves joined at the stems. What a line that guy has. Like Picasso. He presented the sketch to me.

"A rabbit and two leaves," I said, matter-of-factly.

Guddu turned the drawing upside-down.

I shook my head. "Still don't get it."

"The leaves are the Americas. The rabbit is Asia and Europe." The words were flowing more easily now.

"Well, what do you know. That's neat!"

Guddu bowed. "Guddu is pleased," he said, referring to himself in the third person. He turned to look at my cardboard cut-out of Todd Rundgren. "Who is this mage?"

Had a feeling Guddu would have no idea who Todd Rundgren was, so I simply sang the lyrics to "Rock and Roll Pussy." Guddu's face curdled. "You should not have this," was all he said. He had vanished before I could ask him why he came to work. How did he even get in?

Resumed studying the atlas, wondering what it would be like to live in each state. Alabama is out of the question. Alaska is too isolated, Arizona too hot. Had once read of a place in Arkansas with naturally occurring hot tubs. Should try to check it out some time. It is not that far, really. Randy says California is nice. He has an uncle in Ojai, I believe. Colorado? "Friends around the campfire and everybody's high," and all that. Didn't Lucy and Ricky end up in Connecticut? The Mertzes followed them there. Spunt is from Delaware. He pronounces it Dullaware. I cannot imagine ever leaving Texas.

TUESDAY, FEBRUARY 1

Dixie invited me into her office and asked what I have been working on lately. "Others have remarked that they have been unable to find you when they needed you."

"Jo Ann was out, so I had to give a library orientation tour. I've also been spending a lot of time in the Vault." Hoped she would not want to talk about the Vault.

"That's all good and well, but I would like you to finish cataloging the Ignatius Bernhard festschrifts before you start any new projects."

Dixie always says things slightly out of order. And the Baumann Collection is not a new project, but I kept quiet. "Who said they couldn't find me? What did they want me for?"

"Hazel says you're never in your office."

"Not when I'm elsewhere. Jo Ann calls out sick, so I am often at the information desk. But you already know that."

"L.F. was asking for you the other day."

"Was he?"

"He was." We glared at each other for a moment before Dixie dismissed me.

As I was walking back to my office, Spunt stopped me. "Do you party?" he asked in a slow monotone, eyes bulging.

"Not now, Spunt."

Why would L.F. be looking for me?

After work, I headed to the Novel Hovel. Had unloaded my amp onto the sidewalk before Fred came out and reminded me rehearsals were now at the new location. The Novel Hovel closes at six on weekdays. I killed time browsing the occult section where I found Wheeler doing his homework on the floor.

"You have a purse," he observed, mockingly. His lips were a cadaverous Hi-C purple.

"It's a men's macramé handbag."

"Purse!" he cried, jumping up and down and clapping his hands like a chimp with cymbals. He followed me around, talking rapidly about Scooby Doo and cereal. Fred had taught Wheeler how to use the cash register. We watched him ring up a customer, a woman who bought two bottle caps with zodiac symbols painted on them. Fred had put the bottle caps on the counter the other day, boasting that customers would buy anything, including trash.

"How adorable you are!" the woman cooed. Wheeler responded by moving his eyebrows up and down and making smooching noises. Fred and I chuckled, but the lady looked somewhat put off, leaving in a huff with her trash.

I noticed a copy of *The Hobbit* on display in the case by the counter. "When did you get this?" I said.

"We've had that. It's a later printing."

"Let me see," I demanded. Fred unlocked the case and handed me the book. It was a first printing of the second edition from 1951. Very Good in a Good dust jacket. Fifteen bucks. "Can I write you an I.O.U.?"

Fred waved his hand dismissively. "You should really be buying first editions. It's a far better investment."

"Couldn't care less about first editions. Besides, this one looks exactly like the first edition."

"But the dust jacket."

"Are you trying to talk me out of buying this? The wear and tear adds character."

Fred shrugged. The prize went into my macramé handbag.

"Nice purse," he said.

I repeated what I had told Wheeler.

"Ah, an emancipated man."

Smoked a couple of Kents out front while Fred closed up. Wheeler approached me with his calculator held upside down, displaying the word "HELLO."

I wrestled the calculator out of his hand and typed "5318008," then gave it back to him.Flipping it around, he stared at it for a moment before running inside his parents' restaurant shouting "Look, Mama! Boobies!"

Our new rehearsal space is an old brick warehouse. The kind with a long loading platform and big, steel doors. Tim was already inside, making eagle noises into a device with a long hose attached.

"If that's not a bong, what is it?"

"Talk box," he croaked into the talk box.

"What's the bottle of honey for?" I said.

"Bear bong." Tim walked over to the heavy metal door and attempted to pull it down.

"Can I help?" said Bonnie, who sprung to his side.

"Not unless you're a beer."

"Very funny," she said, flopping down onto a couch that looked like a pizza.

Auditioned a drummer this evening. Tall, skinny Mormon with glasses named Dave. Dave, like the last drummer. After setting up his kit, Dave scooted (with her permission) Bonnie's Minimoog next to him. He then laid down a kick-ass groove with his right hand and feet while playing a busy bass riff on the synth with his left hand. He then switched to a polyrhythmic cycle of three beats on the kick, four on the snare, and five on the floor tom. Neither my eyes, ears, nor mind could follow him. Could have been faking it. How would we have known?

As an ensemble, we loosened up with a cover of "Detroit Rock City." Tim playfully sang "Haltom City" instead of "Detroit." We then attempted "The Low Spark of High Heeled Boys" so Dave could stretch out. After a tasteful vibraslap accent, he smoothly transitioned to bongos without missing a beat. No one even saw him bring those in. He turned the spark down low, then switched back to his Ludwigs for a dialogue with Tim's talk box eructations. The chemistry was there.

Bonnie captured "Rock 'n Roll Insanity" on her boombox. When we played back the cassette, Dave shook his head slowly and drawled, "That's bad, that's bad!" by which I believe he meant "excellent." Tim made the obligatory "Is it live or is it Memorex?" joke, which no one acknowledged. Was he trying to one up me?

"Isn't George Hamilton a Mormon?" I remarked, to no one in particular.

"George Hamilton?" responded Bonnie.

"Stephen Bennett in *Roots*. Tan guy." Glanced knowingly at Dave, who was too busy breaking down his kit to acknowledge my comment.

"He sure doesn't act Mormon," said Bonnie. "Doesn't he party?"

After Dave split, we all went over to Fred's house to hang out where it was warmer.

"What did y'all think of Dave?" asked Bonnie.

"Don't believe I ever met him," I said.

"Not that Dave. Dave the Second." I must have looked befuddled. "That's his name."

"Huh?"

"The guy who played drums with us all evening."

"Oh yeah! He blew me away!" I said. Weird how you can spend the entire day with someone and simply not notice them.

We voted unanimously to invite Dave II into the band. We then drank beer and argued about band names for this latest iteration of Aperture. There was Cloud Eater, Chimera, and the Medicine Men, the latter I rejected because it started with the word "the." Bonnie liked Marble Index. From a Wordsworth poem inspired by a bust of Newton, but it too readily brought to mind the Nico album, at least for me.

"*The* Marble Index," insisted Tim, arrogantly.

Half-heartedly offered Deckle Edge. Tim parried with Vera Gemini, which unimaginatively referenced a Blue Öyster Cult song.

"Won't everyone assume Bonnie is Vera?"

"How about Rat Purée?" said Fred. "It's an anagram of Aperture."

"What's an anagram?" asked Bonnie.

"It's where you take the letters of a word and rearrange them to form different words," explained Fred. "Mojo Risin's just an anagram for Jim Morrison. Mine's Ken Derrick Fox."

I rearranged my name in my mind. "I'm Mr. Sleeve Lint," I lamented.

There was a lull in the discussion while Tim and Bonnie contemplated their own anagrams. "Mine's too hard," said Bonnie.

Tim reached for his talk box. "The Eagle Has Landed!" he croaked.

"But that's just the name of your van," protested Bonnie.

Tim petulantly offered Hornswooped Bungo Ponies before sulking off.

"What about Fon?" said Fred.

"Fawn? As in a young deer?" I said.

"F-o-n. It's a character from *La montaña sagrada*."

"Do you want to explain the name every single time you say it?"

"Point taken."

This led to a sort of battle where we tried to top each other with obscure creative works. Shared my favorite movie, *Boom!* (Losey, 1968), which Fred waved off dismissively. He put on a novelty record by P. Vert called "Stickball," featuring lyrics like, "Whip some skull on me, bitch!" I nearly busted a gut laughing.

"You can have it," said Fred, magnanimously.

Tim offered *Cool McCool*. I countered with "Plexiglas Toilet," which was met with disbelief by everyone. "That's not a Styx song," insisted Tim. Bonnie asked if I could prove its existence.

"Hey Fred, do you have *The Serpent Is Rising*?" I asked.

"Hell, no. Can't stand that carnival barker."

After "Stickball" ended, Fred put on an Adriano Celentano record featuring fake English lyrics to which he sang along.

"Was that in English?" I said.

"That reminds me." Fred retrieved the book *English As She Is Spoke* from one of his milk crate bookshelves. He began to read aloud phrases from it. Some of the gems contained within include "At what o'clock dine him?" and "Take that boy and whip him to [*sic*] much." Got a lot of mileage out of the latter, repeating it all evening until Bonnie said she had a headache and was going home.

"Take that girl and whip her to much!" Tim teased. He made a whipping motion with a guitar cable, almost whipping off my glasses.

I turned to face Bonnie. "Whip some skull on us, bitch!" I said, cleverly.

Bonnie did a double take. The others opened their mouths in amazement.

"You do know what that means," said Fred.

Looked at Fred, then Bonnie, and shook my head. Before I could apologize for my innocent *faux pas*, Bonnie had already slammed the door behind her.

WEDNESDAY, FEBRUARY 2

Dicked around for a while at Age of Aquarius. Found a monk robe to wear on stage. Also a red double knit sweater that looks a lot like the one Fritz Reiner wears on the cover of one of his Beethoven albums. The temperature in the library is unsuitable for primates, so perhaps a sweater will help. Could wear it under my jacket, too, when it is as cold as it has been. Also stopped by Toy Chest for a football and a kicking tee.

Despite *Linguae dordica*'s brevity, I managed to finish translating the text from Sherwood's chalk door. *Linguae dordica: elementa grammaticae et tabula verborum* is a grammar of the Dordic language. It is written in Latin, which makes it a bit of a slog. But it is the only Dordic grammar in existence that I know of. Am guessing it is from the 16th century. Its edges have been brutally trimmed, into the text block in places. Came to us bound with additional material tipped in, including a generous typewritten glossary (also in Latin, sadly) and a translation of the "Lord's Prayer" into Dordic. The language superficially shares some features of Indo-European, but I do not recognize it as belonging to any other language family. Could be an isolate. Who the hell spoke this? Where did they live? If Randy knows, he is not talking.

Sherwood had given *Linguae dordica* to Randy to repair. Randy and I made copies for ourselves. Dordic's comparatively simple conjugations had us constructing complete sentences in no time. Soon the two of us were speaking Dordic to each other when we did not want anyone near us to know what we were talking about. Our own argot. We have probably coined dozens of new Dordic words since then, usually just English words transliterated into Dordic (*futbog* 'football'). Or compound words, like 'bull' plus 'shit' equals *boroonyaje*. For ease of pronunciation, we shortened it back to *yaje*, so it now means 'bullshit' or 'shit,' depending on the context.

Sherwood's door text appears to be an incantation for establishing a way or passage (*Lingua dordica* gives Latin *via*). Imagined Sherwood attempting this in his tornado shelter for privacy, failing, then smashing the wall with his cane in frustration. The professor is not stupid. Always considered him a greater skeptic than I when it comes to the supernatural, religion, and what have you. Reading *The Golden Bough* provided me with enough reasons to view Christian myths as no more true than those of, say, the ancient Greeks. Sherwood has always said as much in private conversation, as well as in a draft of an article I found in his satchel with the splashy title, "*E pluribus pauci*: The De-Evolution of Religion." In it, Sherwood explores the competing theories of Gradišnik and Tate. The former supports the idea that all religions evolved from a common source, while the latter suggests something quite the opposite, a gradual homogenization of belief from wildly disparate sources. Tate offers as evidence numerous examples of obscure Amerindian religions which bear little resemblance to any others on earth. Monotheism is far-fetched enough without considering the dubious prospect of many or even an infinite number of gods. Attached to the draft with a paperclip was a nasty rejection letter from the staunch *Bulletin of the E.M.A.W.*

THURSDAY, FEBRUARY 3

A gray, drizzly day. No entry for Dordic in the *Index of the World's Languages* or Katzner's *Languages of the World*, the only two authoritative resources held by Porteous. It also is not one of the thousand listed in *The Book of a Thousand Tongues*, which probably just means the Bible had yet to be translated into Dordic as of 1968. Even if the damned "Lord's Prayer" has. Also looked under 'Anguru' (transliteration mine), the name speakers of Dordic evidently call their own language. Applied my own impromptu Swadesh test to the glossary. Most of the words bear little resemblance to those of any other language that I know of. For example, *bibu* 'water' and *bibulon* 'stream' (these evidently share a root).

While in the staff bathroom, I looked up 'dordic' in a superannuated *Webster's* that lives behind the toilet. The word 'dord' appears. A term in physics and chemistry for 'density.' Curiously, I discovered it is not in the *OED*. Even more curiously, there was no trace of it in *Van Nostrand's Chemist's Dictionary* nor any other similar reference works. Mysteries used to intrigue me. Now I am beginning to find them tiresome. I remain in awe of etymologists.

Was relieved to not find Time Frame in *Schwann* or *Phonolog*. Names that are already taken create perpetual ambiguity and confusion, e.g. Fort Worth's Nirvana and the earlier British Nirvana.

"Is that a new sweater?" said Jo Ann. "It's so…red."

"I'm sweating like a pig."

"Then why are you wearing it?"

"I didn't choose it," I said. "Fritz Reiner did. He chose it for America."

"Not my America."

What a ridiculous conversation. The calluses on my fingertips keep catching on the fabric. And my shirt sleeves bunch up under the sweater sleeves, which I find intolerable. I had almost forgotten why I never wear sweaters.

FRIDAY, FEBRUARY 4

The library closed at two so everyone could attend Sherwood's memorial in the chapel. The library staff departed together, walking naturally in pairs, which is all the width of the sidewalk permitted. Found myself dodging blackened wads of gum, trailing my coworkers while they spoke animatedly to each other. Naturally gregarious, the Bastard led the way, loudly trying to explain stagflation to Guddu.

While waiting for the walk signal at an intersection, Jenny appeared by my side. She lifted her skirt to reveal mismatched socks, then looked up at me coyly. I smiled. She and I walked in silence, sometimes rubbing elbows. We entered the chapel and sat together in the back. Dreary organ music wafted through the rafters amongst murmuring voices, punctuated by an occasional cough. The room was suffused with soft greens and blues from the stained glass windows.

Jenny opened her program. She and I read it together, leaning in close to one another. She smelled like Love's Fresh Lemon. My mind raced, unable to concentrate on the words on the page. She touched my arm and a static charge shocked both of us. I refrained from making a flirtatious comment. She produced from her purse a plastic Betsy Ross dispenser from which she offered me a pink pill embossed with "Z3d."

"What's this?" Usually I did not consume pharmaceuticals before looking them up in the *Merck Index* but I suppose I wanted Jenny to think I was something of a daredevil.

"It's a Pez, dummy," said Jenny, in her sleepy, seductive way of speaking.

I stared at her.

"Candy," she said. "Have another."

I placed it on my tongue. The organ music stopped. The room was now filled with the sounds of creaking pews and throat clearing. Dr. Ziglar rose and approached the lectern. A hush fell over the room. The stained glass went dark as a cloud drifted by. I glanced around the chapel anxiously. Ziglar began to speak, then droned on sententiously for what seemed like an eternity. I contemplated his Fisher Price hair before finally dozing off.

When Jenny nudged me awake, Mrs. Neighbors, who has always had the hots for Sherwood, was saying what a nice man he was and how he will be fondly remembered. She then asked if anyone wanted to say a few words. No one raised his hand. Several moments passed. When I could stand the silence no longer, I rose to my feet.

Mrs. Neighbors peered over her glasses. "Mr. Miller, I believe," she said. "From the library?"

My slacks swished conspicuously as I approached the lectern. As I regarded the mourners, I spotted L.F. in the front row, dressed all in white. I began to feel angry. He knows the truth about Sherwood's disappearance. He may even have had something to do with it. But what? I resolved at that moment to find out one way or another.

Suddenly I became conscious of the fact that I had yet to open my mouth. Thought of Betsy Ross's mechanical yapper dispensing a Pez. I leaned down close to the mic and opened my own mouth wide. "Testing," I said, but it came out more like "toss-ting." Noted with some interest that the mic was a Neumann U47. Those are supposed to be nice. I paused to collect my wits before continuing. "Hello. I'm Steven Miller. I work at the library with Professor Sherwood. Or did, that is. Worked with him for several years." I hesitated during someone's dramatic coughing fit, waiting until they exited the room to go die somewhere of T.B.

Public speaking is one of my worst nightmares. They say imagining everyone naked makes you feel less nervous. Pictured L.F. in his birthday suit, which only increased my anxiety. I mentally tossed him a towel. I then began to slowly undress the Stone Fox, until Professor Ziglar farted. L.F. looked at his watch and whispered something to Mrs. Neighbors.

I leaned toward the Neumann, then continued. "Professor Sherwood was a *sui generis* sort of person, a singularly brilliant man. Someone unafraid to challenge the academic status quo and who had the chops to do so." I dispensed my words one by one, tart and sweet. "I'm aware that some of his ideas were controversial, even outrageous. He was ever willing to discover the truth, however disputed. He always seemed almost as delighted when proven wrong as he did when vindicated. He was similarly pleased whenever I beat him at senet. Which I only did once.

"Professor Sherwood's intellect was so active that sometimes he simply seemed bonkers. When you visited him in his office, he commanded you to pedal his exercise bike. It was connected by wires to an ancient battery. The pedaling charged it." Here L.F. cleared his throat impatiently.

"The professor would then pose a question, usually pertaining to whatever problem he was preoccupied with at the moment. The year he retired, when I was an undergraduate, I took his Cultural Anthropology class. He took my classmates to Mexico over the summer with him to a dig. I regret not accompanying them. Even just standing around in the heat getting eaten alive by mosquitoes and snakes was worth it to be in Professor Sherwood's element. On the final exam, there was a bonus question. We were asked to explain the significance of the phrase 'Uproot the rhumbim, Washoe.' I still have no clue who Washoe is.

"Many here have heard his jokes in Latin. '*Cicero cum apud Damasippum cenaret et ille mediocri vino posito diceret "bibite Falernum hoc, annorum quadraginta est."*'" Here I was distracted by a stark naked Stone Fox. Her mouth was moving but I stink at reading lips.

"I'm sorry, I seem to have forgotten the punch line." The chapel was so quiet I could hear myself swallow. So did everyone else on account of the Neumann. "The professor loved art, music, and games," I resumed. "We used to play paper football for hours. After one game, he gave me a statuette of Horus. He called it the Heisman Trophy. Have seen rather cheap-looking ones at head shops but this one was museum quality. It still adorns my desk.

"Professor Sherwood had no family. Nazis croaked them all. My family is scattered far and wide. I'm ashamed to admit that I rarely make an effort to visit them. Others have no choice. The professor once told me that he considered Porteous his family. Perhaps this explains why he lingered here after retiring." I paused for some passing jets and their afterburners.

"Sometimes the professor would reveal some fact about himself that surprised me. Like his long involvement with the Children's Museum, his sojourn in the Solomon Islands and Japan, or his mastery of calligraphy. I liked the way he said 'thank you' firmly while looking you in the eye. He wanted to make sure you knew he was sincere. He was my friend. I shall miss him." Actually said "shall," which sounded more funereal somehow than "will."

I could not stop myself from continuing. The aftertaste of the Pez was just a phantom by now. "Like to think he's not dead at all, but is simply enjoying the King Tut exhibition at the National Gallery of Art and forgot to tell anyone he was going." L.F. was now staring hard at me.

"Thank you, Mr. Miller," said Mrs. Neighbors, leaping up to the lectern. "Would anyone else like to say a word?"

"That was sweet," whispered the Stone Fox, as I returned to my seat next to her.

Next was Professor Harrington.

"Jim and I met in 1935 during my postgraduate days at Chicopee College in Ontario." Was unused to anyone calling Sherwood "Jim" and I thought at first he had said "Gemini."

Harrington continued, "I was researching my first book on the Hawaiian Kingdom. We shared an interest in Japanese woodblock prints and served together on an advisory committee for a Hokusai exhibition at the De Hart Museum. When my research recently brought me to Porteous, I was delighted to see Jim again. His curiosity and erudition were seemingly boundless. We met a few times to discuss the Baumann Collection and other shared interests. I was greatly surprised to learn of his departure."

I found "departure" an interesting choice of word. From this earth?

L.F. leaped up to the podium. "Much appreciated, Bertie."

Bertie! So this is Sherwood's daft, loathed colleague. He does not seem daft or loathsome to me.

"I'd like to thank you all for coming," said L.F. "Through the door to my left you will find refreshments." The organ music cut him off.

While Jenny was in the ladies room, I scoped out the refreshments, pocketing some fudge for later.

"Mr. Miller, thank you for your kind words about Professor Sherwood."

It was L.F. "My pleasure," I replied, cautiously.

"Did you happen to see the professor at any time during the Christmas break?" He studied my face like some master interrogator.

"Nope. The last time I saw him was the week before that. Middle of December?"

"Mmm hmm, mmm hmm."

Jenny returned from the bathroom. At the same moment, Mrs. Neighbors asked L.F. something and distracted him. "You'll excuse me for a moment," he said.

"Let's get out of here," I whispered to Jenny, putting my hand around her waist and hustling her out of the chapel.

"Why the big rush?"

"Oh, nothing. Just wanted to get away from L.F.," I said. "The man's a talker! Yap, yap, yap, yap, yap!"

"Not many people can pull off that look he's got going. Will you give me a ride back to the Hacienda?"

"Of course!"

On the way to the co-op, Jenny explored my glove box. She read aloud a couple of wadded up receipts she found. "What did you buy for $14.76 at Roy Pope?" She reached up to examine her wide-open mouth in the rearview mirror. "What are these things under my tongue?" She turned to face me, her mouth open like a Pez dispenser. She stayed frozen that way until I pulled into the Dairy Queen parking lot.

I peered into Jenny's mouth. "Say ah," I said. Her breath smelled like candy. "Those little nubby things? I dunno."

We did not speak the rest of the way. We pulled up to the Hacienda. Grand Funk was blaring from a second-floor window.

"See you later, Jenny!"

As I drove away, some guy greeted Jenny on the front porch. Only caught a glimpse of him but he looked familiar. Probably have seen him on campus.

The library was locked but the lights were still on. Assumed everyone had left for the day to go to the memorial. Someone must have remained or else they planned to return.

What was that sound? Entered the workroom to find Spunt throwing knives into a tower of empty cardboard boxes. He did not stop when he saw me.

"What are you doing?" I asked.

"Steven!" he cried. "Do you toss?"

"Not really."

"Let me show you how." Spunt spent the next several minutes explaining the finer points of knife throwing. The proper distance one should stand from the target, the number of turns the knife makes in the air, etc. After letting me try a few times, he produced from a leather bag on his hip a handful of star-shaped metal objects. "These are *shuriken*. Carbon steel. Made in Japan." He let me feel one of the points.

"Sharp!" I said. Spunt grinned.

"You can dip the points in poison."

"What kind of poison?"

"Depends. Do you want to kill them instantly? Or do you want them to suffer a slow, painful death?"

"I don't know," I said, anxiously. My fingertip was now bleeding. Am I poisoned?

"You don't know what?"

"Nothing."

Spunt regarded me appreciatively. How much does he suspect? He let me throw his *shuriken* a few times before Dixie came lumbering around the corner.

"What's that noise?" she demanded.

"We were just breaking down these boxes."

Dixie looked at both of us like we were bugs. She turned to me. "I'd like to show you something." What is everyone doing here? I thought the place would be empty. Followed Dixie to her office, where she presented to me a small pile of books. She opened one. "This book is in Hebrew, so the date due pocket goes in the front, not in the back."

"But don't you want them in the back, where you can find them more readily? Wouldn't it be easier to check them out that way?"

"This is the way we've always done it."

"You're wrong," I said. "But why do you prefer this way?" I was trying to be diplomatic.

"Because Hebrew is read back to front. It's not a matter of preference, Steven."

"I know that, but the pockets are for the circulation desk staff, not the patrons."

"The patron needs to look at the card to see when the book is due."

"I'll be sure to let Edith know." Have no intention of doing any such thing.

SATURDAY, FEBRUARY 5

Saturdays at the library are typically relaxing. No one is in my hair and I am free to do as I please. Today it was just me and the Stone Fox. I try hard not to stare. Was walking by the circulation desk and heard music.

"Are you listening to Bryan Ferry?"

"Yes. I like his teeth!" His teeth? Sometimes I wish I had gotten braces.

During my shift at the information desk, I looked up the tongue in *Gray's Anatomy*. Jenny's little flaps are *plica fimbriata*. They appear on each side of the frenulum on some people and are part of the salivary gland system. Felt my own tongue with a fingertip but it was just wet and slimy. Think I would know if I had *plicae*. *Fimbria*, by the way, is Latin for 'fringe.' The mark of a fringie?

Rehearsal after work. Dave II is in the band! We probably do not deserve a drummer of his caliber. Did we choose him or did he choose us? We started to play him a rehearsal tape, but he said he did not need to hear it. As we played through our entire oeuvre, he made numerous suggestions. Such as slowing "Hail Marys" way down, and having Bonnie introduce it on the Mellotron with Wagner's "Tristan" chord. It is a completely different number now. He also borrowed the thundering brass motif from Tchaikovsky's *Symphony No. 4* to fashion a powerful coda to "Prog Paradigm." After having played only a few songs with him, I am already a better bass player.

The current line-up of Time Frame is, then:

Tim Watson: Gibson SG, vocals, talk box
Bonnie Baxter: Minimoog, Mellotron, Farfisa
"Dave II" McDermott: Stix, kix, and a bag of Trix
Fred "Knoxious" Knox: Part-time knob twiddler, Foley artist
Steven Miller: "Pan" bass, recorder, trombone

Apologized to Bonnie for suggesting she whip some skull on me at Fred's. She said it was fine, that I obviously had no idea what it meant. "Words mean things," she said.

SUNDAY, FEBRUARY 6

I spray painted my old cowboy boots gold. Was careless with the dropcloth and ended up getting paint on the front porch. I put a clay pot over it.

Stayed up watching *Hammerhead*. A killer band name, by the way. Recognized the actress playing Ivory. Remember her vividly from *How to Stuff a Wild Bikini*. One of the characters was said to be a "master of disguise." Of course, he had film studio makeup artists providing his disguises. You would need more than that to pass yourself off as a NATO delegate, especially around people whom you have met. That being said, it is surprising how much cutting off one's beard can change one's appearance. Or by wearing a wig and makeup.

MONDAY, FEBRUARY 7

Got up to take a nocturnal leak. Stumbled back into bed then made the mistake of looking at the clock. That always makes it harder to get back to sleep. End up lying awake and worrying about how late it is. What is the deepest part of the night? If I get in bed at ten and wake up at five, the deepest part of the night would be one-thirty. But people are still awake then. Better make it two-thirty.

It was almost three. There was no sound except for the fan. Something dripped onto my forehead with an audible splat. Reflexively, I wiped it off with the back of my hand, then wiped my hand on the sheet. A moment passed, and then I recognized the sulfuric odor from the Liszt bust. My eyes were now wide open. As I became more aware, I saw movement on the wall above me. A shadow in the darkness, nothing more.

By degrees, I inched my hand toward the lamp switch, until I felt it with my fingertips. Braced myself for something awful, then rotated the switch. For what seemed like less than the amount of time it took for the light from the bulb to fully illuminate the room, I caught a fleeting glimpse of what can only be described as a dark figure the size of a small dog. Mangy, mottled skin, and an elongated head ending in a horned snout. Tall, bat-like ears. Dracontine tail. Its slender fingers and toes were tipped with tendril-like claws. Thought I caught a pale glint in its rheumy, icteroid eyes.

Grunting in fear, I sprung out of bed. Reached for whatever I could get my hands on. Seized a boot jack and prepared to bash something's face in.

But where did it go?

Had difficulty putting on my robe, which in my state of perturbation became a five-sided garment with one arm-hole. After inspecting the wall above my bed, I searched every room, every nook and cranny, every closet and cupboard. Even dumped a basket of dirty laundry onto the floor and kicked clothes all over the place. Remained remarkably calm, however. Perhaps because part of me just did not believe what I had seen.

But that odor! Could still smell it on my hand and sheet. What made it? After washing my hand thoroughly, I removed the sheet from my bed. I lay on the bare mattress for the rest of the night, my thoughts racing. When the alarm went off, I stumbled out of bed exhausted.

Spent the morning at work looking over my shoulder. More than once my eye caught the tip of a tail disappearing around a corner. Probably just suggestion. While searching for a volume of *Zeitschrift für philosophische Forschung* in the upstairs stacks, I noticed at the end of the aisle a discreet metal ladder leading up to a panel in the wall near the ceiling. Of course, I had to find out what was up there. Ascended the ladder and examined the panel, which was fastened by large screws. They were so large you could unfasten them with any object with a flat edge. The Rambler keys were too skinny, but then I thought to use the key ring itself, which did the trick. Removing the panel revealed a spacious, windowless bay. There were numerous vents leading to who knows where, and it seemed sort of windy. A place where hobbits might go to get small. Sarge had rolled by moments earlier on his rounds, so I replaced the panel and hurried down the ladder. Have to take another look when no one is around.

Diane Bollinger started today. A temporary librarian Dixie hired to help with the LC conversion project. Tall, skinny brunette. Late thirties. Hope she is not a hedgehog. When Dixie introduced her to me, I gave Diane one of my matchbooks. She leaned forward and eyeballed it, her arms limp at her side. "Take it. It's for you," I wanted to say, but I put the matchbook back in my pocket. The three of us stared at each other awkwardly for a moment before making small talk about the project, how flat Texas is, and how someone left the Mr. Coffee on all weekend.

"Do say so if you know anything about that, Steven," said Dixie. What a whore for trying to embarrass me.

Gave Diane a casual tour of the first floor and mezzanine. At the alcove at the end of the 700s, I said, "Always thought this would be a good foxhole. In case you need to hide."

"Hide from what?" she said.

"You never know. But there it is."

"Mrs. Womack sure is a battle axe," said Diane, as we filed into the break room. "How can you stand her?" She took a long drag off her cigarette then exhaled through both nostrils. I nervously eyed some old mistletoe above her head, left over from the Christmas party.

Carlos knocked. "No smoking in here." I ushered Diane out to the patio. Her candor caught me off guard. I dislike Dixie, too. But since she is my boss, I was not sure if I wanted to admit that to anyone, much less to someone I had just met. Thought she would leave it at that, but she studied my face and said with a sly grin, "What." I shook my head.

"Miss Bollinger, when you report for work at the library, you will be wearing a brassiere," she intoned in Dixie's haughty drawl. The moment Diane said that, my eyes darted down to her tits, then back to her eyes, which narrowed slightly. "How old do you think she is?"

"Sixty-one?" I said. "A hard fifty-seven. You're working on the Dewey-to-LC conversion, huh? What about 338.761789910922? What would its LC equivalent be?"

"That's a long one! What's it for?"

"*The Longest Cocktail Party*. Book about the Beatles."

"They should call it *The Longest Call Number*."

Doris joined us outside. "Back in my day, we young ladies had to wear skirts. The young men would gather under the ladder when we had to get books down. I used to spit on them."

"Did you get them in the eye, Doris?" I said.

"Damn right, I did!" We all laughed.

TUESDAY, FEBRUARY 8

Spent much of the night lying in bed listening. Every little sound made me flinch. Veronica's pacing was unmistakable. Tiny galloping sounds across the living room floor was Figaro, no doubt. A couple of unidentified thumps got me out of bed but I saw nothing out of the ordinary.

The word of the day is "fecund." Got to use it later in the break room when Carlos moved the icebox and a swarm of roaches were sent scattering.

Spent part of the afternoon in a workshop learning how to be a better communicator. It was held in Shawmut Hall. Non-library staff were present. To my surprise, Diane came in and sat directly across from me. The top button of her blouse was undone. Most people would know if you were checking them out, so I took pains to avoid looking at her. It took more concentration than I realized. Fortunately, the presenter, an ex-cop from New York City, was funny and engaging and slightly intimidating. Actually learned a few things.

We had to do one exercise where we paired up with a partner to demonstrate some of the techniques we had learned. "Mr. Miller, make eye contact with your partner. It shows you are actively listening." If I looked at both of Diane's eyes at once, I struggled to focus on either. If I chose one eye and stared at it, it looked more like I was just staring at her eyeball. Tried scanning back and forth, to catch both eyes in succession, but Diane asked me what I was doing. Felt like she could read my mind.

My driver's license is missing. I never remove it from my billfold, so where did it go? May as well replace it, since it expired long ago.

WEDNESDAY, FEBRUARY 9

Roy Pope's for jelly ingredients. Was wiping a speck off my windshield when a guy in a Firebird rolled his window down and said, "Nice wheels. Looking good, champ!" Was he making fun of me?

Spent the morning preparing a "Jelly of Cherryes so Clear & Vermillion as a perfect Rubey or Claret Wine" from a recipe I found in the Vibius. My expectations for the jelly are low. After all, the recipe follows another for a ridiculous love potion which calls for the blood of seven male sparrows, cinnamon, and mandrake apples. It is written that a mere spoonful causes a fiery passion that can prove dangerous if unrequited. Wonder if they put that on a warning label back in Vibius's day. In fine print, of course.

While boiling the sugar I watched *The Fugitive*. Wanted to see how Dr. Kimble survived as he moved from town to town, adopting various aliases while toiling at menial jobs. I could never go to jail. I would rather be on the lam and would do just about anything to escape.

THURSDAY, FEBRUARY 10

Was raining gently when the carillon tolled five. The Rambler was the only car in Lot C. Wanted to paw through as much Baumann stuff as I could before the library opened. Rather than linger in the Vault where it is either too warm or chilly, this time I took some of the more interesting material back to my office. As my desk lamp was too conspicuous, I read by lava lamp. Its eerie glow suited the esoteric subject matter. By the time the library opened, the lamp was bubbling nicely, so I left it on.

Today's meeting agenda:

> Introducing Diane Bollinger
> LC conversion project
> Library tours
> Date due slips for books in Hebrew, etc.
> Use of Letraset
> Chewing gum
> Professional development opportunities
> Snow days
> Professor Sherwood.

Dixie reported that someone broke into Maxine's supply cabinet, the one in which she locks supplies she doesn't want anyone stealing, like stamp pad inkers, mucilage, and ditto fluid.

"Was anything taken?"

"A new spool of twine and a bottle of denatured alcohol."

Dipso will drink anything. But why twine? Can only imagine a crook's disappointment after picking that lock.

Today was Jo Ann's birthday. Maxine brought a Lord Baltimore cake. A card with a unicorn on it was passed around. "Happy Birthday, Jo Ann!" I wrote. "May your day be filled with magic!" Was reconsidering that last part when Maxine snatched it from me, placed it in an envelope, and licked it shut.

"It is your birthday?" said Guddu.

"It is," said Jo Ann.

"But you are already born."

"The average person has only one birthday," said Doris, helpfully. "The rest are anniversaries."

Guddu looked perplexed but I have no idea why. Surely birthdays are not a difficult concept.

Someone, most likely the Bastard, produced Francis Grose's *Classical Dictionary of the Vulgar Tongue* (1785). People were taking turns reciting magniloquent definitions from it of phrases like *arbor vitae*, a late 18th-century cant word for 'penis.'

"Rantallion!" cried Randy, theatrically trilling his *r*. Everyone stopped talking and looked at him. "One whose shot pouch is longer than the barrel of his piece. See him play at rantum scantum, making the beast with two backs!"

"What's that?" I said.

Diane looked at me like I was a sapscull. "You don't know what a 'beast with two backs' is?" she said.

The Duke of Limbs handed the volume to an eager Guddu, who perused it wide-eyed with wonder. "Tallywags!" he shouted, tentatively raising his fist into the air. "A man's tefticles," he concluded in his buttery accent. He innocently pronounced the long *s* as an *f*, nearly causing me to spew Lord Pibb all over Jo Ann's visage. This elicited chortles from my fellow dandy prats, save Mrs. Fusty Luggs, of course. She guffaws at zilch. She opened up her potato trap and domineered, "No tomes in the leisure chamber!" Assuming this opprobrious vilification was leveled at him, poor Guddu looked utterly betwattled.

A patron phoned while I was at the information desk. It was an elderly person, who called me a "nice library lady" before asking me if we had "the Bible." In my manliest baritone, I replied that we had over forty versions.

"But do you have the one true Bible?"

"We just might," I sighed. "Do you know the ISBN?"

"You're a librarian. You of all people should know what the Good Book is."

I do, and it is not the Bible.

FRIDAY, FEBRUARY 11

Have developed a routine whereby I arrive at the library by five. By the dim glow of exit signs, I make my way to the Vault where I load my book cart with the next batch of Baumann material and take it to my desk to examine. What do I hope to find?

Hazel likes to arrive by seven-thirty, so I head back out to the Rambler before then. I smoke and listen to "Zooloos In Your Morning" until I spot her stepping off the bus.

Boggs asked to have a word with me. "You may have heard about Mrs. Doakes's supply cabinet being plundered," he said.

"Is nothing sacred?"

"Just wanted to let you know I saw you enter the library yesterday at four fifty-four a.m. and again this morning at four fifty-nine." I must have looked alarmed, because then he said, "Naw, I know you didn't do it. Just wanted to tell you to be careful because certain people could get the wrong idea."

Suppose I have been too cavalier about my clandestine bibliographic exploits. Boggs saw me and I did not see him. Am I not stealthy enough?

After work, I was putting an armload of dirty clothes into the Rambler when Veronica shouted hello from her window. When I told her I was off to the coin laundry, she said, matter-of-factly, "I have a washer and dryer." Before I could object, she continued, "Do it with me. C'mon, it beats the Laundr-O-Mat!"

"You don't have to twist my arm," I replied, cheerfully. "Let me run back into my place real quick," I replied, in a bid to collect my thoughts. Was she coming on to me? Should I bring booze? Do I even have any booze? Do I have B.O.? Have not shaved since 1974, but I spotted a bottle of Aqua Velva in the medicine cabinet and slapped some in my armpits. Did not want to be caught unprepared in case the vibe turned libidinous, which was not an absolute impossibility. I am no Burt Reynolds, but I am not grotesque, either. Hastily brushed my teeth and gargled, then frantically ransacked the pantry, coming up with a dusty bottle of Galliano I do not even recall buying. A quick glance in the mirror revealed an outfit that only a loser who was doing his laundry would wear, in my case a threadbare 'Dillos jersey, track pants, and my golden cowboy boots. Commando, natch. Straight off the cover of *GQ*!

Raced up the stairs, then slowed down to compose myself before entering through her open pocket doors. "Nice boots!" said Veronica. She applauded when I presented the Galliano. She unscrewed the cap and took a dainty sip before handing it back to me. "Just started a load of undies. Can I have yours?"

I belched. "Excuse me! T.G.I.F.!" Took a long swig of the golden liqueur.

"Tongue goes in first! Too bad I don't have any O.J. We could have made Harvey Wallbangers!"

Presented her with a jar of the Vibius jelly.

"Thanks, Dollface! Did you make this yourself?" She took my laundry and said, "Eww, I smell rotten eggs," before disappearing into another room.

"Tongue goes in first," I repeated to myself. Never heard that one. Our culture evolves so quickly I don't really notice it, sometimes. Sank into a papasan chair then strained my eyes reading the spines in a bookcase. Spied *Delta of Venus* and a dozen issues of *Partisan Review*.

A magazine with cleavage on the cover caught my eye. "How to Spot a Passionate Man," it read. Am I passionate? Did Veronica spot me? After reading an article about how chicks just want a guy who will listen and not try to fix everything, I stood up and explored the room. I wondered what my pacing would sound like from downstairs. Veronica returned and caught me staring at her books. "Touch them if you want." She took another slug of the Galliano. Checked out her ass as she shuffled through a disorganized pile of LPs, many of them out of their sleeves. She dropped the needle hard onto a K-Tel, which made a horrible sound.

"Whoops!" she said.

Having lived underneath Veronica for several months, this is the first time I have gotten a good look inside her place. Our kitchens are different. We share a front door, and the pocket doors to our individual units do not lock. One does not mind so much when one's neighbor has an ass like that. Would feel very differently if it were Spunt.

Veronica is a tall redhead, a few years older than me. Freckles, aquiline nose, stacked. She is in the French and Italian Department at Turkey Knob. She has a robust social life judging by the number of cars I see parked close behind her Pacer. Can often hear her musical laughter from downstairs. On this evening she was wearing a thick, white terrycloth robe with no clear indication of anything underneath it, and fluffy pink open-toed slippers. How did she get that robe to be so white? Maybe it is brand new.

Veronica's kitty flopped heavily down on my lap while "MacArthur Park" crackled from the stereo. The left channel was on the fritz. "Oh, Figgy loves you!" she cried.

"He visits me sometimes," I remarked. I scratched his neck under his orange bandana. "He brings me taffy." I did not tell Veronica that I also spoke Dordic to him.

"Figaro brings you *taffy*?" said Veronica. She turned to her cat. "Do you visit Steven, Figs? Do you? Did you know you're my lil' pookie dookie face?"

"Did you just call him 'dookie face'?"

Veronica laughed heartily. "Guess I did, huh?" Clutching her robe closed with one hand, she leaned over me and stroked Figaro, her forearm repeatedly grazing my lap. Figgy lay there purring with his eyes half-closed, kneading my belly until a clap of thunder startled him and he peeled out.

"Aagh!" I cried in agony, clutching my groin. Peeked down the front of my track pants to see if I was bleeding.

"Oh my gosh, are you okay?" asked Veronica, craning her neck to see.

"He may have severed my vas deferens," I quipped.

Veronica produced a little stuffed turtle. "Been meaning to ask you. Did you give this to Figs?"

"Yes, a few weeks ago."

"That was so sweet of you!" She kissed me on the cheek. After disappearing into the other room, she reappeared and dumped a bag of nail polish bottles onto the floor.

"Choose."

I sorted through the bottles then handed her Flowering Plum. After struggling with the lid for a moment, she gave it back wordlessly. Using my t-shirt to get a grip, I opened the bottle and returned it to her.

Veronica painted her toenails on the rug while we gossiped about Mr. Hawlie. "Did you ever notice he never speaks in complete sentences?" she said.

"Real nass," I said, imitating our landlord. If he did not think it was "real nass" it deserved no comment. Man of few words.

"You know, he's always lurking. He's a creepy lurker. Haven't you seen him lurking around here? One time, I came home after a date and found his wallet on my sofa!"

"What did you do with it?" Why is she not taking off her slippers to paint her toenails? She is going to get nail polish on them.

"Phoned his house and Mrs. Hawlie answered." Veronica leaned back and wiggled her toes in the air. (Nothing under that robe!) "Now her, I like! She told me to put the wallet in a paper sack and leave it on the front porch. Didn't see him lurking for a couple of weeks after that." She gave me a knowing look.

Veronica shrieked when I referred to Hawlie's slave as Toby. "Kunta Kinte?" she said. "From *Roots*? That's awful!" Have seen the poor guy sitting in Hawlie's junk-filled Town & Country on a scorcher, dying of dehydration, while Hawlie lurked around in the backyard nursing a Lone Star.

"That's Leroy," she said. "He's a sweetie. Hawlie doesn't like it when you talk to him."

"When I first moved here and Hawlie found out I was a librarian, he spoke ad nauseam about his admiration for Kate Greenaway. As if a librarian would automatically know who that is. When I mentioned Beatrix Potter, the only Victorian children's illustrator I could think of, he acted like I had just tried to trump him and changed the subject back to Greenaway."

"You're a librarian?" Veronica looked me up and down, as if she expected to find a horn or scales or something. "You don't meet too many male librarians."

"There are a few of us."

"You work at Porteous, right? What does a librarian do all day?"

"Create order from chaos."

Veronica raised her eyebrows. "There's a book I'm trying to find. Forget the author and the title, but I think it's blue."

"Do continue," I said.

"It's by a British travel writer. Philhellene. Cozy with the Mitfords."

"Nice word!"

"I know! But the book was about the Middle East."

"Porteous has it." I wanted that to be true.

Veronica's face lit up.

"I'll get it for you," I promised. By that, I suppose I mean that I will check it out to myself, give it to Veronica (a violation of library policy), and hope that she returns it. If she does not, it is not like I do not know where she lives.

She scooted across the rug and pulled off my golden boots. "Now let's do you."

While my toenails dried, Veronica taught me how to pronounce *grazie*. Between the two of us, we must have repeated it a hundred times because she insisted I was not saying the final vowel properly. She talked about dating her students, referring to them by the car they drive for my benefit. Gold Cutlass, Brown Pickup, Blue Van, etc.

"I've seen the blue van," I said. "Yosemite Sam mud flaps."

"Blue Van's so good in the sack," she said, softly, taking a slug of the Galliano. "Why don't you ever park in the driveway?" she asked. Uh oh, did she mean that metaphorically?

"Because my reverse button is broken."

"Reverse button?"

"The Rambler doesn't have a stick shift. It has buttons. There's just a hole where the reverse one used to be."

"What do you do when you want to go backwards?"

"I always go forward. Hiawatha's arrow."

Veronica hiccupped. "Why don't you just stick your finger in the hole?"

"There's nothing in it but electricity." My voice trailed off. Spotted a camera on her Mediterranean coffee table and picked it up. "I need a camera. Had one, but my ex took it."

Veronica studied my face for a moment. "That one used to belong to Hawlie. Traded him a bag of petrified wood for it. You can have it, if you want."

I put the camera down quickly. "Oh, no! That's not what I meant."

"I have several. *Prego*."

By the time the Galliano was gone, Veronica was sitting on the rug folding my clean clothes. She slapped my hands away when I tried to stop her. She examined my Holiday Inn towel and furrowed her brow. "What detergent do you use?" she said.

"Sta-Puf, I think."

"That's a fabric softener, silly." Suddenly, Veronica barked out a laugh. "These are so cute!" she shrieked, twirling my King Tut Funtawear on her finger before slingshotting them at me.

"Those were a gift," I replied, sheepishly. "You can keep them." I flung them back. "My ex got them for me a few Christmases ago. Which is probably the last time anyone saw me in my underwear," I joked. That is the second time this evening I mentioned Loretta. Not good.

"Mmm hmm. Most of these are Y-fronts, though," she continued, examining another pair. "Don't you ever wear boxers?"

"Prefer to go commando."

"I noticed," she smirked.

"If I had my way I wouldn't wear pants at all."

Veronica tossed me my Chap Stick. The tube was empty.

"Aw man! Thirty-nine cents down the drain!"

A cuckoo clock chimed midnight and we regarded each other. Veronica looked smoking hot. In a bid to prolong our conversation, I blurted, "Do you want to know why they say a 'pair' of underwear?"

Veronica shrugged. "Well, this was fun! Promise me we'll do this again soon!" she said, giving me a tight, lingering hug. Her hair smelled like Herbal Essence. Picked up my basket of folded laundry. Veronica escorted me to the stairwell as Figaro scrambled by.

"Figs, get back up here!"

"*Grazie*, Veronica!"

"Call me 'Vee.'"

SATURDAY, FEBRUARY 12

With the flashlight from under the circulation desk I explored the hobbit room before the library opened. Could hear the rain hitting the roof. A few empty bottles of brandy were strewn about. A yellowed, brittle essay on *Ethan Frome*. A back issue of *Satan's Scrapbook* and assorted copies of *Creem*. A Triple-A tour book of the Great Lakes region from 1975-76 indicated someone had been up there recently. Carlos must know about this room, but Boggs would have no reason to. Took *Satan's Scrapbook* and put it with the other book sale items down in the Vault. The *Creem*s I am keeping for myself. There must be a good reason someone took that tour book up there. Returned it to the map file where it belongs.

While sitting at the information desk, I looked up several things in the *Dictionnaire pratique des sciences occultes*. Evidently, the library does not own a single occult dictionary in English. Also looked up Kate Greenaway. Showed Jenny the *Creem* magazines but did not mention where I found them.

Feel like Vee and I really hit it off yesterday. What would it be like dating one's neighbor? One, she is older than I am by a few years. Not a problem. Two, we live under the same roof. That could be a big problem. Three, she dates her students. Do not know what to make of that. Would we be exclusive? Four, am I even into her? In my imagination, where anything goes, absolutely. It is February and I still have not gotten laid. But in real life? She is not really my type, but I am not sure I know what my type is. Or if I even have a type. Of course, if she does not dig me, this is all moot.

Caught the Tavares on *Don Kirshner*. To bed at 1:30.

SUNDAY, FEBRUARY 13
Woke up to no smokes. Got dressed and walked down to the Texaco for a pack. Upon my return, I encountered Vee.

"Dollface!" she said, cheerfully. "You're wearing shorts!"

"Going to be warm later."

"Can I talk to you for a minute?" Vee wrung her hands and looked worried. "Something scary happened to me last night. Don't know what to make of it." I went up.

"Scary? What happened?"

"You're going to think I'm ridiculous," she said sheepishly.

"Of course I won't. Tell me."

"It was about two-thirty, I guess. Had gotten up to pee, and was sitting on the toilet in the dark when Figgy came in and tried to climb into my panties. Why do cats do that? Thought nothing of it, until I reached down to pet him. Only it wasn't Figgy."

"Who was it?"

"Didn't know what I was touching at first. Still don't. Guess I was half asleep. You expect soft fur. This was like a plucked chicken. And it kind of stank! I slapped it, which was like slapping raw meat. It made an awful growling sound and disappeared."

"Just vanished?"

"Sort of. It's like it just wasn't there anymore. Turned the bathroom light on, but didn't see anything. I searched the whole house. All the windows were closed. But the pocket doors were open. Figgy knows how to open those, so I thought nothing of it. Except they had definitely been closed when I went to bed and Figgy was inside. But I couldn't find him! This morning, I opened the front door and saw him across the street. He was staring at the house like a sad puss. Had to go and carry him back. He was looking around like he was kind of spooked."

Tried to imagine what a normal response would be. Was going to suggest it was a raccoon or a possum, but those are not hairless. And there is no way an armadillo could have gotten in here. "There must be a simple explanation," I said.

"And what's that?"

"Don't know, Vee." Which was not a lie.

Rehearsal in the evening, followed by a lively debate over the set list. All of Tim's songs made the cut, including "Tim's Bolero." Bonnie wanted "All Tomorrow's Parties" but I held the line against covers. Dave II had us all in stitches over his Frank Zappa impressions, though they went over my head. Frank Zappa is like coffee or smoking a pipe. How do you acquire taste? Should give him another chance. Dave II says he approves of Time Frame, and what Dave II says, goes!

Fred wanted a ride home. On the way, we spoke of Christa Helm's murder. "By the way," I said. "I have your bread for *The Hobbit*." I dug into my mansack and pulled out *Slaughterhouse 5*. "Or, I can trade you this. It's signed. Met Vonnegut when he was at Porteous a couple of years ago. He drew a big asterisk under his name. He then tapped the asterisk twice and asked, 'Do you know what that is? That's my asshole.' This copy has been tainted for me ever since."

"Deal." Fred took the Vonnegut and got out of the Rambler. Not sure who got the better deal. At least I got Vonnegut's asshole out of my house. Feel like I got out from under a curse.

MONDAY, FEBRUARY 14

Spent the morning researching how to be stealthy. Figured my best bet would be hunting guides or Army field manuals. Read almost all of Macrae's *A Handbook of Deer-Stalking* (1880) before stepping outside for a smoke. Sarge was there. He set me straight about stealth.

"Look before you step," he said. "Avoid land mines like leaves and twigs. Tread upon living grass or bare dirt if you can. Walk slowly and think about each step. Map your steps out in advance. Take three or four steps, then pause and regroup. Roll your steps heel-to-toe and bend at the knees; this is 'fox walking.' Soft-soled shoes or light boots are preferred. If you need to move quickly, try walking sideways. If you must run, do so on the balls of your feet."

Wondered if my golden boots were light enough. Regretted not writing this all down immediately. I know I'm leaving something out.

We flicked our butts into the gravel. When Carlos emerged from the break room, Sarge gestured at a pile of butts. "Carlos, police call!"

"Fuck off, Sarge. Those are yours."

Sarge made an expression of great indignation. "Tossing your butts on the ground are a great way to get yourself greased. Keep 'em in your pocket." He pulled one out and held it up as proof.

Carlos waved his hand dismissively.

Lunch with Randy at the Business School cafeteria. A young woman in front of us in line took her time ordering, asking questions, changing her order, digging in her purse in slow motion for her checkbook, etc. Randy was pretty patient about it but I hate standing in line. It is one of the reasons I rarely go out to lunch. When we ordered our sandwiches we gave fictitious names. Randy was Abraham. Not to be outdone, I was Nebuchadnezzar II. After spelling it three times I had to write it down for the nonplussed cashier while Randy gloated. When we sat down I told him about Vee's bathroom encounter.

"That's hot stuff," he said.

"Ha ha, no. You haven't seen this thing."

"Okay, remember when you almost summoned a demon?"

"That's not what I was doing," I said. "But yes."

"Doubt you can summon a demon by casually reading from a book. What was his name again?"

I produced the codex from my mansack. "I'll show you."

"You carry that with you?"

"Always know where it is this way." I found the page and Randy spun the book around so he could see. "Surely this isn't the dude who jizzed in your face?" he said, indicating a woodcut depicting a black panther with tentacles and glowing, green eyes.

"No, it's not. You don't believe in demons, do you?"

"You know me," said Randy. "I approach everything with an open mind. You and your neighbor are dropping acid. Big whup."

"Naw, I prefer to get high on life," I said, sardonically, pointing at Randy with the A.1. sauce. "You know this stuff was invented during the Civil War?"

"Who told you that?"

"Spunt."

"Let me get this straight. Brothers slaughtering brothers, families ripped apart. Carnage everywhere. Some guy chooses this moment to say, 'You know what this nation needs right now? A terrific steak sauce.'"

I slipped the A.1. into my mansack. "Randy, what is this thing?"

Randy finished chewing before answering. "Clearly, it's not a demon. It would have slain you immediately. Or else it's the pussiest demon I've ever heard of."

"How many demons have you heard of?"

"Plenty," said Randy. "You've read Crowley. He and Victor Neuberg are said to have evoked Choronzon, who is malignant, but harmless, and ultimately not even real."

"Is that why you can say his name out loud?"

A voice said our names out loud over the P.A. "Abraham? Nebulous-Cheddar Eye-Eye?"

"Choronzon's not his true name," said Randy when I returned with our sandwiches.

"That name makes me think of chorizo," I said. "I wish I had some chorizo right now."

"They were probably smoking dope, anyway. But then when Crowley split Boleskine for Paris, he did so without dispelling the twelve kings and dukes of Hell he had summoned. They're said to be still running loose."

"That can't be good," I said, unconcernedly, my mouth full of steak. If there is no Hell, then no one can be from there.

Randy shrugged. "Crowley, along with the likes of Kenneth Grant and Franz Bardon, is part of a Western, ultimately Christian tradition of evocation that can be traced as far back as Trithemius. If they were really serious, they would have kept their big mouths shut. These days, their work is only considered occult in the same way, say, Blue Öyster Cult is. Now we shelve Agrippa in the open stacks for any moron to check out and take home. How's that for forbidden knowledge? The choice stuff is locked up in the Vault. Better stuff is probably at the Vatican. The best stuff isn't in any library that you or I have heard of. It's all in private hands. Secrets are worthless if no one can keep them. What are you doing?"

"Huh?"

"Putting ketchup on a steak sandwich like a common criminal."

"What are you, the sandwich police?" I said. "A couple of the Baumann books have a Vatican stamp in them. What if they're stolen? Should I write them and ask?"

"Do you really want to do that? Unless you're prepared to say this creature is a figment of your imagination—and I don't think you are—here is my two cents. This thing is the demon's familiar, or imp, sent to find out who roused him from his ten-thousand-year slumber. You did say, 'Awaken!' Did you not? Now that he's here, he's just going to keep winding you up until you do something decisive. Like banish him. The codex might tell us how."

"That's one way of looking at it. But it might take a while to translate the Dordic. There are too many words I don't know."

"You haven't had a girlfriend in over a year. True or false? You've got plenty of time on your hands, dude."

"True," I said. "But what do you think this has to do with Sherwood?"

"Been thinking about that. Number one: Who is Baumann? Number two: How much of the collection have you cataloged? And number three: Has Porteous publicized the collection in any way?"

"Still know little about Baumann," I said. "But Sherwood surely knew. Everything in the collection requires original cataloging. Do as much as I can but that's on top of my other responsibilities. And have we publicized it? Not *per se*, except for the stuff in the display case. Sherwood might have spread the word in his academic circles. Professor Harrington told me he heard about it in the faculty newsletter. I think we made an announcement when we acquired it, but since then there hasn't been any reason to say anything. It's all languishing in the Vault. Dixie herself has no idea what's down there."

We paused to light cigarettes.

"I'm still reading *Die Tür*," said Randy. "Pretty compelling. Abandoned by their gods, who became *dei otiosi*, Zuberon's followers choose new ones. Some benevolent, some bizarre. Many fraudulent or imagined. Zuberon himself is elected as one. A grand temple is erected in his honor. Zuberon is pleased. Apotheosis is his deepest desire. Then there's more stuff about the world that Zuberon made from the soil of Vul Kar. This place is called Dord and its capital city is Irr.

"Zuberon dwells in Irr for centuries, until he grows bored of his people's affairs and retreats to his vast castle on the edge of the world. Guess his world is flat. In his castle he broods. He tries vainly to create as a god creates. But it's all mere high sorcery. His creations are in his own image. Products of his *qutum*-soaked mind. A perverse mockery of our own world."

"I'm picturing a horrible place of mephitic vapors and crawling things," I said. A business major walked by in a billow of Jovan Musk.

Randy shrugged. "No doubt. But where Zuberon's concerned, *Die Tür* borders on hagiographical, ascribing to him various magical powers, including the ability to control not only elementals but certain major *kakoi*. Can see why Hitler would be interested. Zuberon's bitter over his bogus kismet. Sometimes he visits our world to party, wreak havoc, and interfere with the affairs of those who undeservedly inherited the earth."

"How does he do that?" I asked.

"*Kakoi* travel across the planes at will, going by the book. No doubt one could take you wherever you desire, if commanded to do so. Durchdenmeer also writes of doors, hence the title of the book, despite it being in the singular. The concept isn't his invention. Doors exist in nature. In remote forest glades. At the ends of rainbows, if you can find one. Under certain waterfalls. It's a common theme in mythology, folklore, and literature. The Irish know them as 'thin spots.' Places where you're closer to heaven. Etheric planes can be accessed by oneiric or spiritual means as well. By crossing Bifrost or Styx. Or by dying and doing the Hustle through Heaven's gate."

"Eliade wrote of the *axis mundi*," I said. "The connection between so-called higher and lower realms. Is that the same thing?"

"From what I understand, Dord would be considered a mirror of our own," said Randy. "The concept of *axis mundi* is somewhat relevant. The *omphalos* or sacred center of Dord is quite literally the city of Irr."

"No question that we found a door in Sherwood's tornado shelter," I said. "Or a symbolic representation of one. But that doesn't mean he actually went through it."

"Did you ever translate the text that appeared around it?"

"It's an incantation," I said. "Presumably to activate the door. Some of it's in another language, so I don't know what it means. It's all written in the Dordic runes."

A voice called Guddu's name over the P.A. I turned my head. It was not Guddu, but some other guy. A T.A. from the Engineering department, I think. Can't picture Guddu eating, for some reason.

Randy and I headed out to the quad. A bunch of frat guys were lined up at a kissing booth sponsored by the Omicron Nus.

"Want someone's sloppy seconds?" I asked.

Randy made a face. "I've already had mono once. Hey, isn't that Spunt?"

Spunt was sitting on a bench, squirrel fishing with Cheetos.

"Don't make eye contact," I said. You have to take Spunt in small doses.

Returned to my desk to find a box of candy hearts and a valentine on my chair, the latter which said, cryptically, "The burning hose? Valentine are you?" A little boy fireman was presenting his squirting hose to an alarmed-looking little girl. On the back was written "To Steven, from Jenny." The burning hose euphemism seemed clear enough, though it could also refer to the clap. I panicked inside. Why did she give me this? Are we in kindergarten? What do I say the next time I see her? Should I give her one?

Later in the day, I discovered Jenny had given valentines to everyone. Even Hey Now, who asked me, dreamily, "Do you think Jenny likes me?" When I showed him my valentine, his face fell and he shouted a forlorn "Hey!" Upon closer examination, I suddenly made sense of its typographical spaghetti: "The burning [question mark]…hose [whose] / valentine are you?" Removed a candy heart from the box, which read, "SOME DAY." Tasted like chalk.

TUESDAY, FEBRUARY 15

Worked the late shift. Forgot my Chap Stick today. Keep some for emergencies in my mansack, desk, and the Rambler. Today they were all in absentia. Went to Skillern's to buy more on my dinner break. Bought all they had, seventeen tubes, to prevent this sort of thing from happening again.

This afternoon, while the Stone Fox was working at the information desk, I tossed an envelope onto the counter as I hurried by. As I turned the corner into the reading room, I heard her say, "What's this?" In the envelope was a picture of a toothy Bryan Ferry I had xeroxed from an issue of *Creem*. Onto this I had written in neat cursive, "I like you, too!" After taking my seat at the information desk, I strained to hear her reaction—laughter, a snort of derision, anything at all—but perceived nothing.

At closing time, the staff customarily gathers in the vestibule by the sham Gutenberg. We leave as a group so no one gets locked inside. Carefully avoided eye contact with Jenny. That was weirder than making eye contact, so I now stared at her like a psycho killer. When she looked my way, I had no idea what expression should be on my face. I made what can only be construed as a pained grimace, intended to convey sheepishness, perhaps. She smiled tentatively but probably thinks I am a freak now. Is this the fourth grade?

WEDNESDAY, FEBRUARY 16

Keep a fan going to help me sleep. Woke up during the night and discovered the fan was off. That typically means the power is out, blown fuse, etc. Went into the kitchen to get a flashlight. Turned it on, then walked into the living room to find Figaro near the coffee table, his back arched, ears flattened, tail twitching. He did not respond to my appearance but was staring intently at the fireplace. Pointed the flashlight at it, but saw nothing amiss.

"Figaro!" I called.

Suddenly he bolted for the door to the foyer, which was open. Checked the fireplace more closely, careful not to get dirty. Hope it is not a rat. But would Figaro be afraid of a rat? What if it was the imp again? Have decided to name him Harvey.

Lay tossing and turning in the dark. If Harvey is real, the demon must also be real. That should probably frighten me more than it does.

Figured I might as well head down to the library before it opened. Following Boggs's advice, I walked as stealthily as I could on the scenic route, although I did step on a few twigs. Still, I sounded like the Ghost of Christmas Past, so I paused to secure my jangling keys and coins. When I emerged from the shadows across from the library, Boggs was standing there smoking a cigarette, watching me.

I played it cool. "Beautiful day!" Except it was pitch black out still.

"Every day is a beautiful day," said Boggs, quoting Dowd from the movie *Harvey*.

"Did you just do a Jimmy Stewart impression?"

Boggs continued. "You see, science has overcome time and space. Well, Harvey has overcome not only time and space, but any objections." His eyes narrowed and locked onto mine.

"It seems he has, Boggs." Which Harvey was he talking about?

THURSDAY, FEBRUARY 17

This morning, I practiced being stealthy. Treading lightly. Stepping heels first, then rolling my foot forward smoothly. Just like Sarge said. Chose my path carefully along the scenic route. On a moonless morning, however, it was really too dark to fox walk effectively.

Jo Ann took the day off, so I had to cover for her at the information desk. The moment I sat down, Hey Now walked over to show me some clippings from his monster magazines. He often solicits my opinion, then gets the Bastard to laminate the best ones so he can take them home and pin them to his walls. They must be completely covered by now with iconic images of Barnabas Collins, Charles Whitman, Charles Manson, the Beatles, Robert De Niro in *Taxi Driver*, and J.F.K.'s grassy knoll.

When Hey Now brought up *Dark Shadows* this time, I joked that I lived in "the Old House" on Collinwood Ave. He spoke the words, "Ha ha" and then kept right on comparing the two Burke Devlins. He probably thought I was pulling his leg. When Hey Now laughs at all, he laughs mechanically at surprising things but never at my jokes, which he often takes literally.

"I was there when they filmed *Logan's Run* at the Water Gardens," he often says, à propos of nothing. "Volunteered to be an extra. They turned me away because I shout."

Professor Harrington approached the information desk. "I'd like access to the Baumann Collection, please."

"I'm sorry. It's all down in the closed stacks, which is off-limits to the public."

"I see. That is most unfortunate. I will take it up with the Chief Librarian. Thank you."

All I need is Dixie getting involved. "Let me look into the matter and get back to you soon," I said, to delay the inevitable.

Bonnie phoned me at work and said she got us a gig tomorrow night. She is not screwing around! Spent the evening practicing and memorizing arrangements.

FRIDAY, FEBRUARY 18

Gig at the Tip Top where every vehicle out front was a hot rod. While Max Norm & the Bi-Levels were playing their set, Fred found a rusty gas tank in a vacant lot across the street. He and Dave II noisily dragged it back to the club. A guy in a Mack truck honked as they negotiated a roadside ditch. When it was time to go on, Dave II propped the tank up on a chair behind his kit. He hung a mic inside then banged it tentatively.

"Hell yeah, brother!" shouted Tim into his talk box.

Dave II used the tank as a snare on "Nights in White Satin," which Bonnie begged us to play so she could show off on her Mellotron. I love that thing! The tank was the topic of conversation among some of the Tip Top gearheads.

"That from a '74 Cheyenne?" said one gearhead. "Those are frame-mounted, you know. Don't get T-boned, haw haw!"

"Better than behind the seat," added his buddy. "Eliminates slosh noise, but not the noise from the kaboom." He made an explosion gesture with his hands.

"Makes the Pinto look downright safe," interjected a third.

Tim introduced me to the audience as Neil Armstrong. Did not know what he was talking about until I considered my golden boots. "Armstrong's boots were white!" I muttered.

Someone in the audience mockingly sang, "A ba ba ba, ba Barbara Ann." I shielded my eyes from the stage lights so I could see who it was and recognized a classmate from A.H.H.S. He must have witnessed that botched performance of the Beach Boys tune back when I was in the Cicadas. Very funny, motherfucker.

During "Rat Race," I noticed my bass had fire ants on it. Meanwhile, Bonnie was squirming around and botching notes on her Minimoog. Tim stopped singing. By the time we finished the song it was clear the gas tank had ants in it. We took a break to toss it out, get ants out of our pants, and impose order on chaos.

Turtle Man was there. One of Sherwood's protégés. Did not know he was a gearhead. A bookhead. He sat close to the stage, reading a yellow-spined paperback all evening. At one point he pulled out a camera and took a few photos of us performing. I later found out Bonnie had put him up to it.

SATURDAY, FEBRUARY 19

Jo Ann showed up at the information desk at one to relieve me so I could meet the others at the planetarium. Doris had gotten us all free tickets to *The Texas Sky*. I have been many times but this provided an opportunity to give Jenny a ride. To my relief, she readily agreed when I offered. Hey Now stayed behind, of course.

While I was waiting for Jenny to finish helping a patron, I looked into the shenanigans dish. A new contribution! One of those clear plastic capsules from a gumball machine. It had something in it that looked like aspic. Opened it and immediately recognized the smell. Quickly snapped it shut and returned the capsule to the dish.

"Shenanigans!" shouted Spunt as he leaped from an alcove. He opened the shenanigans dish and inhaled deeply. "It was all over Maxine's supply cabinet the other day. You know, the Great Paper Clip Caper. You should have seen her face when she smelled her fingers."

"What is it?" I knew what it was but I wanted to know what he thought it was.

Spunt shrugged. "I saved the rest of it."

"For what?"

"You never know," he winked. Would think this unusual, but this is a guy who displays canned hams on a shelf above his desk as if they were original Warhols.

On the way to the planetarium, I was too preoccupied with what had just happened to say much to Jenny, who was also quiet.

We arrived a few minutes early. After taking a quick look at the samurai armor guy, we rushed through the Hall of Medical Science. We paused to contemplate the trepanning exhibit, a diorama demonstrating the world's first brain surgery. No matter where you stand, the witch doctor's eyes always look like they are staring at you. He wants your brain! Here we are thousands of years later and we still know so little about the gray matter in our skulls and what it is capable of.

Jenny and I fell into our seats in the planetarium. The twilit chamber soothed my nerves. We pointed out familiar silhouettes along the edge of the circular ceiling: Will Rogers Coliseum, Tandy Center, the C.N.B.

"Look," said Jenny. "Our arm hairs are touching."

Indeed they were. The simulated sunset began. The star projector lit up.

Jenny and I waved playfully to Amber then cozily sunk deeper into the soft seats, our arms now overlapping. I considered taking Jenny's hand. But what if she minded?

While waiting for Tim to show up to rehearsal, Bonnie let me fool around with her Mellotron. It emits unbelievably gorgeous sounds at the touch of a key. Played something that had been bouncing around in my skull for some time, just a melody, really. Improvised a short piece around it. Thought nothing of it until I found Bonnie sulking on the loading dock out front. Said "hey" to her but she ignored me. Maybe she was still mad about my skull whipping quip.

"Did I do something to upset you?" I said.

"No." She took a long drag off her cigarette while I watched, then continued. "It's just that I have all this nice equipment. I have perfect pitch. Took sixteen years of violin and piano lessons and I know my stuff. But I'm nothing special, really. Then you show up, with your shitty technique, sorry, and play this amazing improvisation out of the blue."

"I was just messing around."

Bonnie sighed heavily. "I don't have a creative bone in my body."

"Not true, Bonnie. Your keyboard parts are always just what the song needs. You created those."

"But I can't do what you do. I mean, I have written some songs, but they're so childish."

"Didn't you write 'Rat Race'?" I said. "That song kicks ass! Besides, critics called Bach childish." I do not actually know if that is true. Was vaguely recalling something I had read.

Bonnie glared at me angrily.

"Look, I don't care for my own music, either, if you must know," I continued. "Since it came from my own mind, it contains no wonder for me. How do you surprise and delight yourself? Marlene Dietrich said she could never listen to her own records. Horowitz said the same thing."

Bonnie was not listening. "Sometimes I wonder why I even do this. Play in a band, that is. Almost everything we play is yours or Tim's, anyway. My contributions are slight."

"You write most of the lyrics, dummy! Which are always thought-provoking, by the way."

"Stop trying to make me feel better!" she shouted.

One ill-chosen word at this juncture would just make everything worse. I started to panic. Suddenly, I recalled some advice I read in *Cosmo* at Vee's. What could I say to indicate to Bonnie that I was listening, without making it sound like I was just trying to mollify her? Thought about it for as long as I dared, as my silence might be misconstrued. Too late!

"What are you thinking?" Bonnie demanded.

Tim arrived in his eagle van, tires squealing. Bonnie went back inside the warehouse and that was the end of our conversation.

Rehearsal was the pits. Was overly critical of my bass parts. Began to beat myself up for being unhelpful to Bonnie, for caring only about how her unhappiness made me feel. But what does that mean, to "care"? I care about the people of Kampuchea. A lot of good that does them. You care for someone by showing them. But that can be something you say, because speaking is something you do, right? But if I had taken *Cosmo*'s advice and simply listened, I would have been implicitly agreeing with her. Lesson learned.

SUNDAY, FEBRUARY 20

Laundry at Vee's. Now a semi-regular event. She answered the door in two fluffy towels, one around her torso and one coiled atop her head. Her face was covered in a white substance.

"Make yourself comfortable while I wash this Noxzema off," said Vee. She pronounced it *nog-zee-ma*. She returned in her robe, one towel still on her head. This evening, we listened to Cat Stevens, played Yahtzee, ate Fiddle Faddle, and drank Mateus out of jelly glasses. I do not understand how we were not getting down already. Guess I do believe in demons. Vee put on *The Rod Stewart Album*.

"Who the hell is that bass player?" I said.

Vee handed me the jacket. I perused the inner sleeve. "Says here 'Ronald (Good Looking) Wood.' No wonder!"

"Good looking?" said Vee. "Is there a picture?"

"Here you go." I pointed him out.

Vee grimaced then waved her hand dismissively. "Too scruffy. Say, I'm taking a trip to Italy this June. Would you mind being a dollface and watching Figs?"

"Of course I wouldn't mind!" I blurted, a little too enthusiastically. It would be an opportunity to bring our lives closer together. Glanced down at one of her *Cosmos*. One of its articles was "The Male Orgasm: What Every Girl Should Know." Has Vee read it, yet? What does she know that I do not?

Vee left the room for a moment. I reached for a Polaroid of Figaro when he was a kitten. It was in a clear, hollow, plastic frame filled with colorful bits. I shook it. "What's inside this frame?"

Vee reappeared. "Cat food!"

The cat food looked stale. "I'm so hungry I could eat this," I mumbled.

"What?" She was busy looking for something.

The remark was too dumb to repeat. Presently, Vee knelt before me and unfolded a well-worn map of Venice. I joined her on the rug. The streets had been hi-lited in different colors, indicating where she had walked on her previous trips to La Serenissima. I stared intently at her adventures laid out before me. "Here's a street you haven't been down," pointing out the stubby Calle de Mezzo.

"That's across from San Giacomo and I *have* been down it," she said. She reached for a Hi-Liter and marked the passage. "Have you ever been to Italy?"

"I've been to the truck stop in Italy, Texas."

Vee looked at me in astonishment.

"You'd love it there!" she said. "Rome makes New York look like a bunch of amateurs."

"What do you do when you go to Italy?"

"Oh, *dolce far niente*."

"I've been to Rome, Texas," I said. "Rhome, too. With an *h*."

"You should come to Italy with me! We'd have so much fun!"

My heart raced at the prospect. "That would be fun. But traveling costs money. Doubt I could afford it."

"I don't make a lot of money. But seeing the world's a priority for me." Vee looked into my eyes. "It's been said that if you really want to get to know a person, travel with them."

Is Vee saying that she really wants to get to know me? Already knew a few things about this woman. Her lack of inhibition. Her aversion to scruffy faces. "Hey, do you know how to find Kentucky on a map?" I blurted.

Vee looked at me with pity. I didn't used to be such an asshole. What's wrong with me?

I caught a glimpse of something in the kitchen. "Hey, where'd you get those? The giant fork and spoon?"

"Those were here when I moved in."

"They remind me of something funny that happened with a friend of mine. Sort of an in-joke. He would get a real kick out of those."

"You can have them."

"Really? That's awfully nice of you. First the camera. Now the giant fork and spoon!"

Vee grinned sweetly.

"By the way, I checked out that Robert Byron book for you," I said.

"Which book?"

"That travel book you wanted. By the philhellene. Let me run down and get it for you before I forget." Almost fell back down when I stood. Could hear the booze sloshing around in my empty stomach.

Made my way downstairs slowly, gripping the railing like a seasick passenger. Figs met me at the door. "Permission to come ashore!" I cried. Once in the bathroom, I splashed cold water on my face. The only time I ever pray is when I feel ill. It must work because I have not vomited since 1959. I prayed now. "J.C., if you're up there, don't let me puke. If I am a non-believer, it's only because you made me this way. Surely you can appreciate that."

I went straight to the Byron in the darkness. Turning on the lights had not occurred to me. Did I hear something thumping in the trash hole? As I carefully ascended the steps back up to Vee's, I heard voices and laughter. Some fucker was now sitting in the spot where I had been sitting. The urge to vomit returned.

Vee turned to me and said, "This is Blue Van, I mean, Keith. Keith, this is my neighbor, Steven." He scowled at Vee accusingly. Blue Van! One of her students, no doubt. Probably still has his baby teeth.

I shook Blue Van's hand. He did not get up. He was too comfortable in the spot I had warmed up for him.

"Work tomorrow," I mumbled. "Here's your book. Never mind the due date."

Vee's face lit up. "Thanks, Dollface!" She kissed me on the cheek. I love it when she does that. "Let me get your clothes. They ought to be dry by now." Blue Van cooly lit a cigarette and stared at my golden boots. Vee returned with a warm pile of laundry and dumped it in my arms, then balanced a doggie bag of Fiddle Faddle on top.

"Thanks, Vee. This was fun." I turned to face Blue Van. "Nice to meet you, Keith."

"Whatever, faggot," he mumbled.

"Wait!" cried Vee. "Don't forget your fork and spoon!" She slid them into the crook of my elbow.

While folding my laundry, I discovered a pair of Vee's panties stuck inside one of my t-shirts. Pulled them out in a blue flurry of static electricity. The zodiac symbol for Gemini was printed across the butt. The front bore the words "gracious, intelligent, glib" in small, cursive letters. Vee is indeed gracious and intelligent. But glib? I looked up the word in several dictionaries. Apart from the usual meaning of "marked by ease and informality"—which Vee is to a T—I would not say she is "insincere" or "deceitful." Nor would I say her words "lack depth or substance." From Low German *glibberig* meaning 'slippery.' *Bei Nässe glibberig!*

Sounds like a horse is clomping around upstairs. What the hell are they doing up there? Who is the horse and who is the rider?

MONDAY, FEBRUARY 21

To the library early. Found the faculty newsletter I was seeking, which contained the following notice:

On February 16, 1976, Porteous's Langner Library announced that the Baumann Collection has been received as a legacy from William H. Baumann, Class of 1922. It has been housed at the Seaberg Society Library in Los Angeles, California since 1952. Bill Baumann added new acquisitions to the collection continuously until the Society was dissolved in 1969. Since then, the collection has remained in private hands. Comprising artworks, as well as books and papers on subjects including science, history, and metaphysics, the Baumann Collection will soon become available to scholars on terms comparable to those of the Library's other special collections.

"Who's in here?" shouted Boggs.

"It's me. Steven."

"What brings you to work on a holiday?" Boggs lit a cigarette. "You know," he said. He took a long drag. "I seen your little buddy this morning."

"Who? Harvey?"

"That his name?"

It was my turn to do Jimmy Stewart. "Boggs, I can see that you're disturbed about Harvey. Now, please don't be. He stares that way at everybody. It's his way. But he likes you. I can tell."

"Not talking about a six-foot rabbit."

"Who, then?"

"Little pecker. Looks like a gremlin."

"How unfortunate," I said, feigning ignorance.

Boggs shook his head. "I don't judge. When you been where I've been, you seen it all. Honky gremlin don't faze you none. Look, I seen him sneaking around, but I don't see you two together. So I suppose you either don't know this individual, or you don't know he's following you. But I think you do know something about him. Or isn't that correct?"

I just stared at him.

"You're a nice guy, Steven. I like you. No disrespect, but I thought you librarians just read books and shush people all day. But I seen you working hard. Burning the midnight oil. But if you don't take care of this problem, I'll have to take care of this problem. I like to take care of problems my way. Are we clear?"

"Working on it, Boggs."

"Good man." He walked over to the stairs and mashed out his cigarette in the ashtray. "He's here now," he said, before adding in Stewart's voice, "Well, very glad to have seen you. Goodbye."

After Boggs left to make his rounds, I stood there for a moment, wondering if Harvey was watching me. Boggs said "gremlin" but evidently believes we are dealing with a person. Found his mistake somehow reassuring, as if there might be some reasonable explanation for all of this, after all. Where has Boggs been where a honky gremlin does not faze him?

It is Randy's birthday, so we had a party in the break room to celebrate. I forgot to bring his gift. I also forgot my sandwich, so a slice of pineapple upside-down cake was my lunch. While everyone stood around chatting, I hovered near one group of people, listening but not understanding. I moved on to other clusters of people in mid-conversation, plate in hand, traveling in a slow, eccentric orbit. As there is no smoking in the break room, my empty paper plate gave my hands something to do. I absent-mindedly folded it in half a few times into a surprisingly sturdy shiv. While listening to Hazel talk to Jo Ann about the upcoming Davis trial, I discreetly pretended to stab myself in the abdomen to test the shiv's viability, and was duly impressed. That thing is sharp! As Randy and Guddu appeared to be deep in conversation, I left them alone.

Back at the information desk, I examined my paper plate shiv. On a whim I wrote in Marks-A-Lot one of the words of power on it I had seen in the codex. Just passing the time, really. When Amber appeared, I quickly shoved the shiv into my pocket, then began sorting through a stack of memos and whatnot.

"What did you just do?" she said.

"What?" Had she seen the shiv?

"What's that magazine?"

"What magazine?"

"That one. You wrote something on it then put it on Jo Ann's seat."

"*The Chronicle of Higher Education*," I said.

Amber picked it up. "Why did you put a tick by your name?"

"That means I read it."

"Did you?"

"Can you take over for a minute? Gotta go drain the lizard."

When I returned, Amber looked me up and down. "How much do you actually know?"

"I find soda water and brandy the best guano for the cultivation of my intellect," I said, side-stepping her question.

She paused. "You answer questions all day, right?"

Since when are kids interested in epismetology—strike that—*epistemology*. I am turning into The Space Cowboy! Cautiously, I replied, "Librarians tend to know many things. You could say it's an occupational hazard. But we're skilled at finding things out." Ended up just throwing the question back in her face.

"How does anyone *know* what they know?" This put her into a contemplative mood while I went about my business. My own knowledge is a chunk of Swiss cheese. A generous serving, perhaps, but full of holes of varying sizes, many quite large. But do I know anything really useful? Such as how to fold a fitted sheet or fix the reverse button on the Rambler? Randy once remarked that he and I were over-educated people with no common sense, or some such thing.

Amber was now fiddling with her ant farm. She seemed lost in thought. Presently, she looked up. "Do you believe in the Holy Trinity, Steven?"

"Big Otto, J.C., and Spooky?"

"Who?" she replied, innocently.

"No. I believe Jesus was a man who lived a long time ago. Don't know what the hell a 'holy ghost' is."

"Steven, language! The holy ghost is the Lord, the Giver of Life. And what about God, Steven, do you believe in Him?" Amber emphasized every capitalized word, which lent her speech a strange, halting quality.

"I don't believe in God."

"Then you are an atheist?"

"I wouldn't say that. Maybe 'agnostic' is a better word. To be honest, I don't really think about it."

"Who do you think created us?"

"I don't know why there is something instead of nothing. It hurts my brain when I think about it too much. Books don't help."

"The Bible has all the answers, Steven," she lectured, with wonder in her voice. "The universe is all part of God's divine plan and intention."

"I don't doubt it, Amber. The way I see it, if God made us in his image, he knows I don't believe in him and he knows damn well why. If he's going to condemn me to Hell for that, then he's an asshole."

"Steven! I will pray for you."

"I only pray when I don't want to puke. So far, it seems to be working. Haven't thrown up since before you were born." Amber shook her head forlornly. "I'm sorry, Amber, I don't mean to be disrespectful. Have you always believed?"

"Always."

"Well, I never have. Used to go to church with my grandparents. I was bored shitless, sorry. All I cared about were the maps on the endpapers of the Bible. Those, I would pore over for hours. At least it felt like hours. Would linger in the bathroom, but it had a loudspeaker so you couldn't escape the sermon. Nice people, though. They were very kind when my grandmother passed away."

"What church did you go to?"

"Church of Christ."

"Oh, dear. That's not the One True Church."

"I wouldn't know, Amber," I replied, with a sigh. "Speaking of church, wanna see the Holy Grail?"

"What do you mean?"

"I've got one in my office."

"*One*, or *the*?"

"Follow me." When we reached my office and I handed the Antioch Chalice to her, she turned it over and read the bottom aloud. "Copyright 1966, Made in Japan."

"Nice try, Steven."

TUESDAY, FEBRUARY 22

Slept badly, so I wallowed in bed as long as I dared. Did not know what I was going to face at the library today.

Dixie waylaid me on the way to the break room. "Come into my office." I did so, and took a seat. She let me squirm while she finished laboring over some paperwork. At last, she set her pen down and looked up at me.

Took this moment to present to Dixie a jar of the Vibius jelly. She looked at it, then at me, then waved her hand dismissively and said, "No jams or jellies of any kind."

I returned the jar to my mansack.

"It has come to my attention that you were in the library yesterday."

"Forgot it was a holiday. Is that a big deal?" I stood up to leave.

"You will sit down."

I remained standing, arms crossed.

"Did you see anyone else in the library yesterday while you were here?"

"Besides Boggs? No."

Dixie was taking notes on a steno pad. "I am told you and Miss Fox were amorous at the planetarium."

"Who told you that?"

She just looked at me.

"I have a right to know!" I said. "For the record, we were not amorous. We sat next to each other, that is all. I understand when people come to you with information, no matter how ludicrous, that as head librarian you are obliged by duty to make inquiries. Just want to make sure that when I leave your office that you understand I am innocent of whatever you're accusing me of."

"I'm not accusing you of anything, Steven. But you will watch your tone when you speak to me." Dixie eyes bulged alarmingly. She read aloud from a document. "Library staff shall not consort with coworkers, under pain of dismissal."

"I know," I said, irritably. Was about to return to my desk when Dixie said, "Professor Harrington will be coming to the library on the 23rd. Please show him anything he wishes of the Baumann Collection."

"That's tomorrow," I said. "I won't be here."

"Jo Ann can take him down to the basement. You needn't worry," she said, crossly.

"It's against policy to leave patrons unattended in the basement."

"And so it is, Steven. But Professor Harrington is an eminent visiting scholar and a guest of L.F.'s."

So much for rules. "We wouldn't even let L.F. down there by himself." That is not actually true. L.F. and his cronies used to get liquored up at the Faculty Club then go down to the Vault to guffaw at minstrelsy materials from the good old days. The next day, I would find a big mess and the door to the thesis cage swinging in the breeze.

"Now, Steven. Choose your battles wisely. Will this be one of them?"

I excused myself and went to speak to Jo Ann at the information desk.

"If Professor Harrington comes by tomorrow to look at the Baumann Collection, just ask him what he wants to see and bring it up to him. He can look at it in Professor Whipple's old office."

"Why are you telling me this, Steven? I know what the procedure is."

"It's just that I'm in the middle of cataloging it all and I don't want anything misplaced. But Harrington doesn't know what we have. We don't even know ourselves, yet. Whatever you do, just don't leave him in the Vault to snoop around on his own. Promise me that."

"When have I ever done that?"

"It just seems like there are people down there all the time," I said. "Even Spunt goes down there."

"Well, he's not supposed to."

WEDNESDAY, FEBRUARY 23

A long, sleepless night. Sometimes when I am alone, I feel the Fear. I felt the Fear last night. I lay awake thinking about what I unwittingly unleashed upon the world. Until now, I suppose I have willfully ignored the philosophical implications of Harvey's existence. If Harvey exists, what else exists? It is as if someone is saying to me, "Here is the proof you asked for." But proof of what?

Showering felt like a chore. How many showers have I taken in my whole life? One or two per day, depending on the time of year, minus the years I took baths. When that exercise proved too troublesome, I contemplated the number of remaining showers. The average life expectancy of men in the U.S. is sixty-nine and a half. If I make it to that ripe old age, that would be forty-six more years of showers, multiplied by 1.75 to account for days when it is so hot outside you need to take two or more showers. So, about thirty thousand showers. How many gallons of water is that?

Ran some errands. Piggly Wiggly was out of all toilet paper colors except pink, so I just bought one roll to tide me over. I have never bought white and I am not going to start now. After cashing a check, I picked up Fleetwood Mac's new LP. Realized I had gotten Stevie Nicks and Lindsey Buckingham mixed up because of their names. There is a lot of great music coming out lately. The Eagles, Boston, Steve Miller Band, Al Stewart. It is hard to keep up with it all.

THURSDAY, FEBRUARY 24

Covered for Jo Ann at the information desk. Spent an inordinate amount of time trying to find out how many gallons of water a typical shower uses. Some knowledge cannot be found in books.

A student came up to the information desk asking for Goethe.

"Nice Bruce Lee shirt," I said.

"I am Bruce Lee."

"Show me some moves."

Bruce struck a karate pose.

"Not bad," I said. He could have been faking. What do I know? Should have gotten Randy out there. He is a black belt, or brown. One of the colors. "Goethe, huh? Figured you'd want to read something Chinese."

"I read the literature of all nations."

"As you should, as you should."

Said hello to Guddu as he was walking by, but he snubbed me. What is wrong with that turkey lately? When he returned, we made eye contact and I said, "Guddu, have a seat."

He pursed his lips, then sat down petulantly. He had a book in his hand.

"What book are you reading?"

"*The Electric Acid Kool-Aid Test.*"

"You mean '*The Electric Kool-Aid Acid Test.*'"

"Why cannot you say it the first way?"

"First of all, that's not the correct title. Second of all, in English, adjectives must appear in a particular order. There's a hierarchy: determiner, observation, physical characteristics like size and shape, followed by age and color, origins, substance, then qualifier. For example, one would say, 'the funny little old round blue Chinese *cloisonné* shenanigans dish.' If you mix up the order, you may be misunderstood. Or worse."

"I know exactly what you mean." Guddu reached for pen and paper. "Also, what are shenanigans?"

"Mischievous behavior."

Guddu looked down quickly, as if ashamed, then stood up to leave.

"Don't forget your book!"

"Of course, Steven. Thank you."

After work, a quick supper at Finley's. Dropped my fork on the floor, so ate my Salisbury steak with a spoon. You can eat everything with a spoon at Finley's. Vacuumed down my Jell-O in one boorish slurp while some old biddy in the next booth gave me the stink eye.

I raised my empty dish in a toast. "Ground ligaments and gristle with food coloring. Nectar of the gods!"

"Well, I never!" gasped the old biddy.

On a whim, I bought a rhubarb pie to go. Finley's pies are the best.

The nightclub was packed with high schoolers. The interior was bathed in black light, so everyone's teeth were glowing. Kehoe was there in a fluorescent suit, looking like an oversized Oompa Loompa. He told me to unload through the front door then park around back. A royal pain in the ass. The other band's stuff was already set up on a linoleum rectangle in the corner. Perched on my cab until Bonnie showed up.

"Thought we were playing first," I said. Was looking forward to getting home early.

"Hello to you, too! By the way, Fred's not coming tonight."

"Lucky Fred," I muttered.

After helping Bonnie bring her gear in, I changed clothes in the Rambler. While struggling to pull my jeans on, someone jumped on my rear bumper.

"Security!" shouted a voice. "We've got a pervert over here!"

"Fuck off, Tim!"

We piled up all our gear between the linoleum and the bar. Turtle Man was again present. He had found a seat at one of the club's only tables, directly in front of the P.A. speakers. Reading, of course. Wondered how he could read in ultraviolet light. If he has to take a leak he will probably lose his seat.

Ordered a Harvey Wallbanger and settled down to watch people. A mob of high school girls surrounded me. They had sharp elbows and they shrieked a lot. Took a deep breath and resigned myself to another evening of overstimulation. A girl in gladiator boots asked me for a light. When I produced my Bic, the others all asked me for a light, too. Another one plopped her purse down before me while she went to the ladies' room.

There was a sudden commotion by the entrance. It was the opening act, dressed in theatrical battle costumes. Their faces were covered in war paint, which glowed under the black lights. They started squirting everyone with (what I hoped were) water pistols. I got sprayed a couple of times. "This is suede!" wailed one of the girls.

The singer grabbed the mic. "We're Pantego from Pantego! Are you ready to rock?" Pantego launched into a brash song that evoked Kiss. They were actually pretty decent, but it was too much heaviosity for such a small venue. Between the crowd and deafening noise, I was starting to feel irritable and claustrophobic. Bonnie saved me. "We're out back," she said. Had to wait for the purse chick to return, who was more than happy to inherit my seat.

I emerged from a back door, where I counted the glow of two other cigarettes besides Bonnie's. "I smell skunk!" As soon as I had said it, I realized what I was smelling.

"There's something about skunk odor I like," said Bonnie. "Real skunks, not this." She waved her hands to dispel a cloud of smoke and coughed.

"Me, too," I said. "Unless it's too strong."

Bonnie passed me a bong, which looked like it was made of brass pipe fittings.

"What's the deal with this?" I said.

"Used to make them all the time at my old job," replied Tim. "Invention is the mother of necessity."

"Stoner engineering at its finest. Where did you work?"

"Polyflex."

Was going to ask Tim what the deal was with Polyflex but he was too busy sharing a long-winded anecdote about how grass affects him. His stories pale in comparison to those Sherwood told of imbibing weird shamanic potions beneath the stelae of Yaxchilan.

"Where's Pantego?" said Tim to no one in particular.

"Near Dalworthington Gardens," I said.

"Never heard of it," he said, petulantly.

Pantego stopped playing after a fairly short set. Bonnie and I helped them move their equipment out the front entrance. We waded through the drunken, gyrating bodies while carrying drums, speaker cabinets, and enormous battle axes. We had to take the wheels off a wolf's-head battering ram to get it out the door. How did they get it in here?

No one smokes more than high schoolers. My eyes were irritated from all the smoke. I headed to the men's room to squirt some Visine into my eyes before performing. When I approached the stage area, Tim pointed at my face and howled.

"What happened to you?" said Bonnie. "You have glow in the dark tears streaming down your face."

"Ah, must be the Visine," I said. I bent over to shut my bass case.

"Cute appliqués!"

"Huh?" I replied.

Bonnie patted my butt. Craned my neck to look and saw a Gemini sign across a pocket, surrounded by colorful flowers. All glowing brightly in the black light. "Hey, these aren't my jeans!" I cried. Bonnie reached down and looked inside my waistband.

"Why are you wearing Gloria Vanderbilts?" she said.

Vee's jeans! It was either these or librarian slacks. After Pantego the audience was primed for anything.

Once we started playing, I noticed a few catcalls directed my way. I held my head high. After we blazed through our originals, we wowed the young crowd with our growing arsenal of cover tunes. During Tim's slide guitar solo on "Tush," I turned around and shook my own tush, eliciting shrill whistles and drunken cheers. Tim kicked me in the ass hard. Tim hates sharing the spotlight.

FRIDAY, FEBRUARY 25

Another balmy day. Had a rather nasty headache. 245,000 books in the library and not a single one with a hangover cure. Harrington showed up when I was at the information desk. We talked about Sherwood.

"Jim's work was sometimes far outside the academic mainstream," said Harrington. "One might say it killed his career."

I was not ever aware that Sherwood's career was, in fact, killed.

As for the Baumann material I brought upstairs for Harrington, none of it seemed pertinent to Sherwood's disappearance. Nor did any seem like particularly forbidden knowledge. Treatises on mummification. A book about the Fountain of Youth. Relieved that Harrington did not ask to go down to the Vault.

Before I left for the day, Randy stopped by my office. He dropped some hefty tomes onto my desk, then held up one. "I present to you *Successful Muskrat Farming* by Ralphie Tucker."

"Damn, that's ugly. Aqua buckram?"

"No one would ever want to open that." Randy handed me the original. "By the way, I xeroxed a couple of pages for myself. I want to do an experiment."

"What were you and Guddu talking about the other day in the break room?"

"Oh, nothing," said Randy. He turned away and now seemed lost in thought.

As he turned to leave, I said, "Almost forgot. These are for you." I reached behind my coat rack and produced the giant wooden fork and spoon. "Happy belated birthday, you bastard!"

Randy busted a gut laughing. "Dude! Where did you get these? I can't believe it!"

"Take you out for a drink soon. Can't be this weekend because we got gigs. We're at Double D.'s tonight."

Randy made a face. "I hate that dump. Anyway, I'm busy this weekend."

The marquee said "Welcum El Grito & Time Frame" with an upside-down *m* for the *w*. The cigarette machine was out of Kents, which put me in a mood. Tim greeted the crowd with, "Hello, Big D.! Where the east begins!" Not the way to win over Dallasites. "We are blessed to play upon the very stage where Candy Barlow twirled her tassels, many moons ago. Don't know Candy Barlow? Y'all better read up!"

During our set, some drunk bozo kept demanding we play "Lobo."

"Me and You and a Dog Named Boo?" I said, off mic. I bent down to hear him while still playing.

"You know what you are?" slurred the bozo. "You're just a…kiss my ass." He pounded his fists on the stage. "I want Lobo!"

I jerked my thumb toward Tim. "Ask that guy. 'Lobo' is his favorite song."

When the song ended, Tim announced, "Ladies, our bass player hasn't gotten himself laid since he started wearing women's clothing. Will someone please help him out tonight?"

"Yoo hoo, honey! I'll show you a helluva time." A hag seated near the edge of the stage was now ogling me. She raised her arms and jiggled her double Ds. I waved feebly.

When we were packing up, the hag was giving Bonnie a hard time. "You can't play worth shit! You were only using one finger!" she said.

"Monophonic keys, you dumb-ass cunt," explained Tim.

The hag wagged her finger at Tim. "You don't know shit about fuck, motherfucker. I curse your ass!"

Tim juggled his balls. "Whip some skull on me, bitch!"

The hag was poised to curse Tim's ass when the bartender intervened. "Don't jack with the talent, Shirley."

"Nyou'll nyet nyours!" Shirley gummed, as her teeth tumbled out of her trap. We all watched to see what she would do next. Shirley picked up her dentures and put them back into her mouth without sterilizing them first. Even Lobo groaned.

Discovered someone had bent my radio antenna and hocked a loogie on the windshield. The hag? Why the Rambler and not Tim's van? Of course, it could be my "Foat Wuth, Ah Luv Yew" bumper sticker.

SATURDAY, FEBRUARY 26

Instead of taking the usual scenic route this morning, I took a more circu-itous path. Almost immediately, I saw a deer off to the side of the trail. It was chewing its cud. Or whatever deer chew. We locked eyes and froze. After what seemed like a full minute, it hissed at me. I hissed back.

Looked in the *Encyclopaedia Britannica* to find out if deer chewed cud, but the article dealt chiefly with descriptions of the myriad various species. "For deer in general," it refers one to Lydekker's *The Deer of All Lands* (1908). A few minutes later, I was skimming that tome's pages in vain for any information on cud chewing or hissing. Tried to find Baumann in *The 'Dillo*. Expected he was in the 1922 volume but the page was torn out.

Stopped by the Novel Hovel to pick up Fred. Had some time to kill before closing, so I browsed. While admiring the cover of a *Three Investigators* book, I heard a clattering sound behind me. Wheeler had just dumped a bag of Hot Wheels all over the floor.

"Wow! How many of those do you have?"

Wheeler held up three fingers. His mouth and chin were stained orange from God knows what. Is this kid's mouth never naturally hued?

"Three? Surely you have more than that."

Wheeler just stared at me, then blurted, "Three pajillion."

"That's probably a world record. Let's see." I pulled *The Guiness Book of World Records* off the shelf and began flipping through it. I pretended to read aloud: "The record for the most Hot Wheels is Wheeler, what's your last name, kid, of Fort Worth, Texas, who possesses three pajillion Hot Wheels. That's more Hot Wheels than anybody in the whole wide world." I slammed the book shut and reshelved it. "Way to go, Wheeler!" I said, slapping him five.

Wheeler looked pleased. "Listen to me count to three pajillion. One, two..."

"You know," I interrupted, "These days it's pretty easy to get into *The Guiness Book of World Records*. All you have to do is think of something no one else has done before, like swimming blindfolded while playing the trombone, and do it. Then you'd hold the world record for doing that particular thing."

Asked Fred if he had any Kate Greenaway. "Who?" he replied. When I ex-plained who she was, he said, "Probably." He disappeared into the Children's section. Moments later I was holding *The Two Gray Girls and Their Opposite Neighbors*.

"Keep it?" I asked. Fred looked inside the front cover and thought for a moment. "Sure," he said. "Keep it."

I stepped outside while Fred locked up. Overheard Wheeler talking excit-edly to his mother. "And you can go swimming with a blindfold on and play a trombone!" he said. "That's a world record!" I heard a smack, then a cry.

Opened for Hot Spice at some honky tonk in Weatherford whose name I have already forgotten. The Shed, I think. Bonnie usually plays booking manager, but Dave II arranged this one. When I asked Dave II why he chose this place he said, "So we can share our beautiful music with the good folks of Weatherford."

"Tacos for Two" by Tommy Hancock blared from the jukebox. Man that guy can pick the hell out of the steel. The tables had baskets of peanuts on them. The floor was covered in peanut shells. Turtle Man was there, eating peanuts. He was wearing a cowboy hat. Shoved a couple of fistfuls of peanuts into my mansack to throw at the scenic route grackles.

Beer was free for the band. Before we went on, an entertaining bartender called Billy Webb (which he pronounced 'wayub') told us about all the famous faces he had seen in there. Meanwhile, Tim had to keep going to the bathroom. "What does it mean when your shit is green?" he said.

Fred shook his head. "My last number two was like 'Takin' Care of Business.'" He looked at Bonnie.

"Mine was like John Cage," she said. "Four minutes and thirty-three seconds of silence."

"'December 1963 (Oh, What a Night),'" said Dave II. We all looked at him quizzically. "That's the last time I had a bowel movement." Everyone looked at me.

"'Bunghole in the Jungle,'" I offered, cryptically, using vocabulary Spunt taught me. Thought my clever play on words was hilarious, but I stifled my laughter when I saw no one else laughing. Did not tell them I felt ill.

"Gonna go with 'Green River,' myself," lamented Tim.

"Y'all want to know mine?" asked Billy, while casually drying a mug. We all looked at him. He paused for dramatic effect, then began to sing, "Billy, don't be a hero..."

Home in time to catch Donna Summer on *Don Kirshner*.

SUNDAY, FEBRUARY 27

Sore throat coming on. Should not have stayed up so late watching TV. Went down to the Texaco and phoned Bonnie. No answer, so I dialed Dave II.

"If you don't show up, Tim will play your bass parts on the demo," he said.

"The demo!"

"This gig's a big one. Need you there, buddy. Gotta create some magic with our rhythm section."

Made biscuits and gravy then sat down to read the paper. A space laser is less than ten years away. Its use is ostensibly for defending our own satellites against anti-satellite threats. Will believe it when I see it. "Hawlie" is one of the Jumble clues today. That has to mean something!

A review of Velikovsky's new book *Peoples of the Sea* caught my eye. His latest theory has to do with our timeline of ancient history being off by several hundred years. Some of Egypt's royal dynasties may not have existed at all. Like all his other theories, this one has disturbed academicians. Found myself excitedly reading the whole review in order to see if his "peoples of the sea" were from Vul Kar and not barbarians from the north as is generally believed. But Vul Kar allegedly sank long before the time of Ramses III.

Sherwood always scoffed at Velikovksy. "Because his ideas—*bam!*—are not outrageous enough!" he said. Sherwood thought Velikovksy deliberately held back because he feared he would not be taken seriously by his colleagues. But the public sure ate it up.

Pulled up to Bonnie's parents' house in Denton about an hour later. The idea was to have a quick bite, record a couple of tunes, then play a late gig in town. Bonnie was out back grilling burgers and corn on the cob while Tim and Dave II watched.

It was a great, dark house, only one storey but sprawling. There was no escaping the guitars everywhere. To traverse the interior one had to walk along pathways through them. Most were Gibsons. Did not know they made so many different models. Many were on stands. Others were piled up in cases or just lying flat. Met Bonnie's dad in the control room. Balding guy with indoor sunglasses named Terry.

"You have a lot of guitars," I blurted.

"You dont say," replied Terry flatly, without looking up from his mixing console. "You ever work one of these before?"

"Just a P.A. mixer."

Terry made a sweeping gesture with his hand. "Behold the Yamaha PM-430. Picked this baby up at the flea market last week. Practically brand new." The Yamaha was resting on top of a much larger console. Guess he was not afraid of damaging any knobs. He turned it around so I could see the back.

"Added direct outputs in the rear. Also made it so both aux sends are post mix."

I smiled.

"Get in the booth. When I give the signal, start talking."

I hesitated in the doorway. "What do I say?"

The vocal booth was a small, stuffy room. Its walls were covered in anechoic polystyrene egg cartons. I perched on a high bar stool, facing Terry. He pointed at me, which I took to mean he wanted me to say something.

"Abracadabra," I said into the mic.

Terry gestured for me to put on the headphones. Could hear myself breathing heavily in them, like a perv. Terry got up and left the control room. When it looked like he was not coming back, I wandered back through the guitar maze toward the kitchen. Saw a guitar with seven necks. A ceiling fan had guitars for blades. Found Tim and Dave II drinking beer. Dave II handed me one.

The dinner triangle rang. "That's cow-talk for 'chow time,'" said Dave II.

"Wouldn't cow-talk be mooing?" I said. I realize that people often pretend not to hear what I say.

We funneled into the kitchen. "Drinks are in the icebox," said Bonnie.

I tonged a pattie onto a sesame seed bun. "What songs are we going to record?"

"'X Marks the Spot' and 'Fancy Space Odyssey,'" said Tim.

"Why are we doing a cover?"

"Because some clubs like to know that we do covers. Because the stars are aligned. Because sometimes you want to hear the old tunes. There's power in them."

"Bloodrock's not old," I said.

Tim shrugged.

"Don't really care," I continued. "Those songs just don't really demonstrate who we are." Who are we?

For the next couple of hours, Terry called the shots, and then Bonnie relayed them to the rest of us. "Steven, you're up next!"

"Hey, Bonnie. Can I play that Rickenbacker I saw in the bathroom?"

"Which Rickenbacker? Which bathroom? Sure, whichever," she replied, to my relief.

"Green Bean!" shouted Terry. "Bring him the one by the Christmas tree." Bonnie went away.

I smiled.

"Have you ever played a Rickenbacker?" asked Terry, suspiciously.

Bonnie returned with the instrument of my dreams, except for it being white. Strapped it on and thumbed a few E's. Did not feel like the Pan at all. It was heavier. Playing it felt like work. Bonnie plugged me in.

"Bon, we want the bridge pickup full on. Roll back the neck pickup. Dim both tone controls." Bonnie followed Terry's instructions while I stood like a mannequin. "Crank the mids on the Ampeg, roll off the bass. Add a hint of treble.

I tentatively played "Yours Is No Disgrace."

"You're hearing the brightness of the maple neck and body, with the fundamental of the neck-thru," said Terry. "The pickup placement is different from what you are used to."

I was somewhere else, only vaguely aware.

"Hop on the Squire-Geddy train. Run two pickups to two separate amps. Distortion on the trebly amp. That's the key. You can play a Fender knock-off with a Rick touch, but you can't really do the opposite," continued Terry. I kept playing. Had no idea what a "Fender knock-off touch" might be.

"Steven! You can't just beat on it," continued Terry. "Develop the touch. Don't play it like your Pan." And he was not finished. "Fuck," he spat. I stopped. Was he talking to me?

"Are we ready, Bon?" said Terry.

Recording went off without a hitch. Suggested we start "X Marks the Spot" with the sound of Bonnie ringing the dinner triangle. She loved the idea, and so we did it. It made no sense, but it was fun.

"Let's run it through the phaser," said Terry.

"Let's not," said Bonnie.

We stuck around until we had a rough mix. I unwrapped a brand new C-60 cassette I had brought along and asked if I could get a dub.

"I'm fresh out of cassettes. In fact, we're going to have to use yours, Steven." He held out his hand and I reluctantly gave him mine. Before we left, Terry gave me an old used cassette with the label scribbled out, under which was written, "Time Frame demo 2/27/77." That motherfucker lied!

The Sweat Lodge was near campus. Guarding the front door, a cigar store Indian covered with graffiti and decals.

"If the crying Indian could only see this," I remarked.

"Chief Iron Eyes from the TV commercial?" said Dave II. "He's played by an Italian."

"That can't be true!" said Bonnie.

"The world and its guises," I said, throwing up my hands.

While waiting for the opening act to go on, we drank at the bar. "Louie Louie" blared from the P.A.

"Where did they get their chili pepper lights?" I shouted to Bonnie over a clap of thunder. "We need these at the information desk."

"'Louie Louie' is the filthiest song ever recorded," remarked Tim.

"The F.B.I. concluded the lyrics were unintelligible at any speed," countered Dave II.

"Well if the F.B.I. says so it must be the truth," snapped Tim, sarcastically. Dave II looked hurt.

We played to an appreciative audience. During "Andromeda Suite," a drunk chick joined us on tambourine and none of us even cared. When she collapsed, Turtle Man came and dragged her away. Was surprised to see him in Denton.

By the time we finished, it was well past midnight. At least we did not have to wait around to get paid. Had planned on staying at Bonnie's parents' house with the others. Now I just wanted to get home to blow my nose in the comfort of my own bed. Do not think I could face Terry lecturing me at the breakfast table.

During the drive home, I caught the end of *The Rock & Roll Alternative*. Heard fresh music by the Vibrators, the Saints, and Pere Ubu. Catchy, piquant tunes played fast and hard. The lack of guitar solos notwithstanding, there was something undeniably compelling about the new sound. Especially liked one song by Blondie. Must seek it out. The gulf between these three chords and those of the Kingsmen could not be more vast.

MONDAY, FEBRUARY 28

Walked to the Texaco to call in sick to work. A car had smashed into the phone booth. Was amazed that the phone still worked.

Brought the *Star-Telegram* home. My nose was too runny to hold my head upright for long so I set the paper aside. Not sure why I keep hearing Vee upstairs pacing endlessly. It is like she is stomping from one corner of the room to the opposite. Then she goes back again. Again and again.

Listened to our demo tape. The sound was garbled. The bulk eraser Terry had used ruined it. Thought I could distinguish words, like when you play "Stairway to Heaven" backwards. A word repeated three times caught my attention. A Dordic word. Which coincidentally was one of the clues in today's Jumble. Used to revel in such coincidences, but never put much stock in them. As Nabokov once wrote, "A certain man once lost a diamond cufflink in the wide blue sea, and twenty years later, on the exact day, he was eating a large fish. But there was no diamond inside. That's what I like about coincidence."

No vittles in the house. Nothing that sounded appealing, that is. My pie from Finley's was still out in the Rambler. Brought it in along with my Fleetwood Mac record. The pie looked edible, but I was worried about bacteria. *Rumours* was warped. It was in the eighties the other day.

In the evening, watched *Challenge of the Network Stars* broadcast live from Pepperdine U. Howard Cosell shooting the shit with O.J. Simpson and Bruce Jenner. Telly Savalas contested the results of the last challenge. He claimed the NBC stars should be disqualified for "fragrantly" breaking the rules. I love that guy! Robert Conrad, pointing at Telly Savalas, replied, "You're Greek. The Greeks are famous athletes. Gabe Kaplan's Jewish, so he wants to arbitrate. I'm German. I want to kill both of them." So much talent in one place!

The dunking booth segment could have been the highlight of the program, had the dunkees not been Robert Conrad, Hal Holbrook, and Dan Haggerty.

They must have dunked ol' Grizzly Adams four or fives times. He is not going to get any wetter! Meanwhile, Jane Seymour is standing braless on the sidelines, dry as a popcorn fart.

TUESDAY, MARCH 1

Went to rehearsal sick and coughed in everybody's face. Bonnie played us our demo. Our songs had more muscle than usual. The Rickenbacker, I guess. My personal playing style was less in evidence as I struggled to adapt to an unfamiliar instrument. As demos go, it did not really sound much like us, but did reveal a band that was tight and professional. In that sense, it will serve its purpose. Which is what?

Gig 365 days a year?

Get a recording contract?

Dear Gentlemen, you will forgive me if our reputation has preceded this missive. We submit to you this cassette tape demonstration recording which you will find showcases our manifold talents. It is hoped we may obtain some recording contracts with your distinguished establishment. Should you fail to recognize our potential, I ask that you consider Dick Rowe who passed on the Beatles. Thank you for your time and consideration. Sincerely, Time Frame.

Rehearsal devolved into boozing and bickering. Much nose blowing on my part. While Bonnie worked out a difficult part, the rest of us explored the building. It had been a warehouse for a chemical supply company at one time but had since fallen into desuetude. Discovered a bin of little magnetic pellets, to which we all helped ourselves. Dave II found a machine that said "Magnetic Stirrer" on it. We were soon stirring all sorts of chemicals we found in a cabinet. We stopped when the tetranitromethane odors became overwhelming.

"Better living through chemistry!" choked Dave II. There is nothing a group of drunken cretins cannot achieve. Or attempt.

Fred took the stirrer home. Think he wants to try to use it for musical purposes somehow. Tim took a few canisters of industrial-grade nitrous oxide for laughs. Must remember to look up "tetranitromethane."

WEDNESDAY, MARCH 2

My cold is worse. And that toluene spill at rehearsal last night did my esophagus no favors. During one violent coughing fit, Vee stuck her head through the door. "You poor thing!"

I waved feebly.

Vee returned with a huge bottle of something. She shook it up, unscrewed the cap, then poured what looked like pond scum into a spoon. "My girlfriend Dawn gave me this. Good for you!" She held the spoon up and waited for me to open wide.

Vee made airplane noises and fed me the pond scum while I tried not to laugh. Without warning, she whipped the blanket halfway off me, exposing my bare torso. She then produced a jar of Mentholatum and slathered some all over my chest and neck. The fumes made my eyes water.

"Who's Dawn?" I said, wanly.

"Green Bug. Do you have a t-shirt?"

I pointed at a chair, from which Vee retrieved my 'Dillos jersey. She helped me get my arms and head through the holes. The fabric clung to my mentholated skin. She kissed me on the forehead before departing. "Feel better, Dollface!" Did not tell her I had to get up soon to go to the D.P.S.

While waiting in line, I got a lot of dirty looks over the menthol fumes. Had to fill out a form. Thanks to Loretta, I do not have a phone number, so I put down the one for the circulation desk. The form had parentheses for the area code but they were too close together. Carefully wrote "817" as tall and thin as I could to make them fit, and to demonstrate how thoughtlessly designed their form was. Meanwhile, the line for the zip code took up half the width of the sheet. When getting my picture taken their light malfunctioned. Had to wait for a guy to set up a work lamp. There was a glare, so they made me take off my glasses. You win, D.P.S.

The D.P.S. visit wore me out. Once back home, I took a long nap. When I awakened, I resumed sorting through the contents of Sherwood's seemingly bottomless satchel. Tucked in a pocket was a xeroxed portion of a topographic map, annotated in pencil. At last, I discovered a journal. Was intrigued at first, but the entries were surprisingly mundane. Like the *Yellow Book* but without all the jacking off. The last entry was made on Christmas Eve: "The door is finished. Must take precautions not to draw attention to myself upon arrival." Arrival where?

Read backwards from there, trying to piece together Sherwood's movements before he disappeared. Much was made about what he ate for breakfast, the weather, golfing at Rockwood, etc. He mentions the "grimoire" (undoubtedly the codex) but only in passing. The entry for July 6 reads, "Krolok has instructed me to keep a separate red notebook in which to record details of my remote viewing sessions, to transcribe spells, and to document my magical development." Of the many notebooks in Sherwood's satchel, none are red. Who the heck is Krolok?

THURSDAY, MARCH 3

Had trouble sleeping due to lightning, thunder, hail, and gale-force winds all night. Every time I woke up, I started coughing. All I had in the medicine cabinet was an ancient Contac, so I swallowed it dry. Shambled down to the Texaco to call in sick again. Wore my robe but at least had the common sense to wear my golden boots. Probably looked like a crazy whimsical wizard. Or a bum. A gust of wind almost took my umbrella away. Phone booth still wrecked but I reached through all the broken glass and placed my call just as before. Have not seen Harvey lately. Am I rid of him?

Was tempted to get dressed and drive over to Sherwood's house to see if I could locate the red notebook. After a long, steamy shower, I felt mucho invigorated. Enough to proceed. I knew I would not be able to stop thinking about the thing. It is too bad the Bastard was at work otherwise I would have brought him along.

Parked down by the Bungalow and walked past Polyflex. The exterior of the house was unchanged. I entered through the kitchen window. Inside, it was a different story. Drawers hung open, their contents strewn about. Looked like a crime scene staged by someone who had never seen a real one. Or have I been watching too much *Barnaby Jones*? The bedroom closet door was open. Several coats lay crumpled upon the floor. A slender beam of sunlight spotlit a trail of slime on an oak chest of drawers. Through my one unstuffed nostril I detected a familiar odor. Unless someone had stashed a dead octopus under the floorboards, I would say Harvey had been here.

But how? Could not see Harvey crouching at the bus stop, staring at his watch impatiently, then flashing his Commutercard 13 to the Citran driver. Did no one notice an imp slinking down the middle of Roberts Cut Off? Of course he would have traveled under cover of darkness. Something to think about the next time I hear a dog barking at night. Harvey must have not known what he was seeking because the red notebook was in plain sight on the kitchen table. Was he looking for something else?

A B-52 roared overhead. Was there anything else here of interest? It was too risky to return. The screen door banged. Impulsively, I ducked into the study and hid among the overcoats in the closet.

It was insufferably stuffy. Would my wheezing give me away? Minutes passed. Crouched down and tried to look through the keyhole. Just when I thought it was safe to come out, I heard the floorboards creak. The intruder had entered the study. Could hear him opening drawers and rummaging through papers. Urgently felt the need to cough, which I sought to alleviate with a series of small throat clearings. A loud cough was unavoidable. I sprung from the closet and collided with a tall, thin man in a blue jumpsuit, knocking him down. Carlos! I hauled ass through the living room and out the front door. I ran around to the back of the house, through a copse, and across a field of scrub.

Looked over my shoulder a few times but saw no one. When I emerged from behind the Bungalow, I got into the Rambler and casually drove away. Figured if Carlos had not gotten a good look at my mug, I may as well drive by the house and see what there was to see. Which was nothing. But I did catch a glimpse of someone entering Polyflex through a service door.

Gig at the K.O.C down in Carl's Corner. Fundraiser for some charity that Bonnie's sister or cousin is involved with. Probably gratis. We were not even the headliners, I was to discover. Top billing went to an amateur dulcimer club.

My evasive tactics earlier had aggravated my cough. It persisted all evening despite several slugs of Jim Beam. I am never the most animated performer, but tonight I was a veritable sad sack and played terribly. In anticipation of one of my few background vocal parts, I drew a deep breath. This induced a hacking fit when I was supposed to be harmonizing. The first couple of coughs were directly into the mic. That must have been a wake-up call for the largely disinterested audience. Tim paused mid-lick to flip me off, as if I could have helped it. Through the glare of the stage lights, I saw Turtle Man move quickly away from the P.A. How did he even know about tonight?

While we were breaking our gear down a woman asked if she could use our microphone so they could do a raffle. She pointed at a table upon which were a dozen or so prizes. How long could it possibly take? Well, after the table had been cleared, she pulled out the envelopes. There must have been about a hundred of them. About an hour into the raffle, as I sunk lower and lower into my seat, Bonnie took pity on me and sent me home. We take care of each other, Bonnie and I. I regrettably missed the amateur dulcimer club!

Was headed down Camp Bowie when I was alerted by a revving motor. Looked in the rearview to see a doolie barreling down on me. It kissed my bumper all the way to Collinwood. Did not want the driver to know where I lived, so I veered off on El Campo. Felt around for something I could use as a weapon. Guess I could bonk him over the head with the codex in a pinch. The only spells I know were useless here.

Tried to shake him, as if that were possible in the Rambler. Turned back toward Camp Bowie then swerved into the alley behind the Showdown. There is always a police car parked there. Pulled up behind it and waited. The doolie stopped for a moment. All I could see were its high beams. Presently, it backed up and turned around. Whoever it was probably went home to beat his dogs or slap around his old lady. After waiting to make sure he was gone, I had to get out and push the Rambler backwards to the street while my nose ran like a faucet.

This cold is kicking my ass. Was somewhat worried about disturbing Vee, but if my New Year's party went unnoticed then she probably could not hear me hocking up a lung. Rolled my TV into the bedroom so I could vegetate there. As I did so, I noticed my cigarette ash clung to the screen. Static electricity?

Forgot to wipe for fingerprints at Sherwood's again. There is little I can do about that now.

FRIDAY, MARCH 4

Went to the library but was useless. The heat was cranked up on what was an almost warm, sunny morning. After being cooped up for days, all I wanted to do was be outside. Would have tried to kick a field goal if I did not think it would make me start coughing again.

Looked up tetranitromethane in *Van Nostrand's*. Turns out it is a highly unstable explosive. And toxic, too. Evidently it can cause methemoglobinemia. I examined my skin, which was more beige than blue.

My stomach was upset from all the cough drops. When I went to the staff bathroom, I entered to find Carlos busy ripping the toilet out. "Use the public one," he said, without looking up. If he had recognized me at Sherwood's, he did not let on.

Never used the public one before. I chose a stall and sat down. Disgusting, worse than the ones at the Tip Top. Can you get V.D. from a toilet? The metal dividers were pitted with rust and covered with graffiti and slogans. One read, "For a good time call" followed by the telephone number of the library's information desk. Scrawled in Marks-A-Lot was "Styx sux dyx." Underneath that, a jagged "Perdurabo" in Liquid Paper. As I stood to zip up my slacks, I discovered a three-fingered hand etched into the paint. Randy messing with me, no doubt.

I was so zonked, I put off examining Sherwood's red notebook until the afternoon. No locks or keys. No magical seals. Just an ordinary spiral-bound college-ruled Mead notebook. While examining it at my desk, I came across an unfamiliar word: *eidolon*. Reached for my compact *OED*, but the A-O volume was stuck. Turned the box over and dumped them. Both volumes tumbled to the floor along with the magnifying glass drawer, which I discovered was empty. No entry for "doolie," alas.

Made a xerox of the red notebook for Randy before bringing it to him. Told him about what happened yesterday at Sherwood's.

"Carlos?" he said, alarmed. "What was he doing there? Did he recognize you?"

"I don't think so."

Randy and I also discussed the role of willpower in practicing magic, of performative utterances, and remote viewing. I asked what magic was, just to see what Randy would say. He did not say what it was exactly, but explained that it was about controlling your environment. Did not ask him if people were considered part of the environment.

Gig at the Jug with Lochinvar. Lochinvar headlined, which meant the possibility of being in bed before midnight. Dave II showed me the digital watch he had won at the raffle last night. Told him about being chased by some redneck on the way home, then asked what he thought "doolie" meant.

"Truck with double wheels in back."

"But what does the word mean?"

"Dually, as in two wheels," said Dave II. "If you didn't get a look at the driver, why do you say he was a redneck?"

"Sure it wasn't Loretta?" said Fred. Fred understands well how crazy that bitch was. He still has the scar.

"That's sick," was all I could muster.

While warming up, a scrawny, shirtless black guy drifted in from the street. He stood before me, watching my fingers. Hawlie's slave! Did he recognize me? When we paused, he asked politely if he could play my bass. Handed the Pan to him without a word.

Toby, I mean Leroy, started slapping out a funky riff. Dave II joined in. The handyman proceeded to blow everyone away with his formidable funkosity. Simply by observing him, my bass I.Q. increased ten points. He blew my mind with bends, chirping, and blindingly fast sweep picking. Even controlled feedback, which I could not establish how he was making happen. Toby and Dave II played for several minutes. Found myself becoming impatient so I got up on the stage and reached for my bass. The music ended in a flamboyant finale, eliciting wild hollering from the few barflies in the back.

"That was dynamite," I said, sucking on a cough drop. Toby returned my instrument and I examined it suspiciously. Checked to make sure it was still in tune. It was. Do not have a funky bone in my body, but started playing my own riff anyway. The same one I had once used on "Peace Frog" in my Primary Source days. Obligingly, Dave II waded in.

"Get down!" croaked one of the barflies. I instinctively ducked, like a retard, before I realized what he meant. My nerves are shot!

Was not long before my ambition had surpassed my skill level. Lost myself in a wilderness of scales for what felt like an eternity before simply stopping cold, going out on a flatulent string rip.

No one was paying any attention. Felt like I had somehow dishonored Toby, Dave II, the barflies, any passersby within earshot, all musicians and fans of music everywhere, and Euterpe herself.

The gig was relaxed, with a small, but appreciative crowd of locals and some Academy kids who were slumming it. The hag from Double D.'s showed up. Acknowledged Shirley with a nod and a smile. Did not want to encourage her, but I also did not want to upset her. She walked up and gave me an awkward hug while I was playing my recorder solo, shouting something into my ear.

Shirley sauntered over to the bar. A few minutes later she returned and put her telephone number into my jeans pocket. Shoved it in there real deep while I took a step backwards. Tim noticed and grinned lecherously. After our set, I managed to slip out the door while Shirley was preoccupied playing Barrel-Pong.

Some Academy kids approached me in the parking lot after the show. They tried to sell me a Rolex. After talking me into buying them a six-pack from Kwik Sak, one of them produced an aluminum baseball bat. Thought they were going to mug me, but we ended up taking turns beating the crap out of an old television set by the curb. In bed by midnight.

SATURDAY, MARCH 5

Arrived to campus early to catch up on some work. Witnessed Carlos loading a deer carcass into the back of his pickup. When he looked up and saw me, he said, jokingly, "Are you ready for your breakfast?"

A student requested *The Buckminster Fuller Reader*. After I found it for him, I turned to Amber, who was busy weaving an *ojo de dios*. "Imagine having your own reader," I said. "What would be in *The Amber Womack Reader*?"

"My seminal works on whales," she said without skipping a beat. "What's in *The Steven Miller Reader*?"

"Mostly shit I wrote in grad school. A little music criticism. Some appallingly bad poetry. An incomplete Vivaldi concordance table I made for reference until I discovered someone had already done one. A sad, slim volume. Vanity press. But beautifully bound, naturally," I said. "Oh, and maybe a couple of pieces on demonurgy," I added, recklessly.

Amber's face turned dark. "Demonurgy," she repeated.

Later, a brief and disturbing encounter with Harvey in the Vault. Surprised him when I looked up suddenly. He glared at me like *I* was the problem, then pushed some books onto my face before disappearing along the ceiling. Thought I was rid of the son of a bitch. Is he going to hang around forever? Where is his master?

SUNDAY, MARCH 6

Had to get outside for a change, so I decided to try my hand at gardening. Was still brooding over my encounter with Harvey.

While I was bent over, someone pinched my butt. "Whatcha doing, Dollface?" said Vee. "Aren't you cold?"

"The yard's still a wreck after the winter. Weeds want pulling, grass mowing, leaves raking."

"Toby's falling down on the job, poor dear." Vee surveyed my work, then probed the soil with her toe. "Did you pull up my bulbs?"

"What's a bulb? Guess I did. Sorry!" A cloud passed over Vee's face, but she invited me up to do laundry later.

After cleaning myself up, I went upstairs. Green Bug brought her dirty clothes over, so I guess you could say it was a laundry party. Dawn teaches Art at the museum. Short and marshmallowy, with long mousy hair, feathered bangs, big round Coke-bottle glasses, cherubic moon-face. Gap between her two front teeth. She and Vee met while studying at the Sorbonne. While Dawn was telling Sorbonne tales, I fingered Vee's panties. Pulled them out of my pocket and tossed them to her. Vee held them up quizzically before busting a gut laughing. Dawn stopped talking.

"Wondered what happened to these!" said Vee. She looked at me slyly. Does she think I stole them? She is clearly not upset. She set the panties aside. "Help me fold this fitted sheet."

"Why not just roll it up?" I said.

"Only a guy would say that."

"If you prick me, do I not bleed?" I joked, eliciting polite chuckling from the girls. "You both went to the Sorbonne, and then you came back here?" I asked, incredulously. "You're both from Fort Worth, but didn't know each other before?" Was trying to remark on the coincidental nature of their meeting.

"I'm from Dallas," replied Dawn, after a long pause. "Guess it's a small world!"

I wisely did not belabor the point.

We spent the evening boozing and talking about Hawlie, the Alamo, and travel. Vee and Dawn have visited seventeen countries between them. When Dawn mentions a foreign place, she pronounces it in that language. Instead of saying Paris like an American, she says, "Pa-ree," and instead of saying Cuba, she says, "Koo-bah." When I mentioned Cologne, she corrected me. "It's Köln." But then she said Finland instead of Suomi, so I am not sure what her game is. Dubious.

Dawn disappeared into the kitchen. She returned waving a box triumphantly in the air. "I'm going to make a pizza!"

"Check the expiration date," said Vee. "That's been in the pantry since Watergate!"

At some point during the evening, I recall drinking a Tequila Sunrise during the song "Tequila Sunrise." Too bad it was not also at sunrise. That would have been funny. Raised my glass in toast. "To burn always with this hard, gem-like flame, to maintain this ecstasy, is success in life," I mumbled, quoting Pater. Could feel myself sinking deeper and deeper into the sofa. The libations, my lingering cold, and lack of zees were catching up to me all at once. Was lying flat on my back, eyes half-closed, when Dawn announced she was going home.

"Bye-bye, Steven! It was nice to meet you!"

Reflexively, I reached my hand out to shake hers. I felt pressure and warmth. Then, a piercing shriek and snorted laughter. As Dawn squeezed between the coffee table and where I was lying, she had walked into my outstretched hand, which wedged itself snugly between her legs. By the time I had snapped to attention, the moment had passed. Dawn was now blushing, but also smiling, to my relief. Gingerly removed a lemon peel from my mouth I had been sucking on and forgotten.

"Y'all need to come down and see my new pickup!" said Dawn after regaining her composure.

Wide awake now, I followed the girls down the back steps. A mustard-colored Toyota SR-5 was parked in the driveway. When I got closer to it, I saw it was covered in little indentations, like a golf ball.

"Nice ZooLoo sticker!" I said. "But don't you drive a green Bug?" I said. "With cigarette ads all over it?"

"The Beetleboard. The ads were for Camels. Didn't tell them I smoke Viceroys. Had to sign an agreement not to park near hospitals."

"How much do they pay you?"

"Twenty a month. Had the decals removed because it's not running at the moment. Needed something to haul art stuff in, so I went ahead and bit the bullet." She slapped the hood. "'76 Long Bed Deluxe. Five-speed, with a/c and an 8-track player. Hail damage so I paid below invoice. Its 133.6 cubic-inch four has the torquiest engine and largest displacement of any truck in its class. Zero to sixty in twelve seconds. Might get a camper shell so I can take it down to Padre."

"It has the what displacement?" I said.

Dawn punched my arm playfully. She thought I was mocking her, but I have no idea what a "four" is. Like the number four? Who was this chick? She was talking like her pickup was a hot rod or something.

"Good for you, Sis!" said Vee. "But you don't mind all these pits in it?" She ran her fingers thoughtfully over the hood.

"It needed love! Besides, when I put some Cragars on it no one's going to be looking at the pits."

"Is that a gun rack?" I asked.

"Bought it from Kwality Motors on Belknap," said Dawn. "All their trucks come with them, standard. Must be a promotional thing. But I don't have a gun!"

"What are you going to put in it?" I said.

"I've got an idea!" said Vee. She bounced upstairs and returned with a clear plastic umbrella.

"Perfect!" Dawn put the umbrella into the gun rack. It fit snugly. The girls slapped each other five. As Dawn backed out of the driveway, Vee shouted, "Bye, Dollface!" Seems I have no exclusive nickname with Vee.

Dawn rolled down her window. "Steven, come see me at the museum sometime and I'll show you around."

Not sure what she could show me that I have not seen many times before.

After Dawn left, Vee said, "Look at the moon!"

We stood there for a moment admiring the full moon through a break in the trees. "Hang on a sec," said Vee. She ran back upstairs again then returned with a slice of pizza on a Tupperware plate.

"What do you think of Dawn?"

"She's nice," I said, without thinking. "She has soft cheeks."

Vee gave me a look of amusement.

"I mean, she looks like she would have soft cheeks."

"Dawn's a sweetheart."

I looked up the word "torque" while eating my pizza. It was cold but not terrible. Is there such a thing as terrible pizza?

MONDAY, MARCH 7

Up at the crack of Dawn. A word which I have subconsciously capitalized. Take that how you will.

The new Geweihsessel horn chairs and Leuchterweibchen mermaid chandeliers have arrived. Say that ten times fast! The chairs were upholstered in soft leather the color of baby aspirin. Hideous and wholly impractical for a busy reading room. Jenny estimates two hundred fifty-seven animals died in their composition.

Since it included a stretch of coastline, it was not difficult to figure out that Sherwood's map was a portion of the *Piercy Quadrangle* (1950). The town of Kenny is heavily underlined. Someone drew a heavy circle around a promontory, under which was written "Yaat." I showed the map to Randy.

"Maybe that's where Sherwood went."

"If that's the case he could have just flown there," I said. "Have you been reading Sherwood's red notebook? What does the name Krolok mean to you?"

"Nothing. Many of the pages you gave me are blank, you know," said Randy.

"That's strange." Did the photocopier malfunction? Or was it a Freudian act on my part?

"Krolok. Slavic? Probably some charlatan who promised Sherwood the secret of eternal youth and then bilked him. Bet he wears a cape."

"A modern day Snidely Whiplash," I said. "Did you ever wonder why Snidely's skin is blue?"

"Methemoglobinemia. Probably from mishandling tetranitromethane."

Brought my *futbog* to work with the intention of kicking some field goals, but there were too many students on the field. Left the ball in the Rambler for next time.

TUESDAY, MARCH 8
Found Diane and Guddu conversing in the vestibule. She seemed to be doing all the talking. They were standing awfully close together. Diane stopped speaking when I approached. We traded good mornings. I unlocked the library and we filed inside. What could those two possibly have to talk about? Talk about an odd couple.

I feel like someone has been spending time in my office. Apart from a few missing items, there is no hard evidence, although someone stabbed my Artgum eraser with a pencil many times, ruining it. I suspect Amber for no other reason than she is a child.

Gig at Lord Jim's. More of a seafood restaurant with a fern bar than a nightclub. Decked out in dusty nautical appurtenances like lifebuoys, nets, and glass fishing floats. A lifeboat hung upside-down from the ceiling. Light fixtures made out of ship's steering wheels. What is the word for those? Uncle Daryl would know. He would love this place.

While Tim warmed up at full volume, I excused myself to change in the men's room. It had the highest urinal I have ever seen. Had to stand on my tiptoes to use it. When I emerged in my stage attire, the hostess shushed me. Why are you shushing *me*? Do you see an instrument in my hands? No, you do not.

During our set, the same hostess who shushed me came up during the middle of a song and asked us if we could "turn it down a couple of octaves."

"What are we doing here?" I hissed to Bonnie. Got into it a little bit with her afterwards when I complained that we were playing too many gigs. "I have a job, you know," I said.

"You should have thought of that before," she snapped. Where does she really think all this is going?

It was not until we were packing up our gear that I realized we had been the warm-up act for a jazz duo called Just Tom & Jerry. All limbs and afros. Fender Rhodes and guitar. Both seemed irritated that we were taking so long to get out of their way. They were playing "Cry Me a River" before I could even return for my gig bag.

WEDNESDAY, MARCH 9

Went to the mall to find something for Jenny's birthday. I perigrinated from store to store, searching in vain for something special. When I got home, Hawlie was in the driveway surrounded by a Stonehenge of junk.

"What's that?" I pointed at what looked like a small appliance.

"Bilby. Fridge for motorhomes, boats. Manufactured Down Under. Don't make 'em no more."

"Does it work?"

"Rewired myself." He gestured at it as if to say, "You can pick it up."

The Bilby appeared to be clean and in pretty decent shape. The interior passed the smell test. "How much?"

"Twenty."

"Steep. How about fifteen?"

Hawlie wrote a large "21" on his clipboard, holding it up for me to see. It was oddly convincing.

"But you said twenty."

"That was before I knew it was worth fifteen," he said, in a rare complete sentence.

"I'll think about it." In the short time it took me to set the Bilby down, Hawlie was already fiddling with something else.

Spent much of the morning designing the picture sleeve for our upcoming single. Have been making most of the flyers for our gigs, playing Brother Dominic on the brand ass-spanking new xerox machine outside L.F.'s office. Much of the artwork comes from *National Geographic* and a stack of Dover pictorial archive collections I got at last year's library book sale.

Studied Sherwood's red notebook until my eyes began to glaze over, then watched the after-school special *The Horrible Honchos*. Went out one more time to get Jenny a birthday gift. Usually give books as gifts but I have no idea what Jenny likes to read. Finally settled on a crystal pendant from Baubles & Beads. On my way home, I also got her a Genesis tape from Peaches in case I decided the pendant was too romantic.

THURSDAY, MARCH 10

The word of the day is "analogue." I deliberately pronounced it "anal log" to annoy Jo Ann, savoring the moment her mouth slackened into a frown. "Reynard the Fox has its anal log amongst the Kafirs," I said. I can play Jo Ann's emotions like a pawn shop trombone.

A student came up to discuss a lost book while I was covering for Monty at the circulation desk. I like to joke around with the students. Brandishing my paper plate shiv, I laughed like Snidely Whiplash, then said in his voice, "Ten dollar replacement fee, or...I'll have off your pinky."

Such horseplay usually solicits uneasy laughter. This time, the student, probably some mama's boy from Engineering, regarded me in confusion and alarm. I avoided his gaze and stamped his books in silence. Curses! Foiled again!

"These are due March 31," I said. The mama's boy gathered his books and scurried away.

Today's meeting agenda:

> Access to Baumann Collection
> Who is allowed in the Vault?
> New chairs and chandeliers
> New signs
> Professor Whipple's missing cushion
> Gifts
> Potty incident.

Presented my sign proposal, which is inspired by the signs at the airport. Brown with white lettering. Helvetica type for legibility from a distance. Dixie seemed annoyed that I have taken an interest in the matter. As punishment, she has asked me to go to A.C.L.A. next month. I dread it, although it would be nice to see Danh again.

On my way to Lot C after work, I found a piece of chalk on the ground. When I passed the Benedict Hall sign, I scrawled "Eggs" at the top.

FRIDAY, MARCH 11

This morning I had just sat down at my desk when I realized I had left my Chap Stick in the Rambler. The one in my desk was missing (again), so I walked back out to Lot C. Took the scenic route. When I emerged from the trees, I spotted Diane walking away from the Rambler.

It was drizzling hard so I cupped my hands over my glasses. "Are you looking for me?" I said.

"What? No, why do you ask?"

"Thought I saw you by my car."

Diane laughed insincerely. "That's your car?" A gust of wind blew her hair into her face.

After I grabbed my Chap Stick, Diane and I hurried back to the library together. Along the way, she asked a lot of questions about me, the library, and the Baumann Collection. She had a way of putting me at ease, and I found myself hemorrhaging information. Probably a good thing she did not ask me for my social security number. Tried asking her a few questions, but she was evasive when it came to her own background. When I asked her what a ship's steering wheel was, however, she seized on that subject matter. It is all we spoke about the rest of the way back to the library. She insists it is just called "the wheel."

This, I doubted. "If you said to someone 'I'm looking for a wheel,' they would think you were talking about some other kind of wheel."

"Depends on whom you were talking to," she said.

Harrington showed up unannounced, wanting to go down to the Vault. Decided not to fight it. Discovered boxes of Baumann material had been opened. Their contents were stacked haphazardly on the floor in piles taller than me. I looked at Harrington.

"Someone must be playing a joke," I said.

"A rum sort of joke," he said, ruefully. "No human being would stack books like this."

Harrington has no idea how accurate that statement probably was. But how did Harvey stack the piles so high? And how would he have gotten in? Unless the door did not click shut again. I glanced at an air vent, from which a long cobweb fluttered. I thought about the hobbit room.

Harrington took in the extent of the Baumann material. "How much of this did you say has been cataloged?" he asked.

When I shrugged, his countenance relaxed a bit. We spoke of Sherwood.

"Sherwood solicited the donation of materials from Baumann himself," explained Harrington. "A trinket here. A bauble there." He began to sing: "Baubles, bangles. Hear how they jing, jinga-linga."

I nodded to indicate I knew the song.

Harrington continued. "Mr. Burnside became involved at some point, developing his own personal relationship with Baumann. Baumann was a Porteous alum, you know. Now, a man claiming to be one of Baumann's relatives came forward and contested the gift. He insisted it should have remained part of the estate and thus should never have been given away. He even produced a dodgy document. Baumann's last will."

"Porteous's lawyers squashed the guy like a june bug," I said. "We never heard from him again." Am still having trouble reconciling Sherwood's remarks about Harrington and the man himself. He is clearly not daft. Just eccentric? "L.F. Burnside went fucking crazy."

To show my appreciation to Vee for doing all my laundry, I took her out to dinner at the Italian Inn. We waited to be seated. "I could live here," I said, surveying the cozy interior.

"Me, too!" said Vee. "The bed could go over there, and the TV over there. Even the graffiti is charming. The one on Lancaster has better ambiance, though."

The only table available was in a stall. It was intimate and I assume what most people would consider romantic. A mountain of dried wax with a candle on top emerged from an oversized bottle of chianti on the table. Vee and I ordered the veal parmesan, washed down with a bottle of Meier's Mellow Burgundy. Our Hungarian waitress said "thanks a lot" after everything she did. It sounded facetious but I think English was not her mother tongue.

We examined the graffiti together. I read one aloud. "I asked her for a divorce. And she said yes!"

Vee frowned. "Loretta is sexy but Steve is sexier," she read. "Is this you?"

"I don't know anyone named Loretta," I lied. Of all the booths we had to sit in this one.

The sounds of a mandolin neared, followed by a knock on the doors to our stall. The mandolinist deftly opened them with his foot without missing a note of "Girl, You'll Be a Woman Soon." Cheeky bastard. I watched his fingers carefully as they danced around the fretboard. Man, this guy was good. Beautiful voice, too. When he was done, Vee stood and whispered something in his ear. He grinned broadly and bowed before retreating, bumping the doors shut with his butt. He was now serenading the people in the next stall.

Vee and I were getting along great. She probably gets along great with everyone. She laughed at all my jokes and touched my hand twice. When her leg slid between mine, I resisted the urge to clamp mine around it. "This is not a date," I reminded myself. But what if she thought it was? I cannot rule that out. I never said it was not a date and she never asked. It did not help when she took out a pen and wrote our names on the wall in sloppy cursive. Was that a plus, an ampersand, or a heart?

While waiting for the check, we discussed what to do next. "The tractor pulls start at the convention center tonight," I said.

"Are you serious?" said Vee.

We ended up seeing *The Sting* at the Village Opera House because Vee likes Robert Redford. When we approached the ticket window, the attendant started making *beetle-o beetle-o* noises at us with his voice. It was Turtle Man mimicking my bass playing style. Presented my Q-Card but he waved us in with a grandiloquent gesture. Saved me four bucks. Still have no idea what his name is. Feels too late to ask now. Pretty sure I have seen him talking to Bonnie, but I have never really heard him speak. Am beginning to wonder if he is mute or just communicates with noises.

Vee and I shared a bag of popcorn. My fingertips smelled like butter but I resisted the urge to go wash my hands because I would have had to climb over Vee in the dark. I furtively wiped them on my socks.

Vee talked a lot during the show. One of my pet peeves, even though I am often guilty of it myself. This time I did not mind so much. Had difficulty enjoying the show anyway because of its anachronistic use of ragtime music in the thirties which by then was passé.

"See that guy?" she said. "That's James Sloyan. He's well-traveled. He lived in Rome, Capri, and Milan. In interviews he sounds super intelligent. There's nothing sexier, you know, than a big swinging brain. Did you see *Between Time and Timbuktu*? He played Proteus."

On our way out to the Rambler, Vee walked with her hand in my back pocket. *Play it cool*, I repeated. Like a mantra. Played it cool all the way home and went to bed alone, my friendship with Vee intact.

SATURDAY, MARCH 12

Was disappointed that Diane showed up to work. On Saturdays it is usually just me and a fox or two. She came to see me in my office, sitting on my desk in a knee-length denim skirt. "What are you working on?" she asked, staring intently at a pile of Baumann material. I slapped a stack of Ignoramus Blowhard festschrifts.

"What's this?" she asked, picking up a flier for this evening's gig at the Mother Lode.

"I'm in a band."

"No kidding?" said Diane. "What do you play?"

I pantomimed the bass: "*Beetle-o, beetle-o...*"

She looked at me appreciatively.

"I'll put you on the guest list!" I blurted.

"Show me the Vault," she said.

Only Sherwood and Randy know I call it the Vault. Everyone else says "storage," as in, "Steven, will you please take this item back down to storage."

"Okay," I replied, eagerly. "Have to take these festschrifts down anyway." Could not believe I heard myself saying this.

Diane followed me to the elevator. One of the wheels on my book cart wobbled crazily. We passed Guddu. I swear he and Diane locked eyes as they passed, like they were communicating. Presently, we heard a *boom-tic, boom-tic* coming from somewhere. When the elevator doors opened, Spunt emerged wearing aviators, drumming on an empty book cart. "What's up, pussycats?" he said.

So like Spunt to substitute 'up' for 'new.' Let Diane get in first, and when I rolled my book cart over the threshold, the bum wheel fell off and disappeared into the gap. It landed with a *bang* at the bottom of the elevator shaft.

"Oh, no!" Diane gasped.

I cannibalized a wheel from another cart. Soon Diane and I were alone in the Vault together. I pulled the door shut behind us. We now stood in complete darkness. Thought it would be funny to not turn the lights on immediately, so I just stood still and did not say anything. Diane did not speak, either. Several moments passed. The only sound was the soft rush of air from the ventilation system. Another romantic situation? Something squeezed my thigh and I jumped.

"Yah!" I yelled, and turned on the lights. "The Vault is a designated shelter from tornadoes and the H-bomb," I said, keeping my cool.

Diane inhaled deeply. "I love the smell of old books."

"Oxidative degradation and dust," I said. "If they made a men's cologne that smelled like that, I would buy it. *La Voûte pour Homme.*"

Diane jiggled the door handle of the thesis cage. "What's in here?" she asked.

"Theses," I replied. I guided Diane among the shelves, pointing out the Dalí Bible, Charles Mingus' cat training treatise, and the only extant copy of the 1684 English translation of Chorier's *Satyra sotadica*. Showed her all the Goudiana crap, the *Yellow Book*, first editions of all the horrid "Northanger" novels by Parsons, Lathom, Sleath, et al. and an incunable or two.

"Here's one," I said.

Diane read the title aloud. "*Shindai: The Art of Japanese Bed-Fighting*. This is a hoot! But why is it down here?" I showed her the inscription on the title page.

"Oh, my!"

Diane fondled everything. Did not mention the white cotton gloves we are supposed to wear. "Here's a fine example of anthropodermic bibliopegy," I said. Read the label aloud: "'Skin from around the wrist of a man who died in the North Texas Hospital for the Insane, 1891. Tanned by J.S.B.'" Diane stared at the macabre object wide-eyed while clutching my shoulder, then shrieked when a silverfish wriggled from the spine.

As I shelved the festschrifts, Diane lingered among the uncataloged materials amassed in towering piles. "What's going to happen to all this?" she asked, making a grand gesture with her arm.

"That's all gift material to be evaluated for the library's collection. Those boxes, too. It's been languishing down here for a while. Being chronically short-staffed, we're just now getting around to dealing with it. Most of the art objects are, or were, at least, in Sherwood's office, though I have an Antioch Chalice on my desk that I'm using for paper clips. Suppose L.F. is in charge of that stuff now."

"*The* Antioch Chalice?"

"Reproduction."

Diane produced a joint, which we shared in silence. At one point, she removed her scarf and sweater, revealing a tight black polyester blouse. "Why is it so hot in here? This heat can't be good for the books." Inexplicably, she did a jumping jack. This move caught me by surprise. All I could do was just stare, enchanted.

Coconut's is a restaurant with a stage behind a short wall with a space on top for potted plants. Their fronds drooped down either side of the wall. Diners can only see the musicians from the waist up. Not sure they could see Dave II at all.

Showed up early to eat pizza with the others. Tim flicked a pepperoni onto the back of my hand, which seared my flesh momentarily before I understood what was happening. "Check mate!" he cried. When Tim eats pizza, he sticks his tongue out to meet the slice before taking a bite. It is barbaric.

Just as Hooda Thunk launched into "American Pie," Diane showed up. She smiled and waved. Motioned for her to join us, making hasty introductions between songs. Diane is not Tim's type. Her tits are too small. Nevertheless he spent a lot of time leaning over and making comments into her ear while I expounded upon McLean's lyrics into her other ear. Who knows what kind of *yaje* Tim was feeding her.

By the time we took the stage, I began to realize that not only was I exhausted, my anxiety over Sherwood was taking its toll. Not to mention Harvey's existence. Am I going insane? I would be lying if I said I was not also irritated that Tim was working Diane. Stuck it to him when I plugged my guitar in and it made a percussive pop. This made him jump, which Diane witnessed.

"I can name that song in one note, Tom," I said into the mic, eliciting a few chortles from the audience, though "customers" might be a more apt word. During our set, I saw Diane talking to Turtle Man. Or pumping him for information, rather, judging by her body language. Pump away, Diane! Turtle Man knows nothing.

After we blasted through every song we knew, people started making requests. At first, Tim balked but he relented when the owner's wife came out and said if we played a set of songs people know there is an extra fifty in it for us. My share would pay for the pizza and beer I consumed, so I was hunky dory until someone requested "Respect."

Tim must have heard me groan, because that motherfucker immediately played the opening riff in E flat! "Check mate," he mouthed, wordlessly. Muddled through it the best I could. As the song surpassed the six-minute mark, however, my fingers began to cramp. When the song finally ended, some geezer handed me a drink napkin on which he had scrawled, "Your band is to [*sic*] damn loud. Ruins everything."

The rest of the audience was less discerning. Between songs, a waitress brought me a drink. "Compliments of the young lady," she said, pointing at an attractive woman in a low-cut dress.

For our last number, we played "Respect" again by request. Beat Tim to the punch this time by starting it a step higher than Aretha's. A pain in the ass for me to play, but more importantly a pain in the ass for Tim to sing. Totally worth it. We all played badly (except for Dave II), but the drunken crowd ate it up.

"Thanks, everybody!" said Tim when the song concluded. "Should any of you be in Austin tomorrow night, come see us at Mother Earth. Good night!"

After one upping Tim all evening, I was feeling confident. I approached the young lady who had bought me a drink.

"Hi, I'm Steven," I said. "Thanks for the whiskey!" I offered her my hand but she did not shake it.

"It wasn't for you," she said, sourly. "Told that dumb bitch it was for the lead guitarist."

I picked up the drink, which I had not yet touched. "Well, here, I'll give it to him now." I turned to Tim. "Hey, Tim!"

While we were packing up, Diane approached. "You guys were great! I'm impressed!" As I was rolling up a cord, Diane said, "Could somebody give me a ride?"

"I would love to give you a ride," said Tim, who now towered between us. The young lady who bought him a drink stood awkwardly to the side.

"I can do it, Tim. I know where she lives," I said. Diane looked surprised.

"I choose Steven," said Diane. "But thanks for offering, Tim!"

If Tim was pissed, he did not show it. Check mate, cocksucker.

As Diane and I got into the Rambler she asked, "Why is there a hand painted on the hood?"

Her question caught me off guard. "Deranged library patron," I said. "Where to?" Tim's van was blocking us in.

"I'm staying at the Women's Faculty Club," said Diane. "I thought you knew." She dug through her purse. "Phooey. I forgot my compact. Can I use the rearview?"

Diane leaned in close so she could see herself, then adjusted the mirror so she could apply lipstick by streetlight. While I studied her reflection, she noticed me watching and smiled, then smacked her lips.

"You know, you don't move at all on stage."

I nodded. "So I've been told."

Diane opened her purse. "Dynamint?"

Did my breath stink?

Playfully stuck my tongue out a little bit, and she carefully placed the mint on the end. We both laughed.

"The orange ones are the best," I said.

"So hard to find."

"Isn't that always the case when you like something?"

Tim was taking his sweet time. Finally, his tail lights came on and he slowly rolled away. Have really got to get rid of that hand. I think it is keeping me from getting laid. If not, something is.

SUNDAY, MARCH 13

Slept in. Went down to the Texaco for smokes. Returned to find Hawlie in the backyard. He was squinting in the sun up at Vee's bedroom window, shielding his eyes with a clipboard.

"Ahoy, Mr. Hawlie!"

He lowered the clipboard and regarded me with no recognition in his eyes.

"Got something for you, Mr. Hawlie. Let me go inside and get it." Returned with the Greenaway book Fred had given me.

"Will you take this and ten bucks for the Bilby?"

Hawlie handed me his clipboard so he could examine the book. He held it up and scrutinized it, looking for flaws, I suppose. "Foxing," he observed. When he was evidently satisfied, he clapped the book closed. "Fifteen," he said.

"Twelve." I am awful at haggling, but I also did not want to pay any more than I had to.

Hawlie handed me the book and walked toward the shed. Was that a "yes"? Upon returning from the shed, he regarded the fridge and appeared to be doing math in his head. He scrawled a number on his clipboard and held it up. It said "17."

"Good deal," I sighed. I pulled out my billfold. Hawlie watched my hands closely with his mouth half open, as I removed and counted sixteen bucks.

"That's all I have at the moment." He rolled his eyes toward the sky as if to say, "So help me, Lord," then said, "The book, too."

The Bilby is mine!

Picked up Fred after lunch then hauled ass on the back roads. We got to Austin in four hours flat. The road less traveled is scenic and peaceful.

We arrived early to Mother Earth. There were people sleeping in a couple of the booths. Empty cups and bottles were strewn everywhere. It smelled like cigarette smoke and stale beer. Clubs are disgusting with the lights on. After a quick sound check, we had time to have a relaxing dinner down the street at a Mexican place that had killer margaritas. Ordered the Tres Hombres platter which was way too much food. Of course, I ate it all. Got some hot sauce on my monk robe. Dislike changing in public restrooms, so I had driven down in my stage attire.

"Did your momma make that for you?" said Tim.

Dave II smiled.. When he teases it seems like it is all in good fun. When Tim teases it tends to be mean-spirited.

By the time we got back to Mother Earth, only the stage lights were on. The people in the booths had disappeared and the trash was gone. When I took a seat on a bench to dig something out of my mansack, I sat in a pool of sick. Fortunately, I had a change of clothes in the Rambler. Brown work shirt, plaid work slacks, and golden boots do not look rock and roll. The shirt and pants were a poly blend so at least they were not wrinkled. Went ahead and put on a tie. I hope it made my outfit seem deliberate. Ducked into the ladies' room to regard my getup in the full-length mirror. Who am I supposed to be?

"You're wearing that?" said Bonnie.

Fred shook his head. "Kemosabe," he groaned.

"Job interview?" sneered Tim. "We go on in ten minutes."

Kept quiet about the puke. Tim would have had a field day with that. "I'm making a statement," I explained, enigmatically.

"And that statement is?"

I struggled to think of a witty reply. "Shenanigans!" was the best I could muster.

"Ladies, and gentlemen, Mr. Ward Cleaver!" said Tim when I stepped forward to take my trombone solo.

Tim convinced Fred and me to hang around after our set. He had met some chicks who he said were horny and ready to party.

We all crammed thigh to thigh into a wooden booth. Drinks appeared. Felt self-conscious in my work clothes. The blonde to my left was digging me. She grabbed my tie a couple of times. It tightened uncomfortably around my neck.

"I am Ursula, from Ulm." Ursula from Ulm stuck out her tongue and I placed my cherry on it. After she finished chewing, her tongue reappeared. The stem was tied into a simple knot.

What did we have here? I did not see how such a feat was possible, unless she had ingested a stem earlier and tied it in advance. But no one would do that. I raised my eyebrow in appreciation.

"Your tie. It's so *long*," observed Ursula, playfully. I removed it and she put it around her own neck. In a rare moment of quick thinking, I seized this opportunity to tie it for her. Tying a tie around someone else's neck is not as easy as tying it around your own. Our foreheads touched as I fussed over the knot as long as I dared. Finally settled on a double Flemish loop (from the framed sailor knots chart hanging above the toilet in Aunt Wanda's bathroom).

"You have the cutest nose!" she said, in a thick German accent that recalled Colonel Hogan's. She caressed the tip playfully, then leaned in close to study it. I swallowed hard. "It has a little dimple on the end. You can barely feel it." Her eyes darted from my nose to my eyes, and back again. One of her eyelashes was coming off. Something about this chick seemed familiar, but I did not know anyone with hair that huge. Except for Aunt Wanda.

We shouted over the dueling guitars of Too Smooth. I learned that Ursula is a Virgo and a Poli Sci major. The more we drank the more we touched. She leaned into me when I put my arm around her. Her hairspray fumes irritated my throat. Held my cigarette farther away from her hair, just in case. Whenever I made her laugh, she rubbed my stomach or stuck her thumb into the front of my shirt. When her wandering fingers encountered my trombone mouthpiece, she gave it a little squeeze through my slacks as if trying to figure out what it was. She grasped the end of my belt and held on. It was too noisy to have a conversation. Was afraid of turning her off by repeating "What?" so I found myself nodding and smiling at times without understanding. Who knows what I agreed to.

Tim cut through all the noise by reciting the chorus to "Subways of Your Mind" in a single, prolonged belch, which I could smell. This was a dig at me.

Ursula's fingers found my amulet. I suddenly stood up. "Gotta drain the lizard," I said.

"I'm coming with you," Ursula whispered breathily into my ear. She led me by my belt into the ladies' room. She pulled me into a stall and closed the door, then gave me a long, wet kiss.

"Ladies first, Ursula from Ulm," I said.

"Thank you, Herr Cleaver," she giggled.

While I watched, she squirmed out of her satin hip huggers and started peeing noisily. Noted a birthmark shaped like a butterfly near her bush. I looked away. Undid my belt and unzipped my slacks, letting them fall to the floor.

"How do you go when it's like that?" said Ursula. She mashed it down with her finger, then watched it boing back up with a smirk.

"I don't." Especially not with someone staring at it like that.

When someone began puking in the adjacent stall, Ursula frowned and pulled her pants back up. I reluctantly followed suit.

"*Das ist schade*," she said. What the hell just happened there?

After Too Smooth's encore, Ursula offered to help carry things out to the Rambler. She waited while I collected the rest of my stuff.

As I returned for my gig bag, Ursula said, "I'll watch your purse for you," referring to my mansack, which I was lugging back and forth around my neck.

"Thanks, I've got it."

"Don't be ridiculous." She reached for the strap of my mansack.

"I said I've got it."

When we settled in the Rambler, I momentarily caught a glimpse of Ursula in the interior light. Gaunt features, sunken cheeks. She must have been wearing a pound of makeup. My tie hung loosely from her neck. "Where to?" Could still smell puke from earlier.

"I know a place," she said. "Go out this way and turn left." She curled up and laid her head in my lap. This made it difficult to steer. Had to elevate my arms to keep from elbowing her in the jaw. The Rambler hit a bump in the road.

"What's that sound?" she asked.

"Just my amplifier. Springs will be springs." Still had to piss pretty badly. After several miles Ursula sat up and told me to turn left into a U Totem parking lot. "Get me some Viceroys?"

"You got it." I adjusted my balls.

"And a couple of Tabs." She shook a flask and smiled.

While I was in the U Totem, I had the presence of mind to remove my amulet and tuck it into one of my socks. When I returned to the car, Ursula was fixing her eyelash. Waited until she was finished before putting the car in gear.

"Turn left at the next light," she said.

It was late. We were all alone on the road. Waiting at the traffic light felt unbearably long. I was impatient to get laid. Why was Ursula into me? Guess chicks need to get laid, too.

"Want to see a magic trick?" I said.

Ursula cocked her head.

"Gonna make this light turn green." I turned around and reached way down to the floor where my mansack was. Discreetly took out the codex and shoved it roughly under the seat. Better safe than sorry. The moment I turned to grip the steering wheel the light turned green. "Presto!" I said.

Ursula applauded. "What did you do?" She craned her neck to see into the backseat.

"Nothing. Beer bottle rolling around was driving me crazy. It's just when you're preoccupied with something else the light always turns green."

Ursula directed me to a parking spot at the base of a wooded hillside. It was windy and chilly, so I grabbed a jacket. Ursula took me by the hand and led me up a steep flagstone stair. We climbed carefully to avoid stumbling in the dark. When we reached the top, we found ourselves atop a high bluff. Searchlights criss-crossed the sky from the campus, illuminating the clouds. Something must have been going on, somewhere. We took in the Austin skyline, then found a place to sit on a wide, low stone wall.

Ursula prepared our drinks. We clanked our cans together.

"*Prost!*" she said. Rum and Tab was not as disgusting as I thought it would be. But that was probably because there was so much rum and so little Tab. She held out her palm so I slapped her five.

"No, silly," she said. "Viceroys."

I gave them to her and we both lit up. Something flapped by. "There goes a bat!" said Ursula.

"There goes rabies."

Taking my mansack with me to go take a whizz seemed conspicuous, so I left it behind. Found a discreet spot around the bend and hosed down some cacti for what felt like an eternity. Was starting to feel shitfaced. I glanced over my shoulder but did not see Ursula of Ulm.

On my way back, I worried I was going to walk off the cliff. Was also worried about making a move. Spotted the glow of Ursula's cigarette. As I sat down, she blew smoke out of her nostrils, then raised her flask to my lips. I swallowed every drop.

We kissed. She stood up briefly so she could straddle me. She put her hands on my chest and pushed me back into a stony column. "My neck," I groaned. As she fumbled with my belt buckle, I slid my hands up her blouse. She swatted them away. "Your hands are freezing!" I closed my eyes and let her do her thing.

Woke up alone and shivering. My hands were tied over my head to a pillar with my own necktie. My barn door was wide open. After struggling to escape my bonds, I sat up and looked around wildly. Felt a big hand push me back down. "Ursula!" I hissed. No response. Had a splitting headache. My mansack was nowhere to be seen. After a quick search of the area, I stumbled down the long flight of steps in the dark. My heart was racing. I felt ill.

The Rambler was still there. It was unlocked and the keys were in the ignition. Ursula must have taken one look at the missing reverse button and gotten cold feet. The codex was where I had stashed it but my annotated xerox of *Linguae dordica* was gone. My music gear and football were untouched. An apology on the windshield turned out to be a parking ticket. I got screwed, all right. But not the good kind of screwed.

Released the brake and let the Rambler roll backwards into the street. As the engine caught and my headlights came on I spotted my mansack. Its contents were scattered across the pavement. Got out and collected them. Billfold, gone. My Chap Stick was missing. Found one of Figaro's cat toys in the gutter next to this diary. Must remember to give it to him.

MONDAY, MARCH 14

I-35 home. Thought I might be late to work. In an effort to stay awake behind the wheel, I sang along to the radio at the top of my lungs. When the words failed me, I simply shouted like Hey Now. I rubbed my eyes and slapped my cheeks. Tried to recall spells from the codex, reciting as much as I could. I croaked out phrases in Dordic. I thought of the Stone Fox. Was wary of becoming hypnotized by the white stripes on the pavement. Stepped on my high beams. My head throbbed and my heart was pounding. There was a funny taste in my mouth. I licked my dry, cracked lips and grimaced.

A big rig roared by, blaring his horn. I was idling on the Mixmaster. "Tarkus" blared from the radio. The sun was shining. A spider dangled in my face. I smashed it with my palm, cracking the windshield. Another big rig passed, the driver flipping me the bird. I floored it.

After brushing my teeth, I slapped on some Aqua Velva. It stung but it gave me life. Put on clean clothes and wolfed down a Breakfast Square. Took the back roads to work out of habit and got stuck in North Hi Mount school traffic. Got to the library about forty-five minutes late, which was duly observed by Dixie.

A warm, sunny day, the kind that makes you want to nap under a tree. Getting drugged makes you want to do that as well. When was the last time I stayed up all night?

I quickly lost control of the day. Found myself overwhelmed by festschrifts. Dropped my pencil sharpener on the floor while emptying it, which made a mess. Caught up with Randy on the break room patio, where I recounted my wild night.

"Did she slip you a mickey?" he said.

"My thoughts exactly. Don't think I've ever zonked out like that before. Didn't have that much to drink. Two or three margaritas and maybe four beers. And just the rum and Tab."

"Tab," drawled Randy. "That's what kicked your ass, dude."

"She got *Linguae dordica*. What Poly Sci major reads Latin?"

"Tell me again, why do you carry the codex with you everywhere?"

"Because I'm still translating it. Whenever I have a free moment I chip away at it. Thank [word scratched out] Ursula didn't take this copy. She probably couldn't read my handwriting, anyway."

"You've got to be fucking kidding me! Did you just say the demon's name again?" said Randy.

"Sorry! It just popped out! What's Harvey going to do, kick my ass?"

"Who the hell is Harvey?"

"Jimmy Stewart's imaginary pal from the eponymous film. Except our Harvey isn't imaginary."

Randy raised his eyebrows. "Our Harvey?"

"Fine. My Harvey."

Randy sighed.

"Don't know what his real name is," I said. "Why can't you say a demon's name?"

"You should know better than anyone," said Randy. "But seriously, it's long been believed that knowing one's true name gives you power over them. Isis tricked Ra into revealing his name so she could pass it along to Horus. We all know how that turned out. Marduk has so many aliases no one knows what his real name was. I can assure you it's not Marduk."

"We give our names freely now," I said. "Do you ever notice how people tend to look like their names? I mean, I always thought you looked like a Randall."

"Socrates takes the position that when things are given names, the name reflects some of the essence of that thing."

"Steven is derived from Greek and means 'wreath' or 'crown' and by extension 'reward, honor, fame.' That doesn't sound like my essence at all."

"Not talking about the name your mama gave you. Socrates discusses the difference between conventional and true—or natural—names in *Cratylus*."

"Aw, crap. Just thought of something. If Ursula has my billfold, that means she knows my address. She lives in Austin, though. At least I think she does."

On my way down to the Vault this afternoon, I stepped out of the elevator to discover the metal door opposite that is usually locked stood open. Peeked inside, and saw a long corridor, filled with pipes, meters, panels, and whatnot.

"Hello? Carlos?" I walked down the corridor into what I guessed was a boiler room. Tried another door and turned on the light, to reveal a tiny room with a small desk inside. The wall was covered in keys on hooks. Each key was attached to a wooden keychain bearing a room number. The one for 108 was missing. Happen to know the room number for the Vault is 108 because there is a small tag above its door that says so. Was it taken recently, or has it been missing for years? The one for my office, Room 205, was also missing, which is too bad, because I wanted the wooden keychain for my key. Grabbed the one to Sherwood's office. It might come in handy.

Found the Vault door ajar. The light was on. "Carlos?" I said.

"Hello!" said a voice. It was Harrington. Found him sitting on a stool, digging through a box of Baumann materials. I was speechless.

Harrington must have read the expression on my face. "The young woman at the information desk let me in," he said.

"Jo Ann?"

"The other one."

"The other one?" I repeated. "Amber?"

"That's it."

Does Harrington not understand Amber is just a child?

"Books are a sort of cloistral refuge from the vulgarities of the world," said Harrington.

"Indeed they are. I will leave you to them."

Upon writing this entry, the tip of my pencil encountered a greasy spot on the page. Scratching and sniffing produced the unmistakable scent of Chap Stick. Dropped a pinch of pencil shavings on it which revealed the word "Die." As in croak? Or was Ursula interrupted by the meter maid before she could finish writing something in German? How much did she read?

TUESDAY, MARCH 15

Stone Fox's birthday. Cupcakes in the break room while listening to a cassette of *Wind & Wuthering*. It was my gift to her along with the crystal pendant. Jenny opened them in the presence of our coworkers, which was somewhat uncomfortable. Probably should have given the pendant to her privately.

Guddu was conspicuously absent from the festivities. I had seen him earlier looking like a whipped cur, his tail between his legs. I really wanted him to hear the Genesis tape. What has gotten into him?

"Had a lot of fun the other night," said Diane in front of Jenny. "Don't know many people here, nor do I have a car, so it was nice to get out and paint the town red." She laughed. "The Women's Faculty Club is a bit staid."

"You're working on the LC conversion?" Jenny asked Diane.

Diane nodded. "You know, the LC classification for the Bible is BS. Wonder if Herbert Putnam did that on purpose because he thought the Bible was bullshit."

"I'll find out," I said. Rushed to the reading room to do some quick research. When I returned to the break room I found Diane and Jenny conversing quietly.

"Looks like the word 'bullshit' didn't come into popular usage until World War II," I said. "Mystery solved!"

Diane and Jenny just looked at me. Jenny had a weird look on her face. Diane looked tired.

"Steven, what is 'bullshit'?"

I turned around. "Guddu! Glad you could join us."

"Bullshit is stupid talk," said Jenny. Could have sworn she glanced at Diane when she said that.

"Or nonsense," I added. "It's also a verb. If you're telling me something that's not true, you're bullshitting me."

Guddu nodded gratefully, then grinned. "Are you bullshitting Guddu now?" He then laughed, rather maniacally I thought. He then added, "Thank you for teaching Guddu this remarkable word!"

Was itching to teach him the Dordic word, but held my tongue.

"Can you give me a ride after work?" Jenny asked, once we were alone. Why do all these females need transport?

"Where does your mom live?"

"Over by the zoo."

"You don't live at home?"

"Had to get out of that house," said Jenny. "Mama is exhausting to be around. You'll understand when you meet her."

Was filling in for Jo Ann at the reference desk when Harrington approached.

"Might see the basement again?" he said. "It was most helpful."

Well why the fuck not, I thought, mentally throwing my hands in the air. Accompanied Harrington downstairs and let him into the Vault. "Let me know when you're finished so I can lock up."

"You don't know what this means," said Harrington, enigmatically.

Maybe not but I intend to find out.

We were headed down University when Jenny reached down and picked something up off the floor. "Whose lipstick is this?"

"Might be my ex's." As soon as I said that I thought of Diane. Was it hers? Or Ursula of Ulm's?

Jenny removed the lid from the lipstick and examined it. "Tell me about her. What was her name?"

"Who?"

"Your ex-girlfriend. Why did you break up?" Jenny produced a compact from her purse, then applied the lipstick, which seemed gross since people's feet had probably touched it.

"Loretta. We just kind of drifted apart," I lied. Jenny did not need to know all of that. We were almost at her mom's house anyway.

Jenny smacked her lips. "This color suit me? What do you think?"

Jenny's mom lives in a colonial-style mansionette in a neighborhood tucked behind the zoo. The place reminds me of the sanitorium from *Harvey*. Parked under an oak in the gravel driveway, then entered through the servants' entrance. The house was crammed with an astonishing array of antiques. There were tapestries, armor, and sculptures. An imposing brass Shiva. A decrepit concert grand. A carved walnut table completely covered by a cut-glass Georgian chandelier just resting on it in a massive, sparkling heap. Instantly regretted the crystal pendant I had given Jenny, having just accidentally kicked a stone that closely resembled it across a silk Isfahan rug.

"Holy crap, Jenny."

She shrugged dismissively. "My father's in the art world."

"As opposed to *being* the art world," said a voice behind us. Enter Mama Fox, dropping her keys, purse and shopping bags onto the floor before flopping down with a heavy sigh into an Eero Aarnio ball chair. She kicked off her mules, which whizzed across the room in a breeze of pepper, clove, and carnation. She looked like something from the pages of *Vogue*. Pucci caftan, fingers gilded in rings, wrists hooped in jingling silver.

"You," said Mama Fox, pointing at me. Rub my feet, would you, Darling?"

Do what? I stood with my mouth hanging open.

Mama Fox regarded me over her huge Jackie O. sunglasses. "I don't bite!" she added, in a bid to snap me out of my catalepsy.

I approached Mama Fox cautiously. As I got near her, she slid her butt forward and wiggled her feet in the air, playfully.

My eyes darted around the room. Where was Jenny? I hesitantly kneeled before Mama Fox. The bare parquet hurt my knees, so I repositioned myself as she plopped her feet heavily into my lap. She hiked up her caftan to expose a pair of long, suntanned gams. I took her doughy foot in my hand and began kneading. "Let's make some biscuits," I quipped, idiotically. "My Aunt Wanda says you don't knead biscuit dough because that will make them tough." What would Guddu make of *tough* and *dough*? Words like that must make English challenging to learn.

"What, dear?" mumbled Mama Fox, dreamily. Presently, she began groaning dramatically. "Oh, that feels heavenly!" She clearly dug what I was doing, so I kneaded some more dough before moving up to her ankles.

"Pardon these corny old hooves. I was a dancer for *years*," she drawled. "The Little Rock Civic Ballet told me I was too busty and would never do. But I showed those fuddies! By the end of '66 I was touring with Déjà Phillips. She eschewed the proscenium for other, more unorthodox venues. She brought dance to the people, you understand. Ow! Right there, darling. *Purrrrr.*" She spoke the word "purr," trilling the *r.*

"Mama!" shouted Jenny from above. "I need him!"

When I hesitated, Mama Fox shooed me away with a flick of her wrist. "And I need another husband!"

Dusted off my pants and raced up one of the curved staircases before Mama Fox made me rub anything else. When I reached the gallery, I beheld a multitude of doors. Peered through the open ones as I made my way. One room had a teenager in it, reading on a bed. She looked up from her book.

"Sorry!" I said. I strained to see what her book was.

"Do you want my sister?"

I nodded.

"Straight back at the end of the hall."

Jenny's was a large room which spanned the depth of the house, with windows along three walls, each looking out into treetops. All were open. It was still and pleasantly warm. Incense filled the air. It smelled like rain. Could hear in the distance the occasional sound of whooping gibbons or an elephant trumpeting. Clothes hung from a rack in the middle of the room, while others were flung all over the place. In one corner was a double bed covered in unjacketed LPs, pillows, teddy bears, and more clothing.

Stubbed my toe on a Brannock device, which I picked up. I was holding it when Jenny emerged from the bathroom. She had changed into shorts and a t-shirt.

"You can have it if you want it."

Against one wall there was a bookcase shaped like an irregular polygon. It was filled chiefly with shoes and colorful cats under bell jars. At the foot of the bed was a small table with a hi-fi on it, one of those all-in-one jobs with an 8-track player and built-in tuner. Resembled a console from the *USS Enterprise.* Jenny lay on her stomach, trying to find a radio station.

I crawled over her and sat with my back against the wall. Paused to admire the contours of her calves before I rested mine familiarly on top of them. Jenny found an Abba song and together we sang, "Knowing me, knowing you..." before shouting "Ah ha!" at the top of our lungs.

"Made some banana pudding while you were rubbing Mama's feet," said Jenny. "It's probably ready now. You stay put."

While Jenny was gone, picked up an issue of *Circus* and read an article about bionics. Held up my hand and made a grasping motion. What will our bodies be like in the future? She soon returned with a bowl and spoons. "Do you want animal crackers with yours? I eat animal crackers with mine."

"The ones from the book return? No, thanks. What are all those cats?"

"Those are my Sophisti-Cats," said Jenny. "They're perfume bottles. Hey, you know the Benedict Hall sign? Someone wrote 'Eggs' in front of 'Benedict.'"

I looked at Jenny. "That was me."

"You?" She looked at me searchingly. Not sure she believed me. "I thought that was so funny," she said, in a deadpan voice.

"Do you want a foot rub?" I blurted.

Jenny was silent for a moment. "Shoulders." She placed her bowl on the turntable, then asked, "Where do you want me?"

I repositioned her so she was seated in front of me, my legs on either side of her. I tentatively gripped her shoulders, feeling somewhat intoxicated.

"Hang on." She wriggled out of her bra, pulling it out through a sleeve and tossing it aside.

Gripping Jenny's shoulders again, I gently pulled her backwards and she relaxed, resting her head against my cheek. I pinched and kneaded until I ran out of ideas. My hands grew tired. Her t-shirt was now pushed up exposing her bare back. Slid my hands around her and cupped her tits. Seconds felt like years. No one moved.

Jenny spoke. "I'm going to show you a secret." She stood then turned to face me. She appeared to hesitate, then raised her t-shirt to reveal the sixth and seventh titties I have ever seen in real life (not counting Mom's). They were covered in dark purple marks.

I leaned forward for a closer look. "Who did that to you?"

"Judd," she replied, pulling her t-shirt back down and looking away, her neck aflame. Jenny lay back down on her stomach. I joined her. We lay in silence. She turned the radio dial slowly from station to station:

748-1414, 748-1414, call the Dallas Times-Herald *classifieds, get results that you...at the Spanish Galleon, we'll go overboard for you...if they're not ready, you get a free roll of film! Fotomat knows what...I got a ranch in downtown Dallas, I buy diamonds by the ton, chase cuties in my Cadillac...love ageless and evergreen, seldom seen by two, you and I will make each night the first...jackknifed big rig on the turnpike east of Belt Line...the spectacular musical production of Genesis, the masters of symphonic rock will be at Moody Coliseum, March 19...*

I seized Jenny's hand to keep her from turning the dial.

"Come with me?" she said.

"You want to go?" I was still holding her hand. "Will you marry me?" She squeezed my hand then let go.

We lay quietly for a while, lost in our own thoughts. "The Wreck of the Edmund Fitzgerald" came on which sank the mood. When it was over, I said to Jenny, "Look at me." She turned her head. "Close your eyes for a minute," I commanded. She complied and I pressed my lips against hers. They touched for no longer than three seconds. When it was over, she opened her eyes and said, "I don't think of you like that."

The door to Jenny's room flew open. "Knock, knock!" It was the chick from down the hall. Taller and heavier than Jenny. Unisex hairdo. Freckles.

"Whatcha doin'?" Shannon asked, hurling herself roughly on top of us and shoving her head between mine and Jenny's. Her elbow dug into my spine and I stifled a bark of pain. She smelled like a teenager.

"Listening to the radio," replied the Stone Fox, wearily.

WEDNESDAY, MARCH 16

Went to the museum to visit Dawn. Found her in one of the classrooms. She had just finished teaching a pottery class. Waited patiently until the parents and kids dispersed then stuck my head in the door.

Dawn was perched upon a pottery wheel, contemplating a rude pot. She looked up and smiled. "Steven! What perfect timing! Have you eaten?"

"I have not," I lied.

She stood. "Help me pick up all the scraps and slop. You can dump it in that barrel over there." She indicated a plastic trash can on casters filled with what looked like gray, muddy water.

"I'm not your performing chimp," I said, peering into the muck. Figured I might as well shove my whole arm in. I wiggled my fingers.

"Feels nice, huh?" Dawn said. "Watch out for the needles."

I grasped handfuls of clay and squeezed. While struggling to move my arm sideways, my fingers grazed what felt like something sharp. A needle! Fingers slid into a hole lined with what in retrospect were clearly teeth.

Reflexively, I jerked my arm out. The bucket erupted like Old Faithful. A shadow flew across the room in a blur before vanishing. I was now soaked in muddy water.

Dawn rushed to my side, her Dr. Scholl's clacking against the concrete floor. "Are you alright?" she said. We regarded the splattered trail of muck leading across the room and under a door.

"The kill room," she said.

Dawn fumbled with a ring of keys. She unlocked and opened the door to the kill room and we surveyed the interior. The *kiln* room, of course. With a silent *n*. The breaker panel was ajar and a ceiling tile had been displaced. My heart was in my throat. Harvey's doing. Why had he been in the barrel? If he followed me here how did he get into the barrel without being seen?

Dawn made a phone call. She spoke to someone about a rodent before hanging up. "Otis will find it, whatever it is. Would you look at this mess! But let's get you cleaned up."

Rinsed my glasses off in the sink so I could see better. Dawn tossed me an apron, which I put on over my soiled t-shirt.

"Keep it," she said. "I'll get it back next time I come over. Don't have many of those." While she mopped up, I helped wipe down the walls.

"Let's go down to the cafeteria, wanna?" said Dawn, like nothing had happened. She seemed to have no trouble accepting that an evidently amphibious rodent was hiding in a barrel of muddy water in a museum. I might believe anything now, myself.

Despite having eaten earlier, I ordered the congealed fruit salad.

Dawn looked puzzled. "Are you on a diet?"

Dawn and I took the scenic route through the exhibits. She showed me a storage room full of old taxidermy. This must be where Sherwood got his rhino head.

"This armadillo looks pissed off," I said.

"Take it."

"Really?"

"Give me something later. Surprise me."

Gig at Spencer's with Spanish Fly. That place is always so wild. Banging in the bathroom. Snorting coke off bare flesh. Tonight was the Fine Fanny contest. Many ladies wore hot pants for the occasion despite it being in the fifties outside. Guess they changed when they got here? Saw Turtle Man puking in the corner, book in hand.

"Did that slut whip you some skull?" asked Tim.

"Which slut?"

"Tall, blond skinny chick in Austin."

"Was meaning to ask you," I said. "How did she end up at our table?"

"What do you mean? I dunno."

"Who was the other girl? Were they together?"

"How should I know?" said Tim, nastily. "Hey, why the third degree?"

"Nothing. Forgot to get her number, that's all."

Tim's hostility triggered a reflexive response whereby I hissed a word of power. Either it was effective, or the gods were certainly frowning on Tim this evening. He thought he would show off during "Rock 'n' Roll Insanity" by spinning his guitar around his body. Unfortunately, the headstock punctured an asbestos ceiling tile, pieces of which rained down upon him along with rat turds. The freshly-rolled joint he had tucked behind the nut was now bent at a forty-five degree angle. On the very next song, I guess he got a shock from the microphone. He quit singing and playing momentarily and stepped back, clutching his mouth. I turned my head so he could not see me laughing.

Home late. Too buzzed to fall asleep. Contemplated my disturbing detachment from reality. Is this what being crazy feels like? Reached for Sherwood's red notebook and came across this: "While copies of spells can be made, only a few select spells are seen as worth copying. For they have been used enough times to have a clear outcome and side effects. However, they can only work if they are transcribed exactly as written. A single error results..." The last sentence was incomplete.

Have not been taking the red notebook seriously. I fail to see what it had to do with Sherwood's disappearance. I read it more for its entertainment value than for anything else. However, I found the above passage engaging enough to consider the fidelity of a xerox.

THURSDAY, MARCH 17

Worked the closing shift. It is alright once in a while but I can think of better things to do with my evenings. At least the library is pretty dead after five o'clock. Put the stuffed armadillo on the circulation desk.

"Poor thing!" declared Jenny. She took the black ribbon from around her neck and tied it around the armadillo's. "I will name you Bubba."

Left Jenny and Bubba and headed to the information desk. Harrington was waiting for me.

"Good afternoon!" he said.

I dangled the key to the Vault before him.

Harrington grinned widely. "Are you taking me to my cell?"

"I'll bring you some bread and water later."

"That's all I get for my last meal?"

Our repartee was ostensibly in jest, but this last remark troubled me. Upon returning to the information desk. Amber presented me with a plate of cookies. These turned out to be graham crackers dyed green with food coloring. "No, thanks," I said. Looked too much like Soylent Green. Was pulling up my socks when a hand touched my shoulder.

"Jesus Christ!" I said, nearly jumping out of my skin. Guddu always seems to appear out of thin air. A natural-born fox walker. This time he was wearing a plastic leprechaun mask that was too small for his face. He crumbled a Soylent Green cracker into small pieces and crammed them through the mask's tiny tongue hole. After struggling with this ineffective way of eating, he removed the leprechaun mask to reveal a mouth and chin that had turned lurid green. It was quite horrible, really. "It's people!" I declared, but he didn't get it.

"Who is St. Patrick?" said Guddu.

"A piper in colorful garb hired to lure rats away with his magic pipe," I said.

Amber pinched my arm. "That's for not wearing green," she said. "And for bullshitting Guddu." I must have confused St. Patrick with the Pied Piper.

Was surprised to hear Amber curse. Was even more surprised when Guddu pinched my nose. Hard. Must have broken a blood vessel, because my nose turned the color of a Concord grape. Pointed at my green "100 Proof Irish" button and protested, "Cut it out, both of you. I'm wearing green!"

But Guddu was not listening. He had stormed away, I assume, because I had bullshitted him. I thought about chasing him down but thought better of it.

Spunt called me Rudolph, which irritated me because my nose was purple, not red. Dixie admonished me for wearing the button at work, then asked if I had been drinking. Because of my nose, no doubt. During "Happy Trails" I discovered green puke in the 900s. Could not go home until I had found Carlos to clean it up. I picked up the radio. "Carlos! Break 1-9! What's your 10-20? You got your ears on? Come on back!"

"Why do you talk to me like that?" he crackled.

Harrington was supposed to let me know when he was done in the Vault. Did he croak himself? What was that remark about a last meal? Found the door ajar and the lights off. He probably did not pull the door shut all the way. Come on down to the Vault, where the door is always open!

My new driver's license arrived in the mail. My photo looks like when you shine a flashlight under your chin when telling ghost stories to little kids. I realized that Ursula of Ulm did not get my license, after all and probably does not know where I live.

FRIDAY, MARCH 18

Got to work in time to watch Dixie struggling to park her LTD. She scooched backwards and forwards, her neck sinuously craned out the window. Her bumper came within an inch of touching Spunt's hearse. Dixie pumped the brakes and shrieked, "Who are you? Leave me alone!" Saw Guddu leap out of the way. When I later encountered him in the stacks, he seemed pretty rattled. It is so like Dixie to not know the names of the little people who work under her. When Guddu saw me, he scowled. I left him alone.

Spent the afternoon researching the gods mentioned in *Die Tür*, none of which I could find in any resource.

"What are you reading?" It was Guddu, looking over my shoulder. He seems to have forgiven me. Perhaps he knows I hate Dixie as much as he probably does.

I turned the cover over so he could see.

He read the title aloud. "*Lost Gods of the Americas*. Why are you reading that?"

"I was just reshelving it."

"That is a very bad book, Steven. Not for you."

In the afternoon, I was headed toward the break room when I spotted Jo Ann emerge. To avoid her, I ducked behind the shelf list where I could see her but she could not see me. As she walked by, she dropped her Tab on the floor. The can rolled away, spewing chemicals everywhere. Thinking no one was watching, she slapped herself on the face, and said, "Jo, Jo, Jo! You big dummy."

Drinks with Randy at the Eagle's Nest after work. We had both forgotten that when it is not baseball season, Fridays were Wet T-Shirt Night at the Nest.

"It's open titty season," I said.

"Brings the level of everything down."

We got blitzed fast on Metaxa and talk turned trashy. Randy recounted a recent fling with an American Airlines stewardess. Told him about Mama Fox's feet.

"Dude, you should have nailed both of them!" he said.

"I did try to kiss Jenny later. Evidently I'm not her type."

"What's the deal with Diane?"

When I told Randy about the jumping jack and everything else, he said, "These are pages straight out of *The Sexy Witch*. What did she get you to do?"

"I dunno. Showed her the Vault."

"Dude! She played you like a fiddle," said Randy.

I signaled to Jackie. "Can I get a Harvey Wallbanger?"

"That's going to rot your stomach," said Randy.

"The Metaxa isn't?"

Randy was interested in Harvey's appearance at the museum but was more interested in Dawn.

"How did you meet her?"

"You know. Around. Although I did accidentally get to second base with her. At least I think it was second base."

"Why does that not surprise me?" he said. "Let me get this straight. When you went to see Dawn at the museum, Harvey was already there. When you stuck your fingers in his mouth, he jumped out of a tank of mud and flew away?"

"More or less. I touched his teeth, Randy. Like the edge of a ten-speed pedal. He could have gnawed my fingers off."

The wet t-shirt contest was noisy. I turned my back to it and struggled to understand Randy. He was now talking about Astarian.

"What's Astarian?"

"From Sherwood's red notebook," he said.

I looked at Randy blankly.

"It's a magical language."

"Like Enochian?"

"What do you know about Enochian?" Randy seemed amused.

"Not much," I said. "Other than it was said to be the language of angels. Linguist Donald Laycock debunked it, I think. Said it had inconsistencies."

"Noting inconsistencies isn't the same as debunking. Besides, Astarian serves a different purpose. You're a linguist, Steven. You must have noticed how different Astarian is from, say, English, particularly where grammar is concerned."

"Haven't read as far as you," I said.

"In magical language words are emotive. They're symbols for emotions. Astarian is especially good for constructing metaphors that establish symbols and link magic ritual to the world."

"What do you mean by 'especially good'? How many magical languages do you know?"

Randy did not answer, but reached into his bag. He pulled out a bound volume of *Man* and turned to a bookmarked page. "You should read this," he said. "The author submits that words have an inherent ability to influence the universe. Of what is observable in the universe, anyway."

"How is that different than, say, in believing that the position of stars in the sky influences the universe?"

"Apples and oranges," said Randy. "The way the stars appear in our sky is relative to our position in the universe. Astrology was doomed from the start."

"Have they never heard of precession?"

Randy ordered a Flaming Dr Pepper. Sounded delicious, so I asked Jackie if I could get one with Mr. Pibb. I turned back to Randy and pointed at his bag. "Is that a mansack?"

"No. I'm sitting on mine. As I was saying, immutability is key in a magical language. One of the effects of a language falling from the vernacular is that it ceases to change. Take Latin. In Rome, you wiped your ass with a *tersorium*. Some people still do. But the meaning of *tersorium* remains unchanged. Meanwhile, English is surpassing French as the *lingua franca* of the modern world. So English keeps changing all the time.

"*Gay* used to mean lighthearted," I said. "By the way, the drinks are on me. Your birthday, right?"

"Thanks, dude. And *boners* were honest mistakes. You don't want to pull a boner when you're casting a spell because the meaning of a word changed.

Back when Santa first started slipping his north pole up housewives' chimneys, for example, the *naughty* were those who had nothing, or naught, and the *nice* behaved in a sexually unrestrained way, like the young lady on that pool table." Randy paused to take in the spectacle. He gets even more talkative when he is wasted, so I just let him speak.

"The seven wizards of Vul Kar invented Astarian," continued Randy. "They bestowed new words with the potential of multiple older words in a kind of magical shorthand, thereby creating novel, more potent words of power. So instead of reciting a lengthy incantation to achieve a particular outcome, they now could utter fewer words, or even a single word. Zuberon is said to have created all of Dord with a 353-word utterance. Of course, that's a prime number."

"Oh, no doubt," I said, mockingly. I did not know what the hell he was talking about. "You would think that errors in the original phrases would be compounded when utilizing such a technique," I said. "What if you make a word of power out of a bunch of other words of power?"

"That would be turbo! But that's basically what I'm saying."

I was not completely following him. What part of this conversation is Metaxa, what part Memorex? "If Astarian is derived from Dordic, then they're similar?"

"To a degree. The ambiguity introduced by, say, a lack of verbal conjugations, is compensated for with countless prefixes, infixes, suffixes, and particles, each rendered by a complicated system of diacritics. Without all those diacritics there would be a greater degree of polysemy. Which is why you want to cast spells whose safety and effectiveness have been demonstrated over time."

"Do the diacritics affect how you pronounce a word?"

Randy grinned widely. "Oh, they certainly do."

"How do you know all this?"

Randy sighed. "How far have you gotten in Sherwodd's red notebook?" Leave it to Randy to answer a question with a question.

SATURDAY, MARCH 19

Stashed the Bilby under the desk in my office. Plugged it in and stocked it with a can of Mr. Pibb. Haydn's *Surprise Symphony* was on the radio. Right at the moment of the surprise, I rested my hand on Guddu's foot. The two surprises combined into a single, particularly disagreeable surprise.

"Good morning, Guddu!" I stood up nonchalantly and grabbed the acrylic tarantula paperweight off my desk. I offered it to him.

"What were you doing on the ground?" Guddu asked. He eyed the paperweight but made no move to take it.

"Just plugging in my desk lamp."

"You are plugging in?"

"Yes," I said, firmly. We stared at each other in silence for a moment. Does he know my secret? Will he tell Dixie? I must find out one of Guddu's secrets as collateral.

"This call number is incorrect," he said, curtly. He handed me a book.

"If you find any more, you can just put them here." I pointed at a shelf labeled, "Books To Be Dealt With."

"Your calendar is wrong," he said with a great degree of annoyance.

"It says 1966, but it's the same as a 1977 calendar. Calendars repeat every…" I paused to do the math then gave up.

"Guddu will be checking the book return now," he said. Why would Guddu be checking the book return? That is not his job, is it? What the hell is Guddu's job? My mind must be going.

Stood outside my office and listened for the purr of the Bilby. Remarkably quiet. By mid-afternoon, my can of Pibb was the perfect temperature.

Genesis is playing at Moody tonight. Too bad we have a gig at Fantasy's. They were probably sold out, anyway.

Would not say we have any more equipment than any other typical rock band, but Fantasy's has few electrical outlets. Fortunately, Bonnie had a long extension cord. It went all the way back to and over the bar, which was inconvenient. We tied it around a column to help keep it from being yanked out of the outlet.

The power went out as soon as we started playing. While the barmaid went looking for a generator, Bandidos showed up to settle a score with some rednecks. Grabbed my equipment and quietly fled. Found Turtle Man hiding behind the Rambler. Offered him a ride but he declined. After I loaded up the car and got in, I had to say to him, "I'm taking off now," expecting him to find a different car to hide behind. I slowly drove away. Turtle Man did not budge.

Left behind a slice of pizza I had planned on eating.

SUNDAY, MARCH 20

Studied Sherwood's red notebook. Was hoping to get to the part about Astarian. Instead, I read about some guy named Krolok: "I go to sleep and meet Krolok at our usual place. Still have not told him what I discovered but he must have divined it. He teaches me the words of power. But the dreadful things he asks me to do in return!" Following this passage, a sketch of a robed figure with an elongated head. Krolok?

Set up Todd Rundgren in the backyard and practiced throwing my *shuriken*.

It was harder than Spunt made it out to be. Vee heard the noise and came out to watch for a bit. It made me do worse, though I did manage to hit Todd in the mouth. No offense, Todd. Vee seemed to accept what I was doing without question. She was kind enough to help me search the holly bushes when I missed.

"Poor Todd! What are you preparing for?" she asked.

What am I preparing for?

Another gig at Fantasy's, this time opening for the Rhythm Principle. Rednecks gave Bonnie a hard time while she was carting in her cab. "Why are they making you haul their gear, Hershey tits?" She did not say anything but bitched about it later. Thought about whipping out my *shuriken* but that might not end well.

The slice of pizza I had left on stage was still there. It looked alright, but I knew better than to eat it. There was a guy sleeping on the stage from last time. Am told he lives there in return for cleaning up. Guess he did not want that pizza, either. If he had not thrown it away by now, I do not suppose he is earning his keep. He slept through two songs before rubbing his eyes near the end of "X Marks the Spot" and heading to the bar. Tim gestured at him and said, "Ladies and gentlemen, sitting in with us tonight, the Big Bopper!"

The Big Bopper asked through his nicotine-stained mustache if we played any songs he would have heard of. When I mentioned "Tush," he launched into this long story about how in the late sixties ZZ Top went on tour masquerading as The Zombies.

"How do you know that?"

He put his thumbs in his armpits. "I was the promoter," he said, proudly.

Sounded like *yaje* to me. About the right age, though.

"This was when they were still playing VFW posts and the animal circuit."

"Animal circuit?"

"Elk, Moose, Lion."

For the next twenty minutes the Big Bopper continued to drop names. He had been a roadie for Sam the Sham, had been Goree Carter's neighbor in Houston, and owned a guitar that Johnny Winter gave him.

"Why would Johnny Winter give you a guitar?"

The guy grinned, like I had asked him the exact question he was hoping I would ask. "Because the rascal owed me money."

"Why did he owe you money?" I asked, wearily.

Bonnie saved me by asking me to park her car. I hurried outside to her Pinto. For the life of me I could not find reverse. Just let the car creep forward until I was in the thornbush. Had to put it in neutral, get out, and push it backwards to get clearance. Just like driving the Rambler!

MONDAY, MARCH 21

Got to work early but not before Dixie. Found her in my office sitting at my desk.

"I heard a sound," she stammered, clearly caught off guard. She rose quickly, knocking over the Antioch Chalice. Paper clips went flying.

"Why do you have this?" she said, accusingly, in an attempt to make me the bad guy.

I ignored her question. "A sound?"

"A rattling, or a kind of a hum." She went into great detail about this most unusual sound while gathering up paper clips.

"Ain't that peculiar." I casually positioned myself between her and the Bilby, then started noisily shuffling books and papers as if searching for something until she went away.

Many of our student help ditched work for Puce Week. Volunteered to help out at the circulation desk and ended up working alongside the Stone Fox. She reported for duty wearing a Genesis concert t-shirt under her open puce blouse, which was tied at the waist.

I pointed to her shirt. "You went to that?" I said. Jenny nodded. "Who with?" Jenny held up a guitar pick.

"A guitar pick," I declared.

"The guitarist threw it into the audience and it almost went down the front of my top! It landed here." She stretched her t-shirt collar down to show me her cleavage. Caught a glimpse of one of her bruises, now faded. "Judd fished it out for me. What a gentleman! We were in the front row, you know."

"The front row!" I repeated, with a forced smile. Was she trying to make me jealous? Teach me a lesson? I did not ask her how she skinned her knees.

Felt an urge to be playful with Jenny, but could not muster any enthusiasm. I eyed the dish of shenanigans forlornly.

Dixie had initially objected to Bubba but surrendered due to overwhelming support for the stuffed armadillo who had evidently become the library's mascot. Jenny had knitted him a puce sweater and provided him with a little covered wagon upon which he now perched.

A student in a tight sweater was checking out several books, and I handed her library card back too soon. "May I see your card again?"

She gave me a funny look, then looked down at her chest. "I don't understand," she said.

"I need to see your library card again. Forgot to run it through the Gaylord."

"Oh, ha ha! I thought you were talking about my *cardigan*!"

"It's really lovely."

"Why, thank you! It's Nantuk Ombré. What's your name?"

"Um, Steven."

"Can I take my break now?" demanded Jenny, impatiently.

"Knock yourself out." I am not her supervisor, so why did she ask me?

Dr. Ziglar approached and slammed a book down on the counter. He glared at me rudely, so I just glared back at him until I could no longer bear the eye contact. "May I help you?"

"You may. I'd like to renew this book," he said, acidly. The book was *Minor Sexual Deviance: Diagnosis and Pastoral Treatment.* "How minor?" I wondered.

TUESDAY, MARCH 22

The Stone Fox and I inadvertently wore matching houndstooth plaid cordu- roy pants to work today, which I excitedly pointed out. "Bobbsey Twins!" I exclaimed.

Jenny posed with her butt against mine. Instinctively mimicked her, though I had no idea what we were supposed to be doing. "Charlie's Angels!" she declared.

Did not see how wearing matching pants made us like the bikini-clad gum- shoes, but I played along. "I'm Zero Zero One," I said. "Get to work, Angel!" To my surprise, Jenny wordlessly started emptying the book return.

Stepped out the back door of the break room to read a *National Geographic. The Urantia Book* was gone, so I propped the door open with a mop bucket. Carlos appeared and moved the bucket inside. "You can prop the door open with this here," he said, kicking a gizmo on the base of the door. "If you push here, it does this, and if you release this *blah blah blah…*"

When my break was over, I could not close the door because of that damned gizmo. It was more complicated than Carlos had made it out to be. Why do I not know stuff like this? Had to go find Jo Ann, who was as happy as a dog with two dicks to know something I did not. She explained the mechanism to me all over again while Amber ate her pudding cup and looked on with great satisfaction. Guddu must feel like this twenty-four hours a day.

My *National Geographic* was opened to a topless Neanderthal centerfold. Jo Ann and Amber noticed it and frowned judgmentally like I was a minor sexual deviant.

The phone at the information desk rang. Amber made no move to answer it. I reached over her and picked it up, deliberately stretching the spiral cord across her face.

"Cut it out," she hissed.

The caller spoke with a thick accent. Sounded like they were trying to reach Jo Ann. Made him repeat and spell his name as many times as I dared. "*T* as in toenail?" I said. While I know the International Phonetic Alphabet by heart, I could never get the hang of the NATO phonetic alphabet. My mind just goes blank. Left a message for Jo Ann to call Mr. Dichael Pafquale-Rafmuffen.

Handed the receiver to Amber so she could replace it. "You have ring around the collar," she said. I stared at her, bulging my eyes out thus initiating a staring match. After three or four seconds, I lost.

I pulled out a banana.

"What are you going to do with that," said Amber.

"I like a banana in the afternoon."

"You're going to eat that *here*?"

I made contented chimp noises between bites while Amber glared at me, disgusted. When I was finished with my banana, I tossed the peel into the wastebasket under the desk.

"Take that to the break room!" demanded Amber. "Or do you want to sit here and smell trash?" It is easier to obey than to argue.

Consulted Spunt about *shuriken* technique. He reviewed what he had told me last time, discussing the grip, judging distance, the principle of the turn, and stance. While Spunt was speaking, I overheard Dixie on the telephone saying Diane is helping catalog Baumann artifacts. This news has snapped me out of it. Time to find Sherwood. Why am I so easily distracted?

WEDNESDAY, MARCH 23

Another sleepless night on account of the Fear. The Fear is hard to describe. It is not the same thing as being afraid. It is more fundamental than that. Something on the molecular level. The first time I felt the Fear, I was very young. Had just brushed my teeth, turned out the light, and slid between the sheets. Always shut the closet door because I did not want anything coming through it to get me. On the night in question, I must have forgotten to shut the closet door, for when I opened my eyes and turned to look at it, the closet door was wide open. Darkness surrounding a darker rectangle. For all I knew, beyond that threshold was nothingness. Or worse.

As an adult, I do not feel the Fear often. Sometimes I feel it when I am driving alone at night. Or when I am gazing at the stars. Or when I wake up in the deepest part of the night. Last night I opened my eyes and turned to look at the closet door. Of course it was open. I am twenty-three years old so I know better than to be afraid of the dark. But it is not the dark I am afraid of. I understand that now.

Went to Dillard's to look at billfolds. I have too much on my mind and just wanted to find one and get it over with. They were more expensive than I thought. Was about to leave when I spotted a rack with some cheap-looking nylon wallets on them. Ugly with velcro fasteners. The price was right.

THURSDAY, MARCH 24

While tearing my office apart searching for my missing "Withdrawn" stamp, Amber poked her head in. "Is a fringed jacket a shirt?"

"No. It's a jacket. Why?"

"There's a man at the information desk who is wearing a fringed jacket but no shirt. Our policy says you have to wear a shirt in the library." Amber does not even work here but plainly knows library policies better than I do.

Followed Amber back to the information desk. It was the Doom Hippie. I cleared my throat.

"Are you doing that because of the way I dress?" said the Doom Hippie.

"I'm sorry, what?"

"That sound you just made."

"I was just clearing my throat."

"My lawyers are aware of the situation." The Doom Hippie opened his fringed jacket to reveal a .357 in his waistband. No shirt, no problem. He wanted to know where the Hal Lindsey books were shelved. While I ushered him to the card catalog, he lectured me on Lindsey's "end times" theories and how Satan and his minions "in all their respectable guises" were taking over the world.

"In Revelation 13:1, it is written that a beast with ten horns came out of the sea," said the Doom Hippie. "We now know these words prophesied the E.E.C."

"Amazing. This is an academic library, so we don't have a lot of that sort of thing," I lied. Did not tell him about the Pogue Collection. I searched the card catalog. "Here we go. We have a Finnish translation of one of his books. *Saatana elää ja voi hyvin Maa-planeetalla.*"

"Which one is that?" he said, excitedly.

"*Satan Is Alive and Well on Planet Earth.*"

"Give me it."

"Do you read Finnish?"

"No."

"You might try the public library."

"I'm not welcome in that establishment," he said.

I gave him the book. The Doom Hippie tucked it under his bare armpit and left without checking it out. What the hell is his game?

Got stuck at the information desk for a while so I took a look at the paper. There was a piece in the Reflections section about a witch who lived somewhere in Ohio. Evidently, her coworkers knew she was a witch. Her boss said, "If a witch does a good job waiting tables, she could work here. As long as she didn't carry on with her witchcraft here at the restaurant." I thought about Diane.

Left the information desk unattended to go to the bathroom. On my way past Dixie's office, I could hear raised voices within. No one was around, so I put my ear to the door. Must have caught the tail end of their conversation, but did overhear Jo Ann say something about Diane working here, followed by the sentence, "I don't want that woman anywhere near me. Do you hear me? She is pure evil."

What is going on between those two?

To the Eagle's Nest after work with Randy. Showed off my *shuriken* at the bar. Had to put them away after a redneck wanted to throw them. Randy and I moved to a booth for more privacy. He spoke of the difficulty of translating spells.

"Not a spell book, but consider the Torah. Written in Hebrew, okay? When you produce a new Torah scroll, you transcribe each letter exactly. This must be done by someone not only pious but specially trained. A single mistake means you have to 86 the entire panel.

"The Torah has been translated into pretty much every language known to man, but if you're studying it and care about the precise wording, you want the original Biblical Hebrew. If holy texts require this level of precision, then a grimoire is worse. Any dissimilarity can doom a spell to failure or even catastrophe."

"Can people have a conversation in Astarian?" I asked. "What if you were telling a joke and you ended up turning someone into a chimp?"

"No, Astarian is a magical language. Not a conversational one. Suppose if you spoke it casually there could be unintended consequences, but for the most part, you have to deliberately choose to speak the words in the context of wanting to cast the spell. Sounds carry with them intent, emotion, expectation, dot dot dot. Astarian is more about phonemes rather than morphemes."

"Managed to summon Harvey with no intent whatsoever," I said.

"There you go," said Randy. "But back to words of power. When you create one it becomes divorced from etymology. As a result, written Astarian is far more complex than Dordic. It requires unique characters to render it precisely. Kind of like the difference between writing Japanese in *kanji* and *kana*." Randy surveyed the room. "Looks like they're closing. Bottoms up!"

Sometimes I wonder if Randy is deliberately trying to confuse me. Not sure what his motivation would be, though.

FRIDAY, MARCH 25

A foggy, gray morning. Found a marble on the scenic route. As I was walking past the circulation desk, I decided to add it to the shenanigans dish. The dish had a tooth in it. But whose? Well, well, well. There happens to be a spell for that.

Once in my office, I opened to codex to a spell for discovering. The script was small and fine as filigree. The text was difficult to read. Fortunately, the Dordic runes are distinctive, and there is an economy to their form that promotes legibility. The scribe meant the passage to be legible. The spell contained one Astarian word of power, which I vocalized carefully.

The moment I spoke the word of power, I knew the tooth belonged to Amber. It was like a light bulb turning on in my mind. I just knew it to be true. But was it?

Found this gem in the pamphlet file, from the *Little Blue Book* series: *Shurikenjutsu Fighting Techniques* by Jack Draker. Was standing there looking at it when Amber walked by.

"Birthday party for Spunt in the break room," she said, running her words together. She walked by too quickly for me to notice if she was missing a tooth.

Returned to my office to get my cassette player and party music. Pushed play, went to the men's room. When I returned, everyone was quietly staring at their feet while Chopin's "Funeral March" dribbled from the speakers. Thought I had recorded over that.

Spunt ejected my cassette and put in "Jungle Boogie." He brought his own bathtub liquor, which I sampled. Not delicious, but effective. Am assuming the alcohol neutralized whatever toenail fungus might be present. Dixie was at a board meeting upstairs. Parties at work are more fun when she is absent. Jo Ann was truant as well. She was probably avoiding Diane. Spunt pulled out a knife and tried to stab a fly as it flew around the refreshments. His elbow upset my paper plate and I ended up with frosting on my fingers.

"Don't kill it!" shouted Jenny. "Let it out the back door!"

Amber's mouth was hanging open in surprise. The tooth was hers, alright! Took advantage of the ruckus to fill my cup with Spunt's primitive home brew. I made eye contact with Jenny. She caught my drift and followed me out of the break room. I retrieved a flashlight from behind the circulation desk then led Jenny upstairs. At the end of the bound journals, I gestured to the ladder. "Ladies, first."

"Are you crazy? I'm not going up there."

"C'mon, Jenny. You've got to see it."

"See what?"

"It's a hobbit room!" I said, jocularly. Tried to make it sound fun.

She regarded me with irritation as I prodded her with my foot. She sighed with resignation then ascended the ladder. Averted my eyes in case she spat in my eye like Doris. After Jenny had clambered into the chamber, I followed. We found ourselves sitting cross-legged while I pointed the flashlight around. I shivered. Carlos must have neglected to leave the heat on. It was very still.

"What's all this stuff?" Jenny held up an object. My missing 'Withdrawn' stamp! The flashlight revealed the magnifying glass from my *OED*, several Chap Sticks (mine, no doubt), an embroidered cushion, and an empty bottle of mucilage, to mention a few. Twine was strung about the room like a spider web.

"Stinks like rotten eggs," complained Jenny.

Left everything as we had found it. Did not want Harvey to know his hiding place had been discovered. Was he watching us now? Regarded the shadows uneasily. I left first, then helped Jenny climb down. Doubt she was interested in the hobbit room, and in retrospect, I do not suppose I blame her. I felt a pang of regret. What if Harvey had been there? What the hell is wrong with me?

"Give me a ride home?" said Jenny.

We walked to Lot C in silence.

"What happened to your windshield?" said Jenny.

"A spider startled me. It was all reflex." I changed into a Journey t-shirt.

Jenny scowled but said nothing. When I asked if she wanted to have dinner together she suggested a place called Poker Flat. The place was packed, so we got our ribs to go and brought it back to the Hacienda. When we entered her room, the setting sun was shining through the crystal I gave her for her birthday, making prismatic patterns on her bed and the wall. "It's sparkle time!" she announced, pleased.

I sat on the bed, then removed my wallet because it is too fat. Placed it on a nearby table along with my keys.

"Is that your wallet?" said Jenny. "It's hideous."

I did nor argue with her. Jenny fiddled with a box of jewelry, then put on a black ribbon choker with a little bell on it. "Those ribs look messy," she said. "Let me get some wet paper towels."

She returned from the bathroom. "You moist towelette, Sir."

There was a little black & white TV set with Pong hooked up to it, so we played that for a while until her roommate Misty returned with her friend, Jaclyn. The moment Jaclyn saw my t-shirt, she shrieked, "Oh, my God! I love Journey! Can I have it?"

When I did not immediately agree to give Jaclyn the shirt off my back, she said "Will you trade with me? I'll give you this one!" She had on a waist-length embroidered kimono which tied in the front. It was similar to what Robert Plant wears on stage, I reasoned. Always trying to refine my stage persona, I figured I could wear the kimono with my satin bell bottoms. I love that Journey t-shirt, but when a babe wants to trade shirts with you, you do it.

Jaclyn started to untie her kimono, and before I knew what hit me, *bam!* Bazookas. I found myself nodding, as if in approval or acknowledgment. What was the protocol here? If I looked away suddenly, would I be insulting her? Jaclyn stood casually before me in nothing but a fringed leather miniskirt, so there must not have been any expectation of modesty from anyone. If I blatantly stared directly at them, that would be too lecherous. I played it cool by taking off my t-shirt while casually stealing glances. Two seconds at her tits, then two seconds at a Burt Reynolds centerfold, as if those two things canceled each other out.

I put on the kimono, which actually fit. Jaclyn reached down and tied it for me. What would Robert Plant do? He would admire himself in the mirror hanging on the back of the door, which is what I did. My lips looked very white and chapped.

The kimono was slightly more feminine than I would have preferred. It exposed much of my abdomen, but that is how Plant wears them. If the Golden God can wear kimonos, surely I could, too. After pulling my t-shirt over her head, Jaclyn looked me up and down before pronouncing, "Studly!"

"Guys look great in girls' clothes," remarked Misty, who was now attempting to braid my hair. "Look at Bowie."

That was not the comparison I was looking for, but at least the tone was one of approval. I looked at Jenny who had an enigmatic smirk on her face. What did it mean?

"Didn't know you and Misty were roommates," I remarked.

Misty finished braiding my hair. "Let's put makeup on you," she said. She pushed me down onto her bed, then handcuffed me with a six-pack ring.

"What? Uh…"

"I'll do his eyes," said Jaclyn, who already had her mascara out and was now hovering right in my face. She took my glasses off and placed them on the desk. It felt like we were staring into each other's eyes, but she was looking around my eyes as opposed to in them. I still had to look away. Her cherry lip gloss breath was warm on my face. She stood upright, straddling one of my legs to take advantage of the light. "Look up!" she commanded. "You smell like barbecue." Meanwhile, Misty was banging around in the bathroom. "Found it!" she chirped. Found what?

For the next few minutes, those two chicks painted me up like a cheap tart. "Let's put these in his beard," said Misty, playfully. She dangled a small packet of colored beads. "No!" I squirmed out of the girls' clutches and crouched in the corner. They were all laughing at me.

"You look adorable," said Jenny, flatly.

I put my glasses back on and looked at myself in the mirror. I saw not a golden god, but something closer in appearance to a bearded Alice Cooper. The girls were clearly enjoying themselves, and I would be lying if I said I did not mind two chicks having their way with me, even if their way was humiliating. Pulling my wrists apart, I burst out of my restraints, roaring like a carnival strongman.

As if on cue, everyone settled down. *Wish You Were Here* warbled from a cassette player, which sounded like its batteries were dying. Misty went into the bathroom and got a towel to stuff under the door, while Jaclyn fiddled with a roach. I lay on Jenny's bed against a pile of colorful cushions wedged between her and Jaclyn, our legs mingling. Misty sat near our feet, with her legs over ours. I wondered if the bed would collapse.

While we passed the joint around, I contemplated my surroundings. Numerous lit candles dotted the room. There was a typewriter on a small desk. Next to the fan rested a pink princess phone. A cup of pencils with plastic flowers on the end, which resembled a bouquet. A cork bulletin board was covered in magazine clippings of heartthrobs, surrounded by posters of *Jonathan Livingston Seagull*, Yes, and the aforementioned Burt. A six-can pyramid adorned the black & white TV. I lay back and looked up. A Klee mobile swayed gently overhead, while near the window hung a neglected fern in a macramé basket. A brown and orange string-art owl leaned against a pile of trashed textbooks and a tattered *Siddhartha* paperback. A cinder block and board bookcase sagged under the weight of the *Funk & Wagnalls New Encyclopedia*. Incomplete, alas. A flaccid hammock dangled from a hook in the door frame. On the opposite wall, a hole in the plaster gaped.

Another joint appeared, freshly rolled. I continued my curriculum of long drags, sometimes taking two or three when no one else seemed interested at the moment. Became conscious of my arm falling asleep beneath Jaclyn, but did not dare disturb her. Misty produced a Stretch Armstrong toy, referring to it as "Stretch Johnson." Am pretty certain it is "Armstrong," though. She offered it to me, and it was all I could do to refrain from biting it out of curiosity. David Gilmour serendipitously intoned, "You've been in the pipeline, filling in time… provided with toys and scouting for boys."

"I'm not scouting for boys," I mumbled. It was only when someone knocked at the door that I realized I was unable to move. It was the "haircut and a shave" knock. I found myself laughing idiotically about it for a moment. Misty squirmed over us so she could reach down and remove the towel from under the door and open it. She struggled and groaned to accomplish the feat, while I held her legs so she would not fall off the bed.

Two guys strode in, briefly silhouetted from the light in the corridor before the door closed behind them.

"Jay!" declared the huge one. "Roll me a hog leg," he demanded. Misty obliged while we all watched. She lit it before handing it to him. The huge one inhaled deeply, holding in the smoke for what seemed like an hour, before releasing it all in a loud belch. "Juicy," he declared.

Was too lazy to introduce myself to whom I had decided were the Doobie Brothers. They did not seem interested in me, either.

"Doobie," I thought. What a funny word. I repeated it in my mind. Or was it aloud? "The Scooby Doobie Brothers," I blurted, addressing no one in particular. I was higher than a giraffe's ass.

Jenny elbowed me. "Misty wants to jump his bones," she whispered.

"Huh? Whose bones?"

The smaller guy said, loudly, "Get a load of this queer." Had forgotten about my kimono and makeup. I turned to look at the speaker. The Doom Hippie! Misty wants to jump *his* bones? What does he have that I haven't got?

"Let's get out of here. I want tacos!" said the huge guy.

He scooped Jaclyn up in his humongous, hairy arm. His cowboy hat was rolled up at the sides, like a curly taco shell.

The Doom Hippie addressed Jenny. "You coming or what?"

Jenny knows the Doom Hippie?

"I told you I'm not speaking to you," said Jenny. She burrowed her face into my neck. A moment later, I felt suction. Was she kissing my neck?

"I'll go with you," said Misty, springing up with a sudden burst of energy. She turned to Jenny. "We're done with your boyfriend. You can have him back now!" She sprayed a quick blast of Lysol into the air as the group departed, leaving Jenny and me alone in an acrid cloud of disinfectant spray.

"Boyfriend," I thought. Jenny does not think of me "like that," yet here we are. With my left hand, I clumsily pawed her face and hair until I found the bell on her choker. I tinkled it then casually rested my hand on her tit. No reaction.

Unsure of how many minutes, hours, or even days had passed, I attempted to see my watch but I did not know where my arm was. No visitors after curfew, so I carefully untangled myself from Jenny and stood in an upright position, wondering what time I weighed. Felt like I had the mass of a neutron star. My beard was moist with saliva, most likely my own. Jenny sat up and applied lipstick before studying her own watch.

"Do you know that guy?" I said.

"Who, Judd?" Slowly, I began gathering all the trash from our meal. "I don't even know your phone number," I said.

"Of course you do," said Jenny, in a hurt voice.

"No, really."

Jenny scribbled her number on a "Love is…" pad, then tore off the page and handed it to me.

I translated the digits into letters. "SEAL-ASS," I said, slowly, without realizing what I was saying.

"SEA-LASS," said Jenny, irritably. She did not ask me for mine, which is just as well. I did not feel like explaining to her at the moment why I do not have a telephone.

Had driven about halfway home when I realized I had forgotten my wallet. Flipped a uey and headed back to the Hacienda. Find it hard to believe there are people who claim they can drive when they are baked. How do they summon the willpower? As I turned onto Jenny's street, my headlights illuminated two pale legs swinging into a white dually. I know those calves! Could not see who was behind the wheel. Assume it was Judd. I sped past them. Nothing was worth this humiliation.

SATURDAY, MARCH 26

Opened my eyes to discover Figaro's butthole right in my face. Time for crunchies. Went to bed with mascara still on, now smeared all over my pillow case. Did not know what it was at first. I glanced at Dookie Face and assumed the worst. My hair was still in pigtails. I regarded myself in the bathroom mirror. Is that a hickey?

"Sorry, kitty. I don't have any crunchies." I gave him a Styrofoam peanut to see what he would do. He touched it gently with his paw, once, then walked away.

Stopped by Jenny's on the way to work to pick up my wallet. She was not there, but Misty was. "Uh, I forgot my wallet last night."

Misty rubbed her eyes then silently invited me in. She was wearing a long nightgown, like someone on the cover of a Gothic romance paperback.

"It's, uh, velcro," I mumbled nervously, scanning the room. "Here it is!" I turned around and regarded Jenny's bed, trying to determine if it had been slept in. Misty climbed back into hers, with her back to me.

"Guess I'll skedaddle, then. Thanks, Misty!" *Skedaddle*! Jesus, I sound like a Union soldier. Misty waved feebly, and I left.

When I saw Jenny at work, she took one look at me and wordlessly led me into the staff bathroom. There, she applied makeup to my hickey. As she rubbed my neck, I had to conceal my excitement. Now was not the time to make a move. Later, however, I lamented the missed opportunity. Jenny, what are you doing to me?

Guddu lingered near the information desk. When I invited him to sit down, he did so eagerly. We chatted and he was unusually forthcoming. At one point, I asked him where he was from and he said Michigan, which surprised me. Thought he was going to say Bombay or something because of his accent. I just let him talk, and he told me Mayberryesque tales of growing up in Lansing, of all places. These tales were utterly incongruous with everything I had assumed or thought I knew about Guddu. They also sounded—for lack of a better word—scripted. One thing he said reminded me of an Aggie joke.

"What do you call an Aggie dentist?"

"What is an Aggie?"

When I explained that Aggies were the butt of jokes in Texas, Guddu said in Michigan it was Yoopers. Thought nothing of it, and we kept talking. A while later, Guddu made a comment about something—I forget what—to which I replied, "Spoken like a true Yooper." I was just teasing him, of course, but he must have taken it the wrong way because he got up and stomped away. Someone came up and asked a question just then, otherwise I might have followed him.

It was soon after that my day seemed to take a nosedive. It was just little things at first, like sharpening two brand new pencils down to nubs because the leads kept breaking. My Chap Stick vanished, then my good lighter from Freak Imports. While momentarily covering the circulation desk for Jenny, the Gaylord gobbled up someone's library card. It made a metallic grating sound. startling everyone in the library.

Jenny asked me for a ride to her mom's after work. On our way there, we hit every red light on University. They all took ages to turn green. When I referred to it as the "Rube Goldberg Signal Unsystem," my obvious irritation amused Jenny. She said I sounded just like her father. Her teasing cheered me up a bit, but I was still in a pretty funky mood by the time we got to her house.

We entered the house to discover the furniture shoved against the wall. Mama Fox stood in the middle of the room in a red leotard conducting what she called a "home dance workshop." At first, it just looked like a group of middle-aged women doing the Hokey Pokey.

"Darling, you must join us!" Mama Fox took me by the hand and I quickly found myself in a circle in which we danced our way forward, each of our hands on the hips of the person before us. I craned my neck but could no longer see Jenny.

Mama Fox must have sensed my reticence. When the circle dissipated, she said, "This isn't just simple social fun, Steven. It's a lesson that features dance as a form of healing and community integration. Everybody, please take a seat. Not you, Darling." She placed her hands on my shoulders.

"One of the things we do in this workshop, Steven, is to teach people processes. Ways that we can begin to understand how to physically work with our bodies in a healthy, positive manner. How to use the body and movement to release tension, to allow your feelings to be manifested in a constructive form."

Mama Fox instructed me to sit on the floor, legs extended. She sat behind me, our backs touching. After moving our heads back and forth in unison, she commanded me to lean forward, as she leaned backward, now positioning herself on top of me. Arms extended over her head, she grasped my toes. My own hamstrings were stretched to their limits, but I did not dare speak.

To my relief, we broke the pose and stood, again back to back. This time, Mama Fox raised her arms over her head while I was instructed to reach behind me and support the inside of her thighs with my palms. This placed my fingertips in uncomfortable proximity to her groinal region. She now leaned backward while I leaned forward, until I was supporting her full weight. After letting her down with a thud, I told her that Jenny was waiting for me.

"Go to her! Go have your fun!" urged Mama Fox, while the others applauded lightly.

Found Jenny on her bed, fighting her sister Shannon over a Mayor McCheese doll. "Steven, help me!" cried Shannon. Jenny looked like she was enjoying herself, so I assumed it was okay to join in. I shoved my arm between them, gripped Mayor McCheese's top hat, and held on tight. Soon, the three of us were a writhing mass of sweaty, grunting bodies. Occasionally, someone would shriek after being tickled. It was my turn to shriek when I was given a vicious titty twister, probably by Jenny, but I started to panic when placed in a headlock because I did not want my glasses to break.

The melee ended after what sounded like a couple of slaps, with Shannon storming out of the room and slamming the door, shouting, "Keep it then, you stupid bitch!"

I turned to Jenny, who stood panting and red-faced, holding Mayor McCheese limply at her side. Her hair was a rat salad, and there were red marks all over her arms and legs. "Thanks for nothing, Steven."

"Are you mad at me?" I said.

"Why did you take her side?"

"Sorry, Jenny. I thought we were just having fun."

"I'm sure it was a lot of fun for you. Do you like my sister?"

The question took me by surprise. "What? No!"

Jenny tossed Mayor McCheese onto the bed then disappeared into the bathroom. I sunk into a bean bag chair. Needed to clean my glasses but a polyester work shirt is no good. Used one of Jenny's tank tops, but that only made things worse.

Jenny returned, having calmed down considerably. "You see why I can't live here with these people, can't you?"

"Want to go out to eat? I'll take you to the Carriage House." I was trying to cheer her up.

"Sure. Let me change," she said, disinterestedly. She disappeared back into the bathroom. I reached for a *Creem* magazine. While I was learning the "strange truth" about Jefferson Starship, Jenny reappeared in yellow panties and a pair of large gold hoop earrings. There was a fresh bruise on her left boob, or perhaps a hickey. Judd! Debated saying something, but decided it was not my place. I watched Jenny as she strapped on some heeled sandals then pulled a yellow smocked tube dress over her head.

I stood to face her. "Those heels make you almost as tall as me." For a moment, I thought we might kiss. It might have been nice to just get it out of the way so we could relax the rest of the evening.

"You should wear a jacket and tie."

"I think I have a jacket in the car."

"Go get it so I can see it."

Was careful to avoid getting roped into more dance lessons from Mama Fox. When I returned, Jenny took one look at my crumpled corduroy jacket and sighed.

"Elbow patches?" Jenny led me down the gallery into the master suite. It was decorated with ornate gold and pink flocked wallpaper, colorful silk cushions, and the like. Mama Fox's boudoir. We proceeded through an ostentatious black marble bathroom to Daddy Fox's den. Paneled in mahogany, with shelves filled with books on art and architecture. A display case held various antique pistols. The room smelled of cigars.

"Is that a real Rothko?" I said. Jenny did not answer.

She pulled me into a walk-in closet, then held several ties up to my neck to see which one complemented my jacket the best.

"They're all Pucci. Mom buys them for Dad but he prefers ascots." Jenny chose one and tied it for me.

On the way to the Carriage House, we again hit every red light. Something is definitely wrong. I read they were supposed to fix the timing on all of them. Jenny however did not seem to notice or care.

Had neglected to make a reservation, but Jenny spoke a few words to the *maître d'*, who whisked us into a small, crystal-laden dining room. "He knows Mom," said Jenny.

When Jenny ordered the Escargot Monaco appetizer, I realized this meal was going to set me back. Figured I may as well try to enjoy myself. I ordered the Crab Lorenzo in a lightly seasoned cream sauce. Jenny had the South

African lobster tail. I don't know shit about wine, but fortunately, we stuck with the house red. Conversation was a bit stilted. We spoke of Patty Hearst getting out of jail, work, and the Thai coup. After the waiter brought our food, he produced what looked like a giant, wooden clarinet and asked in a thick French accent, "Would you like some fresh ground *paper*?"

All was well until I spilled house red all over the white tablecloth, then dripped some Crab Lorenzo on my sleeve. While fussing over the mess and cursing my luck, movement overhead caught my eye. Harvey! He waited until I got a good look at him before skittering off across the ceiling toward the kitchen.

When the waiter noticed the tablecloth, he returned with a busboy and made a big production of replacing it with a clean one. I excused myself and headed to the restroom, where I simply lingered before the mirror. When I had been away long enough, I mouthed the word "Fuck" at my reflection and returned to Jenny.

The waiter was just finishing up. I needed carbonation. "Excuse me, can you bring me a Mr. Pibb?"

"I'm afraid not, *Monsieur*."

"Surely you have Coca Cola? Large, *avec des glaçons*," I said, eager to show off my French.

Kept stealing glances, looking for Harvey. What the hell is he doing here? It took a while, but at last the waiter returned with an entire pitcher of Coke with a thousand ice cubes in it and plunked it down heavily before me.

"Will there be anything else, *Monsieur*?" said the waiter, stifling a shit-eating grin.

I was not going to take any more bullshit from this motherfucker, so I said, "Bone ape tit," then picked up the pitcher with both hands and chugged it while he observed. Jenny sat there with her mouth hanging open aghast. Must say it was worth it, if only to see her face change expression for once.

When it was time to settle the bill, I whipped out my checkbook and hoped for the best. I doubted there was enough money in my account. Jenny regarded my act with a look of distaste and produced a Diners Club card. I do not know why it surprised me that she had one.

"But I invited you," I said, feebly.

"Don't worry about it, Steven."

The Carriage House parking lot had been full, so we parked across the street at Brass 'n' Such. When we reached the Rambler, I discovered I had locked my keys inside. Jenny insisted on fetching the *maître d'* while I waited like a fool. While I am certainly capable of locking my keys in the car on my own, I was sure this was Harvey's doing this time. "Is this all you got?" I muttered.

The *maître d'* returned with a coat hanger and fished open the lock while Jenny and I shared a cigarette. Saw her slip something into his hand as he left us.

Had a pretty decent buzz behind the wheel. Good thing Jenny's house was not far. However, I did hit a spot on Camp Bowie where some bricks were missing which rattled our teeth. Compliments of Harvey, no doubt. When we pulled up to the house, it looked like every light was on. There was an orange 911 parked in the driveway.

"Oh, shit, my Dad is here."

Took the servants' entrance and headed straight up to Jenny's room. She changed out of her dress into a t-shirt and shorts. We wrestled a bit, then tried to interlock toes. It was painful but we managed it. Shannon barged in and caught us, then wanted to try it with Jenny, then me. We tried to do a three-way toe clasping, which we concluded was not possible but had us all laughing. Or at least Shannon and me. Jenny's countenance was one of resignation.

The three of us played Uno for a while until Shannon got bored and went back to her room. Jenny and I lay on her bed listening to the radio until she began to softly snore.

I crept down to the reading room. All the lights were off. Figured it was safe to leave by the front door, since I was parked on the street. As I approached the foyer, I heard a strange rhythmic thumping sound. Instinctively, I grabbed a nearby candelabrum and prepared to do combat. As my eyes adjusted to the darkness, I beheld Daddy Fox and Mama Fox up against the front door. He was evidently giving it to her through her red leotard. Mama Fox saw me, and furtively pointed toward the kitchen, indicating that I should use the other door. Which I did posthaste. The grandfather clock bonged eleven.

Hit every red light again, cursing at Harvey throughout each one until I was hoarse. When I got home I headed into the kitchen for a glass of water. Surprise! My kitchen sink is clogged. What else can go wrong? Was too tired to deal with it any more *yaje* and just went straight to bed. I lay in the dark, my head swimming, trying to make sense of the day. I suddenly realized how odd it is that Guddu grew up in Michigan but has never heard of Kentucky.

SUNDAY, MARCH 27

Awoke in a cold sweat, certain that Harvey had tried to throttle me in my sleep. A dream so real, my neck hurt. In retrospect it was probably on account of Jenny's headlock. The last time I had a dream that real, I dreamed I had a couple of rare seventeen-dollar bills with Zachary Taylor's face on them. When I awoke, I almost phoned the bank to be sure.

Despite my Harvey dream, I awoke oddly refreshed. A day of thunderstorms and flash floods. Tried to unclog the kitchen sink with the plunger, which just made a mess. Walked down to Texaco to phone Mr. Hawlie. Mrs. Hawlie answered.

"This is Steven Miller. May I speak to Mr. Hawlie? My kitchen sink's clogged."

"Of course, he's right here."

Hawlie seemed put out that I was calling him on a Sunday. When I explained the situation, he was argumentative.

"Maybe a steel ball down there."

"I'm sorry. What?"

"Steel ball."

"What kind of steel ball? I don't understand."

"Plunge it?"

"I did that but it didn't work." Hawlie and I went back and forth like this for a few moments, until I heard Mrs. Hawlie in the background saying, "You get your tools and you go out there this instant. Do you hear me?" I covered the receiver so he could not hear me chuckling.

Hawlie showed up twenty minutes later with a can of Drano Instant Plunger. After working his magic, he turned on the water, then looked at me with a satisfied air.

Thought about seeing a guy play the Liszt sonata at TCU but then remembered I had rehearsal. Tim brought a chick to it, which did not sit well with the others. Think her name was Kelly. She lay on the pizza couch and chain smoked the whole time, indifferent to our music. I bet Tim hated that. Between songs, Tim would walk over to her. They would chat and he would take a drag off her cigarette. Each time, it took a minute to get him to leave her alone and get back to work. He was present enough, however, to bitch me out every time I made a mistake.

"Steven, you better get your shit together before our gig tomorrow night."

"When have I ever not had my shit together?"

"There have been times."

"Yeah, like when?" Tim really pissed me off, but he was right about tonight. It's like my fingers wouldn't do what I wanted them to do. It was pretty weird.

MONDAY, MARCH 28
Another stormy day. Dixie and Jo Ann barged into my office, with Monty in tow. Jo Ann looked like she had applied her mascara in the dark.

"Monty has ants," declared Dixie. "Do you have ants?" Dixie and Jo Ann scrutinized my office, searching for stray ants.

"No ants in here," I replied, emphatically. They were going to find my Bilby! "You know what? I did see some ants at the information desk. Found a banana peel in the trash the other day." I got up and squeezed past Dixie and Jo Ann, who reluctantly followed, with Monty close behind.

"I never eat at the information desk," said Jo Ann, defensively.

"They might have been driven indoors to escape the flooding," I offered.

After this close shave, I am considering moving the Bilby to the Vault.

Was in the mezzanine searching for a missing volume when I spotted Diane below. The way she was looking around like a shoplifter caught my attention. I observed her cutting something out of a book. When I got back downstairs I saw her casually replace the book where it belongs. When she turned around, she noticed me. I crossed the room on a pretend errand. As soon as she disappeared into the workroom, I hurried over to see what the book was. Took no time at all to discover a photo sliced out of *The 'Dillo* from '73.

Encountered Randy in the break room reading the Sunday paper. He looked up. "Dude, they're cracking down on oracles in Athens. Of the fifteen thousand or so throughout the city, I quote, 'probably only one hundred have some proper psychoanalytic qualification.'"

"Like Ph.D.s?" I said.

Randy joined me on the patio for a smoke. "Get this. I saw Diane cutting pictures out of *The 'Dillo*."

"Pictures of whom?"

"I don't know. Someone at the end of the *D*s."

Randy raised his eyebrows. "Watch out for that chick. We don't know what she's capable of."

Why would what she is capable of matter, I wondered. Told Randy about finding Harvey's inner sanctum. "What do you think he wants?" I said. "Listen to me, I'm talking about Harvey like he's a person. Like he's real."

"We've been over this already," said Randy, impatiently. "If aliens landed and probed your anus in their ship, would you believe they were real?"

"It depends on what I was smoking."

"What if Jesus came up to you and introduced himself?"

"That's already happened to me twice at the information desk," I said. "I need more than that. He'd have to walk across Lake Worth or something."

"We should try to capture Harvey."

"With what, a rabbit trap or something?"

"Caddo-style deadfall trap. Made with dogbane cordage."

"Sounds like you've done this before," I said. "Why not just kill him? Don't you think he'd strangle us if he had the chance?"

"He's had many chances. He's clearly just observing you."

"What would we do with Harvey if we caught him?"

"Find things out."

"Just think if someone overheard us right now," I said. "They would think we were out of our gourds."

"Sherwood wouldn't."

"Sherwood seems to think he can transport himself through a wall."

"You may have a point."

Spent the rest of the afternoon researching traps. Encountered an 1882 patent called "Animal Trap" featuring a revolver pointed at a mouse's head. Eat the cheese, spring the trap. Mouse gets his face blown off. Can't have that in the hobbit room. In the Pamphlet File we have *How To Make a Cat Trap* (1929), but the trap is from scratch. Harvey is not a cat and I am not Handy Dan. The 1957 leaflet *An Improved Box Trap for Small Game and Fur Animals* assumes I have access to a professional sheet metal shop. Found a citation for an article in *The New Yorker* from 1930, but I doubted its usefulness. Besides, I was too lazy to retrieve it from the stacks. The library has no books dedicated to the subject, which is just as well.

"What are you trapping?" asked the clerk at Gibson's.

"Fox," I said.

"Right here. Number 2 Coil Spring with Offset Jaw. Cadillac of traps. Well worth the money. Also the only one we carry. Appropriate for mink and otter, as well."

"Mink and otter," I repeated.

"Gonna need this, too." He took a vial out of a cabinet. "Fox Urine and Tonquin Musk."

"Works for tonquins, too? Good."

The clerk looked at me like I was a retard. Started to register that this trap was for killing. Decided there and then I wanted to be rid of Harvey once and for all.

"Got any rat poison?"

TUESDAY, MARCH 29

Hazel gave me a blank emergency contact information form to fill out. In case of H-bomb, I guess. Took me a while to fill mine out because at first, I could not think of who my emergency contact would be. Dad is out of the question. Mom is a jet setter with no fixed address. Finally decided on Aunt Wanda in Vegas, but had to wait until I got home to look up her address and telephone number.

Almost forgot. Found out Diane is also going to A.C.L.A.

Bonnie phoned as I was leaving the library. "Can you stop by Murray Hill and pick up the P.A.? We're sharing it with Lazer."

"Yes, but I can't bring the P.A. and my own gear to the gig in the Rambler. There's not enough room."

"I'll have Tim drop by your place after he gets off work. Deal?"

"Sure." Find myself saying "sure" instead of "yes" when I don't want to say yes. Had planned on kicking some field goals after work, but my football is deflated.

While we were loading the P.A. into Tim's van, it started to pour rain. Vee shouted from her window, "Hi, Dollface! You got any dirty clothes?"

Tim gave me a sidelong glance. Evidently, I'm Dollface again, unless she was talking to Tim. "Just the ones I'm wearing!"

"Come on up, then, and say howdy to Dawn!"

Tim slammed the doors to his van and we headed up to Vee's. Introductions were made. Vee handed us a couple of Lone Stars.

Dawn was looking fine as hell in a denim jumpsuit. "You guys are in a band?" she said.

Tim did most of the talking and invited the girls to see us tonight. "I'll put you on the guest list."

Back in the van, Tim said, "Are you and Veronica..." He made a circle with one hand while putting his other finger in it repeatedly.

"No, we're just friends."

"She's got chrome, I'll give her that. Dawn on the other hand...not a fan of the turd curls. What a woofer." Tim sometimes says horrible shit like this just to get a rise out of people. Not sure if he means it or not.

"Damn, Tim!"

"That doesn't mean she's not obedient." He then panted like a dog and held his paws up limply.

We arrived at the Mother Lode. After unloading the van, I changed into my kimono. When I joined the others at the bar, they all started laughing. "What the fuck is that?" asked Tim.

"Don't know what it's called."

"I believe it's a *ruana*," said Dave II.

"I'd just call it a blouse," said Bonnie. She fondled the fabric thoughtfully. "I'd wear that. I love bell sleeves! You should wear them with your Gloria Vanderbilts," she winked. I smirked at her.

Turtle Man showed up during sound check, sitting quietly up front with his book. Something bound in plain black buckram, probably a thesis. Was dying to know what it was, but was too timid to ask. Wonder why Turtle Man comes to see us play if he is just going to read the whole time.

The girls showed up halfway through our set. They were dressed to the nines for some reason, in sparkly blouses, their hair and makeup all done. They danced before us throughout much of our set, cheering and hollering, their drinks sloshing out of their glasses.

During our rendition of Space Opera's "Guitar Suite," my strap broke. Unable to support my bass and play it, too, I sat down on a nearby barstool for the remainder of the song, while Tim shot me dirty looks.

After the song ended, I had to use electrical tape to secure my strap to the bass, as the strap pin had come off and vanished. This proved difficult because my strap kept twisting into a Mobius strip. A Mobius strap! Meanwhile, Bonnie improvised something on her Minimoog to keep the audience from wandering off. After I had finished with my repair and was plugging myself back in, Tim leaned over and whispered, "You did that on purpose, motherfucker." He knows I hate covering that song. We do not do it justice because we only have one guitarist. Tim, as virtuoso as he is, just does not have enough fingers to pull it off.

"Clearly my strap broke. I didn't break it on purpose." Tim got a weird look on his face, then launched straight into the opening riff of "Rock 'n' Roll Insanity." I almost missed my cue.

After we were done playing, Vee found us and said, "We got a table!" Took a few minutes to find some extra chairs, order a new round, and get everyone situated. Went to go take a leak, and when I returned, Vee cried, "Hey, your belt buckle's all crooked!" She took hold of it and tried to wrench it back toward the middle.

"Don't want it to scratch the back of my bass."

"XYZ!" Vee grabbed my zipper and yanked it upwards. Her gaze then moved from my crotch to my stomach. She untied my kimono with a quick tug, then said, "Check out Steven's belly. Doesn't he have the yummiest belly?"

Does Vee want me? *In vino veritas.* She ruffled my stomach hair vigorously with her fingers. "Feel it, Dawn!" she commanded. She tried to put Dawn's hand on it, but Dawn jerked her hand back while I stepped backwards, mortified. Maybe Vee wants Dawn to want me. When I made eye contact with Tim, he glanced askew at Dawn then mouthed the words, "Bow wow." Ignoring him, I struck a pose and cried, "I am a golden god!"

Something about the look on Tim's face indicated that he was jealous. Perhaps I was reading too much into it. In an act of certain one-upmanship, he leaned over and whispered something into Vee's ear.

"What is that you're saying?" she slurred, loudly. Tim repeated himself, and Vee cackled. I fastened my kimono and took a seat on the other side of Bonnie, who looked annoyed.

"Hey, Tim!" I shouted over the din. "Is Kelly coming tonight?"

Tim kicked me under the table. Suddenly I felt ill. I returned to the bathroom. Did not vomit, fortunately, but I was in there for a long time. Lazer had started playing. When I returned to the table, only Bonnie remained.

"Where'd everyone go?"

Bonnie pointed with her thumb over her shoulder. I looked and saw Tim and the girls raising hell with a bunch of bikers in the corner. Could hear Vee singing along with Lazer's complex vocal harmonies. Wasn't about to join them, so I nursed my drink and smoked a Kent.

Evidently, I passed out. Next thing I knew, I was flat on my back on the sticky floor. My kimono was open and Tim was rubbing ice cubes on my nipples. I slapped his hands away and clutched my kimono closed like some prudish old lady. Everyone laughed, of course, but none as hard as this one big hairy biker, who was now staring at me hard. I recognized him as the Doom Hippie's buddy from the Hacienda.

"You with the band?"

"Yeah, I'm the bass player."

He kept staring at me. Couldn't meet his gaze anymore, so I looked to the others for support, finding none. At last, the biker grunted and walked away. "A grunt's high praise, coming from a Bandido," said Tim. Bonnie surprised me by chasing after him into the crowd. I thought I heard her shout "Car Boy!" How does she know him?

After Lazer took their bows, we congregated on the sidewalk while waiting for Bonnie to come out. I had parked around the corner, and when I went to get the Rambler so I could load up my equipment, it would not start.

"We'll give you a ride!" offered Vee. Tim looked like he wanted to speak, but was not fast enough. I was off tomorrow, and could just come back for the Rambler. The girls helped me load my gear into the back of Dawn's pickup.

Vee flipped a coin to see who would drive. She, Dawn, and I all shouted "Tails!" at the same time. The coin rolled straight into the gutter where flowing water swept it into the storm drain. After Vee puked in the bushes, we determined she was probably the least wasted of the three of us. We piled into the Toyota with Vee at the wheel and Dawn in my lap.

"What happened to this truck?" shouted Bonnie.

"Hail damage," said Dawn. "Got it for a song!"

"Dawn, can you roll the window down," I said. "I can't reach the handle." It had stopped raining and was now uncomfortably humid.

Tim approached Vee and said forlornly, "Can you fit me in there?"

"You can ride in the back, Mister," said Vee. Tim was not having it and walked toward his van.

As we rolled down Vickery, the damp breeze blew Dawn's hair into my mouth. It tasted like burned hairspray. Desperately needed to adjust my balls but was too gentlemanly to say or do anything. My sweaty arm was mashed against other sweaty arms, and every time Vee shifted gears, our arms moved in tandem.

We rode along in silence. Could feel Dawn's body slowly soften and relax. As she leaned against me, her head tilted to one side. Was she asleep? My legs were asleep. I was sweating like a pig, but I knew better than to complain. Street lights swirled by. Suddenly, my reverie was shattered by the explosive sound of a roaring engine as Tim raced by. I could taste his exhaust fumes. As quickly as he passed, he braked and swerved back behind us. "You're crazy!" screamed Vee out the window, as if Tim could hear her. Is that what women want? Someone who is crazy?

It began to rain violently. We rolled up the windows and I was just about to turn on the a/c when we veered down Collinwood, Tim on our tail. Home at last! Dawn opened the passenger door and spilled slowly out of my lap as I moaned, "My legs!" Grabbed Dawn's umbrella out of the gun rack, sheltering her as I hobbled to the front porch.

"My stuff!"

Raced back to Dawn's truck before my amp got ruined. She helped by lugging my bass and gig bag. The moment we made it back to the porch, lightning struck a lacey oak next door. This was followed by a deafening peal of thunder. Startled, I slipped on the rain-slickened porch and landed on my coccyx.

Dawn helped me up. "Oh, my gosh!" she said. "Are you okay?"

I was more worried about my amp, which is heavier than a black hole. Luckily, it did not have far to fall. Meanwhile, the oak had fallen into the street, completely blocking it and pulling down power lines with it.

Tim was momentarily shaken by the thunder. After recovering, he picked up the umbrella and closed it. He then attempted to ring the doorbell with it before dancing around and poking the girls playfully in the butt. "Quit it!" Dawn squealed, flapping her hands.

"That poor tree," said Vee.

"You drove with those on?" said Tim. We all looked down at Vee's boots, which had spurs attached to them.

"She stole them from one of those bikers," said Dawn with a chuckle.

Vee unlocked the front door and we all clambered into the darkened foyer.

I flicked the light switch up and down. "Power's out," I said. The four of us groped our way up the stairs until we reached the top. Vee slid open her pocket door and we filed inside.

"I'll find some candles," said Vee. She went into the other room, where I heard her cry, "Hey! Where's my…never mind."

She returned carrying a Ouija board with two bottles on it. One was a wax encrusted Mateus Rosé bottle from which a stub of a candle protruded. The other was a bottle of Arandas. Tim did the honors with his Bic. We spread out on the floor around the coffee table.

"Look what I have," sang Vee.

"What's that, a Weejee board?" asked Tim. He lit up a jay. "Let's summon the dead! Pass me that tequila."

Vee grabbed Tim by the sleeve. "Help me get my boots off, will ya?" She plopped down on the sofa and offered her leg. Dawn and I watched as Tim struggled to get one, then both boots off. Vee slid laughing to the floor. "Let me get these jeans off so I can breathe," she said.

"Need any help?" asked Tim, as the girls disappeared into the other room. Tim produced a comb and ran it quickly through his hair. When we made eye contact, he mouthed something to me but I didn't understand. The girls soon returned, having changed back into something more comfortable.

Vee grabbed a big square pillow from the corner and sat on it Indian style. The thunderstorm raged on. As soon as we placed our fingertips on the planchette, Tim asked, "Will something evil happen tonight?"

Vee slapped his shoulder. "Tim! Don't ask questions like that!"

Dawn reached for the instructions. "It says 'to obtain the best results, it is important that the persons present concentrate their minds upon the matter in question and avoid other topics. Have no one at the table who will not sit seriously and respectfully…Tim. If you use it in a frivolous spirit, asking ridiculous questions, you naturally get undeveloped influences around you.'"

"Ooh, undeveloped influences," said Tim, mockingly. Vee cast him a dirty look. "Okay, I'm serious. I'm serious," he added.

After a moment of silence, Tim farted, eliciting objections from everyone.

"What?" said Tim. It's the nachos. C'mon, you all ate some."

"Be serious y'all," said Vee. "I'll start. Everybody put your fingertips on the planchette."

"On the what?"

"This." Vee took Tim's hand and guided it. When we were all ready, Vee spoke. "Will I pass the Civil Service Exam?"

We stared at the planchette. It remained still. But then, it started to move in small increments, slowly, toward "Yes."

Vee clapped her hands. "Oh, good!"

"My turn!," shouted Tim. "Who will get laid tonight?"

"Tim!" cried Vee.

Tim held up his hands in defense. "Dawn said no frivolous."

"'Frivolous' isn't a noun," I mumbled.

As soon as we all replaced our hands upon the planchette, it lurched all over the board. Tim and Vee stared at each other challengingly. Knuckles turned white. "You turkey," said Vee. "You're moving it!"

"*V...*" announced Tim, before the planchette was forced roughly off the board by the pushing and pulling hands. "Hmm, whose name starts with *V*?"

"Very funny," said Vee.

"I'll go next," said Dawn. It took a minute for Vee and Tim to settle down after a brief shushing match. "Who is with us?"

Tim made a dubious expression.

"If you are listening, reveal to us your name."

There was a gratuitous flash of lightning, followed by a long, low rumble.

"Spooky," said Tim. This time he was ignored.

The planchette crawled obliquely across the board, then slid smoothly to the letter *K*. After a brief pause, it slid to *R*. We looked at each other. From *R*, it moved to *O*, then slowly...to *L*. Back to *O*, then *K* again, then nothing.

"Who the hell is Krolok?" blurted Tim.

"Never heard of him," said Dawn.

"I don't know any Krolok," said Vee. "The name sounds foreign."

When everyone looked at me, I shrugged. "No idea."

"Okay shush, y'all," said Dawn. "Krolok, we hear you. What is it that you want?"

"Maybe he wants to get laid," said Tim.

"Well *I'm* not laying anyone," said Vee, sharply.

It was Tim's turn to read my lips, which formed the word "Ouch."

"Suck my dick," he whispered.

"Shut up, both of you," said Dawn. "Krolok? Do you hear me? What do you want?"

The planchette began to stir.

"*Y...,*" said Tim. "*A...*" The planchette now drifted in a slow circle, gradually returning to *A* before stopping on *T*.

"We don't understand," said Dawn. "Krolok? What do you want? Krolok?"

"Maybe Krolok is a serial killer," said Tim.

There was a loud bang outside. When I turned my head involuntarily, I became aware of bright lights coming from the direction of the street, followed by the unmistakable sound of a chainsaw.

Vee crawled over to the window. "That was quick."

Dawn stood up. "Who wants popcorn?"

The thought of eating anything sounded disgusting. Vee put on a Hendrix album and began dancing around in the candlelight. As if in response to the music, one chainsaw turned into a chorus of chainsaws. Returns for remaining upstairs were clearly diminishing. Besides, the juxtaposition of Krolok's name with "Yaat" was unambiguously alarming. Time to crack open some books.

"I'm going to head out," I said.

Tim groaned in objection.

"Aww, are you sure?" cried Vee.

"Yeah, I don't feel so hot. Good night, everyone."

"See the setting sun, the evening's just begun, and love is in the air!" sang Tim, over the Hendrix. The sun set hours ago. That guy really irritates me.

Seizing Dawn's umbrella, I announced in Mary Poppins' voice, "That will be quite enough of that. It's time to go home." As I slid the door closed behind me, I heard Vee sing, "'Scuze me while I kiss this guy!" If I find out she kissed Tim I am going to be sick.

WEDNESDAY, MARCH 30

Stayed up late last night skimming through Sherwood's red notebook for any and every mention of Krolok's name. I then checked the codex to see if it appeared there. As far as I can tell, it does not. While glancing at the spells, I spotted *Hinder* again. Its description sounds sort of like what happened to me. It involves twine and has a page of intricate-looking knots I do not recall from Aunt Wanda's chart.

Tim's van was still parked out front this morning, and so was Dawn's truck. The power was back on. The city forestry crew had done its job. Many logs were lined up neatly by the curb. Will miss that tree. Can already tell my bedroom is brighter than it normally is at this time. Had just washed my hair when there was a knock at the door. It was Dawn.

"Good morning! Come up and have breakfast with us." She smiled sweetly.

"I'll be right up," I said. "Want to come in for a minute?"

Left Dawn to explore my living room while I dried my hair and got dressed.

"Your place is smaller than Vee's," shouted Dawn.

"Vee has a whole room above the front porch that I don't have. She also has a room above the garage."

"You have a lot of books."

"They're all cataloged."

Dawn chuckled. "Of course they are." Was tying my shoelaces when she said out of the blue, "Do you farm muskrats?"

I raced into the living room and snatched *Successful Muskrat Farming* out of her hand. "Where did you find this?" I said, excitedly. "I've been looking all over for it!"

"It was just sitting right here."

"Right there? Wow. Belongs to a buddy of mine. Brought it home by mistake and he's pretty mad," I bullshitted. I put the codex in my mansack then grabbed Dawn's umbrella. "We'd better get upstairs. I'm starving!"

"Terrific!" said Vee when she saw me. "You and Tim can go outside and bring me some of those stumps. I want to put plants on them. How do you like your eggs?"

"Sunny side up."

Tim and I descended the staircase. While I paused to tie my other shoe, Tim sang, "Keep on stumpin', baby...I got to keep on stumpin'" to the tune of "Keep on Truckin'." Found it mildly irritating that both Vee and Tim were calling logs 'stumps.'

"You're in a jolly mood," I said.

"You would be, too, if you hadn't pussied out."

"Why? What happened?"

"The Weejee board doesn't lie."

"Doesn't it, now?"

While wrestling logs up the stairs, I got a splinter. When I told the girls, Vee insisted on trying to tweeze it out at the breakfast table while my eggs got cold.

"Hold still!" she commanded.

"Really, it'll come out by itself. They always do."

Vee admired the logs we salvaged for her. "Are y'all going to leave that on the floor?" Tim and I had left behind a trail of sawdust and bits of bark. Vee tossed a wet dishcloth to Tim, who knew what he had to do. So she was putting *him* to work.

Dawn gave me a ride back to the Mother Lode. She tried to start the Rambler. She jumped it, but the engine was running rough.

"Let's get it towed back to my place," she said. "If you can live without it for a few days, I might be able to fix it. Just give me money for parts."

"Are you sure? That's awfully sweet of you." It took the better part of the morning to deal with that. By the time Dawn dropped me off back at Collinwood, I was ready for lunch. Tim's van was still out front.

Gig at I Gotcha opening for Prowler. Rode with Tim in The Eagle Has Landed. Vee came along, so I reclined on the floor behind them. I marveled at the heavily customized interior. Burnt orange shag carpet; swivel leather bucket seats; and a loud 8-track player with quadraphonic speakers. By the time we arrived, I was a bit vansick. Vee had put her bare feet on the dash, and after she got out, I saw Tim discreetly wipe it off with a chamois.

While we were shooting pool, Bonnie surprised us all with a stack of 45s.

"Our new single!" cried Dave II.

Bonnie gave us each several copies to give away. I handed one to Vee, eliciting a dirty look from Tim.

"Can people buy this in record stores?" said Vee.

"They can!"

I slid one out of its sleeve. "But they're rectangular!" Side A was "Journey to Dord (Radio Edit)" and Side B was "Hail Marys (Slow Version)."

"What's on the cover?" demanded Tim.

"Steven designed the sleeve," said Bonnie, proudly.

"The drawing's by the illustrator Boris Artzybasheff," I explained. It's a piece from a series he did in the late forties on the neurotic symptoms. The title of this one is 'Repressed Hostility.'"

"What does that have to do with the music?"

"Not a whole lot," I conceded. "Although the lyrics to 'Journey to Dord' are arguably of a psychological nature, are they not? I just liked the illustration and thought it somehow fit."

Tim made a face.

"Is that your repressed hostility face?" I asked.

"We should have voted on it," he sulked. Tim regarded the sleeve verso, which featured a photo of the band on stage. "'Photo credit: Turtle Man,'" he read aloud. "Who the hell is Turtle Man?"

"Over there," I said, pointing at Turtle Man, who sat at the bar before two empty pitchers. "Getting his money's worth on 'free brew night' as you can see. Our only groupie. Student at Porteous. Don't actually know his real name. Meant to find out before this went to press, damn it."

"When was this photo even taken?" said Tim.

"When we played at Deuce's, I think," said Bonnie. "I recognize that Rangers pennant."

I turned to her. "Why is 'Journey to Dord' an edit? It's missing over four minutes."

"Dad said the shorter the song, the more likely they would play it on the radio."

"True, but it's two minutes and twelve seconds long now. That's pretty damn short, Bonnie."

"There was only one place where we could have made a clean edit that made sense. But that wrecked the arrangement, so we faded it out after the second chorus."

"But that's before the jazzy interlude! That's the best part!" I protested. Of course, it was too late now.

"I know, but people can hear that on the album," she replied, diplomatically.

Tim now had a spiteful grin on his face. He can be such a jerk sometimes.

One the way home, Vee put her feet back up on the dash. Tim tried to conceal his displeasure, but I am well acquainted with that look even if Vee is not. Upon arrival, Tim followed Vee upstairs, his fist in a ball.

THURSDAY, MARCH 31
Biked to the library. Biking in seventy-degree weather is sweaty work. Had to clean myself up upon arrival. After discovering pee all over the floor in the staff restroom, I taped a sign on the wall that said, "Please leave this restroom slightly cleaner than you found it." Less than an hour later, I found a memo from Jo Ann on my desk which read, "As your bathroom sign is vague, I'm not sure if you are talking about beard trimmings. All the previous complaints I have heard from staff and student employees have been about trimmings in the sink, or the lack of soap or toilet paper. I don't personally use that bathroom, but maybe those of you who do could make a list of agreed courtesies." She cc'ed Dixie and Carlos.

Why are "staff and student employees" complaining to Jo Ann about the staff restroom? Does she solicit complaints? Randy, Lloyd and I are the only ones who have beards. I am pretty sure Lloyd does not groom himself, especially at work. Have not trimmed my beard since '72. Guess it could have been Randy, but I have never seen any hair in the sink. When Lloyd showed up for his shift, I showed him the memo.

"I never trim my beard," he said, handing it back to me. "The last thing I need is Mrs. Womack on my back. She's already mad at me."

"How do you know she's mad at you?"

"You can always tell by what her nostrils are doing. She wrote me up over the way I dress. If she only knew the truth about me."

"The truth?"

Lloyd sighed, then took a long pause. He then opened up to me at length about his thyroid problems and his father's declining health. He seemed to be on the verge of tears.

I nodded sympathetically, but did not know what to say. Presently, I asked him a question about organ music. Lloyd put on an air of forlorn good cheer and began a huge monologue, as I knew he would.

Evidently, a week before those 747s collided in the Canaries, a freshman at Duke predicted the disaster and that five hundred eighty-three people would die. He wrote the prediction down on a piece of paper and locked it in a safe, which was opened after the fact. My *yaje* detector was already going nuts before I got to the part where the student casually admitted he was an "amateur magician." My *yaje* detector remains silent when I read Sherwood's red notebook. Sherwood is not trying to bullshit anyone and clearly believes what he wrote. Now I have to wonder if he was sane.

Brought a cork bulletin board down to the Vault so I could practice throwing my *shuriken* during cigarette breaks. Tacked withdrawn catalog cards on it to make it look legitimate, then assigned a point value to each card. Felt like the techniques I had learned from the Draker pamphlet were beginning to pay off.

Take-out from King Wok for dinner. While waiting for my number to be called, I looked at all the autographed celebrity photos on the wall: Jimmy Stewart, Yale Lary, Icky Twerp, Betty Buckley, Lash LaRue, Peter Ustinov, "Professor Cerberus," the Von Erichs, etc. Imagined them all partying here at once. What, no corporation presidents? What would Joan Crawford say?

Picked at my Temptation Beef with Dark Brown while watching *Fantastic Journey*. It had a sorcerer in it. With the aid of a female werewolf, the sorcerer attempted to possess Roddy McDowell's body in order to escape his imprisonment. Guess I would rather have Roddy McDowell's body and be free than be imprisoned in my own. Wonder if there is anything like that in the codex.

My fortune cookie said, "The best way to get rid of an enemy is to make a friend." I imagined Harvey perched on top of my TV set, me talking to him like Tony Baretta and his cockatoo. Ridiculous.

FRIDAY, APRIL 1

Biked to work again. Forgot to tuck my pant leg into my sock and of course it got chewed up in the chain. My office felt like a sauna. Felt like I needed to shower all over again. Reluctantly put my tie around my sweaty neck, which was the last thing in the world I wanted to do at that moment.

Encountered Randy reading this morning's paper in the break room. "Dude, you're not going to believe this!" he said, excitedly.

"What is it?"

He laid the newspaper flat on the table, then tapped his finger on the Jumble. "All four of these are words of power!"

I regarded the scrambled words. They did not look like words of power. But what do I know?

"Thought a lot about what you said when you called me the other say, and you were right," said Randy.

"I was?"

"Say them!" demanded Randy.

"What do you mean?"

"Just do it," he said, his voice now urgent. "Now!"

I hesitated, then spoke the words aloud with as much conviction as I could muster. "Walog. Siban. Limies! NIGMIT!"

"Now get down!" shouted Randy. He tugged my sleeve and we dove under the table just as Jenny appeared.

"What are you two nincompoops doing?" she said.

Randy's countenance was one of abject terror. Quivering, he looked at Jenny then at me before his face relaxed. "April fool's, dude."

"You bastard," I said.

"What was the joke?" said Jenny.

Randy and I stood up and brushed ourselves off. "Tell her," he said.

"Yes," said Jenny. "Tell me."

"You wouldn't understand," I said.

When Randy and I were alone, I told him about the Ouija board incident with Krolok. He found it significant considering neither Vee, Dawn, nor Tim had ever heard the name, but it appears in Sherwood's red notebook.

"How many Kroloks do you know? What's more, Sherwood wrote on more than one occasion that Krolok visited him in a dream. If Krolok can do that, what else can he do?"

This talk of Sherwood aroused my curiosity. Found the door to the professor's office propped open with a large garbage can. Was dismayed to see the divan, the art, the exercise bike, etc., gone. Nothing sadder than an empty bookcase. The Beam's Choice remained upon the empty desk. Surprised Carlos did not swipe it. The rhino head sat facing the corner. Had I foreseen this ransacking, I might have paid an earlier visit with my key. A missed opportunity! I must be careful not to miss any more. Who knows that was kept and what was tossed (and who kept it). Was just about to walk away when I spotted in the garbage can a box of photographs, along with a pile of handwritten notes and other papers. Grabbed these things and hauled ass before Carlos returned.

Back at my desk, I examined my booty, which included a xeroxed bibliography of sorts containing descriptions of books, pictures, and objects. The list reads like Browne's *Musaeum clausum*. It is heavily annotated in Sherwood's unmistakable hand.

"Please, Steven. May Guddu have this?" Guddu was standing right next to me holding an old geometry textbook. Do not even want to know why. Where did he even find it? Should have asked, although his request seemed innocuous enough. Right after Guddu disappeared, Dixie sent me on a wild goose chase for a thesis that was supposed to be in the thesis cage but was not. Evidence suggested it might be in Sherwood's office, but of course that is empty now. Nothing is where it is supposed to be lately.

Spotted Jenny sulking at the circulation desk. Guess she was mad at me for not telling her my secret. At that moment, I remembered I had brought a copy of our 45 to work to give to her. Maybe that would get me out of the dog house. Played it for her on the library record player. I could not find the 45 adapter, so I centered the record manually. We shared earphones.

"Hey, you guys rock!" said Jenny. "But why is the record rectangular and not round? Also, there's no bass." Damn you, Tim! That motherfucker turned me down!

While Jenny and I were listening to the B-side, Guddu suddenly appeared. Almost jumped out of my skin.

"Jesus, Guddu!"

"Who is Jesus?" said Guddu.

"It's Steven's band," said Jenny, proudly.

Guddu looked at us in bewilderment. "Jesus is Steven's band," he said.

I handed Guddu the earphones, which he held in his palm.

"Hold it up to your ear," I said.

Guddu listened, then pointed his bony finger at me. "This is your band?"

"Yes."

"You, Steven?" he continued, in disbelief, pointing at me.

"Yes."

Guddu grinned widely. "Good show!" His eyes darted back and forth from my eyes to the record player. He snapped his fingers double-time to the funereal dirge of "Hail Marys" just as it was fading out. "This is groovy music, Steven!"

Jenny looked unhappy. "Why do you never invite me to your shows?"

Guess I am still in the dog house. On a positive note, I got the Rambler back. I owe Dawn one.

SATURDAY, APRIL 2

Stopped by Roy Pope on the way to work and after much deliberation bought a box of Twinkies. Which would have to do. They still did not have any Tuna Twist and when I asked about it Bubble Girl said it had been discontinued. She seemed amused, but when she told me the price of the Twinkies and then said, "That was a very good year," I know she found me ridiculous.

Arrived to work early enough to set up the trap in the hobbit room. A word about fox urine. Do not ever open a bottle of it in close quarters, as I unfortunately did. If Harvey is as smart as I believe he is, he will see the trap for what it is and avoid it. Unless he cannot resist a Twinkie.

A student asked if we had a water fountain. No one has ever asked me that question before. Never drink from water fountains (or Petri dishes, for that matter), myself, so they may as well be invisible. Whenever I am thirsty, I just help myself to an ice cold Pibb from the Bilby. What did I do before the Bilby? Guess I just died of thirst.

Professor Ziglar asked, "How do you spell the words 'coruscation' and '*geistlicher*'?" When I spelled them without looking them up, he just blinked and walked away, without so much as a "thank you" or "up yours."

During an afternoon break, I returned to Sherwood's office. Heaved the rhino head onto a book cart and laboriously wheeled it out of the library. Guddu watched me do this with great interest, even following me out to Lot C. Did not see Boggs but that does not mean he did not see me. If he did, I guess my wheeling a rhinoceros head on a book cart out to the Rambler in broad daylight failed to raise any red flags. Went back to take one last look. The Beam's Choice was still there, so I took it. Might as well, if it is just going to be thrown away. It looks fine on my mantelpiece.

After watching me load the rhino into the back seat of the Rambler, I noticed Guddu staring at the hood. His expression was one of alarm. He pointed at the three-fingered hand and said, "This?" I just laughed it off, but Guddu did seem genuinely disturbed. Later, I saw him wantonly shelving books like some sort of wild animal. He seemed quite agitated.

Spent the rest of the afternoon at my desk examining the bibliography and photos. I chuckled at one of the titles, "Leaf in an Unknown Script." Among the other items listed was *Die Tür*, *Chronik von Vul Kar*, and a book about Mt. Shasta in California that Sherwood used to talk about.

Speaking of California, there was a letter to Sherwood from the proprietor of an occult bookstore in San Francisco:

Dear Professor Sherwood,

Regarding the matter about which you were so anxious (again, I appreciate your candor and assure you that your secrets are safe with me), I will only say the coincidences are too remarkable to ignore.

Now, your questions. The Seaberg Society was founded by Virgil Seaberg in 1901 here in San Francisco. Seaberg was a self-described cryptohistorian, a word he coined to mean the study of the kind of history that is shunned by frowsty academians (his words). He founded the Society to bring together like-minded individuals to share recondite knowledge chiefly of prehistoric advanced civilizations, such as that of the Khul of legend. Its members are known for seeking out, collecting, and dealing in primary material pertaining to such civilizations. Such material was procured from far-flung libraries, museums, auctions, and personal collections, and were either purchased, stolen, or traded among connoisseurs of esoterica, practitioners of ars magica, smugglers of antiquities, rival cryptohistorians, and of course, occult booksellers like myself.

In the early days of the Society, its profile was enhanced greatly after sensational discoveries by Count Byron de Prorok in Rockwall County, Texas and at Mt. Shasta. Infighting, betrayal, and the mysterious disappearance of Seaberg resulted in the temporary dissolution of the Society. It was revived in the fifties by William Baumann in Los Angeles, California. At that time, the Society was headquartered in Los Feliz, but it was little more than a tiny, cluttered office where Baumann's secretary answered correspondence. I'm afraid I don't recall her name. She came into my shop a few times when I was still based down there. Flirty brunette. Society meetings took place at various private residences, including Baumann's house on Barton Avenue. In later years, he rarely emerged from it for fear that his priceless collection of Dordiana would be stolen. Which of course it eventually was. Or much of it, that is.

You may be familiar with the so-called Codex Baumann *that was decried as a hoax some years ago. Translated from an unknown language into Greek in 60 A.D. Then again into Latin in the early Renaissance by Gnaeus Vibius who gave it the title* De re dordica. *There are no known extant copies of that book in Greek or Latin. About fifteen years ago, Janus Fraser translated the Vibius into English. It was printed in small numbers and privately circulated among members of the Society. Saw one at auction last year in L.A. Too rich for this poor book peddler's blood.*

De re dordica *described a fantastic place, its inhabitants, and history. The codex was heavily annotated and contained additional matter said to be of great value to occultists. Every now and then we get some kook in here asking for it.*

Baumann was an associate of Seaberg's. His collection included all of Vibius' extant works, as well as the Liber de Hurlis *and the* Shasta Scrolls. *His carved* Head of a Khul, *found encrusted in limestone at Mono Lake, is said to predate the arrival of the Paiute.*

I have some Society material here at the shop, which I will be happy to show you when you visit. Until then, be well.

Regards,

Patrick Odom-Lott

Odom-Lott's letter, dated last September, mentions a visit. Do not recall Sherwood traveling last year, unless it was during the Christmas break. Did he make it to San Francisco? Wish I had the other side of Sherwood''s correspondence with Odom-Lott. Examined several sheets of carbon paper which bore traces of letters from Sherwood, but none were legible. His delicate calligraphic hand had not overcome the resistance of the insert.

SUNDAY, APRIL 3

Pianist Balint Vazsonyi has begun a two-day marathon during which he is to play all thirty-two Beethoven sonatas from memory. I don't see how that is possible. He says he sees the cycle as a musical diary, each sonata reflecting stages of Beethoven's musical development. Reminds me of the Bastard, who can recite large chunks of Catullus and Shakespeare from memory. Randy can also tell you obscure *futbog* statistics, who ran against Warren G. Harding, and where the Summer Olympics were held in 1912. "Must have read it in a book somewhere," he would say. Still recall the agony of memorizing Antony's funeral oration for Caesar back at dear old A.H.H.S. Randy had made it look so easy. I thought of my red notebook and how it reflects the stages of my magical development, such that it is. But my diary? What does it reveal about my development as a human being?

Brought several recordings of Respighi's *Vetrate di chiesa* over to Fred's. He got all of his out, and we spent the evening comparing the lengths of the gong reverberation at the end of the 'San Michele Arcangelo' movement of each. The Doráti won, hands down, clocking in at an impressive twenty seconds. It was fun and took my mind off of Harvey for a while.

Bought lacquer thinner on the way home. No time better than the present to remove the three-fingered hand from the hood of the Rambler. It worked but also removed some of the original paint job. The Rambler is starting to look like a real jalopy.

MONDAY, APRIL 4

Again, I took notes in my sleep. My chicken scrawl looks more like Dordic than English.

Today I had to use the microfilm reader. The take-up reel squeaks loudly. I get much pleasure rewinding film while staring at Jo Ann challengingly. To my great disappointment, it ran smoothly when I used it this morning. Some jerk must have oiled it.

Found Randy in the basement workroom, hunched over a microscope. He was doing something to a document with a plastic hose attached to a roaring machine. "Hey, man!" I shouted.

When I tapped his shoulder, Randy sat up and removed his protective earmuffs. "I'm aspirating mold from the Troutman papers. What are you doing?"

Showed him the bibliography, which he studied with great interest.

"Look," I said. "*Linguae dordica* is described as a 'grammar of a purportedly magickal language.'"

"Magickal spelled with a *k*," noted Randy. "Which means whoever wrote this is familiar with Thelema and understands the difference between Aleister Crowley and Doug Henning."

"But Dordic isn't a magickal language, is it?"

"No, but Astarian is."

"Strange, isn't it? It's almost like the person who wrote that has never seen *Linguae dordica*. Or, he has confused the two languages, which would be easy to do because they use the same script." I read aloud one of Sherwood's marginal notes. "'Ask Randy re: pronunciation.'" I looked at Randy questioningly.

"He did ask me something like that about a year ago. Not about *Linguae dordica* but about the finer points of how Latin pronunciation changed over time. The important thing to understand about *Linguae dordica* is not when it was printed but when it was written."

"Or by whom."

"That's another conversation altogether. But how Latin was pronounced at that time and place is key to how Dordic, and by extension Astarian, is pronounced. You may have encountered, for example, the Claudian half-*b*."

I shook my head. Thought I was supposed to be the linguist.

"It represented the *sonus medius*, a short vowel sound used before labial consonants in words such as *documentum*. This is important. Since *Linguae dordica* is a grammar of Dordic written in Latin, consider how you and I have been pronouncing Dordic. How accurate do you think that is?"

"Not sure why Sherwood would care about that, unless he was reading it aloud for some reason. Or trying to cast spells."

"If they weren't working, his pronunciation might have been suspect."

"Or magic is phony," I said. "That could be your problem."

"Anything's possible, Steven. Do you even party?"

"You were at my New Year's party."

"Q.E.D. Remember at the Eagle's Nest the other day when I pointed at you and said, 'Unmake the face' in Astarian? And you accused me of slapping you in the face?"

"Sounds like something a real bastard might do."

"True, but I didn't. But imagine if I had pronounced it correctly."

"Pronounced what?"

"The spell."

"What are you saying?"

"Think, Steven."

"What the hell, Randy," I wailed. "You tried to unmake my face?"

Randy shook his head. "Drinking and sorcery don't mix," he said.

"These were in Sherwood's office," I said. I handed Randy the box of photographs.

We looked at them together. A man in a hooded white robe standing in the middle of a street in what looked like a small town. Ruins in a wilderness. A deserted stretch of rocky coastline. A stone passageway leading into darkness. "These aren't from someone's family photo album," said Randy.

Meanwhile, I was reading the descriptions of the photographs listed in the bibliography. "'Skeletal remains with elongated skull'?"

"Don't see anything like that," said Randy. "But what do you make of this one?"

"An image of a hand-drawn plan of something. Reminds me of the Palace at Knossos. Kind of weird to take a picture of that. I mean, the photograph documents its existence but doesn't reproduce it legibly. You can't see much detail." I checked the bibliography.

"'Underground colony at Yaat'?" I asked.

"Yaat. There's the name again," said Randy. "I've been thinking. Since we have xeroxed more material than we can ever read at this point, we may as well stash the codex. We could hide it inside the library somewhere."

"But where?" I said. "Harvey's hideout is clearly out of the question. Carlos knows about all the other nooks and crannies, I'm sure."

"Simply misshelve it." Randy cleared his throat. "Don't forget where, of course."

"Or we could replace the Gutenberg with it. No one ever looks at it anyway."

"Hidden in plain sight," said Randy. "I like it."

"Speaking of Harvey's hideout, I set a trap for him."

"You did? What did you use for bait?"

"Poison Twinkie."

"Good luck," said Randy, dubiously. "And I mean it."

Returned to my desk. As soon as I sat down, I heard gunshots.

Diane appeared in my doorway. "What's going on?" she said.

"Probably Carlos scaring away grackles."

Diane seemed not to have heard me. She quickly looked down at a list in her hands. "Have you seen a bronze and alexandrite amulet?"

Felt like she was trying to catch me off guard. I pointed at her list. "What do you have there?"

"I'm taking an inventory of the artworks in the Baumann Collection."

"Professor Sherwood was in charge of the inventory." I hesitated, then added, "Do you want me to help you? I know the collection better than anyone besides Sherwood."

"Yes, you can help me find that amulet."

TUESDAY, APRIL 5

Early to the library to check the trap. Sprung and empty. The maestro lay in the corner of the hobbit room, his eyes gouged out again. Decided to just leave it. No reason to let Harvey know every time I violate his sanctum. Does he understand I am the one who set the trap? But of course, he does.

Later I had to go up to the mezzanine. When I tried to walk up the stairs, something went wrong. Felt like I was on my way up, but somehow made it only to the landing. My lungs heaved, as if I had just run the 100-yard dash. After redoubling my efforts, I stopped short of the mezzanine, exasperated.

Diane paused at the foot of the staircase. "What are you doing?"

"Nothing. Just walking up these steps."

"Why were you walking like that?"

"What do you mean?"

"I don't know. It just looked like you weren't going anywhere."

Thought about what she was saying for a moment, before deciding to trust her. I descended the stairs easily enough.

"Watch me," I said. "I'm going to go up again."

After a few moments, Diane said, "You're doing it again."

Looked around to discover I had not yet made it to the top. What the hell? I crawled up the remaining steps on all fours. I peered down at Diane, who was now staring at me thoughtfully.

As I turned to walk away, I thought I saw Guddu peeking around the corner. He must think I am crazy.

Forgot Amber's name today when introducing her to Professor Ziglar. President Carter has a memory tutor named John Currie whose methods have helped him memorize names, faces, hometowns, and even the birthdays of all five hundred thirty-five U.S. congressmen. Your birthday is September 9th? Currie's code for September is a cow. Nine is a tire. When he thinks of your name or face, he imagines you changing a tire on a cow. Wonder if his methods would work for me? Found nothing by him in the card catalog.

Took the afternoon off so Jenny and I could have a late lunch together. By then I was starving. Did not want to eat earlier because I did not want to have bad breath when I saw her. Jenny wanted to go to Mi Cocinita, a charming little restaurant in someone's garage.

"Why do you have a hand painted on your car?" she said.

"Gets me where I need to go," I said cryptically. "How do you find out about these places? Randy would love it here."

By the time our food had arrived, I had already nearly O.D.'d on chips and hot sauce. That did not stop me from sucking down a three-item combination plate and flan.

Why do I spend so much time with Jenny? Is it because she is there? Loretta had been there, and look what happened. After a long lull in the conversation, I broke the ice when I remarked on the similarities among the logos for Winnebago, Whataburger, and Wonder Woman.

After lunch we went to Age of Aquarius and tried on clothes. Found some peppermint-striped pants to wear on stage which were pretty tight, due in part to overeating. Jenny bought a brown velour tracksuit and some heart-shaped sunglasses. We were both pretty thrilled with our finds and wore them out of the store. Told Jenny that she looked like a teddy bear in her new outfit. Before I had even completed the sentence, I saw the look on Jenny's face and regretted making the remark.

We test drove a convertible Iso Grifo from a dealership on White Settlement. We looked so far out, I think the salesman assumed we were rich and did not ask to accompany us. He just asked for my license and phone number, then handed over the keys. Gave him my work number.

We got milkshakes from a drive-through window. Jenny could not believe it when I told her it was the first time I had ever gone through a drive-through window. Found it nearly impossible to understand the clown through that tiny loudspeaker. Sounded like Charlie Brown's teacher: *womp womp womp.* The milkshake was too thick to suck through the straw. When I discovered it was not even real ice cream, I hurled it out the window. Jenny scolded me for littering. Took the Grifo up to Sansom Park. Slowly ran over a tennis ball while Jenny protested that it belonged to a dog. I then burned rubber in front of a picnicking family. The looks on their faces! The world sure is different in that car. Guess that is what it is like to be rich.

Took the Rambler back to the Hacienda. Jenny said she had a paper due tomorrow for her cataloging class, so I walked her to the porch. We commiserated about Professor Funkweiler's antics in the classroom.

"The textbook is one he wrote himself," said Jenny. "It's got to be over a thousand pages long."

"*The Bibliographic Multiverse.* Still have nightmares about it. What else is he having you read?"

"*Information on the MARC System.*"

"Ugh, MARC. What's next? Machine-readable people?" While we were chatting, I heard a buzzing sound and looked up at a bee that was stuck in a spider web. I rescued the bee with an old bubble wand, but separating the spider web from his wings was no simple task. Jenny gave me tweezers from her purse and looked at me like I was her hero.

After washing my hands, I headed back to Collinwood. I contemplated my bee rescue. Had I interfered with nature by snatching a spider's vittles out from under her? Was my act one of chivalry or selfishness? Randy says everything we do is an act of selfishness. This cannot be true.

WEDNESDAY, APRIL 6
Went to the cleaners to pick up my jacket. When the proprietress presented it to me, I lifted the bag to see if the stain was gone. It was, but now there was a hole where the stain had been. I pointed out the discrepancy.

"Moff hoe!" she snapped, dismissively. "There when you bring to me!"

"*Not* a moth hole. Nor was it there when I brought it to you." The proprietress just kept repeating "moff hoe" and shaking her head until her flunkie emerged from behind the curtain and gave me the stink eye.

"This is *yaje*. I'm not paying for this." I slapped my palm on the bell on the counter and stormed out. Felt somewhat proud for this uncharacteristic act of defiance, but also felt a little ill from all the adrenaline. Like Guddu, I do not like being bullshitted.

Picked up Jenny from the library and took her to dinner at Crystal's. Two dates in a row. If you could call them dates. Let her choose where to sit, which was revealing. Instead of a curtained booth or the cozy den with the fireplace, Jenny chose the theater. There, we sat side by side on a hard wooden bench. Could not hear myself speak over *The Little Rascals*. The little rascals sitting right in front of us did little to enhance the decidedly unromantic atmosphere. Especially when they all turned around and wordlessly stared at us until we left the theater.

Jenny and I paused to try the coin-operated Love Tester. She got "passionate" but I just do not see it. I got "sweet," which might be my problem right there. The Stone Fox received this information stoically and without comment.

After dinner, we went to Putt Putt (for the fun of it, ha ha—now I have that song stuck in my head). On the last hole, I was clowning around and hit the ball way too hard. It flew into the clubhouse and bounced around wildly. The manager was pretty hacked off, so we got out of there. It was funny in retrospect, to me at least. Jenny seemed indifferent about it all.

It was now dark. We drove around aimlessly for a while, talking about what we wanted to do next. Was not really paying attention to where we were going and ended up on an obscure street off Cherry Lane. Suddenly, it seemed the road had disappeared and we were now driving across a muddy field. The street lights had vanished. Not wanting to get stuck, I floored it. The rear of the Rambler slid to and fro while the engine roared. Not sure if one or both of us screamed, but we somehow made it onto a side street, the wheels of the Rambler flinging mud as we slowly gathered speed. I pulled over in front of

Hoots TV. Shadows danced behind its myriad glass bricks. What goes on in that place?

"Just gotta check something real quick." Got out and opened the trunk. Nothing there but books and crap. No room for Harvey to hide. Had half a mind to check underneath the car, in case he was clinging to the muffler, but I did not want to stretch out the knees of my pants. "Where are you, motherfucker?" I hissed.

Drove Jenny back to the Hacienda. When we got out of the Rambler, Jenny took one look and said it looked like mint chocolate chip ice cream because of all the mud splatters. She did not ask me up for a nightcap.

Was too wound up to go home. Found myself on Loop 820. The Rambler shakes every time I hit 47 miles per hour. Guess I must have bent something when I hit that pothole on Camp Bowie. Will have to ask Dawn about it. Every couple of miles I passed signs saying either "Now Leaving Fort Worth" and "Now Entering Fort Worth." Feel like I am entering and leaving reality these days.

THURSDAY, APRIL 7

Worked late. Amber casually told me there was a bat in the library yesterday. She did not see it this morning. I later spied it up in the corner in the reading room, which has a high ceiling.

I grabbed the radio. "Carlos! Break 1-9!"

"I'm right here," said a voice behind me. It was Carlos. "I'll take care of it," he said.

"What are you going to do?"

"Got the Remington in the truck." Holy guano, he is going to fire a gun in the library? I weighed my options, but they all involved Dixie.

"Don't do it now, Carlos. Wait until the library closes," I said.

Carlos regarded the bat, then the clock, then the bat again. He sighed. "I'll be back."

In the meantime, I quietly took the Gutenberg down to the Vault and shelved it by call number among the other rare books. I then put the original codex in the display case where the Gutenberg had been. Opened it to one of the more innocuous pages, one without a demon on it. Was going to place an identifying placard next to it but thought better of it. No one asked me what I was doing.

Carlos returned just as "Happy Trails" was ending.

"20-gauge," observed Hey Now.

Everyone gathered around to watch. Carlos aimed, then fired. What remained of the bat landed unceremoniously on one of the Geweihsessel chairs.

Hey Now clapped and stamped his feet. "Hot damn! You blew that bat clean away! That's Charles Whitman shooting! Hey! Hey!"

"Good show, Carlos!" exclaimed Guddu. Sarge just shook his head.

"Can Guddu hold the weapon?" said Guddu to Carlos, pointing at the Remington.

Carlos looked Guddu up and down like he was a stranger. "No, Guddu cannot hold the weapon," he replied, mockingly. Carlos can be such a dick sometimes.

"You guys can go ahead and leave," I said. "I'll lock up."

After Carlos went to fetch his cleaning supplies, I found myself alone in the reading room. I looked up Slocum Avenue in the *Wallace Street Guide*. It was there. Or at least it was in 1974. On a whim, I sprung up the stairs to the mezzanine and hid in the alcove at the end of the 700s. For a time, all I could hear was a soft rush of air through various vents, and the occasional sound of Carlos wringing out his mop. After a half-hour of silence, I decided he had left.

I went up into the hobbit room to look around. The trap remained as I had left it. For reasons that escape me now, I figured this would be a fine time for a smoke.

Just as I was about to exit Harvey's hideout, I heard soft approaching foot-steps from one of the vents. I put out my cigarette. A pause was followed by a click of metal, then a scraping sound. Then, a gentle thud. A faint odor of sulfur betrayed Harvey's presence.

What to do? While my mind raced, so did my heart rate. Could Harvey see in the dark? Was he observing me? I heard the sniffing of expectant nostrils. In a panic, I lunged for the exit, but collided with Harvey. He yanked at my beard and sank his teeth into my forearm. Thought about biting him back, which would have been pretty gross. Tried to punch his nuts but was not sure where they were or if he even had any. I remembered my paper plate shiv. This, I drew, then shivved Harvey in the neck. He struggled to get away and my glasses went flying.

The imp let out a prolonged, guttural hiss. When I tried to wound him again he nimbly leaped aside then said something. "*Ftung!*" or some such thing.

Immediately, an invisible force, like a solid wall of air, pushed me toward, then out the opening to the hobbit room. I hit the ground like a sack of potatoes. I scrambled toward the stairs then tumbled down them. With the aid of the volute, I pulled myself to my feet and limped out of the building. Remarkably, I had the presence of mind to lock the door behind me. Feel like this library is something right out of *The Twilight Zone*.

FRIDAY, APRIL 8

Awoke drenched in sweat after a troubled night of fevered dreams. In them, I struggled to move against a strong wind along a cobblestone path. I gripped an ancient stone wall for composure as my hair whipped my face, my beard blowing sideways. All was gray. To my left, a declivity into a featureless, darker gray area. No idea where I was traveling, only that my journey was an urgent one. At intervals I was mocked and tormented by elongated, cackling faces that danced before mine. I swatted them away, but they persisted before finally dissolving in the wind. Up ahead in the distance, I sometimes could make out a dark, beckoning figure.

Have a spare pair of army glasses. The prescription is from seven years ago, as is the style of the frames. They must do for now. After showering, I examined my injuries. Nasty teeth marks on my left forearm and a gash above my clavicle. My left wrist is sprained from using it to break my fall. Add to this countless bruises, aches, pains, and one hell of a shiner. I put on Emerson, Lake, and Palmer. Momentarily, the dulcet tones of Tarkus's volcanic geniture chased my troubles away.

Library closed. Surmised I could go down there and get some work done without being disturbed. Found the building dark and quiet, just the way I like it. Was surprised to see the door to Dixie's office ajar. She usually locks it. Did Carlos open it? Was he in the building? I did not think he was, and took this golden opportunity to take a peek at Guddu's personnel file.

It did not take long to find it in Dixie's neatly organized file cabinet. Within the plain manilla folder I discovered something strange. No job application, no notes, none of the usual documentation that one would find in a personnel file. Only a sole sheet of paper, the form that Hazel passed out to everyone the other day that asked for our emergency contact information.

Under Name, it simply said 'Guddu.' No surname. Under Emergency Contact, it said 'Mgliazgobaul.' An Indian name? It did not sound like one. Mgliazgobaul's address was left blank, as was the rest of the form, which was signed, 'Guddu.' The handwriting was the most elegant I have ever seen, ornamented with long curlicues and delicate filigree. Heard the sound of a power drill coming from the vicinity of the reading room. Carlos! I noted Guddu's home address and replaced his file in the cabinet. Closed the drawer and hastily exited Dixie's office. Too bad I did not get a chance to look in Diane's file!

Stopped by Randy's to tell my story, and to be second-guessed and ridiculed. His arguments are always iron-clad. Unless I am prepared to make a case, I keep my mouth shut. Today I talked.

"True or false: Harvey kicked your ass," said Randy.

"Give me a break," I said. "I haven't been in a scuffle since the sixth grade."

I told Randy about all the bullshit that has been happening to me. Spilling things, locking my keys in the Rambler, the muddy field, the traffic lights, and my missing Chap Sticks. He seemed unimpressed.

"But it all adds up! I insisted. When I told him about the never ending staircase, he conceded, "Harvey's definitely messing with you. Maybe he's still pissed that you tried to trap him. Wouldn't you be?"

Randy invited me to stay for a breakfast of what must have been six dollars' worth of bacon. "Had to cook all of it before it went bad."

"Are you supposed to eat bacon on Good Friday?"

"Are you Catholic?"

We ate in silence while reading the morning paper. "Dallas Nazis gearing up for coming race war," I said.

"I hate Dallas Nazis," said Randy.

We decided to drive way the hell out to Richland Plaza for the bargain matinee of *The Song Remains the Same.* Jimmy Page's wanking was hard to sit through. It is a good thing Randy smuggled a bottle of Old Charter into the theater. On our way back out to the Rambler, Randy uncharacteristically stood on a decorative boulder and shouted, "Does anybody remember laughter?" to passersby.

"I'll make you forget laughter," muttered a North Richland Hills Nazi looking for a fight.

"C'mon," I hissed at Randy.

After dropping Randy off, I swung down Alta Mere. Wanted to take a look at Slocum Avenue in the light of day. Sure as shit, there was no construction or mud anywhere. Just a perfectly normal road. What is the meaning of this?

Went home and did my taxes. I then took a much-needed nap. Apart from paying off Uncle Sam, it was nice to have a day of no worries. Faced with a joyless evening of studying the codex, I recalled there is a theatrical production of *Harvey* at the Granbury Opera House. Another one of those coincidences.

Called Boggs from the gas station. He answered. When I invited him to accompany me to see the play, he said, "Steven, you must have read my mind."

Boggs lives across from Lake Como. He was standing by the water when I arrived, watching a low-flying B-52. When the bomber disappeared over the trees, he got into the Rambler.

"That, my man, is the sound of freedom," he said. After I botched our soul handshake, he looked at my shiner and said "What the hell happened to you?"

I hesitated to answer. Did not want to lie to Boggs.

He shook his head. "You and Carlos," he said.

"What do you mean? What happened to Carlos?"

"Something spooked him when he was on a ladder. Fell and broke his arm."

We turned onto Vickery. Boggs pointed out a seedy-looking motel. "Who's the new woman?" he said.

I just looked at him.

"One who don't wear no support."

I laughed. "You must mean Diane. What about her?"

"Saw her coming out of that motel back there."

"That awful place? When was this?"

"It was a Sunday," he replied. "February 6. Early."

"That's strange. What was she doing there?"

"Nothing legitimate happens at that joint," said Boggs. "That's for damn sure."

"She's at the Women's Faculty Club now."

"No! How did she manage that? She ain't faculty."

I shrugged.

"How much do you know about her?"

"Think she's from L.A. Why do you ask?"

"Got a feeling about people, that's all. You should have seen her chewing out Miss Duhig the other day."

"Jo Ann? What about?"

"Something about the basement. I wasn't paying no attention until the discussion became heated. I walked over to the information desk to tell them to lower their voices. I heard Miss Duhig say Diane ain't got no taste. That she dress like a gypsy's nightmare."

"You shushed a couple of librarians?"

Boggs chuckled. "Now how can anyone say that woman ain't got no taste? Boy, Diane didn't like that one iota. Can't say I blame her."

That did not sound like Jo Ann. But then I recalled her outrageous behavior at the Christmas party. Diane must have really gotten under her skin.

The Opera House was in ruins for years. It has been recently restored and on this night looked terrific. The stone structure was outlined in lights. The interior was filled with eager theatergoers ready for a three-act comedy of errors. Ladies' hair in Granbury, I noted, is much more expansive than in Fort Worth. The men wore jackets and ties. Boggs wore what he wears to work: work shirt, tie, Mets jacket. Felt like a slob in my wrinkled velour playboy shirt. And the humidity was doing my hair no favors.

"Don't know how my big black ass is supposed to fit in one of these," muttered Boggs when we got to our seats. My elbows were pinned to my side. We sat between two Kiwanians who evidently knew each other. Glad I left my jacket at home, since it was also hot and stuffy. Boggs left his on.

My discomfort, however, was nothing compared to that which followed the lifting of the curtain. The scene: a rather formal-looking parlor. Enter a diminutive Harvey, who crossed the stage and took a seat in a rocking chair. Apart from being only three feet tall and somewhat moth-eaten, this Harvey looked exactly like the oil portrait in the movie.

Enter Myrtle and Veta who busy themselves tidying up the room. Meanwhile, Harvey is hamming it up. He is smoking a cigar, crossing and uncrossing his legs, and scratching his balls. He rocks wildly in his rocking chair, almost falling over backwards. He snatches a june bug out of the air and eats it. I am busting a gut, but no one else is laughing. A Kiwanian shushes me. When the telephone rings on stage, Harvey acts surprised, falling out of his seat and rolling across the rug like he's on fire. I laugh, but uneasily this time. Again, I am shushed. Does no one see what I am seeing? Boggs is not laughing.

Harvey's shenanigans continue throughout the entire production while I squirm in my seat. At certain times, ignored by the cast and audience, Harvey approaches the edge of the stage and appears to look directly at me while wagging his finger. I say "appears" because of the bunny mask. Its two eye sockets are voids, though I can detect movement within. At the end of the third act, when Elwood summons him, Harvey hurries to his side and they exit stage left.

Next, the curtain call, whereby the cast assembles center stage for a bow. They are joined by Harvey who is now carrying his bunny mask, revealing himself as, surprise, *my* Harvey. After shouting a contemptuous "Bravo!" I give Harvey a standing ovation, eliciting the same from a clueless audience. What else am I to do? Boggs remains seated.

Boggs and I rode in silence. Somewhere on Hwy. 377 he spoke.

"Are you in trouble, Steven?"

"Yes, Boggs."

"Let me know if you need my help."

"I will, Boggs."

SATURDAY, APRIL 9

Another night of fevered reverie. As if an insufferable evening at the theater was not enough, Harvey made a cameo appearance in my dreams, ludicrously introducing himself as a Kiwanian. The name "Kiwanis" is coincidentally (or not) derived from an Ojibwe expression meaning "to fool around" but is also linked to an Algonquin expression meaning "to make oneself known." Harvey's shenanigans are already known to me, so I fail to see the point of last night's farce.

Spent a considerable part of the day studying the codex. If magic is *yaje*, why would someone make so much effort to record spells? What a damn waste of time to write them, but even more so to learn them with no chance of success. The spells are arranged in the codex in order of difficulty. The easiest ones have the simplest names: *Hinder, Warn, Strike*. What would a warning spell be used for? Why not just shout a warning, unless the spell accomplishes that wordlessly? The more difficult ones are several pages long, accompanied by sigils and complex geometrical diagrams. Even their names are long. Tried to translate one but gave up. Something like *Putrefying Orb of Ancestral Reprisal*.

Took a nacho break, though I had no appetite. Walked down to the gas station and bought a paper. It contained an article about the history of Easter which failed to mention Ēostre or any of its cognate Indo-European dawn goddesses. My guess is the truth would not sit well with the *Star-Telegram*'s God-fearing readership. Something Sherwood would certainly understand.

Afterward, I reached for *Decline and Fall of the Roman Empire*. Sometimes I envy Randy, who can read something like this and learn from it, whereas I tend to read for pleasure. Randy can explain at length the reasons for Rome's demise, while I tend to recall only the entertaining parts. "Twenty-two acknowledged concubines and a library of sixty-two thousand volumes attested the variety of Gordian's inclinations; and from the productions which he left behind him, it appears that the former as well as the latter were designed for use rather than for ostentation." If only Sherwood's red notebook were more entertaining. Or transparent.

After dark, I headed down to Spencer's to fulfill my musical obligations. "See Where Foxes Play Every Night" promised the marquee out front.

"This place is crawling with trim," said Tim. The playful foxes hanging onto his arms gazed up at him amorously. It was not long before I had attracted one of Tim's castoffs. "What happened to your eye, Baby?" asked a concerned cutie on roller skates.

"Skydiving accident," I lied. Should have just kept my mouth shut.

"I like your gold boots," she said.

"I like your..." I scrambled for something to compliment.

"You like my *what?*" she said, seductively.

"Your *Logan's Run* getup." She wore a short white belted tunic dress, a metallic choker (made from a strip of aluminum foil?) and an ankh pendant. The effect was futuristic.

Two piña coladas later and I was fingerbanging her in a phone booth. Right at the worst possible moment, Turtle Man banged on the door. He looked like he had just snorted a pound of cocaine. I flipped him the bird with my free hand. Felt my fever returning.

"C'mon, let's find someplace more private," the girl on roller skates whispered in my good ear before thrusting her tongue into it. Her saliva helped create an airtight seal which, when she removed her tongue, almost ruptured my eardrum.

Someone knocked. "There you are," mouthed Bonnie, taking in the scene. She tapped her wrist. The rest of the evening is a blur. You can't regret what you forget. Can you?

SUNDAY, APRIL 10

Was awakened by the sound of an insistent dripping sink. Took a few minutes to realize it was only the locked runout groove of *Atom Heart Mother*. Anxiously checked to see if any of my stuff was missing. Wallet, check. Codex, check. Amulet? After some frantic searching, I found it in my pants pocket.

Figured I should get up and get busy. Found a cast iron reel mower out in the shed and began mowing the front lawn. The handle is broken off near the base. It is just a sharp wooden spike, really. Had to stoop to push it. It was hot, miserable work, and my back is still aching as I write this.

When I had almost finished, Vee appeared, Bloody Mary in hand. A stalk of celery was sticking out of it.

"Happy Easter! What are you doing, Ding Dong?" she giggled. "I know a kid who will do that for a buck." She regarded the mower and grimaced. "You got that from the shed, didn't you? That old dirty thing's just a piece of junk! I can't believe you mowed the entire lawn with that."

Demoted from Dollface to Ding Dong! That hurts. "It's kind of fun, actually," I replied, and I was not lying.

"You're crazy, do you know that? Come upstairs and have some jelly with me."

"Have you tried the jelly yet? If the Cherryes are not Rype, that they are Green even a Bit, they will be so Sour that they will cause Stupefaction to the Teeth."

Vee chuckled. "I'll keep that in mind, silly." She looked me up and down, then took a bite of celery. "You look like you could use one of these," she said, meaning the Bloody Mary.

"Take a rain check. Gotta finish what I started." As I watched Vee saunter up the stairs, I realized I just declined two invitations in a row. Maybe I should have accepted.

While mowing next to the chimney, the wheel caught on a little metal door. Suppose it is for cleaning ash out of the fireplace. Is this how Harvey gets in and out? Or got in and out, past tense. Shudder to think of his recrudescence. Had to trim the grass next to the foundation with scissors. The sun rose higher and higher into the sky. Almost scalded my esophagus drinking hot hose water.

Dave II could not make rehearsal because he was not feeling well. He undoubtedly had important Easter business to attend to. No clue why he would feel the need to fib about Easter. Tim made much of discovering Jesus's face in a tortoiseshell patterned guitar pick. Could just make out His eyes and beard, if you allow that Jesus resembled Grizzly Adams. "He is risen!" Tim shouted. He held the pick aloft before strumming an ominous barre chord. Bonnie scoffed at the whole thing.

"Heard you got to third base with Roller Girl last night," teased Tim.

"Who?" I said. I turned to Bonnie who avoided my gaze. What is third base, anyway? I can never keep the bases straight. I recalled my encounter with Roller Girl and vowed to be more cautious next time.

When it became clear that we were not going to accomplish anything this evening, I made the mistake of accepting a sniff of coke from Tim. "One sniff and you're a golden god," he said.

Headed home and watched the second half of *McQ*, which made me so afraid of being busted I was hyperventilating by the time the end credits spelled out my arrest warrant.

MONDAY, APRIL 11
Slept badly. Dreamed I was kissing Jenny, but she had no teeth. Took an early coffee break at work to wake myself up, but then got engrossed in a newspaper article that quoted one of Sherwood's colleagues concerning archaeological evidence that humans have been in the New World for over 100,000 years. It usually comes down to whether some stone flakes were tools or not. If only there were some really compelling evidence. I would show the piece to Sherwood if he were here. He would have something to say about it!

Jo Ann entered the break room. When she noticed me, she held up a Tupperware container of fruit cocktail. "Taste this."

"Why?" I did not want to taste it.

"I don't know. I think I've lost my sense of taste."

"Well that's peculiar." How do you respond to something like that? Bumped into Guddu on my way back to my desk. He flinched, then would not look at me.

"Little warm for a turtleneck sweater, isn't it?" I said.

Guddu just walked away without answering. Later, I noticed him up on the mezzanine. I do not think he was working, just pacing. Like something was eating him. That guy can be so moody sometimes.

Gig at the Hop with Rambunctious. Dave II was still sick (wink, wink), so we went on without him. Wanted to blow it off, but "the show must go on," and all that crap. Brought along my trusty Rhythm Master. We adapted each tune to one of its ten preset rhythms: Rock 1, Rock 2, Mambo, Foxtrot, etc. We ended up playing "Andromeda Suite" as a waltz. Jeane Dixon's prediction was coming true! Some people booed but most simply looked confused. Tim dubbed the machine Dave III. One day machines will do everything.

At home in time to watch Bob Newhart host the *Tonight Show*. Don Rickles was a guest again. I kept watching to see if he was going to mess with Johnny's cigarette box but he did not.

TUESDAY, APRIL 12

Jo Ann was out sick, so I had to fill in at the information desk for her. While I was playing Solitaire, a patron complained about Turtle Man who was allegedly shuffling papers too loudly. It fell upon me to say something to him, which I was reluctant to do. Judging from the notes he sometimes leaves behind on tables, his research has something to do with human migration patterns following the penultimate glacial maximum. While I was speaking to Turtle Man, Sarge could be heard shouting from the stacks. Someone had handed him one of those cards that say "I'm deaf. Please give me some money. God bless you."

"You lying sack of shit," screamed Sarge. "Get the hell out of my library!" The deaf imposter, who was also bald, had sunglasses on the back of his head. Could not tell if he was coming or going. Then I noticed his fringed jacket. The Doom Hippie! He was taking his sweet time to leave. "Let's go! *Di di mau!*"

"You don't have to shout," complained the Doom Hippie.

By the time Dixie waddled out of her office to see what was going on, it was peaceful again. She looked up at Carlos for a moment, who was on scaffolding scraping bat guts out of numerous holes in the plaster with his one functioning arm. Doubt she knew what he was doing.

Sarge was now examining a small notebook. It caught my eye because it was red. "The dink dropped it," he said.

"I'll take that," I said, firmly. Listen to me barking orders! I outrank the Sarge, after all. Held out my hand and Sarge dutifully put the notebook in it.

Encountered Diane in the break room. She asked me if I had gotten into a fight. She ran her finger along what had become a red streak up toward my armpit. Now regretted not having worn long sleeves.

"Dog bite," I lied, caught off guard. There was no way I was telling her the truth.

"Did he punch you in the eye, too?" said Diane. "There was a rabies scare in Westworth Village the other day. All the animals are quarantined."

"I live in Arlington Heights."

Diane continued to examine my arm. "It's infected," she said. She asked a bunch of follow-up questions like, "Did they catch the dog?" and "Has he ever bitten anyone before?" Was obliged to make up all sorts of *yaje* until I was able to change the subject. Opened a newspaper that was lying nearby.

"Do you like the accordion?" I asked. "Says here: 'Directly from Finland, the Laiho Brothers will be playing on the 16th at Southwestern Union. Their new sound will surpass all previous achievements in accordion music.'"

"That's quite a boast!"

"What's a gentleman?" I said.

"What?"

"Someone who knows how to play the accordion but doesn't."

Diane shook her head. "By the way, Dixie's on the warpath. She said you left the Vault unlocked."

"She suddenly cares about the Vault?"

As I was leaving for the day, I encountered Guddu in the vestibule. He was just standing there, staring at the codex. That guy freaks me out sometimes. If he only knew what was in it.

WEDNESDAY, APRIL 13

Dr. Lanier examined my arm. If I keep saying it is a dog bite, I might believe it, too. "You should have seen me earlier. Have you experienced any tingling in your arm? Any violent movements? Uncontrolled excitement? Fear of water? Inability to move parts of the body? Confusion? Loss of consciousness? Let's start on antibiotics and a rabies regimen. Twenty-one daily injections into the abdomen."

"The *Star-Telegram* said there's a new vaccine that reduces the number of injections needed." I said, anxiously.

"The one developed by the Wistar Institute? It hasn't been approved yet in this country." Dr. Lanier snapped on a pair of gloves. "Nurse Irene is visiting her niece in Sherman so I'll be doing the honors."

Distracted myself from the needle by reading about Goofus and Gallant. Goofus is a shithead, but there is something about Gallant that makes you want to slap him. After administering the injection, Dr. Lanier opened the Dum Dum drawer and I chose watermelon. As I have always.

Tidied up around the house. There was a surprising amount of cat hair for someone with no cat. Was going to hang Sherwood's rhino head above the mantel but a couple of nails are not going to cut it. Put it on the floor for now. It will be safe here until he wants it back.

Sent away to the Rosicrucians for a free copy of *The Mastery of Life*, which explains how to use your "faculties and powers of mind." Benjamin Franklin was a Rosicrucian and look how he turned out. When I filled out the form, however, I ended up putting down Randy's name and address for shits and giggles. And to get him back for signing me up for the Osmond Brothers Fan Club. In retrospect, he seems to already have mastered life. Should have requested a copy for myself.

Found the Doom Hippie's red notebook in my mansack. Believe it is only coincidentally red and not because of its contents, which were the ravings of a lunatic. It is chiefly a lengthy list presented in a stream-of-consciousness style. It begins with things to do, such as "steal something," "break the rules," and "brainwash." I was disturbed to see the word "imp," but saw it was followed by "werewolf" and "dwarf." Likewise, the word "wizard" might be more disconcerting if it did not appear between "gladiator" and "assassin." A page of names includes "Jimmy Carter," "Deep Throat," and "Lee Harvey Oswald." A few pages later, the names become alarmingly familiar: "wheelchair man," "security guard," "Jenny Fox," and "Steven Miller." The last page bore the words "Jesus Christ 1977" superimposed over a large cross.

THURSDAY, APRIL 14

Tornado watch. Early to the library to retrieve my glasses from the hobbit room. They were broken. Considered calling out sick so I could catch Howard Hanson's lecture at TCU, but I have a meeting. Am told I missed yesterday's excitement. Hazel evidently saw "brown movement" coming out of my office. Carlos fired at it. Spunt showed me where the pellets went into the wood paneling by the paper cutter. Everyone sounds insane.

Today's meeting agenda:

> A.C.L.A. conference
> Budget cuts
> Heating & cooling system woes
> CAS internships
> Microfilm reader
> Adjunct faculty borrowing privileges
> Locking the Vault
> Use of break room utensils
> Missing items (office supplies, rhino head, amulet, etc.)
> National Library Week display
> Conduct policy
> Varmint control

Professor Whipple's cushion (again)
Dolph Briscoe library visit.

Word got back to L.F. about the bat stains on the Geweihsessel chair. He is pretty hacked off about it and now Carlos has to do what Sarge refers to as "shit patrol." I do not want to know what that is.

Hazel interrupted our meeting to tell me I had a telephone call from a Mr. Smorin. "He was pushy."

Did not think quickly enough to tell her to take a message, and Dixie glared at me angrily as I left the room. Who the hell is Mr. Smorin?

"Hello. This is Steven."

"Steven, my buddy. How are you today?"

"Who wants to know?"

"Why, it's Abe Smorin. We met when you took the Grifo out for a spin."

"So you did."

"Just a courtesy call to let you know we got a sweet '68 Litri in. Tri-Power version of the 427. It's got a Chevy L71 big-block engine. 435 h.p. at 5,800 r.p.m. Top speed 186 m.p.h."

"Mr. Smorin, if you don't mind, I'm in an important meeting."

"Well, if you would like to…"

I slammed down the receiver.

Saw Dr. Lanier for my second rabies shot. Nurse Irene was still out of town, but a different nurse was there. Nurse Mindy looked younger than me. Her stethoscope was cold on my chest. She made me say "Ah."

"This is the first injection I have ever given," said Nurse Mindy. That sounded like *yaje* because she must have given plenty of injections in nursing school. Educated myself on lunker browns in *Field & Stream* while she jabbed the needle into my abdomen. The pain was worse than when Dr. Lanier did it. Nurse Mindy was taking longer, too.

"Stay put," said Nurse Mindy.

While she was away, I looked down. The needle was still stuck in me. A moment of darkness. I opened my eyes to find Nurse Mindy holding smelling salts under my nose. She offered me a Dum Dum. It was the mystery flavor but I ate it anyway. I want to say it was root beer.

FRIDAY, APRIL 15
The "A Little Noon Music" concerts have started up again. Had considered calling out sick so I could go see the TCU Jazz Ensemble but woke up to rain. Jo Ann is back and looks like crap. Her face was puffy from drinking or crying.

Maybe both. I gave her a wide berth.

Guddu came knocking on my door. He has been sullen lately, even bellig-
erent. "Steven! Can you help Guddu?" He spread some papers before me, then
pointed at the page. "This book has several editors. How many do Guddu cite
before using '*et al.*'? This is maddening."

"Which style are you using?"

"*A Manual for Writers of Term Papers, Theses, and Dissertations.*"

"Ah, Turabian."

Answered this and a few other style questions, after which he took my
hand and gently kissed it. "Guddu is not worthy!" He eyed my Horus statuette
suspiciously before disappearing. Did not realize Guddu was a student. What
the hell is he writing a paper about?

After lunch I was cataloging some government documents when Dixie
barged into my office. "Would you please turn that racket off?" That racket was
Brahms, lady. It was not even loud.

At Dr. Lanier's, I rolled my sleeve up to show Nurse Irene.

"I don't see anything. Are you sure it's not the other arm?" she said. The
wound has disappeared.

"But it was there this morning!" I protested.

Dr. Lanier was astonished but insisted my anti-rabies regimen continue. Not
sure if anything astonishes me anymore. Randy, on the other hand, expressed
astonishment at my stupidity for continuing with this charade.

"Seriously doubt Harvey gave you rabies," he said. "An unknown fatal dis-
ease from another plane of existence? Perhaps."

SATURDAY, APRIL 16

Rain. Nurse Irene was most kind to meet me at Dr. Lanier's office before I had
to be at work. Spent the morning behind the information desk struggling to
make a poster for National Library Week. It is for a campaign to promote the
use of all types of libraries. No one here seems to give a rat's ass. The theme
this time is "Use Your Library." I hope they did not pay someone to think up
that brilliant slogan. They probably ran out of quality ones years ago.

The poster was a royal pain in the neck. Was frequently interrupted by
people with questions like, "Who is Ibid?" Fuck if I know. Back in my office
there were fewer distractions and I worked more quickly. Figured I could
listen to Brahms through earphones and not disturb anyone. Was surprised at
the sound fidelity until Jenny shook my shoulder. Had not inserted the plug
into the jack far enough, thus "Academic Festival Overture" was audible in the
reading room.

"Nice poster," she said.

"Thanks." Regarded my creation in dismay. It featured a badly drawn Burgess Meredith clutching a book to his breast with the caption, "Make Time To Read" in a dozen languages. After that episode of *Twilight Zone*. Apt but hardly original.

Jenny started reading the various phrases aloud. "What language is this one?" said Jenny.

Of course she asked about it. I already regretted including Dordic.

"It's a Native American language," I ad-libbed.

"Oh. Do you want to go see *A Star Is Born* with me tonight?" she asked.

"Okay."

"Will you watch the circ desk for me while I go to the bathroom?"

What was this? If Jenny does not "think of me like that," then I am just like one of her girlfriends. Recalled the *Charm* spell from the codex. If it takes magic to make the Stone Fox mine, I think I will pass. Prefer to get laid the old-fashioned way, I suppose, even if that means not getting laid at all. Once I got the idea, however, it obsessed me. If it did not work then what was the harm? If it did?

While Jenny was in the bathroom, I hatched a devious plan. *Charm* requires a lock of hair or some intimate personal artifact. Retrieved Jenny's belly button lint from the shenanigans dish. She returned from the bathroom before I had a chance to find a place for it. Ended up concealing it in my palm until I was alone. I concealed the lint in my wallet.

Before leaving, I quickly typed some catalog cards; busy work that is relaxing like a jigsaw puzzle.

The preceding sentence is a pangram. Not quite as good as Joseph Heller's 88-letter attempt in *Catch 22*, though. The one about Colonel Korn's friendly shoulder squeeze.

Took the Mixmaster on our way to the Southside Twin and somehow ended up on the Poly Freeway. Should have just taken Hulen. Something about that maze of ramps makes me feel like I am playing a game of chance. Where will I arrive? Almost got us T-boned swerving into Holiday Liquor. Left Jenny in the car. Forgot to ask what she wanted to drink, so I just got a two-buck bottle of White Cobra.

Had assumed *A Star Is Born* was a movie for chicks, but I really enjoyed seeing Kris Kristofferson play a washed-up singer. A cautionary tale! Whenever the window speaker cut out, I found myself brooding over Jenny. If she was not into me, what were we doing at a drive-in? Considered making a move but kept chickening out. Rested my arm behind her until it became uncomfortable. Was eager to try the *Charm* spell. We passed the White Cobra in silence.

Imagine potpourri blended with lemon juice and a hint of anise, distilled into a clear 90-proof liquid. It was close to eleven when the movie ended. Just as I was about to pull out of our space, Jenny leaned out the window and threw up a few dead brain cells.

"We're going back to my place," I said.

Back at Collinwood, I lit some incense and opened all the windows. Jenny kicked off her wedges. She looked a little green around the gills.

"Toss your jacket on the rhino," I said. "What do you want to drink?"

"Ice water."

Returned with Jenny's water to find her stroking Figgy. "He just came through that door."

"My neighbor's cat," I said. "He lives upstairs but he thinks the whole house is his. He meows until you let him in. Don't close the door."

Jenny regarded my overflowing bookcases. "Chomsky. Pretty heavy reading. You have books coming out of your books, you know."

I did not tell her I found Chomsky incomprehensible. Showed her my *OED* (in twenty-six volumes), my *Encyclopaedia Britannica* (11th ed.), Isaac Taylor's *Words and Places* (signed by the author, in full calf binding by Bickers and Sons), and a few rare grammars (not *Linguae dordica*). She showed little interest.

"Are you feeling okay?" I said.

Jenny nodded. "Hey, a card catalog," she said. After idly pulling out a few catalog drawers, she flopped down on the divan. She seemed bored. "I can sleep here. Do you have pajamas or something I can wear?"

I tossed her my 'Dillos jersey. After changing into cut-offs, I went into the bathroom and turned on the faucet to make some noise. *Successful Muskrat Farming* was so tightly bound, I had to crack the spine to get it to stay open on the back of the toilet. The original text was tiny enough, but the shrunken photocopy was even more difficult to make out. Read the incantation aloud in a low, but forceful whisper, utilizing Jenny's belly button lint accordingly. I took off the amulet and put it in my pocket.

Rejection I can handle. If the Stone Fox is not into me, she is not into me. But my curiosity was getting the best of me now.

Found Jenny wearing my jersey. I put on the "Stickball" record and sat down next to her. Solemn church organ issued from the speakers followed by quiet narration.

"What are we listening to?"

I shushed her, but Jenny was not paying attention to the song. She turned to face me then whispered, seductively, "Want to know a secret?" When I replied, "I'm listening," she gave me a Wet Willy. Not the kind of secret I was hoping for.

Made Jenny shriek with an Iron Claw to the belly. We tumbled onto the rug. She attempted a leg scissors choke but ended up straddling my chest backwards, her butt in my face. Her underwear had a hole in them. Before I could stick my finger in the hole, she stopped squirming. "What happened to your thighs?"

"Figaro."

She traced her finger thoughtfully over one of the scars, then slapped it.

"Asshole!" I cried.

"What has it got in its pocketses?" she demanded, sticking her hand in my pocket. She groped around for a moment, then pulled something out.

"How pretty!" she exclaimed.

"What is it?" Her butt was blocking my view.

Jenny held the object up so I could see. The amulet! When I tried to grab it, she put it around her neck.

"Stop wiggling! What else has it got in its pocketses?" she asked, mischievously, before digging into my other one. "Well, well," she said, her voice trailing off.

"Whip some skull on me, bitch!" cried the "Stickball" narrator. Jenny complied, and I did not stop her. Moments after, Vee popped her head through the door. "Yoo hoo!" she sang.

Jenny spun off me and I quickly covered myself. Vee took in the scene, her narrowing eyes darting from me to Jenny. "Oh my gosh, I'm sorry!" she said, pulling her robe closed. "Is Figs in here?"

"He is."

"Was just making sure he was inside for the night," said Vee.

"*That's* your neighbor?" asked Jenny, suspiciously, after Vee had gone back upstairs.

SUNDAY, APRIL 17

"Wake up, Sleepy." Opened my eyes to find Jenny playfully dangling her hair in my face. "I made you breakfast."

I rubbed my nose and sat up. Jenny placed a tray in my lap then joined me in bed. We must have fallen asleep watching *Torpedo of Doom* last night. I regarded the meal before me. Scrambled eggs on tortillas. O.J. in an old plastic cowboy boot cup.

"Where did the orange juice come from?" I said.

"There was a tube in the freezer."

I did not recall having that. "Where did you find this boot cup?"

Jenny did not answer.

I reached for the hot sauce. "Are you going to have any?"

"I'm not hungry," she said. "Here, let me." She took the hot sauce and gave it a good shake. The lid came off and hot sauce flew everywhere. All over the bed, the floor, the wall. Jenny leaped out of bed and returned with a dish rag.

"I've got it," I said.

"Please let me."

Jenny got down on her hands and knees. All I could do was sip my O.J. and watch her scrub my Navajo rug. My eyes followed her tits as they swung back and forth in my dirty, threadbare jersey. Something dangled from her neck. My amulet! Balls of brass on that babe. Should have just demanded it from her, in retrospect. Felt like the guy on the cover of *Rogue of Siluria.*

After Jenny cleaned herself up, I gave her a ride to the Hacienda. She got out of the car, turned, and stooped to kiss me goodbye. I think we have turned a corner, Jenny and I.

Gas, then a rabies jab on the way home. After writing in my red notebook for a while, I decided to type up a catalog card for the codex. Had inserted the card into the typewriter and was ready to start typing when I realized I knew almost nothing about the codex. No title, no author, no publisher, no year. I am skilled at cataloging complex materials, but this was ridiculous. Figured I had better finish translating it first.

When a thunderstorm knocked out the power, I lit candles and curled up with the strange book. The flickering flames cast shadows across the page. I could not however stop dwelling on what went down with Jenny. Was it magic? Or White Cobra? The room still smells like hot sauce.

MONDAY, APRIL 18

To work late on account of my rabies shot. Each time I saw Jenny, I searched her face for any indication of her feelings but it is always that same inscrutable expression. No sign of the amulet. Nor the pendant I gave her, for that matter.

"There's a double feature at the Bowie," I said. "Wanna go?"

"I have other plans," was all she said. What other plans?

My poster for National Library Week is missing from the vestibule. Jo Ann said she had not seen it, nor had Carlos. Dixie probably snatched it. But why?

Was brushing my beard in the staff bathroom when, on a whim, I thought to pull on the edge of the mirror. I did so, revealing a medicine cabinet behind it. Inside were an ancient can of moth crystals and a small box of Unguentine Rectal Cones, which I at first read as "Ungoliant." The box contained a number of small packets, which I left undisturbed. It would make a decent short-term hiding place, I noted.

In Ed Brice's *Ask Me* column today, he writes there is a place in Dallas that buys fingernails. I had to read it three times: "buys fingernails." Wonder how much they pay? There could be a fortune sitting right under our noses in the shenanigans dish. I always envied Brice for getting to be a librarian without having to deal with the Dixies of the world.

TUESDAY, APRIL 19

Expressed concern to Dr. Lanier about going to Philadelphia, who replied in W.C. Fields's voice, "I'd like to see Paris before I die. Philadelphia will do!" He said I could just go to a clinic there for my shots and scribbled an address on a slip of paper. Probably could have used this as an excuse to skip the conference, but I was stoked about seeing Danh again on Porteous's dime.

Picked up my new glasses on the way to work. The frames are similar to my last ones, but not quite as good, of course. Nothing ever is these days. Buy American!

Encountered Randy in the breakroom. "Dude, what were you thinking?" he said.

"Huh?"

"That poster you made. Dordic?"

"I couldn't help it," I chuckled. "So you're the one who took it. You bastard!"

Randy looked hurt, but then said, angrily, "You're going to blow our cover."

Our cover? An interesting choice of words. But he has a point.

WEDNESDAY, APRIL 20

Tashi is performing at TCU this evening. Had they been playing the Messiaen, I would have been pissed to miss it.

Picked up Diane in the Rambler so we could catch the red-eye to the City of Brotherly Love. What did the City of Brotherly Love do to earn that handle? Having heard stories about lost luggage, I decided to take my mansack and a duffel bag. On my weekend book hunting road trips to Austin, Houston, and San Antonio I usually just take a toothbrush. Diane, on the other hand, brought her entire Samsonite collection, which looks like the ape got the best of it, and several clothing bags.

"Is that all you're bringing?" she said. "Do you have a jacket?"

"I'd only end up lugging it around."

"Where are your shirts?"

I patted my duffel bag. "Wash 'n' wear."

As soon as we got settled on the plane, Diane whipped out a tattered Mary

Stewart omnibus. She had not been talkative in the car, either, but perhaps she is not an early bird like me. Passed the time drawing sunglasses, blacking out teeth, and adding beards to everyone in the in-flight magazine before cracking open *Rogue of Siluria*. Diane's skirt was hiked up, exposing a lot of thigh. It always seems like it is on purpose with her. Unlike Jenny's mixed signals, I can tell Diane is not into me. It is more like she wants something from me. But what? Recalling my recent conquest of Jenny, I wondered what a spell on Diane would accomplish. If I called her bluff, how far would she go? All the way? I can see why Randy is cautious.

Takeoff was uneventful, but I found myself gripping my novel nervously. Diane never looked up from her own book, so I assumed she was an experienced flier. Was prepared to admit I had never flown before, but she did not ask. Once the stewardess brought her a Bloody Mary, she loosened up a bit.

"Oh, Miss," she said. "Would you bring me a pack of cigarettes?" Diane turned to face me. "Did you see her outfit? Halston."

I nodded in agreement. "This plane seems really nice. Almost opulent. Feel like I should have worn a tie or something. Damn it, I forgot to bring a tie!"

"I have a scarf you can wear," she said, wryly.

"Is it Halston?" I lisped. What a bitch. Was privately relieved that I did not have to wear a jacket or tie now. Unless Diane narced on me to Dixie. But what would she gain from that?

"Ugh, an infant," said Diane, crossly. Across the aisle, a squirming baby made sounds of discomfort. His mother gave him a binky, which seemed to do the trick. Such easy, natural magic. Meanwhile, the passenger behind me tried to force his knee through the seat and into my liver, lodging it there for the duration of the flight.

After what seemed like an eternity watching baggage on a conveyor belt, we waited an hour for a taxi. Five people begged us for spare change, including a couple of Hare Krishnas. To each his own, but I am not shaving my head for love or country. Already did that once.

The cabbie flipped a uey that sent my head knocking against the window. "We're not in a hurry, driver," I barked. This was my first time in a taxi. "Is it always this hard to hail a cab?" I said.

"Fucking transit strike," muttered the driver.

Diane was flirty with the cabbie, which I found irritating. Was it necessary to touch his arm like that? What did she stand to gain?

At the Commonwealth Club there was a mix-up with our rooms. They had a reservation for Diane but not for me. There were no other vacancies.

"But I specifically asked for two rooms," argued Diane, loudly and somewhat melodramatically. Before I could suggest that the concierge find me a room elsewhere, Diane said, "Why don't we share? We're just going to sleep there. We'll be out doing things."

Was just about to concede when the manager appeared and had a quiet conversation with the desk clerk. "We have a room in the basement," said the manager. "It's rather austere but clean. You may stay in it free of charge."

"That is kind of you," I said. Turned to look at Diane and I swear I saw her shoot the manager a dirty look.

Diane's room shared a lone bathroom down the hall. Imagined long lines in the morning just to brush one's teeth, but then found out there were only six rooms on two floors. Not sure why Diane chose this place to stay. Classy. Felt like one had to be a member to stay here, but Diane probably would not be. Pretty sure she is from California. Know little about her, really. Or California, for that matter. Where did she work before Porteous?

My room was as described, but had its own bathroom. After depositing our belongings in our respective rooms, Diane and I took another taxi to the Bellevue-Stratford, where the conference was being held. The driver played tour guide, pointing out various points of interest in a stream-of-conscious monologue. His cab looked like he lived in it. Next to him on the seat was a cardboard box stocked with beef jerky and tins of sardines and Vienna sausages.

"Behind these handsome walls you got your Eastern State Pen. Al Capone was a guest of honor. Big Joe Bruno. Over there you got your Museum of Art. You seen Rocky. You like presidential plates? They got your American Presidential China exhibition. Caught us at a good time, weather-wise. Freezing sleet in your face, then a week ago we were in the nineties. Ever try wooter ice? Ah, nothing beats Fluffya in the spring."

Philadelphia must have been ground zero for bicentennial madness. Everywhere I looked there were images of Uncle Sam, thirteen-star Betsy Ross flags, and the Liberty Bell. Ben Franklin's smirking mug. Tableaux of Ye First Thanksgiving. Red, white & blue detritus in the gutter. A man in a tricorn hat shouted at us as we passed. Something about Redcoats and big discounts.

"Over there you got your library. Checked out my first book there in '52. *The Codfish Musket*. Ever read *The Codfish Musket*? That's your Logan Fountain. Toss your coins in that beauty. Make a wish. What do you wish for?" After pausing for a reply, he continued. "A cheesesteak from Mickey's, that's what you wish for. There's your city hall. Next stop, the Bellevue-Stratford. Careful don't catch Philly fever in there. Had a bad outbreak last year."

After paying, the driver turned around and looked at us. When he saw my long hair, he said, "You gonna see the Dead at the Spectrum on Friday? I'll be there. Saw them in '73. Terrific show. Was up front at the rail, thanks to my buddy Cheeser who got us in early. There were a bunch of guitar strings from Bob and Jerry on the stage in front of us so they could change strings. See? I still wear mine around my neck."

Diane and I just grinned at each other. Deadheads are nuts.

"Alright, then, youse have a good stay now."

After the mayhem of registration, Diane and I quibbled over what to do first. "The NBTCG Budget Assembly starts soon," she suggested.

"Let's go in here," I replied, pointing into a crowded exhibit hall. A biki-ni-clad model wearing granny glasses and stilettos was chained to a brand-new bookmobile on a slowly revolving platform, shushing anyone who ogled her. Diane and I wandered down the aisles, listening to pitches and taking in the scene. We collected pamphlets and free samples in canvas tote bags with "Gerstenslager" or "F.W. Faxon" on them. One booth featured a pedestal with a granite ball floating on a fountain. The ball was seemingly weightless though it probably weighed about twenty pounds. When I reached for it, some suit yelled "Don't touch!" As Diane and I moved along, we could still hear the guy yelling at other people not to touch the ball. By the time we reached the other side of the exhibit hall, our tote bags were full of notepads, pens, rulers, and other freebies. Scored a "Librarians Do It Better" mug. Diane's prize was a ball-point pen shaped like a syringe and filled with red ink. She brandished it playfully.

"Bend over," she said.

"Where did you get that pen?"

"From a guy in the Medical Institute Press booth. He also gave me his number, like I would ever call him from Texas."

"I'm sure he did," I muttered.

The rest of the morning was coffee and cigarettes until I told Diane I had to run an errand. Her face fell. Felt guilty for ditching her.

"I'll be back in time for the 'Information Please' panel," I said.

The address to the clinic was illegible. I realized no one would know if I blew off my injections. Even if I were sick, rabies shots were not going to help. Instead, I lingered in a record store before racing back to the conference. Took me a while to find the North Hall, by which time the panel was concluding. When I took my seat next to Diane, she looked at me and scowled.

"Sorry I'm late. I forgot which time zone I was in. The banquet starts at six-thirty. That gives us just enough time to have a few drinks beforehand. Saw a bar I want to check out. They must be open by now."

On the way, we got a couple of wooter ices. We ducked into an antiquarian bookstore. I paused to study a Turkish dictionary. When I caught up to Diane, she was reading a book.

"When a man," read Diane, "under some pretext or other, goes alongside a woman and touches her body with his own, it is the 'touching embrace.'" I leaned away from Diane so our arms were no longer touching.

"Let me see that," I said. I examined the title page. "The *Kama Sutra*. Jim Croce's copy—what do you know?" It was only three dollars, so I bought it.

Should have known a place called Bookbinders would be packed full of A.C.L.A. refugees. We ended up sharing a table with a group of librarians from Milwaukee. Handed out a few of my custom matchbooks which were well received. Everyone was drinking heavily.

The banquet was a disappointing affair in a huge hall with too many seats and not enough people. Diane and I sat alone at a table for ten.

Offered Diane some of my spinach soufflé. "It's people!" I cried, impersonating Charlton Heston. Diane busted a gut laughing, but it was not that funny. Someone was making a speech at the other end of the hall, punctuated by scattered applause. After nearly picking clean a crustacean tree, I moved on to the Hawaiian frankfurter platter and salmon avocado mold, the latter compromised by an excess of mayonnaise and olives. The great thing about buffets is that you get to try a little of everything. By the time I got to the Bananas Foster the champagne (and booze from earlier) had caught up with me. Diane ended up helping me to my room after a surreal and embarrassing ride in a taxi I would rather forget. She was kind to me and patiently explained what was happening when I experienced an asparagus urination scare.

While wallering in bed, I felt thirstier than I have ever felt before. Hydrophobia! Skipping my injection was probably a bad idea. But Vietnam did not get me. And neither will Harvey.

THURSDAY, APRIL 21

Too hungover to get out of bed. When I answered Diane's knock, I exaggerated my condition, suggesting partial paralysis while raising a limp arm in the air.

"Philly fever," she said, with sarcastic certainty.

As soon as she departed, I showered and dressed. The towels here are excellent. Suppose they will not miss one of them. Walked along busy streets to the Museum of Art where I spent more time in the gift shop than in the exhibits. They offer merchandise you do not see in ordinary stores. Ended up buying a replica of one of Duchamp's *boîtes-en-valise*, filled with miniatures of his most famous works. A shrunken typewriter cover, a tiny glass ampoule of Paris air (which I was tempted to break open and inhale), postcard-sized reproductions of a mustachioed Mona Lisa with her hot ass, etc. Duchamp's female fig leaf predates the Plaster Casters by nearly two decades. Felt like a traveling salesman walking around with it. "Madame, can I interest you in a pocket-sized urinal signed "R. Mutt"?"

After quitting the museum, I paused to watch a group of Japanese tourists posing like Rocky on the front steps, fists raised in triumph, shouting "Adrian!" My trek down Ben Franklin Parkway took me past the fountain the cab driver had showed us. Sculpted frogs and turtles spouted water at a group of river gods by Alexander Calder. Saw no resemblance between these and the Bank One Eagle back home. A different Calder? I fished a nickel out of my pocket and closed my eyes. I wished for Harvey to go away. If this works, I will believe anything.

Arranged for Danh to pick me up at the Commonwealth Club, where I ditched my *boîte-en-valise* and changed into corduroys. Danh showed up in his '74 Dodge Monaco and honked. When I got in and shut the door, he laid rubber down half a block while I gripped the dash.

Danh's parents live in a suburban brick house surrounded by classical statuary. *The Capitoline Venus* and *David, The Thinker* flanked a wide, pebbled driveway.

"The discus tosser's missing an arm," I said.

"Myron's *Discobolus*. One of the neighborhood kids was hanging off it when it broke."

Danh's father greeted us in the den. He offered me a cup of tea, which I accepted out of politeness. After some small talk during which he learned I was a musician, he reverently presented to me *The Great American Songbook*. Felt it was prudent to bow, so I did. He then gestured to a Kimball Swinger 700 organ. Barely concealing my panic, I looked at Danh who nodded.

Sat down and turned the instrument on, then experimentally pressed a key. Selected the Leslie effect for a nice vibrato, then opened the songbook and searched for any song I might already know. I pressed another key. Something was not right.

"Because I tried to replace the Leslie speaker fuse twice, and both times they blew out, it is my assumption that the Leslie amplifier is out of order, and I cannot fix it," explained Danh's father in halting English.

The occasion called for a slow foxtrot. "This is 'Beautiful Dreamer,'" I announced. As soon as I started playing, singing falsetto, Danh's mother appeared by her husband's side. The rhythm was slower than I had intended, which dragged the song beyond the four-minute mark. When I finished and turned around, Danh's mother had tears in her eyes.

I stood and took a bow. If I ever got fired from the library, I could do this for a living.

"Nobody notices wrong notes," whispered Danh.

"You stay!" his mother begged and took my hand as we prepared to leave.

"Thank you for the tea," I said. Danh hustled me out the door.

Danh turned onto the Baltimore Pike then floored it through a yellow light. "Open the glove box," he said.

"Brass Monkey?" I said. I took a blast before handing him the bottle.

"I haven't forgotten!"

Danh took the scenic route back to the city. We reminisced about our Primary Source days. Told him about the library, Jenny, and Time Frame.

"Do you still play?" I asked.

Danh shook his head sadly. "Working stiff now. By the time I get home in the evening, I lack the will to live. How do you do it?"

"It's the only way to get the music out of my head."

"Well, it was wonderful to see you again. Send Dixie my love."

Returned to my room to discover the contents of my duffel geometrically arrayed on the bed. The *boîte-en-valise* lay open on my pillow. The ampoule of Paris air was shattered. I sniffed the room, half-expecting to smell the Seine. Instead, I smelled Harvey.

Caught up with Diane downstairs in the dining room. "How are you feeling?" she said.

I sighed dramatically for effect. "Still weak. This Crab Louis ought to perk me up." If Harvey visited Diane, she made no sign.

We ate in silence. Out of the corner of my eye I caught Diane stealing glances at me. As soon as I finished eating, I excused myself. Diane started to say something but hesitated.

"What is it?" I asked.

"There's nothing to do in my room," said Diane. "Was hoping we could go for a drink or something. There's a bar a few blocks from here."

"Let me get my jacket."

The same librarians from Milwaukee were at the bar, partying at the tops of their lungs. The place was a madhouse. I winced as one of them danced upon a one-legged round table to Frankie Valli.

"Are you sure about this place?" I asked. Diane pretended not to hear. The only free table was covered in empty glasses. Utilizing a trick from the codex, we were soon seated at a clean table. Diane stared at me searchingly.

"I could really go for a slow screw," she whispered. Her breath was hot in my ear.

Our eyes met for a moment.

"It's the offspring of a Sloe Gin Fizz and a Screwdriver," she explained.

Am always so uncomfortable ordering drinks at a bar. Can never get the bartender's attention, and they always ask me questions I do not know the answers to. Could barely even hear him over the din. "Surprise me," I replied.

Mine was a Harvey Wallbanger. Surprise, indeed. Felt like Vee was looking out for me. Both drinks were garnished with leftover red, white & blue umbrellas.

The librarian on the table ate shit as I made my way back to Diane. Assumed she was okay when I heard cheering and applause. Diane was fussing with a fingernail. "I chipped my polish," she lamented. After setting our drinks down, I noticed I had clipped my own thumbnail too short this morning. Damn it!

"What a meat market. Haven't seen such debauchery since being backstage at the Emerson, Lake & Palmer show at Dallas Memorial in '74."

When one of the librarians put his hand on my shoulder to brace himself and puked, I rose to leave. Enough is enough. We gulped down our drinks and shoved our way through the writhing bodies toward the exit.

Diane pointed at a neon "Psychic" sign across the street. The door was unlocked. The interior was lit by candlelight. Music binged and bonged from speakers concealed behind spider plants. Incense filled the air. A petite old woman in a white silk robe emerged through a beaded curtain. She wore pale lipstick and eyeshadow. Her white wig was balanced slightly off-kilter. "I am Sylvia," she announced.

"Is this Steven Halpern playing?" I said.

Sylvia just looked at me. We settled on a high price. Sylvia explained that the cards help interpret one's subconscious. "Who's first?"

"My name is Diane."

"What kind of guidance do you seek, Diane?"

"Will I regain what is rightfully mine?"

Diane cut the cards. Sylvia arranged seven of them in a V.

"The first card, which represents past influences, is the Three of Cups reversed. It reveals that what might seem to be an impudent undertaking was a sensible step."

"I'm relieved," said Diane. Does she believe this stuff?

"The Seven of Swords. Present circumstances. A dispute involving a friend concerning your personal possessions."

"Yes," said Diane.

The rest of the cards indicated "intrigue and deception" and "delays and disappointments in plans."

"You should accept change if it comes and not act impetuously without wisdom," said Sylvia, rotely.

"I see a profitable partnership. Few obstacles stand in your way. The Queen of Cups reversed tells us that a quarrelsome woman will be thwarted in her attempts to provoke discord."

Dixie! Who else could the quarrelsome woman be? Unless it is Jo Ann. I recalled what Jo Ann had said about Diane.

Sylvia looked at me. "Your turn."

"This is *yaje*," I mumbled. "Can I bum a cig?" I added, patting my pockets.

Sylvia's face darkened. "Knowledge is power," she said while digging in her purse.

"I already know what's going on here," I said, petulantly.

On our way to the next bar, Diane was thoughtful. "Did the cards tell you what you wanted to hear?" I said.

"Yes, I think so."

Diane and I were both pretty shitfaced when we got back to the Commonwealth Club. I ushered her upstairs. When we reached the bathroom in the hall Diane reached for the doorknob. "Oh, no. There's somebody in there," she giggled. "Can I use your bathroom, Steven? I don't think I can wait. Please?"

When we entered my room, I turned on a lamp. "Ah! Bright!" protested Diane, shielding her eyes.

"What are you, a vampire?" I teased.

After Diane came out of the bathroom she dug around in her purse and produced a joint.

I smiled. It was my turn to pee. Thought I might vomit and stood hunched over the sink for some time. When I finally emerged, I opened the door and nearly tripped over Diane's Famolares. A scarf was draped over the lampshade. Diane was lying on her back and had nearly slid off the edge of the bed. Her skirt had ridden up. I stood there for a moment, wondering how to proceed. The gentlemanly thing, perhaps, would be to let Diane sleep in my bed while I took the armchair. As I reached under her knees to move her, I caught a glimpse of a birthmark peeking out from the edge of her black lace panties. The birthmark was shaped like a butterfly. It all came together. Are Diane and Ursula of Ulm the same person?

FRIDAY, APRIL 22

A sleepless night in a stiff chair, the strap of my mansack wrapped safely around my wrist, staring hard at what I suppose is an unquestionably dangerous woman. Diane was probably watching me, too, through nearly closed eyelids. What is her game? I showered and dressed before Diane stirred, then waited for her in the dining hall.

Diane and I had little to say over coffee and croissants. Because she had not registered for the Technical Services Roundtable this afforded me some time to clear my head while she wandered the exhibit hall and waited for me. As soon as I knew Randy would be at the library, I got change for a five dollar bill for the long distance call.

When Hazel answered, I disguised my voice and asked to speak to Randy Kelso.

"May I ask who is calling?"

I said "Mr. Mantee" because Randy would know it was me.

"This is Randy."

"Hey, man, you know that chick Ursula in Austin who drugged me? Guess what? She's Diane."

"What do you mean?"

"I'll explain tomorrow. But what the hell, Randy? Am I in danger?"

"Hazel is standing right here," whispered Randy. "Ursula is who you said?"

"Yes. I'm sure of it," I said. "What do I do?"

"You have the upper hand if this individual doesn't know that you know."

"Understood. Here she comes now, bye." I turned to Diane.

"There you are. Come have a smoke with me." Was determined to play it cool. During "Media Centers in Academic Libraries: A Survey" we were almost asked to leave because we were laughing too hard making *cadavre exquis* drawings of the speakers and attendees. My performance was refined and convincing. Do not think she knows that I know what a treacherous bitch she is.

On the way to the airport I tried not to call attention to my *boîte-en-valise*, which I expected Diane would be curious about. Caught her looking at it a couple of times, but she did not say anything. Found this strange, but Diane is a strange woman.

The flight home was eventful for two incidents. The first was a passenger who became hysterical over something she saw out the window. Harvey, no doubt, jacking off on the wing. Hope he froze to death but something tells me he did not. The second was when we were waiting to disembark. Diane picked up my mansack to hand to me and predictably spilled its contents all over the floor. This game I knew. Picked everything up casually, but Diane got to *Successful Muskrat Farming* first.

The codex had fallen open to an especially provocative page, bearing a potent sigil.

I snatched the book from her. Rather than offer a lame explanation, I held my tongue for once. Let the bitch wonder. On the way out, I asked a stewardess about the hysterical woman.

The stewardess smiled. "Just a nervous flier. Thank you for flying Braniff!"

SATURDAY, APRIL 23

Back on Tejas soil. Three days since my last injection. Nurse Irene was a no-show but I am clearly out of the woods. Jenny had lots of questions about A.C.L.A. She told me about yesterday's Earth Day celebrations. She was still celebrating today by wearing her Earth Shoes and her "Give Earth a Chance" button. She was also wearing the amulet, now attached to her black ribbon choker in place of the bell. I held out my hand and stared hard into Jenny's eyes. She removed the amulet from the ribbon and placed it into my palm without a word.

"Don't those make you feel like you're walking uphill?" I said.

"They make my calves strong. Here, feel."

"Wow. See what you mean." I turned to greet Guddu. "Did you go to the Earth Day party yesterday?"

"No, Steven. Guddu has taken sick leave for the last few days."

Noticed my chipped beige desk is a lovely shade of green underneath. Looks like the Rambler. Spent hours peeling the beige layer off. It is much more work than I realized.

Professor Ziglar came up to the information desk. "I'm looking for *The Virtue of Selfishness* by Ayn Rand."

"Here you go."

When he saw Rand's photo on the dust jacket, he said, "A woman? Never mind. I have never read a book by a member of that species, and I never will."

Noticed my "Books To Be Dealt With" shelf is suddenly overflowing. If Guddu was out sick the last few days, when did this happen? Maybe Spunt put them there.

Gig at a party on Luther Lake in someone's backyard. Parking was a pain in the ass, so I had to dolly all my junk down Rowan Drive. The paving was rough. Thought my speaker wires were going to shake loose. We have hit the big time now.

Luther Lake was paradise when I was a kid. There were only a handful of houses around it. Reeds and moss grew all around the edges of the limpid, spring-fed waters. It was full of largemouth bass, channel cat, perch. There were seasonal migrations of thousands of waterfowl of every description. Year after year Canadian geese, mallards, herons, and red-winged black birds roosted there. Used to see beaver, too. The ravine beyond the dam is now a dumping ground. Coasted across in the Rambler so as not to scare whatever wildlife might remain.

"Luther Lake! Are you ready to rock?" cried Tim as the neighbors all peered out through their curtains at once.

After "Subways of Your Mind" struck out, we skipped our own tunes and played only covers. Bonnie began "One Man Band" in a key which makes the bass riff difficult for me. My hand got tired, so I simplified my part throughout the second half of the song. Nobody noticed. Tim still made a shitty remark afterward. Fortunately, the neighbors called the cops and we got to go home. Funny. Felt like I was well within the pocket.

SUNDAY, APRIL 24

Forgot to wind my clock and overslept. Fortunately it is Sunday and I do not have to be anywhere.

Three early Jean Eustache films were showing at Pigg Auditorium. The first one starred the kid from *The 400 Blows*, all grown up. He took a job as a licentious Santa Claus in order to save up for a nice coat. No subtitles, so I really had to pay attention. Another one, *Le cochon*, was about the slaughter of a pig. It was hard to watch.

The bats are back, which freaked me out a little bit because I did not want one landing on my head or dropping guano on me. *Guano* sounds like it should be a delicious party dip, not excrement. What is so special about bat shit that it needs its own special word?

Hit the restroom on my way out. Down near the floor one of the stall supports bore the instruction "Tap foot to summon Beelzebub." I tapped my foot. Will I ever learn?

Finished *Rogue of Siluria* with Figs curled up in my lap. Murloc is a great example of a villain being drawn as a sympathetic protagonist. A rogue but with his own understandable principles. Sounds like the person I might become if circumstances warranted it. May get there sooner than I think.

MONDAY, APRIL 25

Forgot to spring forward Sunday morning. Have been living in my own personal time zone. No one mentioned it today when I was an hour late for everything. Carlos never changed the clock in the library, so I could perhaps be forgiven for playing "Happy Trails" an hour too late. No idea how I made it through yesterday without noticing. I even went to the movies!

The Bastard has asked me to perform with him at Mayfest. I agreed because it was something we could do together besides dabbling in the occult. Went over to his place after work to discuss our repertoire and rehearse.

"Dude, what took you so long?" said Randy. "Thought we could grab a bite."

"Sorry, the time change screwed me up."

"That happened Sunday."

"How did you get this gig?"

"Just dubbed a David Munrow cassette and sent that in."

"They're going to be disappointed when we show up." Must ask Dave II if I can borrow his bongos.

While Randy flipped us a couple of burgers, I reached for the Sunday paper. "This is the only photograph I have ever seen where Günther Grass is smiling," I said.

"And didn't have a pipe in his mouth," added Randy.

Started to tell Randy about A.C.L.A., but he wanted to hear about Diane. "You really didn't know it was her?" he said.

"She must be the greatest actress in the whole world. What can I say?"

"How can you be certain?"

"Some things Ursula said and did bothered me. But I wasn't sure until I saw that birthmark again."

"It didn't raise any flags when the carpet didn't match the drapes?"

"Why would I? Chicks dye their hair. They wear wigs. By the way, which is the carpet and which is the drapes?"

Randy shook his head. "Tell me about the tarot card reading. What was that all about?"

"Would have gotten mine read, but I didn't want to in front of Diane. What if the psychic had asked about Harvey? Diane's reading was interesting, but I had trouble following what was going on. Said she wanted to regain what is rightfully hers. Surely not the codex. That's not hers."

I gave Randy details about the reading itself. "The horseshoe spread," he explained. "Effective but not nuanced. Prefer Papus' method, myself. Check out *The Tarot of the Bohemians* if you want to read about it."

"Sounds like you know something about the tarot."

"It's sort of like the western equivalent of the *I Ching*. For my first novel, I used the entire Rider Waite deck as a rough outline of the characters and plot. The tarot deals with universal archetypes."

TUESDAY, APRIL 26

Porteous has the Papus. Amber made a face when I brought it back to the information desk. She will probably run to Dixie and tell her I am consorting with the devil. Of course, she has no idea. Later, Amber caught me peeling paint off my desk. Was scraping away with a letter opener, really going to town, and I guess I was making a lot of noise.

"That's vandalism."

"No, it's not. I'm just removing the layer of beige paint."

"Beige looks more professional, though."

"I will not live in Beige World, Amber!"

She rolled her eyes and left me alone. When I thought I was finished, I discovered I had forgotten about the side facing the wall. This is going to take a few more days.

The *OED*'s entry for *guano* was more than satisfying. "I find soda-water and brandy the best guano for the cultivation of my intellect," wrote Ouida in her novel *Held in Bondage*. Emerson's usage was far more ominous: "The German and Irish millions have a great deal of guano in their destiny." No doubt they would, 'destiny' being a clear euphemism for 'fan.'

Noticed something odd about the titles on my "Books To Be Dealt With" shelf. Books on witchcraft, the tarot, the paranormal. Many bore defects that would seem inconspicuous if they all were not the kind of books Guddu would call "very bad."

WEDNESDAY, APRIL 27

No laundry parties at Vee's lately. Dirty clothes are piled high on the couch. Every fork and spoon is in the sink. When I am not at work or rehearsal, I am usually studying magic. Even when I am at the library, I try to get my work done as quickly as possible so I can go down to the Vault. Today was no exception. Read the codex until it was time to leave for our gig at the Bunker.

Even though I had it Martinized, I never wear my monk robe anymore because I know what happened to it. Besides, if I showed up to the Bunker in that goofy shit I would get my ass beat. Even during the day, I am uncomfortable even driving past the *de facto* headquarters of the Bandidos.

On this evening, I swaggered in through the Bunker's iron saloon doors with pistol handles like I owned the place. There was no other way, I reasoned. "They pay well," explained Bonnie, "because their treasurer Car Boy is a buddy of Bobby's."

Car Boy must have been the one who left a bottle of White Cobra in the back of Bonnie's Minimoog. That stuff is nasty. I discreetly moved the bottle in case it spilled. Car Boy is the one who led me out to a streetlight post with the bottom plate removed. After all the outlets had been taken, Car Boy had hotwired me to the post. "Compliments of Reddy Kilowatt," he said. What does it say about me that I thought of how handy it would be to have Sherwood's ancient battery before I thought of a generator.

"Can we smoke grass in here?" said Tim.

Car Boy poured a pile of cocaine onto a table, snorted it, and walked away.

Tim looked at me. "Will take that as a yes," he said.

While we played, the Bandidos projected eight-millimeter films onto the wall of centerfolds behind us from their last run to Lake Texoma. If the stage lights were not already bright enough, I felt like the light from the projector was burning holes in my retinas. One time I turned around and it was a scene of them slitting the throat of a pig. Their little slice of *cinéma vérité* gives Jean Eustache a run for his money.

We performed all night long. The Bandidos made us play "Midnight Rider" repeatedly. For one iteration of the tune, I wanted to change it up for variety. Tim and I disagreed on the tempo and we ended up playing it at our own tempos while staring angrily into each other's eyes. At one point I thought it might circle around and wind up back in time. Dave II managed to hold the shambolic tune together, somehow. Bonnie just stood there with her arms crossed. A Bandido ripped off his undershirt (while still wearing his leather jacket—a neat trick), set it on fire, and swung it over his head like a lasso. Meanwhile, Car Boy was now standing in front of the stage playing an invisible guitar like he was part of the band. No one seemed to notice when I turned the melody from "Cielito Lindo" into a tasty bass lick, a sly reference to the Frito Bandito.

When the song ended, Car Boy turned around and bared his fangs at me like a Doberman. Thought he was mad about the Frito Bandito lick. "You're not as fucked up as us." He held his filthy palm out with a bunch of pills in it. His other arm was around me. He smelled like grease and b.o.

"Why do they call you Car Boy?" I asked.

Car Boy held his hand up closer and nodded. I opened my mouth. He popped the pills inside. A few of them missed and scattered across the stage. Washed them down with a little sip of the White Cobra. The *Merck Index* would have to wait. "I want my spurs back," he hissed into my ear. He then made us all smoke some angel dust.

The frets on my bass were now moving like an escalator. "The escalator of life!" I marveled. My amp cut out, so I shouted my parts like Hey Now. Bonnie was watching Dave II trying to find the down beat. Tim had staggered off the stage before vanishing in a column of white smoke. The last thing I remember before waking up on the floor of the thesis cage was a glowing eyeball hovering over me like a will o' wisp. Something far more ominous than Harvey, I felt. Probably just a bad trip. It would be the second time I have passed out this year. On my way to breaking my old record of four set in 1970.

Theses lay jumbled upon the floor. Some of the ceiling tiles had been pulled down, along with a few electrical wires and a fair amount of dust, debris, and what looked like goat bones. Did someone bring livestock in here? Did not think of Harvey at first, until I detected his faint tell-tale odor.

Took a while to clean up. Could not replace the ceiling tiles, so I will have to file a maintenance request with Carlos. I will suggest a heavy rat crashed through the ceiling. Discovered a couple of theses soaked in slime. *Religion of the Americas Back to 110,000 B.C. Discovered by Remote Viewing*. Must find out what remote viewing is, exactly. The other one was *Understanding and Obeying the Inscription at Rockwall, Texas*. These, I discreetly trashed.

Harvey must have followed me into the thesis cage and then got trapped inside. Broke out through the ceiling while I lay there passed out. No idea what time I got home.

THURSDAY, APRIL 28
Made a couple of phone calls when I got to work. Bonnie has my guitar, trombone, and amp. With that out of the way, I got busy withdrawing the slimed theses from the card catalog. Sorry, K. Cooksey (Class of '51) and S. Hurlbut (Class of '56). Their thesis advisor was Sherwood, which does not surprise me. Most old theses, while non-circulating, are still shelved in the open stacks. But riddle me this: Why do we keep certain theses in a locked cage within a locked basement while the Dalí Bible and other valuable items are shelved outside the cage?

Thought I might still be high from last night when Jenny hopped into my office and said, "Look at me, I'm a pregnant bunny!"

At that moment, Dixie walked by. "Don't say that word!" she said, sharply.

Jenny looked confused. "What word? Bunny?"

"No."

"Look?"

"You know good and well to which word I am referring."

"Pregnant?" blurted Jenny, incredulously.

"We will speak of this later," snapped Dixie. "And you," she continued, looking at me, "Did you steal a towel from the..." She paused to look at her steno pad. "The Commonwealth Club?"

I just looked at her.

"We'll discuss the matter later," she said before walking away."

"Matter? What matter?" I muttered.

Jenny looked at me and whispered, "What in the world?" She pulled Professor Whipple's cushion from under her blouse. "You look awful," she said.

FRIDAY, APRIL 29
Have been avoiding Diane. My poker face was always poor so I am afraid that if she looks me in the eye, she will know that I know she is Ursula of Ulm. She

will know everything! Whenever she is near I find myself sneaking peeks at her, wondering if she is really working or is up to mischief. Or peeking down her blouse. I will admit it. I am oddly attracted to her and I do not know why. That is probably what she wants so she can manipulate me.

Drinks with Randy after work at the Eagle's Nest. He has this idea in his head that he wants to try something. He spoke of Sherwood and the tornado shelter, and told me to come over on Sunday evening. An excuse to drink and listen to music. And to create a door to another dimension.

Told him about the problems I was having reading tarot cards. I fished them out of my mansack and slapped the box onto the table.

Randy laughed. "Zolar's? Dude, where'd you find these?"

"Last year's book sale. Thought they were neat."

"No, these are no good," he said. "There's only fifty-two cards here. They had to print some of the major arcana on the back of minor arcana. That's not right. Get yourself the Rider deck. It's pretty straightforward. There is some subtle symbolism that only Golden Dawn and similar orders would need to know about."

The tarot cards can wait. I have enough to worry about right now. A song about Luckenbach, Texas twanged from the jukebox. Never heard it before. "Hey, is this Waylon?" I said to Jackie.

"Sure is, hon," she said. She reached for my empty glass. "Can I get you another Metaxa?"

"Where is Luckenbach?" said Randy.

"Hill Country." For once I knew something Randy did not. Thanks to my love of maps. "Are there any songs about Fort Worth?"

"Moe Bandy just recorded one."

"I mean songs that aren't country."

"There's that Leadbelly tune. Woody Herman."

SATURDAY, APRIL 30
Stayed up late so I could see half of Yes on *Don Kirshner*. Was reminded of Squier's picking technique and tried it myself later while playing along to "The Gates of Delirium." This morning I have a blister on my thumb.

Slow day at the information desk. While reading the newspaper, I noticed something alarming about one of today's Jumble clues. I dialed Randy's number with a pencil.

"One of the Jumble clues is a word of power," I said. "For real this time."

"How about that," he said. "I'm hanging up now. I'm right in the middle of something."

"What about the word of power?"

"If you say it out loud, maybe you can solve the Jumble."

"Don't you think it's a coincidence, though?"

"There is no such thing as coincidence," said Randy.

"Auric Goldfinger might agree with you. 'Once is happenstance. Twice is coincidence. The third time it's enemy action.'"

"Who is the enemy?"

"I don't think I have any enemies."

"You sure about that?"

"Besides Dixie? I don't know. Dixie's more of a natural enemy. Foxes versus hedgehogs. The Doom Hippie worries me."

Randy chuckled. "The Doom Hippie?"

"Remind me to tell you about him. Car Boy, possibly. Diane, no doubt. Is Harvey an enemy?"

"Are you asking me?" said Randy.

Took a long lunch break and went to a rummage sale at Casa Mañana. They were selling items collected from the costume shop and scenery storage area. Thought I might find something interesting to wear on stage, but ended up going back to work with Professor Moriarty's ornate chair from *Sherlock Holmes* strapped to the roof of the Rambler.

Left Amber in charge of the information desk while I headed down to the Vault to check out the thesis cage. What I discovered was intriguing, to say the least. Every single thesis was written by students of Professor Sherwood. All were on esoteric subjects that would not be out of place in the Baumann collection. Found Diane's joint from last time and took a few puffs while reading the introduction to *The Ieya Cults of the Great Basin*. Saved the roach because it is something that belongs to Diane. You never know when that might come in handy.

Amber was hacked off that I was gone for so long. As I took my seat at the information desk, I heard her mutter something under her breath.

"Pardon?" I asked.

"Do you realize what time it is?"

"Half past the monkey's ass and a quarter to its balls."

"*Yubou stubink*. Have you been smoking the devil's lettuce?"

"*Hubow wubould yubou knubow whubat dubevil's lubettuce smubells lubike?*"

"*Ub-I'm nubot stubupid.*"

"Miss Womack! Follow me to the C.P.!" barked Sarge.

"*Subit ubon ubit,*" I said, getting the last *wubord* in as Sarge conducted Amber to the circulation desk.

Between then and "Happy Trails," I read the newspaper at the information desk. Evidently, a recent Brisco appointee to the Health Advisory Committee died in 1975. Whoops!

As I was going around pushing in chairs in the reading room, Amber said, "Why are you pushing all the chairs in? Carlos is just going to pull them out when he mops." I am sick of that kid making me look foolish. But she is right, damn it.

Considered going to see Ralph Bakshi's *Wizards* to learn something about wizards. But decided to stay in because I have a real wizard book to look at.

SUNDAY, MAY 1

Met the band at Bonnie's boyfriend's house. He converted his garage to a recording studio. He and Tim were arguing about wow and flutter when I approached. We shook hands, but for the life of me I could not recall his name. All I could think of was a cow changing a tire. Fortunately, I overheard Bonnie refer to him as Bobby.

"Nice rig," I said.

"MR-70. Brought it back from 'Nam. It's all about the tube type and output transformer. How would you like to tape in mono?" asked Bobby, persuasively. "Bonnie and I were discussing it."

"Mono?" blurted Tim. "You mean, like, dog shit?"

"What? No, man, *not* dog shit. You've got it all wrong. Stereo's a swindle. Think about a hot piece of ass you want to nail. Now think about a black and white photo of that hot piece of ass lying on your waterbed, legs spread wide open as far as they will go. She's making her 'come screw me fast and hard' eyes at you. Mono is just like that. Stereo's a cheap whore with too much makeup."

Bonnie punched him in the arm. "No mono! I told you!"

This is the guy Bonnie opens her legs wide for? I grok what he is saying about black and white, though.

Bonnie played some albums from Bobby's extensive collection. Heavy-duty stuff. *Loud 'n' Proud* by Nazareth. Uriah Heep's *Demons and Wizards* piqued my interest for obvious reasons. When Sabbath's "Sweet Leaf" came on, Fred suggested we steal the cough intro for the beginning of "Psyche!"

"Why not use Tim's? His cough is worse than that."

"No. Sabbath's. People will get it," he assured us.

"You like that, huh?" teased Bobby. "You're listening to glorious, unadulterated mono!" He carefully adjusted one of the knobs on the amplifier. Where the hell did he find Sabbath in mono?

Wondered aloud what copyright laws would say about using someone's cough without their permission. Can you copyright a cough? Could a spectrograph identify the cougher? Fred was dismissive. Doubt he would be so cavalier if Don Arden filed a lawsuit against us. Have no desire to be sued. Or famous. Especially not for something that trivial.

On one of our many, long cigarette breaks while Bonnie was dubbing her vocals, Tim and I walked down the street to a park, where we shared some sweet leaf while standing on the edge of a bluff overlooking Vickery and the train tracks.

"Used to live in this neighborhood," Tim reminisced. "See that barn over there?" He pointed to a rickety barn on the other side of the tracks. "Popped my first cherry there." We both stared at the barn, letting Tim's statement sink in. Pictured two lovers rolling in the hay in soft focus to the accompaniment of romantic banjo music. By degrees, the banjo increased in intensity and velocity. The lens of my mind's eye, as it were, began to zoom violently in and out on Tim's bare white ass, which jutted indecently into the air from behind a hay bale. What in tarnation? Handed Tim his joint back.

"Potent," I wheezed, releasing a thick cloud of smoke.

As a train approached, I noticed the barn releasing its own cloud of smoke. Moments later, one could clearly discern flames. The fire department was on the scene quickly. They parked on Vickery and waited for the train to pass, lights flashing. The barn's roof began to collapse.

"Oh, no!" lamented Tim. We watched in silence as the firemen fought the flames until there were only smoldering ruins.

"*Now* it starts to rain," moped Tim.

When we returned to Bobby's, everybody was laughing because Bonnie was holding a microphone up to his cat's face, who was snoring into an Echoplex.

"Let's put this on the album!" exclaimed Fred. If Fred had his way, Side A would be nothing but cat snoring.

Tim got in his van and peeled out as Dave II waved forlornly.

"What's eating him?" asked Bonnie.

"Tim's virginity barn just burned down."

A neighbor banged on Bobby's door to complain. Nothing productive was happening anymore.

Headed to the Bastard's. Randy's xerox of the codex lay open on his brass trunk coffee table. He had bound it in three-quarter green leather with marbled paper sides. It was flanked by lit candles, even though it was still light out. "Was thinking we could use this," he said, gesturing to a gold-veined decorative mirror. "I'd like to recreate the door Sherwood drew in his tornado shelter as exactly as possible. Chalk won't work on a mirror."

Recalled what Loretta had written on our mirror in lipstick that moonless night. "There's some lipstick in the car," I said. Returned to find Randy talking to himself in the mirror.

"The Chinese once believed that our reflections weren't reflections at all, but demons," said Randy. "The fauna of mirrors. They mimic us to learn our ways. Someday they will emerge and conquer our world. Did you bring your camera like I asked?"

I handed it to him.

"Leica," he said. "Nice lens, too."

"My upstairs neighbor gave it to me. Did you ever meet her?"

"She the one who sleeps with her students?" We sat down on the sofa. Randy gestured to the codex.

"Found the key to making the mirror work," said Randy. He pointed at the relevant text, which I studied.

"This is the word for *door*, isn't it?" I said.

"*Ostium*, if you'll recall your *Successful Muskrat Farming*. In Latin it means door or a mouth. Or an entrance. The mirror is the *ostium*."

"The *ostium* to what?"

He tapped the page. "*Ad ignota*. Wherever it is you're going. Sherwood's text repeats some of the phrases. This could be a place name. Your Dordic is better than mine."

"A place," I repeated. "Or a state of being. Like *nirvana*? I mean, the mirror obviously isn't an actual door. If Sherwood thought he could walk through a wall, that explains his overnight bag."

The mirror leaned against the wall next to an aquarium full of bettas. I paused to admire the latter.

"Their names are Dorian, Phrygian, Lydian, Myxolydian, Aeolian, and Locrian," said Randy. "The only way I can tell them apart is by their scales."

"What?" It took me a moment before I got Randy's uncharacteristically cheesy joke, but then it was too late to laugh without seeming awkward. I approached the mirror and carefully reproduced the text in lipstick exactly as I had copied it down. Randy asked if I could read it aloud. "I suppose so, but what if I mispronounce something?"

"Do your best. Put your will behind it. Have you read the Martin Solis, yet? Or what Sherwood wrote about it in his notebook?"

"His notebook?"

"His *red* notebook. C'mon, Steven. Never mind, just start reading." Randy grabbed me by the shoulders and positioned me before the mirror. "Enunciate, Steven. Enunciate."

I did so, as slowly and clearly as I could, concentrating especially on the upside-down text at the bottom. We then stood there, staring at the mirror for a few moments in silence. Recalled the artwork on Black Sabbath's *Sabotage* where the band is emerging from a mirror. The image of Bill Ward's red tights made me snicker.

"Move," demanded Randy impatiently. He changed places with me and faced the mirror. He then read aloud the text in a clear, stentorian voice, raising his palm at the end and symbolically pushing open a door.

The acoustics of the room changed, as they do when a real door opens. This was accompanied by a soft rush of air toward the mirror. Randy seemed to be frozen in the same position. I shouted his name.

The surface of the mirror rippled. Before I could contemplate the meaning of this, a tenebrous form unfolded from the glass, momentarily taking on an aspect of quicksilver. Randy fell.

The mirror reflected Randy's upper body blanketed in shapeless gloom. But when I looked directly at Randy I saw only him, flailing his arms and legs on the shag carpet. Shadows danced about the room as the swag lamp swayed. Water sloshed from the aquarium. The ferns toppled.

I dropped to Randy's side, grasping for anything that was not Randy. My fingers tore into a spongiform membrane, revealing a chitinous structure underneath. Gave it a hard yank and heard a snap.

Scanning the room for a weapon, I spotted a brass heron. Its neck and beak made a large hook. Used this to pull at the creature. The heron's base was heavy, which made it difficult to wield. Gave up on hooking and started smashing. Each time I smashed, something snapped. Randy now grunted like someone doing deadlifts.

The heron became heavier. Caught a glimpse of the scene in the mirror. And I was dismayed. The shadows had broken up and now covered Randy's torso, much of the floor, one of the ferns, and part of the heron. They crawled up my calves. It was difficult to move my legs.

Tossed aside the heron and drew my paper plate shiv. The primary bulk of the thing surmounted Randy. Stabbing proved ineffective, so I used the shiv to snag. This activity produced diminishing returns. Randy raised his arms above his face. The veins in his forehead pulsed. He was clutching something. Instinctively, I reached for whatever he had, which felt in my hands like a flattened, bony disc covered in a thick layer of friable material. Ripped something from Randy's grip, but once I seized it, I hesitated. It was as if I had forgotten where I was. The next thing I knew, someone was slapping my face. Opened my eyes and saw Randy staring down at me. "How many fingers?" he said.

"Three."

"Who's the president?"

"I'm fine," I insisted. I sat up slowly. The room was in shambles.

"This proves several things," said Randy.

"Such as?"

Randy wiped something off his arms. Felt compelled to do the same, though I saw nothing on them.

"It's like I was sinking in mental quicksand," said Randy. "The room went completely dark, and what little I could hear sounded like everything was under a thick blanket. I remember struggling but then moments would go by where I would forget to struggle. I'd think to myself, 'Where am I?' and have to discover all over again what was happening. Utilizing Solis' willpower techniques, I was gradually able to regain the presence of mind to fight back. You probably saved my life, or from a fate worse than death. Thought I had yee'd my last haw. By the way, where did it go?"

What things did this prove? How could Randy speak so well? I was still having trouble finding my words.

"How long was I out?" I said.

"Not long at all."

"Seems like there should be debris everywhere. That black stuff just came apart in my hands."

"We need to do some research before we try this again."

"You want to try this again?"

"You want to find out what happened to Sherwood, right?"

"Of course," I said. "By the way, what happened to the heron?"

"It might have gone into the mirror. Not sure."

"*Into* the mirror?" Spotted my shiv on the floor. Waited for Randy to turn away before I reached for it. Had he seen it?

MONDAY, MAY 2

Was struggling to make sense of a journal that had gone through several changes in its title, frequency, and numbering when Randy came rushing into my office. He slammed the door behind him.

"Dude," he said.

I looked up reluctantly. "What is it?"

"First of all. We neglected to shut the door."

Randy had my full attention now.

"I'm lying there reading Sherwood's journal last night and must have dozed off. I wake to a crash from the other side of the house. I get up and sneak down the hallway. Takes me a minute before I notice the sliding glass door to the pool area is wide open. Can hear crickets and frogs and whatnot. I'm crossing the living room when it hits me. The glass door isn't open, it's completely smashed. One of the curtains is gone, and the rod's on the floor. The moon is full and bright. I can see it reflected in the tank.

"I turn on the lights out back. There's shattered glass everywhere, okay? But it's all outside. I turn on the inside lights, and sure enough the room's wrecked. Mainly just shit knocked over. Nothing appeared to be missing. So, not burglars.

"The front door's locked. Then I see it. A trail of dust leading outside from the wall."

"I know what you're about to say," I said.

"Something else came through," said Randy. "As soon as I understood that, I reversed the spell. That was probably stupid. Could have made a mistake. But I didn't want anything else coming through and croaking me in my sleep.

"Was too psyched to go back to bed, so I got a flashlight and followed the trail. It's like someone dragged a filthy rug out the door, past the garage, across the field to the property line, knocking down the fence, over the levee, across the bridle path, and down into the West Fork."

"No way," I said.

"When we opened the door," said Randy, "we may not have specified where we wanted to go. So, what was on the other side was a null value, so to speak."

"A door to nowhere, then? How did you reverse the spell?"

Randy ignored the second question. "A door to the place between other places," said Randy. "The void. Whatever denizens exist there must have been drawn to it. That thing had no idea where it was or who we were. Probably took one look at me and thought, 'Dinner.' By the way, where'd you get this kick ass wizard throne?"

"Casa Mañana. It's from *Sherlock Holmes*."

"Good deal," he said, gripping the armrests. "All you need now is a wizard hat."

"I don't think I do."

How did he reverse the spell?

TUESDAY, MAY 3

Turtle Man left his tent and sleeping bag at the library. Hazel was going to throw them away, but I convinced her to let me keep them in my office in case he returns. The tent appears to be in acceptable condition. On the other hand, the Geweihsessel chair he claimed as his own is filthy, as can be expected. He sits in it all day, every day. Feel like if I mention it to Dixie, it will somehow be my fault. L.F. is going to blow his stack when he notices.

Was chatting with the Stone Fox at the circulation desk when I casually stood a sheet of paper on end. When it stayed that way, Jenny exclaimed, "Hey, magic!"

I motioned for her to remain still, lest a current of air knock the paper over. I thought I caught a faint whiff of sulfur. Suddenly I noticed Guddu standing right next to me.

"Steven, it is magic?" said Guddu. He reached for the paper but it collapsed before he could touch it. Guess the movement of his hand created a slight breeze. His expression of wonder quickly turned to fear and he flinched, like I might hit him.

"It's okay, Guddu." I picked the paper up off the floor. When I looked at Guddu again, he seemed relieved.

WEDNESDAY, MAY 4

To Bobby's to see how the sessions were progressing. Was instantly drawn into a debate over some narration Tim did for "Andromeda." I argued that narration was unnecessary, that the music capably expressed what he was trying to say with words. Besides, he sounded bored. Meanwhile, Fred was busy providing various embellishments, including a perfectly spliced Sabbath cough. Thought we had agreed not to use that.

During a creative impasse, Fred produced *Oblique Strategies*, a deck of cards designed to encourage lateral thinking. Each card bore a gnomic suggestion, or an aphorism, such as "Honor thy error as a hidden intention," or "Repetition is a form of change." They must have helped, because he was able to progress.

I asked if I could borrow them. Fred put the cards back into their box and tossed them to me.

"These ought to come in handy when I can't decide what to have for dinner." Some of the suggestions recalled those in the Doom Hippie's red notebook.

On a piece of masking tape on the mixer was written, "Please don't get coke in the faders." One fader was conspicuously labeled "Tim's Guitar." I commented on it.

"A private joke," said Bobby. "Tim's always turning his guitar up in the mix, so I labeled an unassigned fader and kept an eye on him. Saw him walk by and move it a couple of times." He looked up. "Speak of the devil," he added, as Tim arrived with alcohol in both hands. Though it was not that warm outside, he was sweating like Chuck Barris. When he thought no one was looking I saw him tweak the fader. For all his macho posturing, Tim is just an egomaniac.

Bobby recorded Bonnie playing a Minimoog part through one of his guitar amps. After a take, Bonnie asked me if I could turn the vibrato intensity up and then back down when she gave me the signal. I did so and it turned out pretty neat.

"Hey Bobby, Steven's over here twiddling your chick's knobs!"

"She asked me to, Tim," I said, defensively.

Bonnie asked me if I wanted to hear what they recorded that morning. She fiddled with the tape machine for a moment then handed me the head-phones. Presently, the sounds of a church organ filled my skull. As I listened, Bonnie's eyes searched mine. When the piece had concluded, I removed the headphones.

"Well, what did you think?" asked Bonnie, eagerly.

"That was beautiful, Bonnie! Did you do that?"

Bonnie beamed. "Bobby knows a guy who has a studio across the street from a church that has a humongous old pipe organ. You should have seen it! When I used the 32' stop, plaster dropped from the ceiling."

"Want to see my organ?" said Tim. He grabbed his crotch in case we missed the innuendo. Bonnie and I ignored him.

"How did you record it?" I said.

"We ran the cables across Montgomery street. Of course, a Mack truck ran over them immediately, but they were okay. Was thinking it could be the finale of the 'Andromeda' suite. What do you think? By the way, we still need about three minutes to fill out Side Two. The perfect amount of time for your recorder solo!"

"Are we in the fourth grade?" cracked Tim. He does not take the recorder seriously.

"If so, then John Paul Jones was in the fourth grade when he laid down a four-part recorder harmony on 'Stairway to Heaven,' or have you heard of it?" I turned to face Bonnie. "Really? I only do that live when someone needs to tune up or take a leak. But okay!"

Started with the opening notes of Debussy's "Syrinx," which quickly gave way to improvised variations on a melody from "Tim's Bolero." It was tough because I do not know how to breathe properly, but we somehow managed to get something down in a single take.

"It's a wrap!" declared Bonnie. We all slapped each other five. "Wish we had some champers!" she lamented.

"Forget champers," said Tim, as he tapped his finger pick against the side of a canister of nitrous oxide. Might need to get some of that for Jenny. I do not think I have ever made her laugh. Wonder if there is a *Laugh* spell?

THURSDAY, MAY 5

When Professor Ziglar approached me at the information desk for assistance finding a book, I ominously replied, "Let us consult the cards." I whipped out *Oblique Strategies*. "Ask your body," I read aloud, which seemed somewhat irrelevant to his needs. Another card read, "Try faking it!" which I thought was funny. Certainly faked my way through a few essays back in the day.

"I don't know what you're doing," he said, dryly.

"Gardening not architecture," I said, reading another card. "That's deep."

"Stop doing that. I need *Astrology: A Christian Perspective* by Norman Farnsworth."

Of course Porteous has it. If there is no god, and astrology is *yaje*, then why do we need seven hundred ninety-four pages of Norman Fuckworth's perspective? But I bit my tongue.

Despite being the end of the semester, the information desk was busier than it should be. As soon as I had finished helping one patron and settled back into my newspaper, another one walked up. Or the phone rang. Sometimes both at once. Their inane questions were perversely timed, roughly one every ninety seconds.

"Where are we?" said one blithering idiot.

"The library."

"No, I mean *where* are we?"

"Fort Worth, Texas?"

"No, uh…"

"Tarrant County?"

"That's it!" said the blithering idiot. I may as well have said Kentucky. He scribbled "Tarrant County" on a scrap of paper. "Oh, do you have comp exams from the last few semesters?"

"Comp exams are over, dumbass," I said, to myself. Felt a migraine coming on.

Looked up to see the Doom Hippie standing there, dangling a Thermos from his finger.

"Can I help you?" I said.

"Can *I* help *you*," he said, reversing the emphasis.

"What?" I said, put out.

"Do you have *The Necronomicon*?"

"We do in our Pogue Collection, but I'm afraid it's non-circulating."

"Can I look at it or not?" said the Doom Hippie, impatiently.

"You *may*. Please fill out this form. Will need to see some identification."

The Doom Hippie opened his jacket to reveal his pistol. "Here's your identification."

"Fair enough." We should have a gun at the information desk. I placed the form before him, and handed him a pen. After printing the title of the book (misspelling it, naturally), he signed his name, "Perdurabo."

The Doom Hippie shoved the form toward me, then stared at me hard.

"Please take a seat. I'll be back in a few minutes." As the elevator doors opened, I glanced his way and he was still watching me.

Every time I go down to the Vault, things are not where I left them. Stacks of books disappear and reappear. Boxes move. Gaps in shelves widen. A clipboard I had left behind was now missing.

I located the book in question, *Al Azif (The Necronomicon)* by Abdul Alhazred. An unassuming hardback from Owlswick Press, 1973. I flipped through its wavy, already heavily foxed pages, which featured in facsimile (according to L. Sprague de Camp's preface) a necromantic treatise. That is all I need, this joker commanding the dead in the reading room.

When I returned to the Doom Hippie, the few other patrons had cleared out and we were now alone. The reading room was darker than I had left it, evidently on account of some passing clouds. Not a sound from the circulation desk around the corner. When I handed *The Necronomicon* to the Doom Hippie, a fire lit in his eyes and he grinned maniacally. As he walked away, he stopped suddenly and turned. He held up his Thermos and said, "Can you go into the break room and fill this up with water from the water cooler?"

"No, but you're welcome to use the water fountain in the vestibule." How did he know we have a water cooler in the break room?

"That's not the right water."

Might have done this for another patron, out of the goodness of my heart, but not for the Doom Hippie. He was starting to get on my nerves.

"Jenny does it for me," he continued.

"I'm not Jenny."

The Doom Hippie stared at me searchingly. "I'm the last hippie in Tarrant County, dontcha know."

"Sorry, you're not." Don't know why I chose to argue with him.

"Where were you in '67?" he demanded.

"Where were you in '70?" I countered. I knew I could hit him with more truth than he could handle.

"Not with a noose around my neck."

The combination of my long hair and beard with the tie was blowing what was left of his drug-addled mind. "I love wearing a tie," I lied. "I'm not afraid of your handle."

The Doom Hippie became agitated. Was he going to start shooting up the library? "Ah, but the *man* wears a tie! When you dress like the *man*, you become the *man!*" He pronounced 'man' with emphasis, much like Amber pronounces 'Him.' He brandished his Thermos at me. "You won't even fill this up with water for me like a decent human bean." Did he just say "human bean"?

While the Doom Hippie was reading *The Necronomicon* at a nearby table, I watched him carefully out of the corner of my eye. He could not stay still for one minute. When his knees were not bouncing up and down, he muttered and fidgeted. He lit some incense. While roughly picking his nose he looked up and saw me watching him. He did not seem to care. At last, he let out a cry. "I can't understand it!" He swiveled to face me. "Don't you have this in English?" he demanded.

The catalog card describes the book as being written in Duriac, a language even I have never heard of. "That's the only edition we have, I'm afraid."

"You're lying," he hissed. "I'm going to find out what you love and make it cease to exist." The Doom Hippie then left the library with *The Necronomicon* in one hand and his Thermos in the other. What if he thinks I love Jenny?

Escaped early with Randy to head over to Mayfest. It was a relief to be away from the chaos of the library. Parked the Rambler at Farrington Field and took the shuttle. Some people on the bus wanted us to play for them. I just smiled and tootled out "The Eyes of Texas." This is the first time it has not rained during Mayfest. It was so muddy last year!

By the time we found our spot, I was starving. Sucked down a chili dog from a nearby vendor. The nourishment improved my mood considerably. My headache dissipated. Announced our presence with an out-of-tune fanfare on the trombone. Our setlist was mostly Renaissance, medieval, and folk pieces, mixed with quasi-medievalized instrumental treatments of a few Top 40 hits. Randy and I are billed in the program as Fowls in the Frith, which describes us as "soft folk rock." Of course we did "Scarborough Fair" and "The Battle of Evermore." A little Fairport. Some Amazing Blondel and Pentangle. Randy on lute and mandolin. Me on recorder, trombone, and bongos. Arrangements were largely improvised. One piece was extrapolated from the butthole music from Bosch's *The Garden of Earthly Delights*. Randy transcribed it for lute and trombone, employing the "devil's interval" during the intro. That was a nice touch.

The butthole music had a curious effect on the crowd. Some bore expressions of disgust as if they suspected its rectal origins. A retarded child bawled in distress to his scowling young mother. Unperturbed, a Scottish Tartan Thistle Dancer observed me closely. She seemed particularly interested in my trombone. Made her jump when I trilled right in her face.

"You play the trombone really good," she said, when we finished. She then whispered in my ear, "But I can blow good, too, laddie."

"Here you go!," I said and handed her the trombone. "Play me something."

Needless to say, she could not get a single tone out of that instrument. I do not know what her game was.

A rodeo clown kept bothering people who were trying to dig us. Every time I got the chance, I just aimed my trombone at him and blasted away. He finally got the message and fucked off. There were times when the Civil War reenactors stole some of our thunder. Otherwise, I would say we held our own. Lack of amplification notwithstanding, I enjoy playing with Randy more than Time Frame. Wish we could play together more often.

Playing music requires concentration and it takes my mind off things. But after we finished and were packing up, there came a girl's scream from the direction of the river. Randy and I exchanged concerned glances while a feeling of dread came over me.

"I'll check it out." I hurried toward the scream and found two members of the TCU Jazz Ensemble attending a sobbing young woman. She was soaking wet and shaking. Others stood on the bank, scanning the water. Wondered what could be lurking beneath its surface.

FRIDAY, MAY 6
It was warm and stuffy at the information desk. Do not know how Jo Ann can sit there without a fan. The telephone rang. "Good morning, it's a great day at the Porteous Library's information desk. This is Steven. How may I help you, please?"

"Steven? Why are you talking out of your asshole?"

"The boss makes us. I'm working, Tim. Make it quick."

"We're mixing tonight at Bobby's. Be there at nine."

Even though I am off tomorrow, I did not feel like staying up late. All these late nights are wearing me out. "Are the others going to be there?" I asked.

"Probably. What are you doing? You sound like you're in a well."

"Sorry, I'm trying to work out a kink in the telephone cord. Naw, too many cooks in the kitchen. Besides, I'm playing at Mayfest with Randy after work."

"That's just great, you two-timing jerk."

"Gotta go, Tim."

Everyone who could was asked to help shelve books. This time of the year they are all returned at once. Students wheel them through the door in wagons, wheelbarrows, and suitcases. "I will Dewey decimate you all!" bragged Sarge, brandishing his Extend-O hand menacingly. An experienced shelver, Sarge has the foresight to sort his piles first. It also helps that he speaks fluent Dewey and knows the stacks like the back of his Extend-O hand. It's going to go hard for Sarge after we switch to LC.

After Randy and I each shelved one book cart, Dixie grudgingly let us leave early again. She asked about my Sherlock Holmes chair but I waved her off. "We're going to be late!" I lied. Threatened rain, but fortunately cleared up. Basket of fried okra for dinner, washed down with lemonade. The okra was filling, and there was a moment when I flashed on how meals do not have to be square. There is something to be said for eating while standing up and getting it over with.

"Let's set up over here this evening. Don't want to be next to the Civil War again."

"Are we allowed to?"

"If anyone says anything, we can just say we didn't know."

The new spot was next to an elderly lady teaching people how to make lace by hand, so we did not have to struggle to make ourselves heard. Of course, we were now drowning out the old lady. Sorry, lady!

At one point, I took a break and found myself in the First of F.W. tent where they were playing a short film about Fort Worth, narrated by none other than Jimmy Stewart. Stewart was magnificent, and the film really hits the nail on the head. The old cowboy playing "You Are My Sunshine" is coincidentally playing through a Peavey. The scene passed too quickly to identify the model, though. I am guessing a Century, but his looks taller, more like a Roadmaster. This is going to haunt me. The score itself, by Bob Farrar, was really terrific. Pretty sure Farrar is the same guy who did the music for *Scum of the Earth*.

Throughout the evening, Randy and I took silent cigarette breaks. Recent events undoubtedly weighed heavily on Randy's mind as much as mine. Some guy recognized me from Time Frame, which bugged me for some reason. Not sure he was very impressed by our lugubrious "What power art thou, who from below…" In retrospect, the song was perhaps ill-chosen for a summer festival.

On the way home, we decided to stick to more upbeat tunes tomorrow. Like "Tempus transit gelidum," "Washington Square," or some dances from *Terpsichore*. And we could certainly play that galliard faster.

"What do you think busted through your back door?" I said.

"There's a spell in the codex whose name translates as *Inveniet*," said Randy. "It means 'to discover.' It requires something of the person or thing you want to learn about, such as a lock of hair. Whatever came through the door left a trail of what I suppose is skin or hide. Little leathery flakes. Propose we try the spell and see what we find out."

"When, tonight?" I started to argue. Did not tell him I already knew about *Inveniet*. It took an effort to convince myself that what happened with the mirror had really happened. And let us not forget Harvey. It is too much to deny anymore.

Back at Randy's, we cracked open a couple of cold ones and got comfortable in the den at the coffee table, he on the sofa, I in the La-Z-Boy. Randy opened the codex to the page with the *Inveniet* spell on it. Before us was the smashed back door, now boarded up.

He sat down next to me and placed the flakes in an aluminum ashtray.

I picked it up. "Did you steal this from McDonald's?"

"You do the honors. Your pronunciation is better," said Randy.

"I guess so." I flicked a dead dirt dauber off the table.

"You must direct the energy with your will."

"What if I do it wrong?"

"Who knows? Magic begins with the discipline of the human will. Recommend Martin Solis's book on the subject. Cheesy but the principles are sound. He explains things well."

"Don't you con me with your mind expansion slop," I said, in Sergeant Friday's voice. Randy was not amused. "And if I mispronounce something?"

Randy shrugged. Did not really want to go through with it. Part of me was filled with wonder at the prospect of becoming a card-carrying sorcerer. "If this is all it takes, why aren't there more sorcerers in the world?"

"You know the answer to that, Steven," said Randy. "Look around you. There are people who would do anything for this book. Even if magic was *yaje*. And you now know it's not."

Would sooner believe Harvey came from the fourth dimension than, say, Lansing. Sorcery brought his ass here. I brought him here. And I had already successfully cast this very spell. Hell, I have even committed it to memory.

In that communication workshop, the ex-cop said that before you begin to communicate something, you want to have a goal in mind, then say and do things to reach that goal. So I said to Randy, "I'd like to receive a clear picture of what this thing looks like, and where I can find it."

"That's a lot to ask."

"I feel like you're the sorcerer and I'm your apprentice," I said. Does Randy know more than he is letting on? He just smiled. "Should we dim the lights, or light incense, or something?"

"Anything that promotes concentration." Randy lit a couple of spiral candles. They looked like unicorn horns. Knowing Randy, they probably were. He turned off the lamp and sat down.

What was I afraid of? Tanking? Finding out something I wish I had not? After confirming what I was supposed to do with the material in the McAshtray, I closed my eyes and cleared my mind.

I read the words aloud, speaking as slowly as I needed to, pausing at times to avoid becoming tongue-tied. Became aware of a certain cadence, or rhythm, but had the remarkable presence of mind not to become distracted by wondering about meter, or how many syllables there were. Not unlike playing trombone inside an improvised arrangement. The somatic components, which had seemed superfluous at first, came to me naturally as if I had rehearsed them. When I reached the end of the text, I instinctively closed my eyes. And I waited. Through my eyelids I could faintly discern the dancing, red glow of the candles. Heard a truck in the distance. By degrees I became aware of a series of clear images, as if dreaming. A wrecked fence. The pedestrian path on the levee. The river. A creek. A tunnel.

When I opened my eyes, Randy was staring at me.

"I know where it went," I said.

"Did you see it?"

"It's holed up in one of those concrete tunnels by a creek."

"Where?"

"I can take us there."

Randy looked at me admiringly.

"That's it?" I said. "That's how magic works?" I pretended to know less than I did. Randy seemed irritated, then went off on this whole long explanation. I let him speak, only paying half-attention. But one thing stayed with me. While distingushing Dordic magic from the Western magical tradition, Randy said they were very different in that Dordic magic often relied on the assistance of other entities, "be it the service of cooperative elementals, the control of *kakoi*, or the powers granted by gods forgotten or unknown, as those are the most likely to respond to requests for aid." A light bulb went off in my head.

"The spell I had used this evening did not require anyone's aid."

"That was an easy one, just a bit of mental sleight of hand."

Randy is either wrong or lying. I changed the subject. "How can you use magic to better your life? Make it so you don't have to go to work, for example."

"Can think of a couple of things."

"Like what?"

"Control a *kakon*," said Randy. "Let him do all your dirty work." I noticed he used the correct singular form of *kakoi*.

"Like my laundry!" I said. Guess I was thinking of Harvey and not Harvey's pompatus. But what could I make Harvey do? Hold up a Kwik Sak? Loot the Kimbell? What is he capable of?

"Think big, Steven," said Randy. "Hang on, there's something I want you to read." He disappeared down the hall. What now? Another red herring, no doubt. Randy returned with *Mastering Witchcraft* by Paul Huson.

"Witchcraft?" I said.

"You don't have to give it a name. This book explains the importance of ritual in mystical endeavors. The magician fully prepared, the ritual carries out a dramatic presentation of verbal, somatic, and material components."

"Are we talking about witches or magicians? Aren't they the same thing?"

"Both use ritual to temporarily induce certain mental and chemical reactions in the mind of the operator. This in turn fosters particular atmospheric conditions in the immediate surrounding area. At the very least, it will help you understand where Diane is coming from."

Spent the evening reading the Huson until I zonked out with it on my chest. All this reading Randy gives me makes me wonder if he is trying to distract me sometimes. Despite always appearing to be relevant, the material is too diffuse for me to ever correlate. But why?

SATURDAY, MAY 7

On my bedside table were several catalog cards covered in notes, scribbled in haste throughout the night. Most of it was gibberish, but one card bore a musical passage in my customary notation. Below that were the same notes rendered in Astarian. Had never noticed before how suitable Astarian was for this purpose. Brilliant, really. Did I think of this in my sleep?

Walked down to the gas station for a newspaper and cigs. Read the news with scant concentration while my mind wandered. The subject of today's Mini Page was magic. That caught my attention. A photo of a chimp bore the caption, "Lots of folks are going ape over magic these days." Indeed they are.

Spent an inordinate amount of time studying the Magic Try 'n' Find. Besides the expected words like "abracadabra" and "spell," I noted "glib," which conjured up Vee's panties in my mind's eye. I lingered over the word "hecnos." Where have I seen that word? Or is it a name? A panel on optical illusions asked "Is seeing believing?" I tossed the paper aside in irritation.

Throughout the morning, errant melodies nagged at me, as if crying for attention. What if a melody could serve the same function as a word of power? Found myself reaching for blank catalog cards until the activity of jotting ideas down became repetitive. After dressing myself, I stopped by Mott's to buy a red notebook. Before I had reached Randy's, I had pulled over twice to scribble in it. Should have done this sooner.

Mayfest was much more crowded today. It was Saturday so kids had no school. Once the clouds dissipated, the sun beat down on us mercilessly. The upper 80s are pretty warm when you are in direct sunlight for prolonged periods.

Today's strategy to eschew sadder songs in favor of gayer tunes paid off. A frenzied "Saltarello" drew a small enthusiastic gathering. After Randy sang a rousing "In taberna quando sumus," we moved on to more modern fare. "Lady" by Styx, "Those Were the Days," and "The Entertainer" brought the house down. We played as if our lives depended on it. The chicks were digging it, too, until I hit a little boy hard in the mouth with my trombone slide during "Aqualung." His face was painted like a grotesque bird with two huge black eyes, like something from a Bosch painting. Like his siblings, he wore filthy rags. His pig-faced mother glowered at me as she shepherded her children away.

Without me holding him back, I returned from a bathroom break to find Randy playing "Invocación y Danza" to an appreciative audience. People were dancing. I stood back and gave him his moment in the spotlight. Just as he finished, someone smashed a confetti egg on top of my head. Turned around to see two teenage chicks running away, squealing. After a short pursuit, I caught up to them behind the porta-potties and was stung by several yellowjackets. The girls hopped onto the back of a hayride and waved.

Despite the indignity of the moment, or perhaps because of it, I felt menacing. Like I wanted to turn them into frogs. Who was I? It was time to face certain truths. After pausing to observe a pie eating contest, I returned to Randy sweaty and somewhat humiliated.

Randy set his lute down and pulled out a cigarette. The crowd reluctantly dispersed.

"Let's ditch," I said. "I'd like to go look for that thing. The tunnel is stuck in my mind's eye. Like when you stare at the sun then look away."

"Don't stare at the sun, dude."

"Like when a song gets stuck in your head, then." This simile was less apt, but I did not want to belabor the issue.

On the way to the Rambler Randy and I formulated a plan. First, we must locate the tunnel in question, the odds of which were at this point still unknown. Provided it existed, we might need a flashlight, rubber boots, and a camera. Weapons were discussed. Carlos is off on Saturdays. He keeps his 20-gauge in his work truck. We would need a hanger to unlock the door, which I am a pro at, having locked my keys in the Rambler many times.

"Can we not just buy a gun?"

Randy looked at me like I was stupid. "Don't worry, dude, we'll put it back."

First stop, Collinwood. Do not own rubber boots, so I wore my golden ones. Grabbed my guitar case to conceal the gun. Could not find a hanger.

Next stop, Porteous.

Carlos parks his truck in the spot near the break room patio. I picked up a pebble. I whispered the word of power and flicked the pebble at the passenger window. No hanger required. Less than a minute later I was briskly walking away with Carlos' Remington and a box of shells. The gun was too long for the guitar case. So much for that idea. Maybe no one will notice if I just casually carried it at my side.

At Randy's house, he grabbed the giant wooden fork I had given him for his birthday.

"What are you going to do with that?" I said.

"This could be an effective weapon."

Randy was right, but he hurt my feelings. Of course, it is his to do with as he pleases.

Randy and I walked toward the back of the property and scaled the fence where it was bent over.

"Which way?"

"Downstream," I said. We walked along the river trail atop the levee. The only sound was our feet crunching in the gravel. The sun was starting to peek through the clouds. It was still muggy. A kid on a minibike roared by and gave us the finger. Randy brandished the giant wooden fork at him. After about a half-mile, we spotted a culvert under the levee and paused. "Is that it?" asked Randy.

"No." How could I have been so certain? The culvert was a note out of tune.

We continued along the trail for some time. Kept switching arms, as the Remington was unwieldy.

"Is that a creek?" asked Randy.

"It's creek-like," I said. "But that's not the one."

"Do you have any idea how far away it is? You're not thinking of those old tunnels that run underneath downtown?"

"It's not that kind of tunnel."

"They say there was a tunnel under Throckmorton," said Randy. "Connected the city jail to the library. The secret door was behind the circulation desk in a closet."

"What was it for?"

"Who knows? Spunt told me about it. Sounds like *yaje* to me."

"Did you hear about the proposed tunnel linking the library and the Tandy Center?"

"No, but I heard the new subway will stop at the library."

But will the subways of my mind stop there?

Near Rockwood Park we paused and regarded the creek on the other side of the river.

"That's not it," I said.

We continued under University. Randy feigned excitement over a drainage ditch. By the time we got to Northside, we were both miserable. "It's been three hours, dude. We should have driven."

"Walking is the only way. We're almost there." It was like playing a song from years ago, like your hands knew their way across the measure and home to the key note. We were somewhere near the Stockyards when we saw it.

We turned along the creekside, scanning. We went under a train trestle. The trail crossed the creek. We went up the embankment to the street. "This must be 23rd," I said. From the vantage point of the bridge, which overlooked the creek, my eyes knew exactly where to look.

We got over a railing. We waded through dense weeds. The shadows were long under the bridge. At the tunnel's entrance, the footing was wet and slimy. The light of day was fading. Randy changed into his rain boots.

Followed Randy into the passageway, with waddling gait to avoid stepping into the stagnant water. More like hedgehog walking than fox walking. The ceiling was arched, about seven feet high in the middle. The tunnel was not quite wide enough to walk two abreast. Turned now and then to regard the entrance behind us, which grew progressively smaller. Spray-painted graffiti soon gave way to bare concrete, punctuated now and then by dripping water or stony debris. A train horn reverberated faintly in the distance.

"Wasn't Caligula murdered in a tunnel?" I said.

"What?" said Randy.

We walked for some time until I slipped in some muck and cursed. Randy shushed me, but his shush echoed just as loudly as my voice. Relieved myself against the wall, pissing as quietly as possible. Fox pissing. There was no point in announcing our presence, but even using stealthy techniques such as fox walking, my footsteps resounded as if I had clown feet. Kept fox walking, anyway, even if Randy was not.

After some twenty minutes, Randy stopped in his tracks. "This looks like the end. What now?" he asked, wearily.

The tunnel ended abruptly in a wall. Unlike the sides of the tunnel which were relatively smooth, the wall before us was rough, and had a mottled, charred appearance.

"Get back!" hissed Randy.

A rheumy orb the size of a softball danced in the light on the end of a slender stalk. Recoiling in fright, I bumped my head hard on the ceiling. After regaining my composure, I aimed and pulled the trigger, only to find I had neglected to release the safety. I released it, aimed again, and fired.

I was unprepared for the noise or the kick. The stalk lunged and swayed. It was attached to what appeared to be a mound of debris, which had not been there before. The mound now stretched upward into a slender column. The gun was now jammed or fouled. Did not have time to clear it so I dropped it. Randy jabbed at the stalk with the giant wooden fork in one hand, the flashlight in the other. Was obliged to pirouette out of the way a couple of times, though he did nick me on the ear.

Backed off and reached into my pocket where I had stashed my *shuriken*. I hurled them one at a time but they seemed to be ineffective. No choice but to retrieve the gun and try again. It still would not fire. Fiddled with it until I was finally able to extract the shell. "Get down!" I commanded.

Something grabbed my foot and yanked me off my feet. Hit the ground with a splash, and was dragged violently into the dark.

The interior surface of the creature's maw was covered with shiny, black *plica fimbriata* which undulated perversely. I beat with my fists upon the edges of its lipless orifice as it pulled me inside. Something punctured my boot.

"Randy!" I cried, urgently.

I cast an upside-down glance in Randy's direction, and thought I saw him tracing patterns in the air with his finger. The stalk began to weaken and droop. Its eye had become too heavy to support. It bounced off my face on its way down. Presently, the undulations ceased. The creature made a deep yawning sound which gave way to an ululant, forlorn cry. Randy stomped on the orb, which burst like an overripe persimmon. The maw was now a liquescent, black slit, from which viscous, greenish-brown bubbles dribbled, soaking my jeans. I struggled free from its dead weight and struggled to my feet.

Randy trained the flashlight upon our foe, which now resembled nothing more than a pile of rotten seaweed. It smelled worse. But that cry! I had looked into its eye. I had seen intelligence there.

"We need to dispose of the carcass properly," said Randy. "Its discovery could cause trouble for us."

"How's that?" I said.

"Say someone finds it. Word gets out and next thing you know everyone's talking about the extraterrestrial remains they saw on *Eyewitness News*. Call me paranoid if you like."

"You're paranoid," I said. "But let's get out of this place. I'm sick of hearing my voice echo." Once we finally debouched from the darkness, I took off my boot and inspected my bloody foot.

"We'd better split," said Randy. "Someone may have heard the gunshots."

"Look what it did to my boot." Something had abraded away the leather at the vamp.

"You're fine. Got you on the ear, though. Sorry, dude."

I felt my skull for a bump. "Damn near got brain damage hitting my head against the wall."

"How would you be able to tell?" said Randy.

"Ha ha. Guess we're walking back."

"Do you know how to get home?"

"Well, if we walk that way," I said, "we should run into Jacksboro Highway." Handed the Remington to Randy. "Here, it's your turn to carry this." Washed my hands and face in the creek.

"Hurry up," said Randy.

I dried off with my t-shirt. "I'm starving. If we weren't so filthy I would say let's go to Joe T.'s. Damn, a margarita sounds good right now."

"Margaritaville can wait," said Randy. "We have a job to do."

"I know that. I was just saying."

"Don't forget the fork."

Pulled up my socks and off we went. It was not until we had crossed the train tracks that I realized we had walked the wrong direction.

"I have no idea where we are," said Randy.

"I do," I said. "See that parking lot? That's where the Niles City canning plant used to stand."

"Someday the whole nation will be one giant parking lot."

Ten minutes later we were plodding down 23rd. Stuck my thumb out a few times but no one stopped for two dirty vagabonds. It took almost two hours to get back. Randy rounded up a broom, some gloves, a machete, and a box of Hefty bags. My trunk was full, so I had to unload it onto Randy's porch before we could leave.

"Almost forgot," said Randy. He ran into the house and returned with a bottle of Kentucky Gentleman.

Hacking up a carcass this size was hot, sweaty work. The flesh was tougher than we expected. We worked through most of the night. There was much dense, sinewy matter, and miles of entrails. Did not find anything resembling flippers or feet, so I am not sure how the thing moved around. Randy held up a dripping gland before placing it in a margarine tub. This I observed without comment.

"Think I found my curtain," said Randy. He poked something with his boot. "What's this? A half-digested critter. And here's one of your stars. You were tossing these like a fucking ninja."

"A lot of good those did," I said. "Just leave it."

We filled numerous Hefty bags, trading swigs of Kentucky Gentleman like it was canteen water. We left the empty bottle behind, along with the rest of the gloppier remains.

"I hate this," I said. "You know Roy Orbison's playing at Six Flags as we speak. Can't believe I missed him again. How come blind people are always such amazing musicians?"

"What do you mean?"

"Like Roy Orbison. Have you seen the guy play?"

"Roy Orbison isn't blind."

Why did I think he was?

Hauling bags of monster meat up the embankment to the Rambler was no easy feat. After some deliberation, we decided the safest place to dispose of the bags was in the well in Sherwood's backyard. I drove around to the back of the house. In case Roof Guy guy was watching, I waved my middle finger out the window. I backed right up to the well and we quickly did what we came there to do.

"I'll get some lye tomorrow," said Randy. "Do you think you can pitch in for that, and for the trash bags?"

Took out my wallet and handed him a fiver, still moist from tunnel water. Recall having a vague feeling that we should be documenting this better. I am doing the best I can here, but I am sure I have forgotten something.

"What if something came through Sherwood's door and got him? What if that door's still open?" I said.

"It didn't look like it was open. It just looked like a wall."

"And the mirror looked like a mirror."

I was filthy, sore, tired, and drunk. My brain was overwhelmed with thoughts, some of which trickled out of my ears before dissipating.

"Hey, can we go downtown?" I said.

"You want to go downtown? Now?"

"I want to take a look at something."

"It's three o'clock in the morning. I have nothing else better to do," said Randy, sarcastically.

I tossed Randy the keys. "You drive."

On the way, we passed a McDonald's.

"Over twenty-five billion served," I read aloud. "That's six hamburgers for every man, woman, and child on the planet."

"Some people ate more than one," said Randy, thoughtfully.

We waited at a red light. "See that parking lot?" I said. "My Uncle Larry used to sell furniture there. Old Phoenix Building. He's got these huge carved cat faces he salvaged when the building was demolished."

"This whole area has changed so much," said Randy. "Danciger Building. Edison's. Collins Art Company. The blood place. All gone."

When we got to Commerce Street, I told Randy to turn right. I strained to see the street numbers on passing buildings. We passed 14th. "Pull over here."

"Why are we stopping?" said Randy.

"Guddu said his address was 1502 Commerce."

"1502? That's the Water Gardens. I could have told you that."

"That motherfucker. What's Guddu's game?"

As we headed home, I looked around in wonder at what was once Hell's Half Acre, the roughest neighborhood west of the Mississippi. We pulled over so I could take a leak under the zipper mural. We then made our way back to Randy's, pointing out landmarks, both current and bygone, along the way.

"Who the hell's idea was it to paint St. Andrews white? You don't paint stone," I griped.

"That's just limestone, not paint," said Randy.

"It looks different in the dark."

At the five points intersection, the light was taking forever to change. There is a word of power for this. I rendered its Astarian syllables into a brief melody then softly whistled it. The light turned green. As we swerved up Bailey, I heard blaring horns and the squeal of brakes, accompanied by the telltale crunch somewhere behind us of colliding steel. Felt like I was going to puke. Then I dozed off.

When I awoke in Randy's guest bedroom, I turned on the lamp and reached for my red notebook. I began writing as fast as I could. After a while my mind started to wander as I recalled bits and pieces of all the crazy shit I have been reading. I put down my pen. The room was stuffy and too quiet. I could hear my own breathing. I rose from bed and went into the bathroom where I splashed water on my face.

I recalled Randy's remark about enslaving a demon. He said it so matter-of-factly that it seems he must be convinced of its plausibility. Sometimes I feel like he is keeping secrets from me. I know I am keeping secrets from him.

Dug around in my mansack but there is too much crap in it. Am I turning into Sherwood? Dumped everything out onto the bed. Two Chap Sticks. My Q-Card. My diary. There it was: the film canister with Harvey goo in it.

Did not want Randy to know what I was up to just yet, so I stayed in my room and made do with two red tapers and a Firestone ashtray. The kind with a rubber tire around it. I must get one of these. Scraped some of the dried Harvey goo into it, careful not to take a whiff. No sooner had I spoken the words of power, I knew Harvey's true name: SHAGDUK! (The spelling is mine.)

SUNDAY, MAY 8

Slept in. While brushing my teeth, I regarded myself in the bathroom mirror. Evidently, I got some sun yesterday. I tapped the glass for reassurance. The fauna of mirrors! In the privacy of Randy's guest room, I dialed Mother's number. It rang twice before a man's voice said, "Hello?" I hung up. After a quick breakfast of leftover Chicken à la King, Randy and I hauled ass to Mayfest to fulfill our musical obligations.

A C-5 roared overhead while we loaded the Rambler. "The Pentagon wants to close Carswell," said Randy, who seemed surprisingly bright-eyed this morning.

Randy must be in better shape than I am. My elbow was killing me and a quarter-sized blister on my palm stung. Could barely lift my arms to play the trombone. Did not have it in me to be musical at all.

By late afternoon, Randy and I were taking turns playing so the other one could wander off for beer. Felt uneasy the times he was gone. Am not used to entertaining crowds solo. The fuzz strolled by. Kept my eye on him until he was out of sight. What if he knows what Randy and I have been up to? Felt like I had committed a crime, and I suppose I have. Stuck to songs I could sing and play on Randy's lute at the same time, like "Heart of Gold" and "Rocky Mountain High." I have never played a lute, but a few kids and old ladies picked up what I was laying down. "I Am, I Said" was harder to sing and play at the same time than I thought, and I am afraid I botched it. Nailed the vocals, though.

Played my "Andromeda" recorder solo, extending it with numerous variations. Recalling how words of power can be expressed musically, I tried one. The fingering came effortlessly. A strange melody from no pop song issued from my recorder and floated over the crowd until...KABOOM!

What a fucking careless thing to do. But what about intent? Must I now think before I play? But then I noticed the cannon nearby. They were getting ready to fire it again.

Randy returned with his face painted like a lion, a blonde in tow. He introduced her as Mary Ellen. She hung out while Randy and I played together for a while. When it was my turn to get my face painted, Mary Ellen led me to a nearby table where her friend had just finished painting whiskers on a child.

"Hey, Dawn!" I said.

"Hi, Steven! Oh my gosh, what happened to your ear?"

"My neighbor's cat."

"You two know each other?" said Mary Ellen.

"We do," said Dawn. "She offered me a seat. "Let me do him."

"What am I going to be?" It was difficult to feign interest. I could not stop thinking about Shagduk. I wanted to say his name aloud.

"You'll see." Dawn tied a bib around my neck, then, after applying red, white and blue tempera to my cheeks and forehead, she held up her compact.

"The Texas flag?"

"When you look at me with those stars in your eyes, I could waltz across Texas with you," she sang. Before I could respond, "Like a storybook ending, I'm lost in your charms," my words were drowned out by an abrupt cacophony of bagpipes. The Scottish Tartan Thistle Dancers were upon us! Dawn laughed. A gentle breeze, punctuated by a strong gust of wind. Followed by another, stronger gust. Paints and brushes slid to the ground or flew away. The table flipped over rather violently. Darkness fell.

The Thistle Dancers were now moving out of sync as whatever time signature had guided them now dissipated into the rising tempest. They began to balter and soon were lurching about like they had been poisoned. The tempo of the bagpipes slowed from *lento* to *grave*. The notes throbbed and grew flatter. My head swam. I felt weak and I slumped in my folding chair. The Thistle Dancers scattered, shrieking.

I looked up to witness a single torch of green flame. It illuminated a wall of iron bars, like those of a prison cell. The bars in the center glowed orange before melting away. Through them sprung a black panther, followed by its handler, a dark-skinned dwarf in a leather cowl. The panther froze, assuming the manner of a big cat who had just spotted its prey. The dwarf shouted a command and cracked his whip. The panther flinched, then turned its head and hissed at the dwarf. I fled toward a bandstand. The panther followed, dragging its handler who screamed commands in a familiar language.

I found myself under some bleachers, my escape blocked by a section of chain link. As I turned, I almost ran straight into the dwarf, who punched me in the nuts. I hit the deck, tears of pain and white-hot rage flowing down my cheeks. I duked it out with the dwarf in a desperate struggle. The harder he hit me, the harder I hit back. Instinct guided my blows. When I used the "Iron Claw" on him, he let out a wail of anguish before shoving me away. I leaped to my feet. I seized a nearby stanchion but it proved too unwieldy. Unhooking the velvet rope, I swung it overhead, its weighted hook connecting once with the dwarf's temple and again with his wrist before he yanked the rope away. When he tried to garrotte me with it, I shoved my palm under his jaw. Something crumbled. Flinging him against a shoe shine booth, I fell upon him. Next to us was one of those electric shoe polishers. Mashing his face against one of the buffers, I reached across with my hand and pushed the red button. The dwarf bucked wildly under me, gurgling incomprehensibly as his gums were polished to a gory pulp. Presently, the buffers ceased spinning. The dwarf displayed a broad, bloody grin and held up the power cord, triumphantly.

From behind, I was savagely grabbed by the collar and tossed into one of the shoe shine chairs. The panther, standing tall on hind legs, cursed me in an unknown language. He banged on the armrests and rattled me in the chair. When I shrank from him, he pinned me down and hissed in my face. A black rope of drool dangled toward my mouth. The weight of its paws upon my shoulders made it impossible to struggle. Felt heat and pressure near my butthole, as if being probed with a searing brand. I squirmed in fear as the panther's wizened snout nuzzled my neck. It snorted hot breath and spoke, haltingly. Phonetically, like someone reading English aloud but not understanding.

"Have you seen anything of an old tome?" it croaked. Its eyes searched mine with a gaze so penetrating, I felt the beast could read my thoughts. It had other questions. These it asked without words. I felt my will weakening to the verge of submission.

I felt the beast hesitate. Then, its head recoiled as if avoiding bad breath. As soon as it released my shouders, I held up my amulet like a crucifix. What did I have to lose? It drew its head away from mine and looked away for a moment.

"Well, well," it said, backing away from me. The beast made a few turns in the dirt, evidently agitated by my bluff. The ambiance of the vicinity changed, as if one had stepped from outdoors into a cavernous room. In my mind's eye materialized a confusion of blurry images, like a double-exposed photograph. A massive, ornate candelabrum came into focus, its light forming woolly streaks across my field of vision., its light forming hazy streaks across my vision.

The beast crouched in a corner and eyed me warily, its spiked tail flopping heavily back and forth. Meanwhile, the dwarf had reappeared and was now standing before a large stone table upon which rested a massive folio. I remained seated upon the shoe shine chair and watched as the dwarf scanned each page with his fingertip. With each passing minute, I began to realize I was not going to be killed, at least not just yet. The bagpipes seemed so faint and distant now, and for a moment I had the presence of mind to wonder about Dawn.

The dwarf looked up from his book, then turned to the panther and nodded. At this sign, I leaped from the shoe shine chair. The beast lunged toward me with a vicious snarl. No sooner had I landed on my feet, I heard a voice call out a command. Or perhaps a name. The last thing I recall was the beast's cry of dismay, before the scene faded to black. Just before it did so, I caught a glimpse of Guddu on the bandstand, rubbing his hands together.

"Steven?" Someone was patting my cheeks. Reviving me. I gasped, then opened my eyes to see Dawn's moon-face looming above mine.

Dawn helped me to my feet. I brushed myself off and watched in wonder as a couple of fallen Civil War reenactors were wheeled past us on gurneys.

"What happened?" I said. I knew what happened, but I wanted to hear Dawn's version.

"There was a hail storm," she said. "Oh, Steven, it was awful! And then it rained so hard." She ran her fingers through my hair. "But you're dry," she said, quizzically.

Randy holds his booze better than I, so I let him drive. "Where to?" he said.

"The Eagle's Nest, of course."

"To the Eagle's Nest!"

Realized too late that I had assumed shotgun before Mary Ellen had a chance to call it. "Why don't you...never mind," said Randy, who was clearly irritated as Mary Ellen took her seat behind him. Reached in the glove box for smokes. No smokes, but I did discover a tape labeled "Steven & Randy Rock 'n' Roll." I waved it provocatively in Randy's face. "Look what I found!" I sang.

"A tape. So what."

Retrieved my cassette-corder from under my seat and inserted the tape. I hit play. As soon as our caterwauling began, Randy recognized it.

"Dude, don't play this," he moaned. He reached for the cassette-corder, but I playfully held it out the window. It was a tape he and I had made in our dorm room one Schlitz-faced evening. Just the two of us and a couple of guitars, and a kazoo, if memory serves. Spontaneously playing whatever song popped into our heads. We made up lyrics and forgot chords. There were competing guitar solos, retarded outbursts, and off-key harmonizing. Between songs there were snatches of Catullus and filthy limericks. Impassioned quotes from *Soylent Green*. When my croaking baritone rendition of "Brand New Key" began, I sang along and mouthed the kazoo parts.

Randy groaned. "We should have burned that. Sorry, ladies!" Felt satisfying to embarrass Randy for a change.

"We should send it to the *O.D.*!" I suggested.

"They'll play it, for sure," said Randy, sarcastically.

Pressed the rewind button but the tape jammed. A nasty warbling sound issued from the speaker. Randy groaned in mock sympathy.

"Oh, no! Anybody got a pencil?" I said.

The vibe at the Eagle was laid back. Mary Ellen lit up and we passed the joint around. Fortunately, Randy did most of the talking, for I was too zonked to say much. After a day like we just had, how Randy could drone on about the Kentucky Derby to total strangers was beyond me. For a moment, however, I felt almost relieved to be among people who knew nothing of sorcery, doors to the void, or the likes of Shagduk. But Dawn has seen him. A group of Thistle Dancers came through the door, their tartan and tulle costumes bloodied.

This was the girls' second Mayfest to paint faces. Was itching to wash my face but wanted to spare Dawn's feelings. But then Randy had to open his big mouth.

"What's with the Chilean flag?

"What do you mean?" said Dawn.

Randy pointed at my face. "The Texas flag has a long rectangle...here."

"No, that's the Texas flag. Wait, you mean I painted the flag of Chile on six faces today?"

Randy raised his beer in a toast. *"Por la razón o la fuerza!"*

I raised my glass and repeated the slogan in Dordic. Randy glared at me, while the girls simply looked confused.

"So you teach kindergarten," said Randy, in a bid to change the subject.

"Yes," said Mary Ellen." Her arm jostled her beer, some of which sloshed harmlessly onto the table. I avoided Dawn's questioning gaze. All the beer I drank just made me sleepier. Kept chewing on my cheeks, though I muttered "Do not!" to myself repeatedly.

"When you're taking a shower, do you ever think of how many more you will take before you die?" I said to no one in particular. It was high time I faced reality. Enough of this fucking around in reverse. "I am your master, now," I said, under my breath. Shagduk can kiss my ass.

Whoever was laughing stopped. Even the jukebox now sounded sad. Why do I have to be such a drip sometimes? Ward Cleaver did not come home to June and tell her about the dead rat he saw downtown. He kept that darkness to himself. Or maybe he told Wally later. When the time was right.

I became aware of a voice.

"Steven?" said the voice. "Steven?"

"What?"

Randy snapped his fingers. "Where are you, dude? Dawn asked you a question."

"I'm sorry. I can't keep my eyes open," I said. "Can you guys take me home?"

"We took your car," said Randy, irritably.

"Do y'all mind if we leave, then?"

Randy must have closed the deal with Mary Ellen, because he directed me to drop them off at his house. Dawn lives near the Church of Christ. We did not speak the whole way there. She did not invite me in nor did I try to kiss her. I just wanted to get home. Ran two red lights on the way back to Collinwood.

I knew what I wanted to do but correlating the contents of my mind turned out to be more difficult than I thought. The spell itself seemed straightforward enough. It was right there on the page in plain Dordic in thirty-nine easy steps. Parts of the binding ritual gave me pause, for either the language was ambiguous or simply mysterious. Was Shagduk "shy" or "young"? Well, he is not shy. That much is certain. But how am I supposed to know how old he is? The text suggests I needed to know this information in order to proceed, but does not explain why.

Much time was wasted referring to Sherwood's red notebook (as well as my own new one). Half-remembered bits of Randy's long-winded monologues competed in my mind with definitions of Dordic words I thought I knew. When Randy and I speak Dordic, we speak our own dialect and there is no one to correct us. What if I said something wrong? Mispronounced a word of power? The most likely outcome, I figured, was that jack shit was going to happen.

It was almost sunrise when a scratching at my door snapped me out of my reverie. Figaro. If I did not let him in he would just keep at it. Oddly, he sat down near me and watched me as if he knew what I was about to do and wanted to witness it. Why not?

I regarded the scene before me: the open books, the candles, the chalk lines on the floor. The Beam's Choice decanter which seemed perfect for the occasion. I admired the sigil I had made before taking a photograph of it. Might need it again. The air in the room was charged with anticipation. I felt a little sick. After perusing the text one last time, I began.

Not including the hours of preparation, the ritual itself took no longer than the time it takes to prepare a sandwich. I held up the decanter into a beam of sunlight which streamed through a gap in the drapes. Movement within the smoky purple glass gave evidence of some inner agitation.

"*Shagduk nene kha*," I said to Figaro, "Shagduk is mine."

Figgy licked his paw unconcernedly.

Mashik baya!

Norberto, the Bastard, Eddie Black, M., Huffman, Lloyd Llewellyn, Ryan, Bryce, Matt, Mom, Dad, George Gimarc, Ernie Gygax Jr., Kirston Fortune, Jimmy Grider and the freaks at Peavey Cvlt, Memories of the DFW Music Scene, and Fort Worth Memories & History.